TERROR TALES
OF LONDON

TERROR TALES
OF LONDON

Edited by Paul Finch

TERROR TALES OF LONDON

First published in 2013 by Gray Friar Press.
9 Abbey Terrace, Whitby,
North Yorkshire, YO21 3HQ, England.
Email: gary.fry@virgin.net
www.grayfriarpress.com

Typesetting and design by Paul Finch and Gary Fry

ISBN: 978-1-906331-39-9

TABLE OF CONTENTS

THE TIGER
Nina Allan

There is a bed, a wardrobe with a large oval mirror, a built-in cupboard to one side of the chimney breast. The boards are bare, stained black. There is a greyish cast to everything. Croft guesses the room has not been used in quite some time.

"It's not much, I'm afraid," the woman says. Her name is Sandra. Symes has told him everyone including her husband calls her Sandy, but Croft has decided already that he will never do this, that it is ugly, that he likes Sandra better. "I've been meaning to paint it, but there hasn't been time."

She is too thin, he thinks, with scrawny hips and narrow little birdy hands. Her mousy hair, pulled back in a pony tail, has started to come free of its elastic band. Croft cannot help noticing how tired she looks.

"Don't worry," he says. "If you can let me have the paint, I'll do it myself."

"Oh," she says. She seems flustered. "I suppose we could take something off the rent money. In exchange, I mean."

"There's no need," Croft says. "I'd like to do it. Something to keep me out of mischief." He smiles, hoping to give her reassurance, but she takes a step backwards, just a small one, but still a step, and Croft sees he has made a mistake already, that the word mischief isn't funny, not from him, not now, not yet.

He will have to be more careful with what he says. He wonders if this is the way things will be for him from now on.

"Well, if you're sure," Sandra says. She glances at him quickly, then looks down at the floor. "It would brighten up the walls a bit, at least."

She leaves him soon afterwards. Croft listens to her footsteps as she goes downstairs, past the entrance to the first floor flat where she and Angus McNiece and their young son live, and into the pub where she works ten hours each day behind the bar. Once he feels sure she won't come back again Croft lifts his luggage – a canvas holdall – from where he has placed it just inside the door and puts it down on the bed. As he tugs open the zip, an aroma arises, the scent of musty bedsheets and floor disinfectant, a smell he recognises instantly as the smell of the prison, a smell he has grown so used to that he would have said, if he'd been asked, that the prison didn't have a smell at all.

1

No smell, and no texture. Being outside is like being spun inside a centrifuge. He keeps feeling it, the enthralling pressure on his ribs and abdomen, the quickfire jolts to his brain as he tries to accustom himself to the fact that he is once more his own private property. Just walking from the station to the pub – the long, straight rafter of Burnt Ash Road, the blasted concrete triangle that is Lee Green – gave him a feeling of exhilaration so strong, so bolt upright it still buzzes in his veins like neat whisky, like vertigo.

The pub is called *The Old Tiger's Head*. Croft has read it was once a coaching halt, a watering hole for soldiers on their way to the Battle of Waterloo. More recently it was a tram stop, where trams on their way down from Lewisham Junction would switch from the central conduit to overhead power. Photographs of Lee Green in the early nineteen-hundreds show the place when it was still a village, a busy crossroads between Lewisham and Eltham, creased all along its corners, faded, precious.

He begins to remove his clothes and books from the canvas holdall. The clothes will go in the wardrobe. He tries the door to the built-in cupboard but it appears to be locked. Croft wishes the woman, Sandra, had felt able to stay with him in the room for just a few minutes longer.

Why would she, though? What is he to her, other than the sixty pounds each week she will get from him in rent money?

Croft wonders what, if anything, she has heard or read or been told about his case.

The child, Rebecca Riding, lived less than two miles from the place where he is now standing. A decade has passed since she died. In an alternate world, she would now be a young woman. Instead, she went to pick flowers in Manor Park on a certain day, and that was that.

Abducted and raped, then murdered. Her name had joined the register of the lost.

Did Croft kill Rebecca Riding? The papers said he had, for a while they did anyway. He has served a ten year prison sentence for her murder. Even now that the charges have been overturned, the time he has spent living as a guilty man is still a part of reality.

He is free, but is he truly innocent?

Croft cannot say yet. There are too many things about that day that he cannot remember.

*

His first meeting with Symes consists mainly of Symes cross examining him on the subject of how things are going.

"Did you manage to sign on okay?" As if penetrating the offices of the Lewisham DSS was a significant accomplishment, like shooting Niagara Falls in a barrel, or scaling Everest.

Perhaps for some it is. Croft thinks of the faces, the closed and hostile faces of free people who through their freedom were unpredictable and therefore threatening. In prison you became used to people doing the same thing, day after day. Even insane actions came to make sense within that context. In the offices of the Lewisham DSS, even getting up to fetch a cup of water from the cooler might turn out to be a prelude to insurrection.

All the people he encounters make him nervous. He tells Symes everything is fine.

"It was lucky about the room," he adds, as a sweetener. "I'm grateful to you."

The room at *The Old Tiger's Head* was Symes's idea. He knows Angus McNiece, apparently. Croft dislikes Symes intensely without knowing why. In prison you come to know a man's crime by the scent he gives off, and to Croft Richard Symes has about him the same moist and fuggy aroma as the pathetically scheming lowlifes who always sat together in the prison canteen because no one else would sit near them, suffering badly from acne and talking with their mouths full.

Symes wears a lavender-coloured, crew-necked jersey and loose brown corduroys. He looks like an art teacher.

That Symes has been assigned to him by the probation service to help him 're-orientate' seems to Croft like a joke that isn't funny.

Symes is telling Croft about a group he runs, once a week at his home, for newly released offenders.

"It's very informal," Symes says. "I think you'd enjoy it."

Offenders, Croft thinks. That's what we are to people. We offend. The idea of being in Symes's house is distasteful to him but he is afraid that if he refuses Symes will see it as a sign of maladjustment and use it against him.

Croft says yes, he would like to attend, of course. It would be good to meet people.

"Here's my address," Symes says. He writes it down on one of the scraps of paper that litter his desk and hands it across. "It's in Forest Hill. Can you manage the bus?"

"I think so," Croft says. For a moment, he imagines how good it would feel to punch Symes in the face, even though Croft isn't used to fighting, he hasn't hit anyone since he was fifteen and had a dust-up in the schoolyard with Roger Burke by name, Burke by nature, Croft has forgotten what it was about now but everyone had cheered. He imagines the blood spurting from Symes's nose the

3

way it had from Roger Burke's nose, the red coating the grooves of his knuckles, the outrage splayed across his face (how fucking dare you, you little turd), the pain and surprise.

Symes is finally getting ready to dismiss him.

"Tuesday at eight, then. Are you sure you don't want me to email you directions?"

"There's no need." Croft isn't online yet, anyway, but he doesn't tell Symes that. "I'm sure I can find you."

*

"I'm just popping to Sainsbury's," Sandra says. "Can I fetch you anything?"

The supermarket is only across the road. Croft can see the car park from his window. Sandra knows Croft could easily go himself, if he needed to, but she asks anyway because she's like that, kind, so different from her husband, McNiece, who hasn't addressed a single word to Croft since he moved in.

Sandra has her boy with her, Alexander. He gazes around Croft's room with widening eyes.

"You're *painting*," the boy says.

White, Sandra bought. A five-litre can of matt emulsion and a can of hi-shine gloss for the woodwork.

The smell of it: bright, chemical, clean, the scent of new. It reminds Croft of the smell of the fixative in his old darkroom.

"That's right," Croft says. "Do you like it?"

The boy stares at him, open-mouthed.

"Don't bother Mr. Croft, Alex," Sandra says. "He's busy."

"It's no bother," Croft says. "And it's Dennis." The presence of the boy in his room makes him more than ever certain that Sandra McNiece does not know what Croft was in prison for. If she knew she would not have brought her son up here. If she knew, she would not have allowed Croft within a mile of the building.

She will know soon though, because someone will tell her, someone is bound to. Croft is surprised this hasn't happened already. Once she knows she will want to throw him out, though Croft has a feeling Angus McNiece won't let her, he won't want to lose the extra income.

"I could do with some tea bags," he says to Sandra. "If it's really no trouble."

*

"Were you really in prison?" the boy says. *Alexander*. He sits on the edge of Croft's bed, swinging his legs back and forth as if he were sitting on a tree branch, somewhere high up, in Oxleas Woods perhaps (do kids still go there?) where it is said you can hear the ghosts of hanged highwaymen, galloping along the side of the Dover Road in the autumnal dusk.

"Yes," Croft says. "I was. But I'm out now."

"What were you in for?"

"Does your mother know you're up here?" Croft replies. The idea that she might not know, that the boy is here in his room and that nobody has given their permission, makes Croft feel queasy. Or perhaps it is just the smell of the hardening gloss paint.

"Yes," the boy says, though Croft can tell at once that he is lying, that the child has *sneaked upstairs to see the prisoner*, that in the boy's mind this is the bravest and most daring feat he has ever performed. Croft wonders if Sandra realises she has given her son the same name as her. Perhaps she does, perhaps the boy was named after her.

Alexander the Great.

Alexander Graham Bell.

Alexander Pushkin.

In Russian, the shortened form of Alexander (and Alexandra) is not Alex, but Sasha. Pushkin was shot in a duel. He died two days later in some agony from a ruptured spleen. He was thirty-eight years old.

"Shouldn't you be in bed?" Croft says. The boy looks at him with scorn. How old is he, exactly? Six, seven, eight?

"What did you do before you were in prison?"

"I took photographs," Croft says. "That was my job."

"Would you take one of me?"

"I might," Croft says. "But I don't have a camera."

The boy reminds him of someone, the lad who betrayed him perhaps. The boy is younger of course, but he has the same bright knowingness, the same hopeful aura of trust as the lad who seemed to become his friend and then called him a murderer. Croft wonders what his Judas – Kip? – is doing now. Has he become a photographer himself, as he intended, or is he cooped up in some office, serving time?

*

Croft never dreamed in prison. The air of the place was sterile, an imagic vacuum. The outside air is different, teeming with live bacteria, primed to blossom into monstrosities as soon as he sleeps.

5

In his dreams of Rebecca Riding, he begins to remember the way her hair felt, under his hand, the soft jersey fabric of her vest and underpants.

"Will you take me home now?" she says. Croft always says yes, though when he wakes, sweating with horror, he can't remember if this really happened or if it's just in his dream. There's cum on the bedsheet, still tacky. He steps out of bed and goes across to the window. Outside and below him, Lee Green lies hazy in the light of the streetlamps. In the hours between two and four there is little traffic.

His legs are still shaking.

If he waits until five o'clock a new day will begin.

Croft opens the window to let in the air, which is crisp, tinged with frost, the leading edge of autumn, easing itself inside him like a dagger. The orange, rakish light of Lee Green at night reflects itself back at him from the oval mirror on the front of the wardrobe.

Croft wishes he had a camera.

If he cannot have a camera, he wishes he could sleep.

*

The bus to Forest Hill is the 122. They run every fifteen minutes, approximately. There's a stop more or less opposite the pub, at the bottom end of Lee High Road. It's the early part of the evening, after the main rush hour but still fairly busy. When Croft gets on the bus is half empty, but after the stop at Lewisham Station it's almost full again.

Croft moves upstairs, to the top deck. He does not mind the bus being packed, as Symes seemed to think he would. The crush of people, the sheer weight of them, makes him feel less observed. None of them know who he is, or where he is going. Friends of his from before, police officers and journalists living north of the river (Queen's Park and Kilburn, Ealing and Hammersmith, Camden Town) liked to joke about southeast London as a badlands, a no-man's-land of scabby takeaways and boarded-up squats. Croft looks out at the criss-crossing streets, the lit-up intersections and slow-moving traffic queues. Curry houses and fish-and-chip shops and eight-till-late supermarkets, people returning from work, plonking themselves down in front of a cop show, cooking supper. All the things that, once you are removed from them, take on an aspect of the marvellous. He feels southeast London enfold him in the darkness like a tatty anorak, like an old army blanket. Khaki-coloured, smelling of spilled beer and antifreeze, benzene and tar,

6

ripped in several places but still warm enough to save your life on a freezing night.

The sky is mauve, shading to indigo, shading to black, and as they pass through Honor Oak Park Croft thinks of Steven Jepsom, who once lived not far from here, in a grubby basement flat on the Brownhill Road. It was Jepsom they arrested first, but a lack of real evidence meant they had to let him go again.

Whereas in Croft's case, there were the photographs. It was the photographs, much more than Kip, which had testified against him.

Now, it seemed, Steven Jepsom had been Rebecca Riding's killer, all along.

Croft remembered Symes's first visit to the prison, Symes telling him about Jepsom being re-arrested, almost a year before he, Croft, had been set free.

"It won't be long now," Symes had said. He gave Croft a look, and Croft thought it was almost as if he were trying to send him a signal of some kind, to claim the credit for Croft's good luck.

"Is there new evidence, then?" Croft asked.

"Plenty. A new witness has come forward, apparently. It's strange, how often that happens. There's no time limit on the truth, Dennis."

Croft dislikes Symes's insistence on using his first name. Using a first name implies familiarity, or liking, and for Symes he feels neither. He has always tried not to call Symes anything.

He tries not to think of Steven Jepsom, who is now in prison instead of him.

A guilty man for an innocent one. Straight swap.

Richard Symes lives on Sydenham Park Road, a residential street leading off Dartmouth Road, where the station is, ten minutes' walk from the bus stop at most. The house is unremarkable, a 1950s semi with an ancient Morris Minor parked in the drive. The porch lights are on. As he approaches the door, Croft thinks about turning around and heading back to the bus stop. There is no law that says he has to be here – the group is voluntary. But Symes won't like it if he doesn't attend. He will like it even less if he finds out that Croft turned up at his house and then went away again. He will see it as a mark against him, a sign of instability perhaps, an unwillingness to reintegrate himself into normal society. Could Symes report him for that? Perhaps.

That would mean more meetings, more reports, more conversations.

More time until he's off Symes's hook.

Croft decides it is better just to go through with it. It is an hour of his time, that is all, and he's here now, anyway. It's almost more trouble to leave than it is to stay.

He rings the bell. Someone comes to the door almost at once, a balding, fortyish man in a purple tank top and bottle-glass spectacles.

"You're exactly on time," he says. He steps aside to let Croft enter the hallway. Croft notices that in spite of it being November and chilly the man is wearing leather sandals, the kind Croft used to wear for school in the summer term and that used to be called Jesus sandals. Croft feels surprise that you can still buy them.

The Jesus man has a front tooth missing. The light of the hallway is sharp, bright orange. Croft follows the Jesus man along the corridor and through a door at the end. By contrast with the garish hallway, the room beyond is dim. The only illumination, such that it is, appears to be coming from a selection of low-wattage table lamps and alcove lights, making it difficult for Croft to find his bearings. He estimates that there are eight, perhaps ten people in the room, sitting in armchairs and on sofas. They fall silent as he enters. He looks around for Symes, but cannot see him.

"Our mentor is in the kitchen," says the man in the sandals. "He's making more drinks." He has an odd way of speaking, not a lisp exactly, but something like it. Perhaps it's his adenoids. Each time he opens his mouth, Croft finds himself focussing on the missing front tooth. Its absence makes the man look grotesquely young. *Our mentor?* Does he mean Symes? He guesses it's just the man's attempt at a joke.

A moment later Symes himself appears. He is carrying a plastic tray, stacked with an assortment of mugs and glasses. Croft can smell blackcurrant juice, Ribena. For some reason this cloying scent, so reminiscent of children's birthday parties, disturbs him.

"Dennis, good to see you," Symes says. "Take this for me, would you please, Bryan?" He eases the tray into the hands of the Jesus man, who seems about to overbalance. "What are you drinking?"

"Do you have a beer?" Croft says. His eyes are on the Jesus man, who has recovered himself enough to place the laden tray on a low wooden bench. The thought of the Ribena or even coffee in this place fills him with an empty dread he cannot explain. A beer would at least be tolerable. It might even help.

"Coming right up," Symes says. The baggy cords are gone and he is wearing jeans, teamed with a hooded sweatshirt, which has some sort of band logo on the front. His wrists protrude awkwardly from the too-short arms.

8

He's dressed himself up as a kid, Croft thinks, and the idea, like the thought of the Ribena, is for some reason awful. Symes tells him to find himself a seat but all the sofas and armchairs appear to be taken. In the end he finds an upright dining chair close to the door. The chair's single cushion slides about uncomfortably on the hard wooden seat. Croft looks around. He sees there are more people in the room than he thought at first, fifteen or twenty of them at least, many of them now talking quietly amongst themselves. Immediately opposite him an obese woman in a brightly coloured smock dress lolls in a chintz-covered armchair. She has shoulder-length, lank-looking hair. Her forehead is shiny with grease, or perhaps it is sweat.

Her small hands lie crossed in her lap. The hands, which are surprisingly pretty, are adorned with rings. The woman smiles at him nervously. Quite unexpectedly, Croft feels a rush of pity for her, a sensation more intense than any he has experienced since leaving the prison. He had not expected to see women here.

"Hi," Croft says. He wonders if the woman can understand him, even. There is a blankness in her eyes, and Croft wonders if she's on drugs, not street drugs but prescription medicine, Valium or Prozac or Ativan. There was a guy Croft knew in prison who was always on about how the prescription meds – the bennies, as he called them – were deadlier than heroin.

"They eat your fucking mind, man." Fourboys, his name was, Douglas Fourboys, eight years for arson. Croft had liked him better than anyone, mainly because of the books he read, which he didn't mind lending to Croft, once he had finished them. He had an enthusiasm for Russian literature, Dostoevsky especially. Douglas Fourboys was a lifelong Marxist, but at some point during the six months leading up to Croft's release, he had found God. He claimed he'd been sent the gift of prophecy, though Croft suspected this probably had more to do with the dope Fourboys's girlfriend occasionally managed to smuggle past the security than with any genuine aptitude for seeing the future.

"You've got to be careful, man," Fourboys had said to him, just a couple of days before his release. "They're waiting for you out there, I can see them, circling like sharks."

Fourboys had definitely been stoned when he said that. He'd reached out and clutched Croft's hand, then tilted to one side and fallen asleep. Croft misses Fourboys, he is the only person from inside that he does miss. He supposes he should visit him.

"We know who you are," the woman says suddenly. "You're going to help us speak with the master. We've seen your pictures." She smiles, her thin lips slick with spittle. Her words send a chill through Croft, though there is no real meaning to them that he can fathom. The woman is obviously vulnerable, mentally challenged. Clearly she needs protection. Croft feels anger at Symes for allowing her to be here unsupervised.

Suddenly Symes is there, standing behind him. He pushes something cold into Croft's hand, and Croft sees that it's a bottle of Budweiser. The thought of the beer entering his mouth makes Croft start salivating. He raises the bottle to his lips. The liquid is icy, familiar, heavenly. Croft feels numbness settle over him, an almost-contentment. Whatever is happening here need not concern him. It is only an hour.

"I see you've met Ashley," Symes says. He squats down next to the armchair, leaning in towards the fat woman and taking her hand. He presses his fingers into the flesh of her wrist as if to restrain her, as if she is something dangerous that needs to be managed. The woman shifts slightly in her seat, and Croft sees that her eyes, which appeared so dull, are now bright and alive. He cannot decide if it is wariness he sees in them, or cunning.

She doesn't like Symes though, this seems clear to him. Join the club.

"Ashley is my wife," Symes says. He grins into the face of the woman, a smile of such transparent artifice it is as if both he and she are playing a practical joke at Croft's expense.

Suddenly, in the overheated room, Croft feels chilled to the bone.

Is Symes serious? Snatches of words and images play themselves across his brain like a series of film stills: Symes's grin, the woman's slack features, the sticky word 'wife'.

You're wondering if they fuck, Croft thinks. Is that all it is, though? He takes another swig of the beer and the thoughts recede.

"Would you excuse me, just for a moment?" Symes says. "There's a phone call I need to make. I'll be right back." He stands, and walks away. The woman in the armchair looks after him for a second, then strains forward in her seat and puts her hand on Croft's knee. Croft can smell her breath, a sickening combination of peppermints and something else that might be tuna fish.

"You know him," the woman says, and for a moment Croft imagines she's talking about Symes, though the words that follow make his supposition seem impossible. "Even though you don't know it yet, you know him. He'll steep all his children in agony. Not just the agony of knowing him, but true pain." She tightens her grip on his knee, and Croft realises that she is strong, much stronger than she appears, or than he would have believed.

The mad are always strong, Croft thinks. He does not know how he knows this, but he knows it is true.

"Who are you talking about?" Croft says quietly. "Who is the master?"

The woman leans towards him. Her face is now so close to his that her features seem blurred, and Croft thinks for a confused moment that she is about to kiss him.

He sees himself straddling her. Her mounded flesh is pale as rice pudding.

"He is the tiger," she says. She grins, and her grin is like Symes's grin, only just like the Jesus man she has a tooth missing. The sight of the missing tooth fills him with horror.

"I need to get out of here," he says. "I mean, I need to use the bathroom." The room feels unbearably hot suddenly, stifling with the scent of unwashed bodies. He places his half-drunk beer on the coffee table, and as he makes his way back to the hallway he finds himself wondering if the woman will take advantage of his absence to taste the alcohol. He imagines her thin lips, clamping themselves around the mouth of the bottle in a wet, round 'o'.

He can hear Symes's voice, talking softly off in another room somewhere, but Croft ignores it. The staircase leads upwards to a square landing, with four doors leading off it, all of them closed. Croft tries one at random, not through any logical process of deduction but because it is closest. By a stroke of luck the room behind it turns out to be the bathroom, after all. Croft steps hurriedly inside and locks the door. He sits down on the closed toilet seat, covering his face with both hands. The room feels like it's rocking, slowly, back and forth, like a ship in a swell, though Croft knows this is only the beer, which he is unused to. He has barely touched a drop of alcohol since leaving prison. He presses his fingertips against his eyelids, savouring the darkness. After a minute or so he opens his eyes again and stands up. He lifts the toilet seat, pisses in an arcing gush into the avocado toilet bowl. He washes his hands at the sink. His face, in the mirror above, looks pale and slightly dazed but otherwise normal. It is only when he goes out on the landing again that he sees the photographs.

There are six of them in all. They are arranged in two groups of three, mounted on the blank area of wall at the far end of the landing and directly opposite the bathroom door. He had his back to them before, Croft realises, which is why he didn't see them when he first came upstairs. He recognises them at once. He thinks it would be impossible for an artist not to recognise his own work. One of the photos is of Murphy, or rather Murphy's hands, secured behind his back with a twist of barbed wire. The Kennington case.

Four of the other photos are also work shots, all photos he took for the Met in the course of his twenty-year career as a forensic photographer.

Lilian Beckworth, an RTA.

The Hallam Crescent flat, gutted by fire.

The underpass near Nunhead Station where the Cobb kid was found.

The sixth photo, not a work one, is of Rebecca Riding. The police believed it had been taken less than thirty minutes before her death.

Croft told his lawyer and the police that the photos they found at his house were not taken by him. His camera had been stolen, he said, and then later returned, placed on his front doorstep, wrapped carefully in a Tesco bag. Whoever left it there had not rung the bell. When Croft later developed the film, he found pictures he remembered taking at various sites around Lewisham and Manor Park. He also found the photos of Rebecca Riding.

"The photos are good though, aren't they, Dennis?" the cop kept saying. "They're no amateur job. You're a professional. You remember taking these, surely?"

Croft said he didn't, and kept saying it. In the end he could hardly remember, one way or the other.

It was true that they were very fine photographs. He'd spent some time working on them in his darkroom. The excellence of the results surprised even him.

Croft turns away from the photographs and goes back downstairs. In the stuffy living room they are all waiting, and for a moment as he returns to his place near the doorway Croft gets the feeling that he has been lured there on false pretences. He brushes the thought away, sits down on the uncomfortable wooden chair. The hour passes, and at the end of it Croft cannot remember a single thing that has been said. People are standing, going out into the hallway, pulling on coats. As Croft moves to join them, he feels a hand on his arm. It is Richard Symes.

"Some of us have clubbed together to buy you this," he says. "Your work means a great deal to us here. We're hoping this will help you find your feet again."

He hands Croft a package, a small but heavy something in a red-and-white bag. Croft knows without having to be told that it contains a camera. The gift is so unexpected that he cannot speak. Symes is smiling but it looks like a snarl, and finally it comes to Croft that he has been drugged, that this is what has been wrong all along, it would account for everything.

Drugs in the Bud.

12

Bennies in the beer.

It's the only thing that makes sense. Fourboys was right.

Outside, he feels better. The air is cold, bright as a knife. The sensations of nausea and unreality begin to recede. Croft walks smartly away, away from the house, along Sydenham Park Road and all the way to the junction with Dartmouth Road. He stands there, watching the traffic, wondering how much of the past hour was actually real.

*

The camera is a Canon, a top-of-the-range digital. It is not a hobby camera. Whoever chose it knew exactly what they were getting.

He has given up asking himself why this has been done for him. Having the camera in his hands is like coming alive again. He remembers the dream he had before he was in prison, his idea of giving up the police stuff and going freelance.

He has been taking photographs of the boy, Alexander. They are in the old Leegate shopping precinct just over the road. The boy is in a T-shirt and clean jeans, it is all perfectly harmless. When Croft returns the boy to the pub afterwards, Sandra is behind the bar. There is a complicated bruise on her upper arm, three blotches in a line, like careless fingerprints.

Croft has a bank account now, with his dole money in. He has filled in a couple of application forms for jobs. One is for a cleaning job with Lewisham Council, the other is for a shelf-stacking job at Sainsbury's. He can afford to buy a drink at the bar.

"Why is the pub called *The Old Tiger's Head*?" he asks Sandra McNiece.

"It's from when it was a coaching inn," says Sandra. "Tiger used to be a slang word, for footman. Because of the bright costumes they wore."

"Is that right?" Croft says. Croft briefly imagines a life in which he asks Sandra McNiece to run away with him. They will travel to Scotland, to Ireland, wherever she wants. He will take photos and the boy will go to school. He does not dare to take the daydream any further, but it is sweet, all the same, it is overwhelming.

"That's boring," Alex says. "I think it's because they once found a tiger's head inside the wardrobe. A mad king killed him and brought him to London, all the way from India."

Sandra laughs and ruffles his hair. "What funny ideas boys have," she says. "What are you doing in here, anyway? You should be upstairs."

Croft buys a small folding table from the junk shop at the end of Lee Road that sells used furniture. He places objects on the table – an empty milk carton, two apples, a Robinson's jam jar filled with old pennies he found at the back of the wardrobe – and photographs them, sometimes singly, sometimes in different combinations. He places the table in front of the wardrobe, so the objects are shown reflected in the oval mirror. Croft experiments with taking shots that omit the objects themselves, and show only their reflections. At first glance, they look like any of the other photos Croft has taken of the objects on the table. They're not, though, they're pictures of nothing. Croft finds this idea compelling. He remembers how when Douglas Fourboys was stoned he became terrified of mirrors and refused to go near them. "There are demons on the other side, you know," he said. "They're looking for a way through."

"A way through what?"

"Into our world. Mirrors are weak spots in the fabric of reality. Borges knew it, so did Lovecraft. You have to be careful."

"You don't really believe this stuff, do you?" Croft knew he shouldn't encourage Fourboys, but he couldn't help it, his stories were so entertaining.

"I believe some of it," Fourboys said. "You would too, if you knew what I know. There are people who are trying to help the demons to break through. They believe in the rule of chaos, of enlightenment through pain, you know, like the stuff in *Hellraiser* and in that French film, *Martyrs*. They call themselves Satan's Tigers." Fourboys took a coin out of his pocket and began swivelling it back and forth between his fingers. "If you knew how many of those sickos were on the loose it would freak you out."

The next time the boy comes to visit him in his room, Croft shows him how to set up a shot, then lets him take some photographs of the Robinson's jam jar. Afterwards, Croft takes some photos of Alex's reflection. He has him sit on the edge of the bed in front of the mirror.

"Try and make yourself small," Croft says. "Pretend you're sitting inside a cupboard, or in a very cramped space."

The boy lifts both his feet up on to the duvet and then hugs his knees. In the mirror shots he looks pale, paler than he does in real life. It's as if the mirror has drained away some of his colour.

"What's in there?" Alex says. He's staring at the chimney alcove, at the built-in cupboard that Croft has been unable to open.

"I don't know," Croft says. "It's locked."

"Perhaps it's treasure," says the boy.

14

"If you can find out where the key is, we can have a look."

"I know what it'll be." Alex grins, and Croft sees he has a tooth missing. "It'll be the tiger's head." He throws himself backwards on the bed and makes a growling noise. "I bet that's where they've hidden it."

"Isn't it time for your tea yet?" Croft says.

"I'm scared of tigers," the boy says. "If they come on the TV I have to switch off."

That night, Croft dreams of Richard Symes. There has been a break-in at Symes's house and there are cops everywhere. They're trying to work out if any valuables have been stolen.

Symes's throat has been cut.

There is no sign of Ashley Symes, or anyone else.

*

At his next meeting with Symes, Croft is able to tell him he's been offered the shelf-stacking job. Symes seems pleased.

"When do you start?" he says.

"Next Monday." He wonders if Symes will say anything to him about a burglary at his home, but he doesn't. Instead, Symes asks him how he's getting on with his new camera.

"It's great to use," Croft says. "The best I've had."

"Why don't you bring some of your work with you to show us when you come on Tuesday? I know Ashley would love that. Bring the boy with you, too, if you like."

How does Symes know about Alex? For a moment, Croft feels panic begin to rise up inside him. Then he remembers Symes knows the McNieces, that it was Symes who found him his room. "I couldn't," Croft says. "He's only eight. His mother wouldn't allow it."

"What she doesn't know won't hurt her. It would be an adventure for him. All boys love adventures."

Croft says he'll think about it. He thinks about himself and Alex, walking down the road like father and son. On his way back to London Bridge station, Croft buys Alex a present from one of the gift shops jammed in under the railway arches near Borough Market, a brightly coloured clockwork tiger with a large, looped key in its side. It is made of tin plate, Made in China.

The journey from London Bridge to Lee takes seventeen minutes. As he mounts the stairs to his room, he meets Sandra coming down.

"I've just been trying to find you," she says. "I found this. Alex said you were looking for it."

15

She holds something out to him, and Croft sees it is a key. "It's for that cupboard in the chimney alcove," she says. "We've not opened it since we've been here, so God knows what's in there. Just chuck out anything you don't need."

"That's very good of you," Croft says. He searches her face, for tiredness or bruises, anything he can hate McNiece with, but today he finds nothing. He thinks about asking her to come up for a coffee but is worried that his offer might be misconstrued. He closes his fingers around the key. Its hard, irregular shape forms a core of iron at the heart of his hand.

It is some time before he opens the cupboard. He tells himself this is because he has things to do, but in reality it is because he is afraid of what he might find inside. Late afternoon shadows pour out of the oval mirror and rush to hide themselves in the corners and beneath the bed. As the room begins to fill up with darkness, Croft finds he can already imagine the stuffed tiger's head, the mummified, shrunken body of a child, the jam jar full of flies or human teeth. When he finally opens the cupboard it is empty. The inside smells faintly sour, an aroma Croft quickly recognises as very old wallpaper paste. The wallpaper inside the cupboard is a faded green colour. It is peeling away from the walls, and in one place right at the back it has fallen down completely. The wooden panel behind is cracked, and when Croft puts his fingers over the gap he can feel a faint susurrus of air, a thin breeze, trapped between the wooden back of the cupboard and the interior brickwork.

Croft puts his whole head inside the cupboard and presses his opened mouth to the draughty hole. He tastes brick dust, cool air, the smell of damp earth and old pennies.

He closes his eyes and then breathes in. The cold, metallic air tastes delicious and somehow rare, like the air inside a cave. He exhales, pushing his own air back through the gap, and it is if he and the building are breathing together, slowly in and out. It is then that he feels the thing pass into him, something old that has been waiting in the building's foundations, in the ancient sewer tunnels beneath the street, or somewhere deeper down even than that. Its face is a hideous ruin, and as Croft takes it into himself he is at last granted the knowledge he has been fumbling for, the truth of who he is and what he has done.

Strange lights flicker across the backs of his closed eyelids, yellow stripes, like the markings on the metal tiger he bought for the boy near Borough Market.

You are ready now, says a voice inside his head. Croft realises it is the voice of Ashley Symes.

And in the end, it is easy. Both McNieces are downstairs, working the bar. Alex is alone in the living room of the first floor flat. The carpet is a battleground, strewn with Transformers toys and model soldiers. The tin-plate tiger is surrounded by aggressive forces. The TV is playing quietly in the background.

When Croft sticks his head around the door and asks if Alex would like to come on an assignment with him, the boy says yes at once. The boy knows the word 'assignment' has to do with photography because Croft has told him so.

"Where are we going?" Alex says. It is getting on towards his bedtime, but the unexpectedness of what they are doing has filled him with energy.

Croft knows that unless he is very unlucky the boy's absence will not be noticed for at least three hours.

"To visit some people I know," Croft says. "They keep a tiger in their back garden."

The boy's eyes grow large.

"You're joking me," he says.

"That's for me to know and you to find out."

The boy laughs delightedly, and Croft takes his hand. The journey passes uneventfully. The boy seems captivated by every small thing – the pale mist rising up from the streets, the lit-up shop fronts, the endlessly streaming car headlights, yellow as cats' eyes.

The only glances they encounter seem benign.

When they arrive at Symes's house, Alex rushes up the driveway to the front door and rings the bell.

"And who is this young man?" Symes says, bending down.

"Dennis says you've got a tiger, but I don't believe him," says the child. He is beginning to flag now, Croft senses, just a little. He is overexcited. The slightest thing could have him in tears.

"We'll have to have a look, then, won't we?" Symes says. He places a hand on the boy's head. Croft steps forward out of the shadows and towards the door.

Once he is inside, he knows, it will begin. He and Ashley Symes will kill the child. The rest will watch.

"You have done well," Symes says to Croft, quietly. "This won't take long."

"Will there be cookies?" Alex says.

Croft stands still. He can feel the thing moving inside him, twisting in his guts like a cancer.

He wants to vomit. Croft gasps for breath, sucking in the blunt, smoky air, the scent of macadam, of the hushed, damp trees at the roadsides and spreading along all the railway lines of southeast London. The fleet rails humming with life, an antidote to ruin.

He smells the timeswept, irredeemable city and it is like waking up.

Above him, bright stars throw up their hands in surprise.

"Come here to me, Sasha," Croft says. He is amazed at how steady his voice sounds. "There's no time now. We have to go."

"But the tiger," the child whimpers. He looks relieved.

"There are no tigers here," Croft says. "Mr Symes was joking. Come on."

The boy's hand is once again in his and he grips it tightly.

"Will we be home soon?" says the boy.

"I hope so," Croft replies. "We should be, if a bus comes quickly."

He does not look back.

LONDON AFTER MIDNIGHT

O*ne of the most famous London horror stories of all time did not actually have its origins in London, but in sun-soaked California, at MGM studios, and in some respects – or so the purists would tell us – it wasn't really a horror story, though it did have a horrific outcome. On its release in 1927, London After Midnight, directed by Tod Browning and starring Lon Chaney Snr, was heralded as Hollywood's first attempt at a proper vampire movie. But in fact this, like so many 'facts' where London After Midnight is concerned, was a deception.*

The movie was a traditional Gothic melodrama of a type very common in Hollywood in that pre-talkie era, and similar to many contemporary productions, it was set in fog-shrouded London, a city that American audiences assumed was still reeling from the depredations inflicted on it by a top-hatted, knife-wielding phantom called Jack the Ripper. In brief, it concerns the shooting in his home of aristocratic Roger Balfour, and the resulting unsuccessful investigation by Inspector Burke of Scotland Yard (Chaney Snr). Forced to deduce suicide, the Yard lets the case drop – until five years have elapsed, when two very mysterious individuals take charge of the disused property: an eerie woman with long, dark hair, and even more frightening, a grinning ghoul with bug eyes and sharp teeth, known only as 'the man in the Beaver hat'. Inevitably, the conclusion is drawn that this devilish duo are vampires, and that their arrival is connected to the suicide of Sir Roger. Equally inevitably, the Man in the Beaver Hat, (Chaney Snr again, this time in his trademark spectacular make-up) begins to terrorise the neighbourhood.

The denouement – and we can safely give away this spoiler because the last known print of the film was lost in 1967 during a fire in an MGM vault, and despite myths to the contrary, no known copies exist – is that the Man in the Beaver hat is actually Inspector Burke, attempting by an elaborate ruse to smoke out the real murderer.

So there we have it – the real twist is that London After Midnight was never a horror movie at all, but a complex murder mystery. But this didn't stop cinema-goers of the time lapping it up. It made an amazing $540,000 profit for MGM, one of the largest of any of Chaney's films, though the critics were not too generous. The

New York Times described it as *"incoherent,"* while *Variety* said that it was *"not of the quality that results in broken house records."*

But in fact, this is only the beginning of the grim tale that was *London After Midnight.*

Within a few years, MGM had withdrawn it from circulation. Rumours soon spread that this was because it was too disturbing, and that viewers had stumbled out of the theatres spellbound and disoriented by Chaney Snr's terrifying performance. When the movie was lost in 1967, even though by then it had not been seen widely for over 30 years, these rumours became part of movie-going legend.

The film had been an absolute shocker!

There was something about it that was malevolent!

It should never have been made, and maybe the fire that finally consumed it had been lit deliberately!

All of these stories were undoubtedly aided by the memorable image of Chaney's demented, shark-toothed grin, as immortalised in several surviving stills. But the truth is a little more mundane. Browning re-shot the movie in 1935 as *Mark Of The Vampire*, this time with sound, and starring Bela Lugosi as the titular bloodsucker and Lionel Barrymore as the policeman. MGM had simply withdrawn the original from circulation several years earlier so as not to overshadow this later release.

However, while the stories that *London After Midnight* created mass hysteria on its first showing may not be true, it wasn't without at least one tragic casualty. In October 1928, in Hyde Park in London, an Irish girl call Julie Mangan was murdered when her throat was slashed with a razor. When the perpetrator was apprehended by the real Scotland Yard, he turned out to be a young Welshman called Robert Williams. Williams admitted his guilt, but said that he had been accompanied into the park that night by Lon Chaney Snr in his monstrous make-up and Beaver hat, with his bulging eyes and grinning fang-filled mouth, who had screamed at him to kill.

Williams was condemned to death, but later examination by psychiatrists provided testimony that he was suffering severe delusions – which, if not caused by the movie, were certainly enlivened by it – and the sentence was commuted to confinement for life in a secure hospital.

THE SOLDIER
Roger Johnson

"A Christmas ghost story?" I prompted.

Julia Kirkby's eyes widened. "Did I say that?" she murmured. "Perhaps I was exaggerating a little."

"Oh, I do hope not," said George Cobbett, in a dangerously polite tone that warned of dyspeptic ill-temper. Its import wasn't lost on Julia.

"Well, at least it took place towards Christmas, and if there was an end to the story, then it came on the day itself." She flashed us a brief, slightly nervous smile. "Mystery there to start with – and more to come. As to ghosts ... I think you'd better make up your own minds about that."

"Straightforward advice," said George. "Here's some for you. There's a good fire going, your glass is full, and you're among friends – so begin at the beginning and stop when you think you've reached the end."

"Very well," said Julia, "though I should tell you that it isn't actually *my* story. If it were, perhaps I'd be able to understand it more clearly." She took a sip from her gin and tonic, and continued: "As far as I was concerned, it began with some research I was doing for an article on the City of London and its peculiar institutions – the Livery Companies, Gog and Magog, the Trial of the Pyx – that sort of thing.

"Well, I came across a letter in an issue of *The Athenaeum* from some time in the 1890s. The writer simply asked for information about the Worshipful Company of Militia – 'said to be the oldest volunteer corps in the British Army, and drawn entirely from men of the City.' The name meant nothing to me. You may not think that's surprising, but my father was a military historian, and I actually do know something about the subject. I looked through the following half-dozen issues of the magazine, but there was nothing further. Perhaps someone had got in touch directly with the enquirer. There was no way of telling. It did seem a little odd, though, that he'd been unable to satisfy his curiosity by simply asking at the War Office. I wondered idly whether the whole thing was a mistake. Maybe the body in question was actually the Honourable Artillery Company.

"Still, I had work of my own to do.

"The article eventually appeared a few months later in a magazine called *Your England*, which is distributed only in North America, aimed at expatriates and potential tourists. By the time it was published I'd written a lot of other pieces and had quite forgotten about the Worshipful Company of Militia. I'd certainly forgotten making a brief reference to it in my article, so the Worshipful Company wasn't the first thing I thought of when a package arrived from Canada.

"Inside the package, which had been forwarded by the publishers of *Your England*, was a small batch of typed sheets and a covering letter. My correspondent – his name was Davies, which is of no importance whatsoever – had been interested by my reference to this mysterious body, because it was something he'd known of, by name, for several years. And he had run up against a blank wall in trying to find out more. He actually had written to the War Office and the National Army Museum, but the replies had been courteous and completely unhelpful. He could add nothing concrete to the little I already knew, except what I should read in the enclosed pages. Yours sincerely, etc., etc.

"The typed sheets were a transcript from a notebook, kept in about 1880 by a boy who was some sort of cousin to Mr Davies's grandmother – the relationship wasn't entirely clear. Although more obviously important and valuable items had been discarded over the years, this notebook had somehow survived. There wasn't much to tell about its owner. His name was Richard Henry Wenlock, and he was nearly sixteen years old when he wrote this brief journal. Physically he was stocky and well proportioned, but mentally – well, I don't know. Not actually backward in any usual sense, but distinctly strange.

"He was the youngest child by several years, which wasn't uncommon, I suppose, in those days of large families. At least one sister had died in early childhood, and there was a brother killed at Balaclava. Perhaps it was the brother's career that had set the boy to the notion of becoming a soldier himself – or perhaps it was just the experience of being brought up in a garrison town. I can imagine the clash there'd be between that military ambition on the one hand and the over-protectiveness of an ageing mother for her last and youngest darling."

Julia paused and looked pointedly at the glass in front of her. George hastily emptied his own glass of bitter and handed it to me. Plainly this was my round. When I returned from the bar, I found that Julia had taken from her briefcase a neat loose-leaf folder. She thumbed quickly through the pages before turning back to the beginning.

"This is young Wenlock's story," she said. "I can grasp the significance of some of it, but... Well, let's see what you two make of it."

And she began to read.

*

I really did not think that I should be happy when I came here. They told me that it was not just London, but the City of London. Of course I knew that London is a city. It is the greatest city in the world. But that was not what they meant. The City of London is a very small place, they said, like a village, and the Queen does not live here, nor does Parliament meet here. It does not seem to me very much like a village, but I have learned that the City is very special.

It was strange at first, not being able to go out into the countryside, and not seeing soldiers everywhere, as I used to in Colchester. I loved to visit the Garrison in Colchester. It was even exciting to go to the chapel there, because it was a soldiers' church and had regimental flags and battle trophies. I made up my mind quite early on that I wanted to be a soldier, but somehow things did not seem to go right. My Father had served in the army, and he used to tell me wonderful stories of wars and campaigns, but Mother never liked to hear them, and she never wanted me to be a soldier. When Father died she tried to stop me going again to the barracks, but it was not hard to go there without her knowing. But then Mother died too, of what the Doctor said was her weak heart, and I was sent here to the City of London, to live with my Aunt. I have been here now for nearly three months. Soon it will be the twenty-fifth of December, God's birthday, and then I shall take my first steps towards becoming a real soldier.

It did not take me long to find out that where we live in Spicers Lane is not very far from the castle which is called the Tower of London. I think it is rather strange that the Tower of London in really in Stepney and not in London at all, but there are many strange and special things still to learn about this City. There are soldiers at the castle, and just occasionally I am allowed to see them. Some of them are old men and wear funny old-fashioned clothes. I have read also that soldiers come to the great Bank of England, which is quite near, but they only come in the evening to stand guard, and I have not seen them yet.

I am going to be a very special kind of soldier, and that is only right, for I am a special person. I know that, for Mr Pater told me so. I must write down all that has happened so far, so that it is clear in

23

my mind. It is most important for a soldier to have a clear mind. Father told me that. Some things, though, are secret things and must not be written down, and if the wrong people were to find out about them I should not be allowed to become a soldier.

So I must not tell where the Church is, except that it is only a short distance from Spicers Lane and it is in a little square churchyard which you get to by going underneath a building and along an alleyway.

There is a metal gate with a bull's head on it, and Mr Pater told me that it is usually locked, but I have never found it locked.

Many of the churches in the City have strange names. I have found this out while walking about the streets, with my Aunt or on my own. There are Saint Katherine Cree and Saint Dionis Backchurch and Saint Andrew-by-the-Wardrobe. So I was not surprised when I saw the board just inside the iron gate with the name upon it, Saint Denis Mitre. But I was surprised and excited to learn that it was a soldiers' church, the first I had seen since I left Colchester. I knew, because under the name on the board was written, The Church of the Worshipful Company of Militia. Militia means soldiers, so this church was a soldiers' church.

It was a Sunday afternoon, and the City was very quiet, like death. It was as if there had never been anybody alive there. Even the public houses were shut, and there were no shops open at all. If I had chosen to walk towards the Tower of London, then there would have been many shops open and busy street markets, because so many people who live just outside the City of London are Jewish and do not keep Sunday as a day of rest. But in the City all was still. I like to be here on a Sunday, because then I can feel that I have the whole special place to myself, and even the Lord Mayor is not more important than I am. It is even more peaceful than on Saturday afternoons, when so many of the people who work here go home for luncheon and do not come back until Monday morning. The stillness on Saturday afternoons is one of the reasons why the City of London is so very special.

My Aunt had been taken ill with a headache while we were at church, but it is not that church that I shall tell of. It was only our parish church, which is called Saint Michael Cornhill and which is old and gloomy and rather dull. After luncheon, Aunt said that she would lie down for a while, and as Cook and Ann, who is our maid, said that they were very busy, I asked if I might walk about the streets for a while. I said that I had not lived in London long, and it was important that I should know where famous places were, like the Guildhall and Saint Paul's Cathedral. That is what I said, but really I wanted to get out of the house and away from Aunt and

Cook and Ann, because I could not make them see how very important and special it was to me that I should become a soldier. When I mentioned it to them they would laugh, but in a secret kind of way that they hoped I would not understand, but I did.

The sky that Sunday was grey and watery, and the sun looked like a dull sixpence, casting uncertain, fleeting shadows. It was the sort of day that suits well the greyness of this City, which was now mine. I am of a clever and enquiring mind, and I already knew where the Cathedral was, and the Guildhall in its secret square, back from the empty road. However, I resolved to follow the streets wherever my nose led me, now this way and now that, so that I might know my new home fully. In this way I discovered many special and important buildings and places, such as the Royal Exchange and the Mansion House, which is where the Lord Mayor lives, and the Founders' Hall and Leadenhall market, and it seemed to me that I ought to return to Spicers Lane and my Aunt's house. But my nose led me to turn to the left off one of the main roads and into a narrow lane where tall grey buildings seemed to reach up to the grey sky, almost shutting out the light.

As I walked along this lane I noticed, for I am very observant, that there was a number of older and generally smaller buildings among the big grey ones. One of these, which looked very old indeed, had a narrow passage or alley underneath it, leading away from the lane. I should have passed this by, thinking it a private way, if it had not been for the sign. It was just inside the passage, screwed to the wall with bolts that had rusted over very many years, and there was an arrow painted upon it, which pointed away from the street. Underneath the arrow were the words, To The Ch –. But that is all it said, because the rest had faded entirely.

The passage was rather dark beyond, and it still looked to me like a private and secret place, but if I had not been meant to go in, then there would not have been a sign with an arrow. So I went along the dark and narrow alley and found at the end of it a gate made of strips of black iron, shaped into strange shapes, and with a metal bull's head in the centre of it. Beyond the gate I could see a small square, whose grass looked colourless and unhealthy. There were tombs of blackened stone and patches of bare earth, but the grass was neatly shorn. Someone tended this little churchyard. Looking to the far side of it, I saw the church itself.

At first, and for a moment, I was disappointed, because I had seen several churches that afternoon, and even the dullest of them were more handsome than this one, which seemed rightly to hide away from the streets where people go. But then I saw the notice-board which told me that this was a very special church. It stood just

25

within the gate, and it was cracked and faded, but I could clearly read the words, The Church of Saint Denis Mitre, and underneath, The Church of the Worshipful Company of Militia. So then I knew that it was right that I should go on, because this was a soldiers' church.

I pushed open the iron gate and walked across the grass to the big wooden door of the church, where I lifted the heavy latch and pushed, but the door was locked. I was about to go away, disappointed, when I noticed the knocker on the door. It was made of iron, black like the gate, and shaped like a bull's head. Almost without thinking, I raised the knocker and rapped smartly upon the door. The sound was very loud, like a martial drum. I expected to rouse angry people in the buildings that surrounded the little churchyard, but nobody appeared at any of the blank windows, and I remembered that it was Sunday. Probably these houses and offices were all deserted. Almost before the sound of that loud rap had died away, the big door was opened, and in front of me stood a tall man who wore a dark robe and had a curious kind of cap upon his head. As he saw me, he smiled. This was my first meeting with the Priest.

He said, My dear son, I have been waiting eagerly for you. I thank God that He has led you to us this day.

This was strange, because I had not known myself that I should even find this hidden church, so how could the Priest know that I would come?

But he was speaking again, and he said, Come in. It is good to have another soldier to swell our ranks.

I started to explain that I was not really a soldier, but that I hoped to become one, and he said, In God's good time you shall. We must give thanks to God and to the Mother of God that you have arrived. This is a special church indeed, and you are a special Son among the Sons of God.

He said that he was the Priest of this Church of Saint Denis Mitre, and that he was called Pater. Because of the cap that he wore, I was so bold as to ask if he was a Roman Priest, and at that he only smiled in a singular way and did not reply. But I thought that he was a Roman, because of the smell of incense that was all around the church. It was not very strong, but it was like the incense they use in the big churches in Flanders, where my mother had taken me when I was quite a small boy. I found this rather exciting, but I was not sure that my Aunt would like the thought of my visiting a Roman church.

It was a soldiers' church, though, and I had been welcomed as a soldier. That was very special and important.

I asked if the church was very old. Was it as old as Saint Michael Cornhill, which was our parish church? And Mr Pater said that it was very much older, older than all the churches that stood in the City of London, even Saint Paul's Cathedral. And it had always been a church of soldiers.

He said that he would show me something of the upper part of the church, and tell me a little about the soldiers who worshipped there. Alas, he said, there are very few of them now, but once they were numerous. They were the strongest and bravest of all the soldiers of the Empire, and they worshipped God from all its wide dominions. Those who are left still remember in their bones the great deeds that were done, and even now those few are proud to be of the Worshipful Company of Militia.

I said that I had never heard of this Company of Militia, and Mr Pater told me that it was very old, like the church. It is the oldest company in England, he said, and for a long time now it has met only here in the City of London. Ah, my son, he said, this City of ours is a very special place. It is more strange and special than you can imagine, and you are a privileged young man to be admitted to its secrets.

He took me to the altar and made me swear that I would say nothing to my Aunt or to anyone else of what he told me and what he showed me, and his eyes were dark and terrible as he spoke. When I asked why, he said that a soldier must be a fit person to have secrets entrusted to him, and that if I could not keep the secrets of the church then I was unfitted to be a soldier. Besides, he was an officer of very high rank, and I must learn to obey his orders. So then, of course, I swore as he commanded, by God and His great sacrifice, by which the world was saved.

Then his lifted up the embroidered cloth and showed me the altar itself. It was made of a single great block of stone, and on it were carved the signs of the stars and the words, LORD OF AGES, only the words were in Latin, and I could not read them. This, he said, is the altar of our Lord, even as the other is. Now come, and see what a proud tradition we soldiers have.

The stone walls, and even the strong low pillars with their rounded arches, seemed to be covered with plates and tablets of stone, recording the lives and deaths of soldiers who had worshipped at this church. All the names were of men. There were no women's memorials here at all. Many of these monuments were framed with stone wreaths, and above them was written the word, DEO. Mr Pater explained to me that this too was Latin, and meant simply, TO GOD. The names on some of the stones were quite ordinary, but many of them were strange names. They are among

27

the secret things, and I must not write them down. Mr Pater was able to tell me a little about these soldiers, how they fought bravely for their country and for their God, and how they died uncomplaining when they were called. It was remarkable that he could tell me something about every man whose name was there, no matter how long ago he had lived. This one, he said, was a valiant Lion, and this a faithful Persian. I may not mention the name, but it did not seem Persian to me.

Before I left that afternoon, Mr Pater asked me to kneel with him in front of the altar and say a prayer of thanks to God for sending me to the Church of Saint Denis Mitre. The battle continues, he said, and we must have soldiers. Life and Death, Light and Darkness await the outcome.

When may I come again? I asked.

When you will, he said.

And will you be here?

When you come I shall be here, he said.

That was my first visit to the Church of Saint Denis Mitre, and my first meeting with Mr Pater.

When I got back to my Aunt's house in Spicers Lane, I found that I had hardly been missed. I was able to tell of the streets I had walked along and the buildings I had seen, but I said nothing about the church and the Worshipful Company of Militia.

In the evening, while Aunt read to me from the Bible, I thought of the stories that Mr Pater had told me. Stories of great battles, of brave soldiers and mighty deeds, of victories won and enemies defeated. The stories that Aunt was telling me were not exciting, but those that Mr Pater had told me thrilled my martial blood even as I remembered them. I called to mind the great wars in which the Soldiers of God had fought, the mighty clash at Maranga and the battle of Chalons, when the plains were rich with the red blood of brave men. I thought upon these secret and terrible things, and I said no word to anyone.

It was not always easy for me to leave the house alone and to go about the City. On the next Sunday I was kept indoors because my Aunt fancied that I did not look well, and that the winter chill would be unhealthy for me. Twice at the weekends Aunt told me to stay with her because special company was coming to tea. The people who came were not special at all, though perhaps Aunt truly thought they were. They were an old woman, who was about Aunt's age, and her son and daughter. I had hoped that the son might be a soldier who could tell me exciting stories of wars and battles, but he was only a lawyer and very smartly dressed and dull. Aunt told me to be very agreeable to the young woman, and I did as well as I could, though I could not think why. She was pretty enough, but not interesting. I wanted more than anything to visit the hidden church again and to learn more about the soldiers.

Once, on a weekday afternoon, which I think was a Wednesday, I was sent on an errand to Aunt's bank, and I thought that I might return by way of the church. The day was covered in a greasy yellow fog, so that I could not see many paces in front of me, and I had to take care not to jostle people or step into the road. There were boys here and there with torches in their hands, to guide gentlemen along their way, and after I had called at the bank I followed one of these boys because it seemed to me that he would lead me in the right direction. As he passed the corner of a counting-house I saw in the light from his torch the sign with the name of the lane that leads to the secret narrow passage and the church, but when I walked along the lane all was so dark and uncertain that I could not find the old building with the entrance to the passage. When I got back to Spicers Lane I tried hard to hide my disappointment, but my Aunt noticed that something was wrong. Happily, she thought that I must have taken a chill, and she made Ann light the fire in my room and give me a hot drink and see that I went to bed early. I did not mind this in the end, because in my sleep I dreamed of being a soldier and fighting in the most glorious battles.

I was at last able to visit the church again, and it was on a Sunday afternoon, just as before. Three weeks had passed since my first visit, but Mr Pater was there as he had said, and he greeted me like an officer welcoming a faithful soldier. I felt very proud and very humble at the same time. With the Priest was an old man who must have been over fifty years of age. I may not tell his name, but Mr Pater said that he was a brave and loyal member of the Worshipful Company of Militia. He had risen high in the ranks and was soon to be promoted again, to the rank of Courier.

I said that I had not heard of an officer being called a Courier, even though I knew of Captains and Generals, but he explained that it is a rank that is very special to the Worshipful Company of Militia.

I asked the old man when and where he was to receive his new rank, and at that he pointed to the rounded west end of the church and said, I am to be buried at the great Festival on the twenty-fifth of December, when we celebrate the birth of God and His coming into the world.

I did not like to hear that, because he was a fine old man, and I did not want to think of him dying, but the two of them just laughed kindly and told me that no harm would come of it. He will pass

29

through Death to a new Life, said Mr Pater, and on that joyful day he will be reborn. God will take care of him. You have much to learn, my son, but if you are willing to be taught you too shall share in our feast, and be recruited with the rank of Raven. God has shed the Eternal Blood for you. Can you refuse Him your service?

So then I knew that this good man had accepted me as a fit person to be a real soldier. It was the most important thing that had happened to me, and I resolved that I should be brave and strong and worthy of my brother, who died in battle far away. How proud he would be! You will be a true Servitor of the Lord, said the old man, and my heart rejoiced.

Mr Pater left me in the care of this good old soldier, and he told me many things about the great and honourable company that I am soon to join. Some of them are secret things and may only be spoken of among those who know. They made my head swim with the wonder and the glory of it all. At last Mr Pater came back and told me that it was time for me to go. They will miss you at home if you stay longer, he said, but you shall come once more before the great day.

That was my second visit to the soldiers' church, and it was near the end of November.

The third time I went to the church was on a Saturday afternoon, just two weeks ago. Of course, there were more people about in the streets, and the public houses and some of the shops were open, but all the City seemed very quiet when I thought of how it had been only that morning. The sky was all over clouds of a greyish blue, and towards the west was a great uncertain patch, so dark that it was almost black. The air itself felt heavy with excitement, as if it had been charged with electricity. But I did not need excitement from the air, for this was my third visit to the secret church, and my last before the great Festival, when God is born, and the year turns.

The Priest and the old soldier were there again to greet me and to conduct me into the church. We knelt before the altar to offer our eternal service to the God of Battles, and the flames that burned in the little pottery bowls shook a little, even as my heart shook, with the majesty and the glory.

Mr Pater said, Now, my son, you have seen what may be seen of this church above the ground. Today you shall see beneath, where lie the heart and bowels.

They led me behind the altar, to where an archway was covered by a hanging curtain. In the archway was a wooden door, which the Priest unlocked. Then, with two candles to light us, we proceeded down a narrow and winding stone stair to the church beneath the church.

It is the same shape as the church above, and no smaller. The walls are of a plain white, and on the floor is a design in stone to remind us always of God and His sacrifice. Behind the door that we had entered through stands a statue of a most beautiful Lady, whose face is proud and commanding. She is the Holy Virgin, Who is to be revered. The smell of incense and wine was strong.

Mr Pater said, Here is the real church, of which that above is but a shadow. See the benches and tables, where the Communion Feast is taken! See the High Altar, where the Holy Mysteries are celebrated! My son, this shall be your glory when you join us.

He told me and showed me much more: of the roaring of beasts and the croaking of birds, of the liquid sweetness of the honey wherein the Lions bathe, of the spiced sacramental wine. This much I may write down, but the rest is secret. I knew and gloried that I was to be admitted to the ranks of an ancient and blessed company.

When the time came for me to leave, Mr Pater said to me, You are God's gift to our cause, for we are few in number now and grow old. Our faithful friend here is the youngest of our company. I myself am older than you think, old beyond your imagining. Your youth and vigour are sorely needed in the great fight.

How shall I arrange to leave the house and come here on the day of the Festival? I asked.

Never worry, he said. I shall arrange that. Pay no heed to those who celebrate other gods upon the twenty-fifth of December, but set your heart and mind upon the one true God. They have kept us under foot for so long! But we are soldiers, you and I, and we will prevail. If by chance you cannot come to us upon the great day, then we shall come to you. Be assured!

And so I left the Church of Saint Denis Mitre and the Worshipful Company of Militia, but soon I shall return, for soon it will be the twenty-fifth, the day of the Festival of God's birth, and I shall hear in my ears the terrible pain in the bellowing of the dying bull.

*

"Yes," said George. "It's certainly a strange story. Powerful strange. What became of the boy?"

Julia took a thoughtful sip from her gin and tonic. "There," she said, "we have to rely on third-hand evidence. Some while ago my Canadian correspondent found a letter, written to his grandmother by a cousin, who tells what she had heard from someone else in the family – oh, dear! This is getting very complicated. What it comes down to is a very brief report on the death of a younger cousin, who isn't named but is certainly the Wenlock boy.

"You'll remember how amused he was at his aunt's notion that he'd taken a chill? Well, apparently he really had, though he'd ignored it. He was such a withdrawn, secretive lad that he managed to keep the worst of it from the rest of the household until a few days before Christmas, when it became clear that he was seriously ill. His mother had a weak heart, and it looks as if the complaint was hereditary. At all events, he was confined to his bed, and the doctor was called. Pneumonia, that was the diagnosis, and the boy wasn't to be left alone. The pneumonia aggravated the heart condition, and he died shortly after ten o'clock on Christmas morning. Not a very merry Christmas in that household, I fancy. He ate little and spoke little, though he seemed, they thought, to be waiting for something to happen. When he died, he was smiling.

"There. Now you know just as much as I do. What do you make of it?"

I started to say, "One or two things seem pretty plain – " But I was interrupted by George's voice. He spoke in an almost dreamy tone, quite as if no one else had said anything.

"Some years ago," he said, "your old friend Michael Harrison wrote a book setting out the theory that much of Roman London can still be traced in the names of the present City – street names and so forth. He went into considerable sound detail. One point I particularly remember is the notion that a few of the churches, too, have names that indicate Roman origins. Dionis Backchurch and Magnus Martyr, for instance, at the very least suggest *Dionysus Bacchus* and the *Magna Mater*."

"Now that," said Julia, "is something that hadn't occurred to me. And you think – ?"

He waved a hand, deprecatingly. "Well, the City certainly is a curious place – very secret and special, as young Wenlock put it. And I suppose that a hidden cult would tend towards corruption, mental or spiritual. My knowledge of the later Empire is limited, and I wouldn't dare offer it as proof, but – well – to me, at any rate, the name Denis Mitre strongly suggests *Deus Mithras*."

"I think you've got it," I said. "*Mithras, also a soldier...* The highest grade was *Pater*, if I remember rightly. And wasn't Cybele – the *Magna Mater* – also known as the Mother of God?"

The old man nodded in approving silence. Then he turned his sharp eyes to Julia. "Young lady," he said, "you haven't told us everything, have you? I appreciate that you weren't able to find out any more about the ancient militia company, but what of the church, heh?"

She laughed. "You're right, of course. I've been doing some research there, and I can tell you that St Denis Mitre was one of the churches that escaped the Great Fire. The parish was small and neither rich nor populous, so in about 1710 there were proposals to demolish the church. Instead, it was extensively renovated. Some of it was attributed to Hawksmoor, but the few surviving pictures of the building don't show anything that looks like his work.

"The church did exist, though it was eventually pulled down. It had stood empty for something over twenty years, having been closed on the authority of the Archbishop of Canterbury on account of 'certain un-Christian practices'."

She hesitated for a moment, looking at each of us in turn. "Now," she said, "here's the twist. That journal was written in about 1880. The Church of St Denis Mitre was destroyed in December of the year 1855. Make of it what you will."

"George," I said, "you've got your Christmas ghost story after all. How about another drink?"

QUEEN RAT

To say that the life of the poor in Victorian London was tough would be the understatement of all time. The few jobs available to them demanded long hours of tedious, physically exhausting work, often in insanitary and dangerous conditions, and were rewarded with the most menial wages. But many of London's underclass in those days didn't even enjoy these meagre privileges. They had to invent their own jobs and do what they could to eke a living from them, which hope was often based more on fantasy than reality. For example, the 'mud-larks' prowled barefoot along the muddy banks of the Thames, searching for any bits of discarded ironmongery they might be able to sell. The 'pure-finders' scoured London's pavements, collecting dog turds, mixing them with mortar and taking them to the tanneries in return for a copper or two, a morsel of food, a candle, a piece of coal – who knew? But perhaps the most horrible homemade job of them all was that of the so-called 'tosher', a man who did not just have to endure terrible risks, and navigate his way through unimaginable ordure, but who also had to brave the terrors of the supernatural.

In a nutshell, the toshers were scavengers in London's sewers.

These men and boys would go out – usually at night, because from 1840 onwards entering London's sewer system unauthorised was punishable by imprisonment – and venture down into an odious, filth-ridden netherworld of pipes, culverts and tunnels so vast and fathomless that even today no accurate map of it exists, searching for 'valuables' – the odd coin perhaps, a bent nail, a rusty spoon. Many were trapped in flash floods and drowned; some caught hideous infections; others were overwhelmed by toxic gases and suffocated. Many more were simply lost, never to be seen again.

Little wonder the toshers' folklore was filled with eerie tales about the mysterious beings and creatures they encountered down there. In those dank, twisting bowels of the city it seems that ghosts and goblins were legion. Disembodied voices claiming to be deceased relatives would call to the men from the darkness. Imps and kobolds would play tricks on them. Savage, white-skinned hogs – so accustomed to the unlit world that they'd lost the power of vision – were believed to roam the endless passages, supersensitive noses drawing them always to the presence of human flesh.

But the most frightening story of all was told by a former tosher, Jerry Sweetly, as he lay on his deathbed in the year 1890. The tale was passed down through his family, and eventually told to the world by his great-granddaughter in the 1990s.

Sweetly was 15 when this incident allegedly occurred, and had been working as a tosher since earliest childhood. Somehow or other he'd made a sufficient living, but at this stage of his career he'd become uneasy during his subterranean ramblings, suspecting that something was always close behind, observing his every move. After one unusually successful day he was able to forget these troubles as he had earned enough to go drinking in a Bermondsey gin-house. While in there, he was approached by a comely young woman who sought to make his acquaintance. Sweetly had never seen her before but was entranced, despite the curious way her eyes reflected firelight and the curved claws on her fingers. Later that night, when both he and the alluring lass were wildly drunk, they repaired to an old warehouse and made love. But during the course of this pleasure, she bit him fiercely on the neck, drawing gouts of blood. Angered, Sweetly attempted to strike her – at which point he realised that he was alone. He came quickly out of his stupour as he searched the room, only to hear a voice say: "You'll get your luck, tosher, but you haven't done paying me for it yet."

Glancing up, he saw a large female rat perched on a rafter above his head, peering down at him. Terrified, Sweetly fled and later told the story to his tosher companions, who advised him that he had been lured by the so-called Queen Rat, a wanton she-devil who haunted the London sewers, seeking husky young men and either rewarding them or punishing them depending on the outcome.

From the cryptic words the creature had spoken, it sounded as if Sweetly was to be both punished and rewarded, and in a strange way this is exactly what came about – he lived a long life and eventually made good financially, but he was forever unlucky in love, consecutive female partners dying young and in tragic circumstances. Legend also tells how a man who has made love to the Queen Rat will sire generations of children in each of which there will be one born with a grey eye and a blue eye – this also happened with Sweetly's family.

Despite this last compelling detail, there is no way to either prove or disprove the tosher's story. In modern times, the ghosts and spirits of London's underworld have become more associated with the underground railways than with the sewers. These tales are eerie enough in their own right, but none describe anything similar to the voluptuous, shape-shifting demoness known as the 'Queen Rat'.

35

TRAIN, NIGHT
Nicholas Royle

Alex, I never said it *was* you. I never said the man on the tube *was* you. I said he *looked like* you. So much like you it was like we were back together again. And since I couldn't be with *you* any more, I could be with this *version* of you. That's what I was saying. That's what I said.

His head was shaved. You would never do that. You're too proud of your hair. You wouldn't deny yourself the pleasure of wearing it long. He was also younger, ten, maybe fifteen years younger. But his bone structure was the same, his eyes were identical. You know what, I'm coming round to the idea that he was you, after all.

Nor was it on the Central line that I saw him. It was the Hammersmith & City line. That's what I said and that's what it was. I got on at Shepherd's Bush, you got that bit right. I got on at Shepherd's Bush and he was already on, having boarded at Hammersmith or Goldhawk Road. There he was, in my carriage, and there was a seat right opposite him, so I took it. Because it was the Hammersmith & City line, I saw him in natural light, and natural light leaves no room for doubt. The Central line is underground at Shepherd's Bush and while I'll admit the Central line does have a peculiarly attractive light, it's not the same. I might not have been so certain. Plus, if it had been the Central line, how would I have followed him off the train at King's Cross?

I didn't say I followed him into an abandoned building either. I followed him into an art gallery, that place on Wharf Road, that big one with the exposed brick walls. I said it *looked like* an abandoned building. Just as the man on the train *looked like* you. Geddit?

Anyway, I found out who he is. OK?

Maybe this will make you happy, because it should demonstrate to you once and for all that I don't think he's you. I know he's someone else. He's an actor. I know because I saw him in something on TV. I was watching this crime drama, alone in the flat, because, you know, I live alone these days, with my unwashed towels and chipped cereal bowls dusted white with crushed paracetamol. That's another thing about your email. You contradict yourself. One minute you say I walked out on you, then you're saying *you* left *me*. Make your mind up. You can't have it both ways. So I'm watching this thing. It was ITV but it was quite good.

You wouldn't have given it a chance, of course. That was how I knew you wouldn't be watching it, because it was on ITV. I presume you don't watch ITV with Fareda, either. I presume you're as judgmental as you ever were. See, I don't mind writing her name, now I know what it is. I don't bear her any ill will. As a matter of fact I feel sorry for her. Are you going to do to her what you did to me? Poor girl.

There he was, in the background in one scene. Little more than an extra but he did have a line of dialogue. It was him, I was certain of it, and he looked as much like you on TV as he had on the train. His name was in the credits. Let's call him Anthony.

I discovered something else. That film you showed me shortly after we first started seeing each other – *Un soir, un train* – that black and white Belgian film from the 1960s. You said I looked like Anouk Aimée. Looking back, maybe you wanted me to infer that you looked like Yves Montand. I watched it again the other day. As you know, when I say the other day, I generally mean the other week. You used to find this charming. The way the film pans out is a bit like what happened to us. That village where Mathias and his two companions end up, where they can't understand a word the villagers are saying, that's a bit like us at the end. It was like we were speaking different languages, and not just different languages from the same group, like two romance languages, but two *completely* different languages from different origins entirely. Arabic and Hungarian, Inuit and Welsh. Although, of course, only one of us had changed the language they were speaking.

It's scary, a bit creepy, that film. Maybe you shouldn't give a copy to Fareda. Maybe you shouldn't take her dancing, either. That's when I fell in love with you, you know. When we were dancing at that party in Shepherd's Bush and every five minutes a train went by on the elevated line above the market. You grabbed me and made me watch as one went past.

"Look at them watching us," you shouted into my ear. "They think we look good together."

I watched the figures silhouetted by the yellowish light inside the carriage, while you held me around the waist.

How I wish now I could have been one of those passengers inside the train looking out at the people dancing. You would have been no more than a frame-grab to me and I would have got off at Hammersmith and carried on with my life. A different life.

A couple of days after the party, we watched *Un soir, un train* for the first time.

I guess you thought the two of them – Mathias and Anne, Yves Montand and Anouk Aimée – were supposed to represent the two of us. If so, then the flashback in London is probably when they are happiest. The way they sit in the back of Michael Gough's car when he takes them on a drive through Rotherhithe, both of them in the back so they can be together, leaving the front passenger seat empty, like it was a taxi. The way they hold hands, later when they're out of the car. The look Michael Gough gives them when he sees them holding hands. I think he's envious of them because they're so happy together. Like we used to be.

The tape was recorded off Japanese TV. Do you remember that? A friend of yours had taped it for you because it was so rarely screened. So it was in French with Japanese subtitles. We had to watch it six or seven times before we knew what was going on and we laughed when we realised that Mathias and his companions couldn't understand what the people in the village were saying either.

I started looking out for Anthony on the Hammersmith & City line. After all, I'd seen him twice, so there was a good chance he worked or lived somewhere along the line. A good chance I'd see him again. I didn't carry my DV camera. I wasn't going to film him this time. The reason the footage I sent you was so uneven and featured other people as well as him, especially the stuff I shot in the gallery, was because I was having to do it on the sly. It's not easy filming from inside a half-fastened coat.

I tried boarding the same carriage as the last time I'd seen him. Then I tried varying which carriage I got in. I still didn't see him.

I was looking out for him on TV, too, and in *Time Out* and online, but it seemed like he wasn't doing anything that was listed anywhere.

I watched *Un soir, un train* yet again, rewinding the tape endlessly to study the scenes shot in Rotherhithe. Both locations were previously unknown to me, yet notable enough to appear in *The London Encyclopaedia*, which you may remember buying me.

I hung around the gallery on Wharf Road, but I didn't see Anthony there either.

Then one morning I got on the train and there he was again. Sitting more or less in the same place. Looking every bit as much like you as he had done before.

I didn't stop to think. If I had done, I might have got tongue-tied and everything might have played out very differently. I contrived a conversation. It was easy. He was reading a script. I asked him if he was an actor and he smiled and said he was. It was so easy. Because his bone structure is the same as yours, his smile is the same as yours too. His teeth are slightly whiter, but that's OK. It really did feel like I was sitting there and talking to you. Except it felt like talking to you at the beginning, not the end. And not now. Talking to you now – writing to you now – feels very different.

We talked until King's Cross, where he said he had to get off. I said I was getting off there too. I wondered if he was going to Wharf Road again, but I didn't ask him that. I said, "Where are you going?" He said he was going to a rehearsal. He had a part in a play and they were using the director's flat on Gray's Inn Road as a rehearsal space. I said that sounded exciting. He asked me what I did. It wasn't like he'd only just thought to ask. I'd just not given him the chance.

"I'm a film-maker," I told him, as we were about to part on the street.

"Really?" he said. "Now *that's* exciting."

The way he said it, I could tell he meant it. I guessed he preferred film to the stage.

"Do you have a card?" he asked me. A card! Me!

"I've run out," I said, and as I scribbled my number on an old receipt, my sleeve rode up and I realised he'd be able to see the marks on my forearm.

"Well, I never had any," he said carefully, then wrote his own number in small, precise figures on an empty page of a little notebook that he produced from his shoulder bag. He tore the page out along its perforation and added: "I should probably get some."

We said goodbye and I set off in the opposite direction to his, but then turned to watch him go, weaving through the commuters. He's even a similar height to you.

I waited for him to call me and when he did I said there was a location in Rotherhithe I needed to have another look at and would he like to meet there for a drink? Before leaving the house I slotted the tape into the VCR again. The thing I discovered about *Un soir, un train* is that it's not actually a black and white film, after all. I looked it up to check something, and every source that lists it, from *Time Out* to the IMDb, has it down as colour. Maybe some incompatibility between Japanese TV and the UK standard. I couldn't – and still can't – figure out why you gave it me so close to the end. What was it – a week, two at the most, before things fell apart? Were you trying to convince yourself we still had a future? Was your butterfly mind already selecting a new film to show to Fareda?

I picked up the remote and had a last look at those London scenes. In the back of the car. Michael Gough telling Mathias and Anne how Rotherhithe is "notorious". His dialogue, of course, is in English. Their arrival at Bermondsey Wall East, walking on to Cherry Garden Pier, then the visit to the Angel pub. Some kind of

39

balcony, sitting down, holding hands, Michael Gough remaining standing, but that's when he notices their clasped hands.

I also opened a file on my laptop and brought it up to date. When I've finished with it, I'll print it out and close the machine down.

I'll take the tube to London Bridge and walk down impossibly narrow streets between fantastically tall buildings. Converted wharves. Exclusive flats, apartments. Portered, gated. The kind of place we could have ended up sharing in another universe. I'll skirt the Design Museum, cross a bridge of wire and stainless steel. The river a constant presence on my left, tide creeping in.

Bermondsey Wall West, cut inland, along a bit. Derelict wharves and warehouses. Gaps in the gentrification. Back towards the river. Bermondsey Wall East, Cherry Garden Pier, the first of the two static locations. I can't walk on to the pier as they did in the film. It's owned by a private company now. City Cruises plc. I'll walk up the ramp towards a blue door with a no-entry sign on it, barbed wire coiled above. A security light will flick on, blinding me.

A hundred yards further downstream, the Angel. Lights burning at the windows will turn the blue air a half-shade darker. The light won't last much longer. In the film, Mathias and Michael Gough enter the pub while Anne remains outside. Next shot, the two men are on a balcony, where Anne joins them.

I'll push open the door and go inside. The first thing I'll notice, like the last time I was there, will be the Sam Smith's logo on all the taps and bottles and I'll think to myself, as I did before, that you wouldn't have liked that. This pub has been there since the fifteenth century, and the moment you come along, you find out it's a Sam Smith's joint. Beer's just beer to me, as you know. But I remember how Sam Smith's used to provoke extreme reactions in you. I'll look around. There'll be a handful of locals in. Sam Smith's or no, it's a decent-looking old-fashioned boozer, lots of wood and brass, comfortable seats. I'll move through into the back bar and my eye will be drawn to the picture window. On the other side of the window a balcony, and out on the balcony I'll see Anthony's shaved head shining under the artificial lights. As if sensing my arrival, he will turn round.

Anthony will already have a drink. He won't be bothered by it being a Sam Smith's pub. He'll be trying their own-label wheat beer, which is OK, he'll say. I'll get him another as I buy myself one. We'll sit on the balcony overlooking the river. I'll make sure he's sitting on my right, like in the film. I'll imagine Michael Gough leaning on the handrail looking alternately out at the river traffic

40

and back at the two of us. Anthony will ask me about "my work". I'll take out my DV camera and tell him I'm in the middle of making a short film. I'll say I'd be grateful for his help and he'll say he'd be glad to provide it.

"Samuel Pepys used to drink here," I'll tell him, "and Judge Jeffreys, the Hanging Judge, so called for obvious reasons."

"A strict disciplinarian, I presume?" he'll say.

"He would sit here and watch pirates being hanged on the other side of the river at Execution Dock," I'll tell him.

"Execution Dock?" he'll ask.

I'll point across the river to Wapping Old Stairs.

"They used to bring convicted pirates from Marshalsea Prison. The rope they used to hang them only had a short drop, which wasn't enough to break their necks, so they'd do 'the Marshal's dance' as they slowly suffocated."

"And people call us uncivilised today," Anthony will say.

"They'd be left there until three tides had washed over them," I'll say as I balance my camera on the hand rail to get a shot of us sitting side by side, me and the man who looks like you. This is the shot from Michael Gough's POV. I'll ask Anthony if we can hold hands for a moment. He'll agree. He's a professional.

I might hold his hand for slightly longer than I need to for the shot. Then I'll explain that the next shot is more complicated and that his role will be to act as cameraman. I'll tell him I'm going to disappear for a bit. I'll walk to the tube at Rotherhithe, which is only a couple of minutes from the pub. Take the East London line one stop under the river to Wapping, then walk to Wapping Old Stairs. I'll ask him to stay on the balcony and watch out for me coming down the steps on to the foreshore and then film me, zooming in for a close-up.

"Won't it be very grainy?" he'll ask. "The river's wide here."

"That doesn't matter," I'll say.

I'll produce a stamped padded envelope with your name and address on it and ask him, when the shot is complete, whatever he thinks of it, to stick the tape in the envelope and post it. He'll nod, but look puzzled.

"You'll be coming back, right? Or do you want me to come round there?" he'll ask me.

"Neither," I'll say.

Still he'll look confused.

"I want you to hang on to the camera for me. Post the tape and hang on to the camera." If he remains silent and just sort of frowns at me, I will go on: "You've heard of Dogme? Lars Von Trier? His set of rules for film-makers?"

"It's something like that?" he'll say, brightening up. "Why didn't you say?"

"Great," I'll say. "But I want you to promise me you'll keep filming, even if it looks a bit weird. A bit extreme. Just keep filming. There's only about ten minutes' space left, in any case."

"And then I post it to this –" he'll look at the label – "Alex guy? What's he, your editor? Your collaborator?"

"Something like that. Promise?"

He'll promise.

"OK, I'm going to go now," I'll say to him. "Thanks for your help. Thanks for everything."

I might kiss him, or I might make do with having held his hand.

When I've gone, he'll sit and wait for a bit, then start to get impatient as he watches the stairs across the river. It is a long way, almost three hundred metres. He may experiment with the zoom on the camera, see if that gives him a better view. What he gains in image size he'll lose in definition. He'll keep checking, both with the camera and the naked eye. He'll pick up the padded envelope and perhaps feel the outline of something already inside it. I think he'll take a look, see it's a sealed envelope bearing the same name as on the label, and quickly put it back. He'll check his watch, see it's been fifteen minutes already. How long can it take to go one stop? He'll think about having another drink, but will decide he's too nervous and mustn't risk missing me.

Eventually, just when he's about to try my mobile number, he'll see a vague shape coming down the steep slippery steps of Wapping Old Stairs. He won't be able to recognise me, but he won't question that it's me for a moment. Why should he? In a slight panic, although he'll have had almost half an hour to prepare, he'll fiddle with the camera, trying to frame the best shot. He'll press the red button before I'm quite ready, but that won't matter. He'll squint at the tiny screen, trying to work out what I'm doing. He'll wonder if I'm waving or semaphoring or doing something weird with a rope. At that distance, he won't be able to tell, not even on full zoom. He might be able to see my feet leave the ground. He'll need to rest the camera on the hand rail to keep it steady, while on the screen he'll watch a grainy, degraded image of me dancing.

THE HORROR AT BERKELEY SQUARE

There are few more prestigious addresses than Berkeley Square in London's fashionable West End. But in the late 19th century the entire city was rocked by a shocking event said to have occurred there.

It was a rainy night in the year 1887, and two sailors, having come ashore from the ship HMS Penelope and spent the evening roistering in various London taverns, were roaming the empty streets looking for free lodgings. By pure chance, they happened upon No. 50, Berkeley Square, a swish, four-story townhouse which appeared to be untenanted. Breaking in, they found the building empty and filled with dust – there was a cold, musty atmosphere but at least it was dry. Satisfied, they ascended to a room on the top floor and bedded down, intending to leave first thing in the morning.

A short time later they were disturbed by the sounds of heavy feet ascending the staircase towards them, and a weird grunting noise. Thinking they had disturbed a den of thieves, the two sailors panicked and tried to bar the room, only to hear snuffling and snarling on the other side of the door, and the scratching of animal-like claws. One sailor was so frightened that he attempted to climb from the window, but fell and was impaled on the spiked railings far below. He was found later that night by a patrolling constable, who then discovered the other sailor cowering in the darkness inside. In his few moments of lucidity, the deranged survivor explained how his friend had died, and then described an abominable entity forcing entry to the room – some dark, shapeless mass, which made hideous sounds as it lurched towards him. Why he was spared is unknown because he descended into raving madness before he could complete his narrative.

Naturally, there are question marks against the truthfulness of this account. For example, might one sailor have murdered the other by pushing him from the window during a quarrel, and then made up his ghost story?

In actual fact, there was no certainty the incident had ever occurred at all – no names were given, either of the sailors or the police officer who discovered them. But regardless of this, the rumour caused a sensation in London in 1887, not least because there was already much focus on 50, Berkeley Square as a haunted house thanks to an investigation held ten years earlier by *Mayfair* magazine.

Reportedly, things had first started to go wrong at the swanky address in the 1850s, when its owner, a man called Myers, suffered a nervous breakdown after his bride left him at the altar. Prior to this event, none of the domestic staff who had worked there had experienced anything unusual, but after being jilted, Myers dismissed them all and lived alone, becoming progressively dirtier and more misanthropic. The once fine townhouse degenerated into an eyesore with filthy windows and broken guttering. Whatever happened to Myers is uncertain, but later tenants were disturbed by the property's forlorn and menacing atmosphere. One room in particular, on the top floor, was regarded as having a positively evil aura.

Mayfair journalists commenced their enquiry in 1879, having heard all kinds of strange stories. They reported how a new maid had fled from the top floor, screaming: *"I have just seen it!"* before literally dropping dead with fright. A short while later, a steadfast young man insisted on spending a night alone up there, saying that he would ring the service bell if he needed assistance. Some time that night, he rang the bell wildly, but before help could ascend to him, a shot rang out – he had committed suicide in the room, and his dead face was written with indescribable horror.

If an unearthly presence existed at 50, Berkeley Square it was an evil one, and yet the Victorian gossip columnists were as baffled that this should stem purely from a man's depression as contemporary parapsychologists would be. Other theories were put forward. One held that Myers, in the midst of his madness, had resorted to black magic, and had used the top room to perform rituals and incantations. Another held that before Myers was the occupant of 50, Berkeley Square, a more ruthless individual had converted the top floor into a prison for his demented brother. A third stated how, long before any of these events occurred, a young woman had thrown herself from the top window to avoid molestation at the hands of her wicked uncle. There is no known factual basis for any of these lurid tales, but of course they made good reading at the time.

One thing is certain: 50, Berkeley Square has remained firmly on London's paranormal map even into the modern era. The property was purchased by Maggs Bros, the famous antiquarian book-dealers, in 1937, and is still in their possession. Investigators have been allowed inside, but apart from occasional unexplained sounds and a curious brown mist said to float in the stairwells, no major incidents have been reported recently.

As a footnote, Prime Minister George Canning, who resided at the address from 1770 to 1827, also alleged that it was haunted, which may hint at a much earlier origin to the disturbances than was previously thought. In addition, Lord Lytton's classic horror story, The Haunted and the Haunters, is believed to have been inspired by the events at 50, Berkeley Square – and this was written long before Mayfair popularised them.

THE ANGELS OF LONDON
Adam Nevill

F rank stared at the mess, still a little surprised such things were tolerated in the city. Soon he would stop caring like everyone else.

At the base of the lamppost on the street corner the rubbish bags spilled their entrails across the pavement. Someone had dumped a bin bag. Others followed their example until a pyramid of refuse rose up the lamp post to his waist. The core of the structure was rotten as if the body of the king the pyramid honoured was poorly embalmed. A mattress had been thrown against the pile. Rusted springs were visible and watermarks formed continents on the quilted fabric. Now a broken pushchair, with canvas rags hanging from the aluminium frame had been added to the installation. A disturbing element of squalor and human fragility, something London's occupants became immune to or a part of. He wasn't sure which of the two paths he would follow: indifference or collaboration.

He thought of submitting the entire mess for the Turner Prize but never had the energy to smile at his own joke. And he had no one to share it with.

Above his head the pub's sign creaked. The sign was wooden, the mounting of iron and nearly rusted through. He wondered how long it would stay up there. It was amazing how many old and broken things just kept going in the city.

The actual picture of The Angel of London was painted on the wood inside the corroded frame. The paint had weathered and acquired a wholly different aspect to that originally intended. Featuring a scaly-looking face, wearing a tight skull cap and a wreath of leaves, the angel now resembled something Van Gogh might have painted after a maniacal bout of self-examination. Whenever Frank saw the hideous peeling face he knew he was home.

Through the grimy window panes he could see the silhouettes of wooden chairs upside down upon tables, a long bar that resembled an unused plinth inside a dusty tomb, and a poster for a long expired competition connecting rugby to Guinness. The pub was dead, had been closed for years.

Indicating a high-turnover of tenants, masses of uncollected post were slung along a shelf inside the neighbouring door that led to the rooms above the bar. Some of the mail was on the floor. Why was the old post not forwarded to past residents? Or did it belong to the current tenants who operated a wilful resistance to the outside world? Few of his questions about people in the city were ever answered.

There was no post for him. Someone was taking his mail, not even the junk reached him.

After four months as a tenant in a room above the derelict bar, Frank acknowledged he was probably vanishing from the world entirely. Becoming a thing withered, gaunt and grey, shabby and less substantial. Anxiety about money, finding the right kind of work, his future, isolation, all seemed intent on reducing him to a ghost, and one that few dimly remembered. He wondered if his image in photographs was disappearing. If he didn't find a better job and get out of the building, he imagined himself disintegrating into a stain on the murky wall paper of his wretched room. He'd already disappeared from the social radar of his two friends. A relocation to London to catch up professionally, still hadn't landed him a job anywhere near the film industry. His plummet to the bottom had been immediate.

London had golden rules. Never take the first accommodation you view, but he had done because the room above *The Angel* in Dalston was the only place he'd found on *Gum Tree* at £100 a week, which was all he could afford. Never take the first job you're offered, but he had done because the one grand he came to town with was gone in a month. He worked security in Chelsea, on shifts, which was nowhere near Dalston. Poorly paid jobs for the semi-skilled were plentiful, but affordable accommodation in the first three zones was scarce enough to not exist.

Frank wearily made his way up through the dimly lit dilapidation to his room. Familiar smells engulfed him: damp carpet warmed by radiators, cooking oil, an overflowing kitchen bin.

When he reached the first floor Granby was waiting outside his room. Frank jumped. "Fuck's sake."

Fright subsided into loathing. Granby knew what time he came in from work now, had surreptitiously learned his movements by watching him from inside the building. If anyone came out of their room, Frank would immediately hear the click of Granby's door on the third floor. Like a spider behind a trapdoor the landlord appeared to do little but watch his captives. Frank had never heard the murmur of a television, or music from Granby's attic room, had never seen him prepare food in the sordid kitchen, or even leave the building. He was so thin the landlord didn't appear to eat.

"Right, mate," the whispery voice came out of the gloom. His bony face with its watery eyes and peg teeth was barely visible. The figure sniffed, was always sniffing hard up one nostril. Frank knew what was coming.

"Need to speak wiv you 'bout the rent, mate." Granby had no conversation beyond insincere small talk and attempts to scratch money from people who barely existed within the building.

Frank had come to wonder whether *The Angel* was an abandoned building that utility companies had forgotten to disconnect. Maybe Granby had assumed proprietorship of the rooms upstairs. Whatever was going on was some kind of dodge and it contributed to his doubt that Granby had any right to charge rent on the squalid rooms. He'd once attempted conversation with Granby, but the shifty creature never revealed any details about himself, or the property, beyond claiming *The Angel* had been in the hands of his family for years.

After deductions from his wage packet, Frank took home £900 a month. Nearly half of that went to Granby. Food took another £200, and credit card debt £100. That left £100 for transport. Frank saved as much of the remaining £100 as possible for a deposit on a room he hoped would be less wretched than the one he lived in at *The Angel*.

ATM machines informed him he had saved £300, but Frank hadn't seen a bank statement in four months. He suspected Granby was opening his mail to learn about his finances. Which would mean the lies he had told Granby about his earnings and savings his landlord would be wise to. Granby must know about the £100 he saved each month and wanted it for himself.

The small figure moved in front of his door as Frank released his keys from his jacket pocket. "Ain't just you, mate. Times is hard for all of us. But fings go up like. For everyone." The weasel's harassment was becoming predictable.

He had no idea how old Granby was. He could have been thirty or sixty. His movements were agile, his voice wasn't aged, but his face was worn. The eyes had seen too much. The spirit inside them was blunted, and only occasionally enlivened with a feral intent when money was being discussed. Because money was his only purpose. The same vulpine self-interest applied to the teeming millions in the city.

What was most remarkable, or memorable, about Granby's facial features was that they reminded Frank of a particular kind of working class face, the type you saw leering out of a black and white photograph taken during the Second World War. Granby's face was not contemporary at all. But the white sport leisure wear and curly hair were utterly incongruous and made Granby look ridiculous. He was like a person from the forties masquerading as someone from the eighties.

"That right?"

Frank's irritation cooled when he detected a tension in Granby's wiry arms, and a narrowing around his eyes. When angry, Granby also paled in a way that was horrible to behold. Resistance to Granby took things to a new level quickly. Disappointment when his loquacious wheedling for money fell flat accounted for this. Physical confrontation never seemed far away and Frank suspected there was a great capacity for violence in the man. He communicated the sense that everything was at stake, that he would be ruined if Frank didn't pay up.

Frank intended to find another place and leave *The Angel* anyway, and within four weeks. But four weeks was an eternity in the same building as a man determined to make life a condition of incremental blackmail, with insinuations of terrible consequences if his demands were not met.

His inherent caution around the unstable took a backseat. "We've been through this before, Granby. There's no shower. One bathroom. I'm washing in a sink."

Granby didn't like the disadvantages of *The Angel* being pointed out to him by the tenants. "Everyone has to put up wiv it, mate. That's life. What you fink you should be in, some top hotel on a hundred a week? You is 'aving a laugh, mate."

"What improvements have been made that can justify another rent hike?"

Granby was also a firm believer that if a conversation remained one-sided for long enough the tenant would see his point. His Cockney voice rose to drown Frank out. He started bouncing on his heels like a wiry puppet, or something much worse, a bantam-weight boxer. "I gotta look after my family. My family's the most important fing in the world to me. If our personal financial situation is freatened, I tell you something, mate, I don't know what I'd do. What I'm capable of."

Frank had never seen any evidence of this 'family'. The hard-pressed 'family' had initially been used as a sob story during the second month of his tenancy, when Granby first asked him for more money, with tears in his doleful eyes. Frank had only been allowed the first month, without harassment, to get settled in. Something that also stank of a well-rehearsed tactic.

"What fucking family?"

Granby's fists clenched. Frank sensed they would feel like wooden hammers against his face. He lowered his voice but kept an edge in his tone. "There are four tenants in this building all paying you four hundred quid a month. For what? Half the lights don't work. The furniture's either totally wrecked or barely serviceable. My post isn't delivered. Or is it? And you've got nearly two grand a month coming in. For what?"

"What you mean two grand a mumf? Vats got nuffin' to do wiv you." Granby started walking backwards and forwards. He took his white tracksuit top off. Rolled his head around his shoulders as if preparing for physical exercise. "Nuffin. Nuffin. That's personal. Now you is going too far."

"There's no inventory. No contract. Cash in hand. Do you even have any right to collect money on this place?"

"What you talkin' about? Aye? You're freatening me? You is freatening my family. You need to watch your mouf. I've warned you."

"I'm leaving. This last month's rent comes out of my deposit."

"You're going nowhere. Free month's notice. We agreed."

Sleep deprivation from night shifts, three hours a day travelling on the bus between work and a dark shabby room, the sight of his clothes on the floor because there was no chest of drawers or wardrobe, the endless trips to the laundrette, the indifference of strangers, being dead on his feet, never having any money, the fidgeting anxiety that surrounds failure like a crowd of children, the cold terror about his future, it all seemed to rise through him like a terrible pressure and release itself in a steam he could not cap. "Agreed? We agreed one hundred a month. In my second month you try and hike the rent twenty five quid a week. So am I to stay here for as long as you decide, while you keep upping the rent? And making threats? Do I sublimate my life to your 'family's' financial security? You don't scare me. One visit to the police, the DHSS, whoever, and you're little operation's over. I bet you're signing on too, aye? You've not done a day's work in your life, have you?"

By the time he'd finished, Frank knew he'd gone too far, had tripped every wire in the little man's mind by using off-piste words like 'sublimation', by mentioning sub-legal diction like 'rights', and adopting an ironic tone about the man having a family. This was no place for a concept like fairness. *The Angel* was an extortion racket, run like a prison, and the tenants were inmates.

Granby circled him. "I gotta go. I gotta go. Get out my fuckin' way." He made for the stairs. "You is taking me for a cunt. A cunt! There'll be trouble. There'll be trouble if I don't go right now."

At first, Frank assumed Granby was all mouth about not being held responsible for his actions and was backing off. And he felt triumphant as if a bully had been faced down, a petty tyrant dethroned. But Granby's bloodless face and glassy eyes, the muttering of the lipless mouth, the repetition, suggested Frank had committed a terrible offence. And Granby had barked at him as if he were less than human. *Cunt* wasn't just a word to Granby, it was a statement of unfairly conferred status that should be countered with the most severe reprisal. Frank understood this in a heartbeat. Once you'd taken someone like Granby *for a cunt*, anything could be done to you. That's what the word meant down here. In places like *The Angel*.

He also had a suspicion that direct action, one on one, might not be Granby's style after all, and his skin prickled at the thought of his throat being slit in the night. Or maybe the curly head would move swiftly through the dark, peg teeth grinning, before the steel went in, deep into the meat, as he bent over the sink to wash his armpits. What a time to realise this now; and those words could not be taken back, or ameliorated.

Granby had keys to his room.

He should leave now.

But what about his stuff? If he abandoned his CDs and books they were gone forever. They were all he had. And where could he go? Were there any couches he could borrow? Three nights in a London hotel was his limit, so what came after?

"Look, Granby. Hang on."

Granby was already on the staircase rising to the second floor. Why was he going back to his room? To get a weapon? Recent news stories of people burned alive, of acid thrown in faces, of knifings closed Frank's throat and made him feel cold and sick. He wanted to make amends and hated himself for being craven.

Granby's feet bumped up two flights of stairs. At the top of the house a door slammed.

Frank let himself into his room.

In less than a minute there came a gentle tapping at his locked door. Sat immobile on the end of his bed, Frank swallowed but failed to find his voice.

"Frank. Frank." It was the Irishman, Martin. An old decorator with haunted astigmatic eyes, who hung off the payphone in the entry most evenings, muttering into the plastic handset, usually in defence of his involvement in some protracted dispute that Frank only heard one side of. The man's voice would flute up the stairwell to Frank's room on the first floor. They were on nodding terms, but never spoke, despite sharing the first floor. London was that kind of place. The other tenants of *The Angel* were either disinterested in him or wary of a new arrival.

Frank approached the door. "What?" he whispered back.

"Can I speak with you? It's all right, Granby's back in his room."

The insinuation that he was hiding from Granby behind a locked door made Frank feel ashamed. He opened the door. His hand trembled on the handle.

"Can I speak with you?" The man's eyes looked in two different directions and the skin of his face was a yellow-grey from smoking. The first floor reeked of hand-rolled cigarettes amongst other things.

Frank let his neighbour inside, closed the door, and locked it as quietly as he could. The small man spent a few seconds looking about his room, studying the walls, though there were no pictures, just wallpaper thick with paint the colour of sour milk. There was little else to look at if you discounted unpacked boxes of possessions and an incongruous office chair before a sash window that overlooked a yard, the space filled with broken furniture.

Without looking at Frank the man said. "Oh you're all right, son. For a few days. And *he* won't come down to sort you out. Don't operate like that."

"Then how does it operate?" The question was out of his mouth before he could consider it.

Martin turned around. Frank didn't know which eye to look at. He chose the one that wasn't dead, bulgy, and always directed at the floor. "You want to be careful, son. You don't want to mess with Granby. You might have a day or so to straighten this out, but not much more."

"I'm not letting him rob me. We agreed a hundred a week. He tried –"

"I know. I heard."

"So?" Frank held out his hands, questioningly, at the man's presence in his dismal room. If he'd just come to reiterate Granby's threats he might as well leave.

"Take it from one who knows, my friend, you best pay the man what he asks for to avoid trouble. Serious trouble. He's very upset." Frank opened his mouth to protest but Martin held up one thick-fingered hand. "You have to adapt. You're with the Angels now, my friend." The man's use of 'with' confused Frank, as if his neighbour was suggesting he'd joined a community established around angels. *With the angels* was also a phrase too uncomfortably close to an expression of death.

"I'm leaving. So there won't be any trouble."

Martin smiled. "Oh, they won't let you leave, son."

"What do you mean, they? Granby can't stop me."

"No, true. But *they'll* come and find you to collect the debt."

"There is no debt."

52

"In your mind, son. But not in theirs'."

"What? Who's *they*?"

"It's been decided. See if it hasn't, my friend."

"This is crazy."

"I'll tell you what I'll do. You've a good heart, son. I can tell. So, I'll go and – "

"No. I'm not mixed up in anything. I took a room. A piece of shit in a broken-down building. And now I'm leaving it because I am being threatened. Simple."

"I wish it were, son. But at *The Angel* there are different rules, ones we've all had to learn."

"This is getting silly."

"Oh no, son, it's deadly serious. You can trust me on this. I shouldn't even be here. There'll be hell comin' down those stairs if he knows I'm in here, talking like this." The way the man mentioned the stairs made Frank's legs feel weak.

"He's bullying you all. Robbing you."

"Oh, it ain't just Granby. No, no, son. It's those he has the ear of, if you know what I mean."

"I don't."

The man whistled between what was left of his brown teeth and raised an eyebrow. "Granby works for *others*. A bad lot. Very bad. He's the last of your worries."

"What, lone-sharks?"

"No, no. Worse than that, my friend. A *family*. A very old London family. Granby don't have much say in things. He just does favours for them."

"You mean organised crime. Like the Krays?"

"No, son. But not the kind of family you or I would want to belong to."

"I'm really not following. I appreciate the heads-up, but –"

"I'll tell you what. You give me the money and I'll go and see Granby about the disagreement."

"What?"

"Before it gets out of hand."

Frank shook his head. The old scratcher was trying to get a cut of Granby's scam. More threats from Granby delivered by a patsy. "No way. I'm not giving you any money. I'm not frightened of him."

Martin smiled at the lie. "It's no place to go taking a stand, my friend. Not here. Won't get you anywhere. I've seen what happens. And as I said, it ain't him you need to worry about." Martin dropped his voice to a conspiratorial whisper. "It's them *others* he's got up there with him at the top of the house. They's running things.

53

Always have done. Granby's a go-between. But he has their ear, like I said."

Frank swallowed the lump in his throat that kept reappearing to shut his voice off. "He's alone up there. Surely?"

Martin shook his head, his expression grave. "No, my friend. You don't want to go believing things like that. And it's best to keep them up there. Keep the peace, like."

"So ... what ... what do you mean? They attack people, this family?"

"When Granby came here he brought a bad lot with him. An old family that's been in this city a very long time. Long before Granby and most of that out there." The man waved one hand at the windows. "This used to be a different place, I can tell you. Was once called *The Jerusalem*. Clean. Good sort of people lived here. We used to drink in that bar when it was open. Even women lived here. But there's not been a woman here in fifteen years. Not since *they* come and changed the name. It all went downhill when Granby brought them here."

"Fifteen years. You've lived here for fifteen years?" He nearly added 'Jesus Christ' to add weight to his horror.

"Twenty." Frank could see the man wasn't joking. "I used to be upstairs. On the second floor. Better room. But Granby moved me down here. I couldn't pay enough, see?"

Frank slumped more than sat on his bed as he tried to comprehend what the man was alluding to, some kind of hierarchy of favouritism connected to the rooms and rental rates. "You mean ..." He couldn't form the words.

"What, son?"

"He demoted you from the second floor. Because you wouldn't pay more rent?"

"Couldn't keep up with the cost. Down here I can manage. But think of this, son. You're on the first floor. Where can you go that's further down? There's no rooms on the ground floor. Nowhere to live. So you're already on your last life."

Frank thought of the dusty abandoned bar, then became irritated with himself for even considering the man's nonsense.

"You can't afford to make enemies when you're already at the bottom."

"I can't believe you put up with this. Do the other two upstairs?"

"Oh, yes, we all keep to the rules, son. There's no other way. I've been here long enough to know that. Jimmy on the second floor still works in the City, and he's been here as long as me. The only one left who has. So why do you think a man like that lives in a place like this? You think he chooses to?"

Returning from night shifts Frank often saw an elderly man in a suit. He always left the building early. They'd never spoken and the man always refused to meet his eye. "How much does he pay?" Frank's curiosity had taken over.

"That's between Jimmy and Granby. You never discuss money here. *They* don't like it. That was your first mistake."

"Oh, they don't like that? Is that so? What a surprise. This just gets better and better. So some guy in finance is trapped here and has been shaken down by Granby for fifteen years? Fuck's sake. This is unbelievable. What about the drag queen?"

Martin didn't return Frank's grin. "The fella who dresses like a woman. Lillian. That's what he calls himself now. And that's a bad business right there, my friend. Oh, Lord. But it shows how bad it can get if Granby is upset about rent not being paid."

Frank had caught sight of a frail and elderly cross dresser more times than he wished to remember, but never outside the building. As a habitual haunter of the bathroom and its speckled mirror, the cross dresser often clattered around inside the bathroom while Frank waited on the stairs to use the toilet. 'Lillian' also played opera records and made the stairs stink of perfume. Frank didn't know anything else because they'd never spoken. The man may have once been a convincing female mimic as he was small-boned, but now looked haggard and was always drunk.

"He was an actor once."

"What?'

"Oh, yes. On the stage. West End. Long time ago. Work dried up and he couldn't keep up with Granby. That's when he made the change. To go on the game."

"Game?"

"Whore."

"No ..."

"These days he sucks cocks down *The Duchess* to keep up with Granby."

Frank started to grin. He was close to screaming with hysterical laughter.

"It's terrible. He lost everything. Drinks too. He let this place get to him. But you can't afford to let it do that. Never. You have to learn to adapt if you want to enjoy any kind of life here. This is how it is once they let you in. And Lilly can't keep up with his rent now. He'll be the next to go, unless he gets your room at the reduced rate."

His visitor never intended for the story to be amusing, but Frank couldn't stop grinning. "Go? Go where? Where will Lillian go if he doesn't get demoted into this shit-tip of a room?"

"What I am trying to tell you is that I've known others here too who thought like you, who held out on Granby. But they're not around now." Again, Martin dropped his voice to a whisper. "But they never left either." He winked the eye Frank had been looking at. "Granby will give anyone a few months to make arrangements and you've had that. But then the collecting goes to others. And Granby don't like that because it makes him look bad. And *they* are all he's got going for him. If he can't collect *they* have to get involved. They *come down*. You follow? And them coming down to sort things out makes them very angry at being disturbed. Angry at Granby, angry at us. And I'd guess we're close to that time now."

"He and his imaginary family up in the attic are not getting another penny from me. I'll be gone in four weeks, or less."

"Oh, son, don't be go getting ahead of yourself. There'll be no four weeks. Like I said, you have to pay now. That's how it works here. To keep them others up there. And no one leaves unless they say so. That's the arrangement."

Frank had heard enough. "Okay. Okay. I appreciate the advice. But I know a racket when I see one. This is bullshit. Do you honestly think I'll stay here and let myself get threatened? Maybe for fifteen years, while Granby takes my money, whacking up the rent whenever he wants to? And if I can't pay then I have to put on a friggin' dress? Christ almighty, what is wrong with you people?" Frank briefly entertained an image of himself as an older man, wearing a dress in *The Duchess*, wherever that was. He wanted to howl with laughter.

He stood up and unlocked his door. Martin understood it was time to leave, but hesitated. "You're in *The Angel* now. You're in *their* house."

"Yeah, yeah. Thanks. I get it. But no thanks."

The old man stepped out of his room into the half-darkness of the corridor. The one begrimed window of the stairwell let a little light through. A silvery-grey infusion illumined half of the decrepit old figure's silhouette, which stood perfectly still. Without blinking either of his mad eyes, Martin watched Frank's door close.

Outside his room Frank could hear a faint trace of opera music. A muted fanfare. He shuddered.

*

Night fell and Frank paced his room, from the windows to the radiator, back and forth. The carpet looked as if it had been worn down by the similar movements of previous inmates.

Neither of his friends, Nigel or Mike, would help him out with a sofa to sleep on: girlfriends were cited as reasons in both cases. *Cheers.*

Frank had twelve hour shifts across the next three days, so looking for a room was not an option he could pursue in the morning. As a temp he could not afford to lose the money by taking a day off work. He'd have to stick it out at *The Angel* for a few days. Maybe return to his room late after work, keep a low profile. Once the shift pattern concluded he could find a new place and split.

Worn out by his nerves and thoughts, Frank placed the office chair under the door handle and flopped onto his bed.

Sleep came quickly. Sleep hectic with dreams.

He saw a fat man stood by a window that opened above the pub's sign, in a room that must have been at the front of the building. The man fed pigeons and shouted "Bitch, fucking Bitch" at most of the women who passed in the street below.

In another room similar to his own, an old man crawled in circles on the carpet. His false teeth were lost and the host of a quiz show spoke about angels to him through the window of an old television.

In a chaotic and nonsensical carousel of what resembled excerpts from a seemingly unending collection of ethereal footage, his own room was featured several times. The carpet was brighter, the walls not so sallow in each brief episode. In one scene he vividly dreamed of a bearded man with hairy arms lying on his bed. A yellow candlewick bedspread covered him to his stomach. In one hand he held a two litre bottle of vodka. The man stared at the ceiling with what looked like revulsion and terror.

In another dream a yolk-eyed drunk also appeared on his bed, this time the mattress was partially covered in a tatty purple sleeping bag. The man sang a music hall song while someone shouted "Cunt!" through the door. In that scene there was a strange sound too with no visible source. It sounded like a large bird was stuck inside the room and was beating the walls with its wings to get out. Either that or it was desperately trying to flap its way inside.

Frank woke and sat up in his bed.

His face was wet with tears, he was exhausted. And he was so shaken by the dreams he didn't go back to sleep. He got up and dressed into his security guard uniform. It took him a while to summon the confidence to open the door of his room and to enter the dark passage outside. He urgently needed to empty his bladder.

As he came out of the bathroom before his scrabbling fingers could locate the switch and turn the light on, he realised he was not alone in the dark passage that passed between his room and Martin's.

At first he thought the scuffling sound was being made by a dog, until the thin bluish light that fell through the one sash window over the stairwell illumined something rising from the floor outside his room to stand up on two thin legs.

Someone frail with unkempt hair. Perhaps an elderly woman, because of what may have been a nightgown falling to the scrawny knees. But then the arms of the figure appeared to be too long for a person of any age. And behind the figure something thrashed the air with what sounded like a pair of broken umbrellas.

Frank whimpered and slapped the light on to reveal an empty corridor. Paper peeling from the walls, red skirting boards, faded green carpet, but no sign of life.

He stood still, stunned immobile. The thud of his heart filled his head. His thoughts groped for an explanation. The light was on a timer and clicked out, leaving him in the dark again.

*

At work, Frank was often stood before the plate glass doors of the entrance of the residential building he guarded. Staring at the forecourt of Clarendon House, without really seeing the parked cars, he contemplated the hallucination and his dreams from the night before. He wondered if the building was some kind of hellish trap, where alcoholics and the unstable came to die. Or maybe the building damaged the occupants.

But by the end of the afternoon he'd more or less convinced himself that the tourniquet of stress currently constricting his life, worsened by the sense of entrapment, Granby's threats of violence, and Martin's elliptical suggestions of a sinister 'family' housed within *The Angel*, were the cause of the bad dreams and the remnants of a nightmare glimpsed in the half-light of a dingy corridor.

After he clocked off he whiled away four hours in Islington, sipping beer that he could ill afford to buy, before making his way back to *The Angel*.

At ten pm, he opened the front door incrementally, removed his shoes, and crept up to the first floor, using the sides of the stairs to reduce the noise of his ascent. Despite his best efforts to move silently, once he reached his room, keys in hand, he heard the distant, yet distinct sound, of Granby's door opening two floors up. The idea of something slipping out of the attic room was too horrible to entertain, and Frank eschewed all precautions of keeping quiet in his haste to get inside his own room and to lock the door behind him.

From ten until midnight the total absence of Lilly's opera music, the mutter of Martin's television, or any congress in the communal areas beyond his door, Frank interpreted as an unwelcome sign of anticipation, if not apprehension, among the other occupants of *The Angel*. As if something was about to happen. And the suggestion by his neighbour the previous evening that something would come down from the top of the house to 'collect' rent from him, no longer seemed as absurd to Frank as it had done during daylight hours.

He managed to stay awake in the large silent building until two when sleep overcame him.

At four am he sat up with a small cry, convinced the group of thin figures stood around his bed had come out of the dream with him. He removed his hands from his face and sat still in the darkness. The details of the dream faded quickly.

Some ambient light from a distant streetlamp distinguished his thin curtains from the surrounding walls. The rest of the room remained dark. Which was galling because the sound of scratching from the wrong side of the ceiling, directly above his bed, was not something he could investigate with his wide open, beseeching eyes.

He turned sideways and scrabbled for the switch of the bedside lamp. He was so frightened, and his cringing among the bedclothes impeded his movement to such an extent that it seemed to take about a minute for him to get the lamp switched on.

During the appalling wait for light he imagined that something was hanging from the ceiling by its feet, and that a face was no more than a few inches from his own.

Moments before the room was lit he heard what he thought was a sound of determined wings beating against the plaster of the ceiling, as if something was struggling to get back through a small hole.

With the overhead light on, as well as the lamp, Frank could see that there was nothing on the ceiling, and no evidence of any intrusion to account for the sound of the commotion above his bed. But he was left with an enduring fear that something within the building was now determined to show itself.

Frank dressed hurriedly and picked up his wallet and phone. He decided to leave the building and wait out the remainder of the night walking the streets, because it was infinitely preferable to staying inside.

He never made it to the stairs.

Once the door to his room was open he became too afraid to enter the corridor outside.

The air cracked with the sound of dry wings, like a dirty pigeon rising from the greasy cement of Trafalgar Square. At the end of the passage what light fell through the window over the stairwell silhouetted the outline of someone who wasn't Martin, Jimmy, Lillian or Granby. Nor could he be certain that the wizened figure's feet were even on the ground. He lacked the presence of mind to speculate how it was possible for the figure to hover like that, as well as flicker in and out of his sight, like an image appearing and then disappearing from before the window.

But whoever, or whatever it was, the intruder was in a state of great agitation at the sight of him.

What he could see of the figure shook its tatty head about, whipping stiff strands of hair through the air. What might have been fingers, at the end of the long arms, repeatedly clenched into fists and then unclenched. The idea of turning the corridor light on and seeing the figure in more detail was something Frank found too unbearable to contemplate.

Cringing inside his doorway he only found his voice after swallowing the constriction in his throat. "Money. I'll get it. Please don't. The money. I'll get it."

Somewhere upstairs in the house he could now hear Granby over the sound of the beating wings. "Cunt! Cunt! Cunt! Cunt!" the man screamed in a kind of mantra, as if he had entered into an animal frenzy of both fury and intense excitement at the thought of violence and blood in the wretched building.

Frank was sure he was about to be torn apart, or even worse, taken somewhere that the building appeared to offer access to through the ceilings of its scruffy rooms. And it was at that point that enough clarity returned to his mind for him to offer a suggestion to the noisy and foul air batting against his face.

He was never sure whether he spoke, or whether his offer was a thought, or even a prayer to whatever unnatural thing was gradually moving from the window and up to the dim ceiling of the first floor. But he closed his eyes and made a pledge that he would collect money on behalf of the thing before the window, and to it he boasted that he would be better at collecting than Granby ever was.

When a stench fouler than anything he had ever experienced engulfed his face and made him vomit on to his shoes – a miasma that might have hung over a cluttered battlefield or a plague pit – Frank collapsed upon the hard carpet as if overcome by sewer gas.

What revived him was the commotion of old wings moving upwards through the stairwell. Followed by screams from the attic amidst a terrible thumping of something solid making contact with a wall.

Eventually the noises ceased and silence returned to the building. A respite blessed to Frank's battered senses.

When he got to his feet he knew what to do.

*

The door to Granby's room was open, but Frank never entered the room. Instead, he peered inside from the doorway.

Frank never turned the light on either. What he could see was half-lit by the residual street light coming in through the skylight. He found the dim light more than adequate.

The ceiling sloped either side of a central roof beam.

Bulging black bin bags covered the floor of the room. The nearest bag was packed taut with bank notes. He assumed all of the other bags were too. On the table under the window, wristwatches and items of jewellery glinted. In one corner of the room a large collection of shoes formed a pile.

In the centre of the room, as if adored by the congregation of rubbish sacks filled with used bank notes, there were four stone columns, each with a small stone figure mounted upon it.

Frank could only glance at the stone figures; was unable to look upon them for longer. But as he stood in the doorway, he was in no doubt that they were rifling through his mind. Inside his thoughts he could hear a flock of little wings.

Being so close to the figures for so long must have driven Granby half mad. For a man with more intelligence and imagination, even though the inanimate quartet only appeared to have been carven from rock and rusticated by a great age, cohabitation with the figures would have been a sure course to full insanity. To withstand the angels for so long, Frank could only assume that Granby had entirely sealed himself inside the old sleeping bag that was rolled up beneath the table covered in watches and rings.

There wasn't much of Granby left to ask about the sleeping arrangements. What remained of him was mostly still inside the white tracksuit. The fabric was near luminous in the faint light; a sodium light occasionally supplemented with bursts of red from the flickering signage of the fried chicken takeaway across the street from *The Angel*. But the former landlord of *The Angel* had recently been rearranged into new configurations and contortions of limb and posture. The curly hair had been completely torn off his head, along with most of the scalp, which shone wetly upon the floor

61

directly beneath the closest plinth. It was not possible for the legs and arms of the living to bend in the way Granby's now did, and the man's spine resembled broken crockery beneath a handkerchief.

As his eyes became more accustomed to the light, Frank also became aware of the shapes hung from the picture rail on what looked like wire. There were at least a score of them. At first he had mistaken the shapes for overcoats, but now realised that although he had correctly identified that at least two coats did hang from the picture rail, the owners were still inside the garments. The other hanged figures were naked and withered to not much more than bones. Frank was relieved he could not see them in any greater detail.

Below him in the vast house he heard the first signs of life; Martin closing the bathroom door and running the only working tap over the basin.

On the second floor there must be two empty rooms. He was sick to death of the sight of Lillian, so make that three empty rooms.

Frank took one final look at the smashed figure of Granby at the foot of the plinth, and noticed the man's teeth were missing. He thought it a strange city that allowed its old Gods to keep such odd tokens.

He decided to get the empty second floor rooms occupied quickly. £125 a week seemed like a reasonable rate. At least to start with.

BOUDICCA'S BANE

L ondon has seen many incidents of homicidal violence during the two millennia of its existence, but without doubt the worst single event occurred when the city was still in its infancy, and it was caused – ironically enough – by a historical personage who has been lionized by the British ever since.

Thomas Thornycroft's bronze statue of Boudicca on Westminster Bridge depicts an archetypical warrior queen: beautiful, charismatic, powerful, fearlessly leading her people to war against the foreign oppressors. In that respect, it is perhaps no surprise that she is held in high esteem by populist historians, who throughout the ages have drawn parallels between Boudicca and women of note in their own eras – Elizabeth I, Queen Victoria, even Margaret Thatcher – but it is curious that Londoners regard her so fondly given that, to date, she is the only British potentate to order every occupant of the city put to death.

Boudicca's annihilation of London, or 'Londinium' as Britain's early Roman settlers called it, happened so long ago that sheer passage of time has reduced its horror in our eyes. But the known facts in the case speak unparalleled atrocity.

Boudicca was Queen of the Iceni, a Celtic tribal people with strong aristocratic tradition and a warlike culture. They lived in what are now the counties of Norfolk and Suffolk in southeast England, and so had fallen under Rome's influence at an early stage of its British conquests. Boudicca's husband, King Prasutagus, was a clear-headed monarch, who, recognising superior military forces, had surrendered to the Romans on their first arrival under Emperor Claudius in AD 43. He thus became a client-king of the Empire, which meant that he respected the Roman Governor of Britain's authority, and in return was allowed a nominal independence in his own realm. On his own initiative, Prasutagus also made a new will in which the Roman Emperor was named co-heir to his kingdom, to rule it alongside Prasutagus and Boudicca's two daughters.

The Romans, in response, made generous loans to Prasutagus, which enabled him and his people to prosper. But Prasutagus died in AD 60, and Rome's financial agents – as might have been their plan all along – called in these loans, and in addition demanded soaring interest payments. Boudicca, whose people had long grown used to their comfortable lot, protested angrily, and in retaliation

Roman forces plundered their land. The queen was publicly flogged and her two daughters, whose names may have been Heannua and Lanossea (though this is factually uncertain) were brutally raped, thus rendering them unmarriageable – which in effect destroyed the royal house.

Boudicca's fury knew no bounds.

Rousing her warriors to war and calling on the neighbouring Trinovantes tribe, who had even more reason to detest the Romans – their land had actually been stolen from them – she was soon able to put an army of 120,000 men into the field. This was many more than the Romans in Britain could have mustered at the best of times, but as it was, the Governor, Gaius Suetonius Paulinus, was campaigning with the bulk of his legions hundreds of miles away in what is now North Wales.

Boudicca fell first upon the Roman garrison town of Camulodunum (modern day Colchester). The garrison fled and she burned it to the ground, along with the Temple of Claudius, which had caused much anguish to the Trinovantes as the Romans had insisted on building it on their sacred soil. Cohorts drawn from the Ninth Spanish Legion now came against her, but Boudicca routed them and afterwards placated her religious lieutenants – the druids – by offering all her prisoners as human sacrifices to the war-goddesses, Andraste.

Her next target was Londinium. This wasn't the main colonial settlement in these early days of Roman Britain, but it was still a busy port on the north shore of the Thames estuary, with growing commercial and mercantile interests, so it was deemed important enough to be walled and manned by troops. It was also increasingly viewed as the Romans' main springboard into Britain, the place where all their soldiers and supplies were landed, and it was understandable that the rebels now made a beeline for it.

Governor Paulinus got there before Boudicca did, but he was well ahead of his own army too, and quickly recognised that the city could not be defended. Despite the pleas of its populace, he withdrew, taking away with him all administrative staff and military forces – even the auxiliary troops who had previously guarded the city walls. A population of around 30,000 was now entirely unprotected. Many of these were Roman citizens, merchants and colonists, but a significant proportion were native Britons: traders and their families, artisans and shopkeepers, journeymen, dock-workers and day-labourers who had come in from the country, even slaves. It made no difference. All would meet the same appalling fate.

A few military veterans who had stayed behind attempted to resist when Boudicca's horde arrived, but they were quickly overrun. The rampaging Iceni then set about enacting their queen's vengeance on the city that had become the bane of her existence. In three days of blood and rapine, they comprehensively sacked Londinium, killing almost everyone they found there, women and children as well. According to the Roman historian, Tacitus, the few they took prisoner were hideously tortured. Once again, a number were sacrificed to Andraste, enclosed in wicker cages and burned alive amid drunken, orgiastic revels. Others, in an ironic mirror-image of the fate suffered by so many barbarian peoples who had fallen into Roman hands, were taken outside the city and crucified. Still more – primarily the Roman women, or so the historians tell us – were impaled upright. Others were dismembered, having their limbs and breasts cut off.

Even allowing for the breathtaking cruelty so common to warfare in the Ancient World, these horrors sound excessive. It is highly possible that Tacitus, and the Greek author Cassius Dio – who was writing at a much later date, and drew his Boudiccan information from sources now lost – were exaggerating her depredations in order to demonise her, and yet both are regarded as reliable historians, and in any case this wouldn't fit with other references they make to the Iceni queen, in which they speak admiringly of her fine stature and fierce beauty.

What is not in doubt is that London's first incarnation – Londinium – was razed to the ground when it was only 20 years old, and its ruins burned to cinders. Nothing was left of the largely timber city – not even its cemeteries, which were ritually desecrated – and it genuinely seems as if the entire population was murdered. Archaeological excavations have uncovered nothing but a layer of fine, blood-red ash were it once stood.

Though she was later brought to battle by Paulinus and comprehensively defeated – and though she herself took poison rather than face capture, and never saw her people be punished by the Romans almost to the point of extinction – Boudicca will always be portrayed as a heroine of the British because she has become an icon of courage and independence. These days, it doesn't matter so much what she actually did as what she stood for. But to be honest that's a rather simplistic viewpoint.

Victorian artist Thomas Thornycroft sculpted his famous image of Boudicca from imagination – no accurate portrait of her exists. But it is difficult, standing in the heart of London – a modern, vibrant city, which these days welcomes all creeds and cultures and is a racial melting-pot, so close to the Houses of Parliament, one of *the seats of Western democracy – and knowing what happened on that exact spot, not to gaze up at that stern bronze visage and wonder perhaps if it doesn't contain just a hint of insanity.*

CAPITAL GROWTH
Gary Fry

*... London, if it be not one of the masterpieces of man,
is at least one of his sins.*
G K Chesterton

Dishonest people had a certain look in their eyes. Mary, her instincts honed by motherhood, had always been aware of this furtive truth. On the train to London, however, she and her family were lucky to have a table to themselves. Her husband Joe sat opposite, while their son – Jason – was directly beside her. Nevertheless, Mary remained vigilant until they arrived at King's Cross, carefully scrutinising other passengers and making sure none interfered in this unwanted daytrip.

It had been Joe's idea. He had business to conduct in the city and had finally persuaded her – with the help of her insistent therapist – to "loosen the apron strings" and let Jason "see a bit of the real world." Mary had assumed the seven year old boy had seen quite enough of that. Their home in the Yorkshire Dales was insulated from the worst society could throw at youth, but there were always school friends whom Mary was unable to police; there was always the ubiquitous TV; and there was always Jason's father, with his interest in the stock market and other dubious, money-oriented pursuits.

Indeed, as the train rolled into the station, Mary spotted her husband using his mobile phone to search the Internet. He'd no doubt be checking for text messages or assessing the FTSE index for buying or selling opportunities. This was all adult stuff and had always scared plain country girl Mary ... As the three of them got off the train, she saw many other people walking along the platform, that familiar dishonest look in their eyes. London was an experienced city; this was why she hadn't wished to come today, nor bring her innocent son.

"Jason, stay close to your mother," Mary announced, as crowds thickened near the exit.

"He's okay," Joe replied, snapping away his phone as if putting a gun back in a holster. Then he glanced at the boy and smiled broadly. "Nothing troubles you, does it, lad? You're going to help show your folks around today, aren't you?"

67

"I want to go in the London Eye," Jason replied, his voice nearly lost among all the booming, rattling sound inside King's Cross Station. But then they emerged into a bright day, with many other people – most meeting-bound, presumably – falling away to the left and right.

"Why don't we start at the British Library," Mary said, and this was far from a question, because she'd already taken her son's hand and started leading him towards the nearby building.

"I'm sure Jason would prefer somewhere a bit more exciting," Joe replied, following with resigned obedience. His voice was loaded with a sigh as he added, "Isn't that right, son? You tell her. It's okay to do so – you certainly have *my* approval."

Jason clearly didn't know how to respond, and Mary hoped his silence implied agreement with her. His father could be such a bully at times, always bringing his coarse occupational attitudes to the private realm of the family. This was like the world at large – now represented by noisy, traffic-filled London – violating an idyllic, personal space. Mary had always done as much as she could to resist that.

Joe had offered to provide guidance with his GPS-enabled phone, but Mary had brought along a paper map. When they reached the British Library, her husband said he'd remain outside to make "a few important phone calls", which suited Mary just fine. Then she took her son inside the building to show him original manuscripts of great chaste works by the Brontës, Eliot and Austen. Jason nodded with sensitivity, even though Mary had the impression that he wanted to do something less stuffy.

Only so much could be done to prevent a boy being a boy; Mary was aware of this truth and willing to be flexible. Her therapist had made many convincing points about the dangers of overprotecting children, and more recently she'd tried to worry less about Jason's psychological development. She supposed her own upbringing had a lot to do with her concerns – an only childhood spent on a remote farm, with just reclusive parents for company – but she was seeking to overcome these weaknesses, however challenging that might be.

They took a tube journey to Oxford Street and spent an hour shopping in high street stores. Jason wanted a new game for his console, but was less interested in the puzzle-solving ones Mary pointed out than the war efforts his dad enjoyed. When they reached the till, Joe took out his wallet and paid with his plastic, which, in Mary's opinion, did little to teach the boy the value of money ... But as they stepped outside, her attention was distracted by the sight of a beggar on the pavement, his aged face a mass of wrinkles, as if constantly huddling against the English cold had withered him prematurely.

"Spare some change, please?" this man asked in a London accent, the vowels presumably stretched by his latest intake of alcohol.

The truth was that Mary *could* spare change – she had a purse full of it, left over from the generous allowance her husband deposited in her account each month. He wasn't always unsupportive, and could be quite tender at times – when it suited him. All the same, she was loath to interact with the tramp, who, she now noticed, was wearing an incongruously pricey-looking sweater with a designer logo stitched to the front.

"Come away from him, Jason," she said to her son, again taking the boy's hand and leading him back to the tube entrance. The sooner they were away from this Mecca of consumerism, the better she'd feel. But then her husband stopped her dead in her tracks.

"I thought we might *walk* to Trafalgar Square, Mary," he called, holding out his mobile as if it was some kind of lifeline. Mindful of the lack of telephone reception underground, he was probably expecting another communication. After all, when had he ever expressed a preference for exercise when taxis or alternative forms of transportation were available?

But conscious of her son's health, she agreed to her husband's suggestion, and they'd reached only Soho Square before his phone rang, just as she'd known it would.

"Yes ... Buy at three-sixty, not a penny more ..." Joe said, his voice echoing off the capital's age-old walls, "... then hold for the dividend and put in a sale order for when it hits the same price . . ."

His latest stock deal was far from the first furtive transaction made in this area and wouldn't be the last. Glancing around, Mary couldn't help feeling as if the urban environment around them could absorb such experiences, as if the history of human endeavour, ignoble or otherwise, was woven into its foundations. This had stained the stonework and dimmed the windows; it rendered all the people working in such property slaves to an undying legacy: London affairs.

Looking back to see how much distance she'd put between herself with Jason and her wheeler-dealing husband, Mary noticed a figure following them along the backstreets. This man would resemble little more than a mass of rags if not for the fashionable sweater he wore – the same troubling garment she'd noticed back in Oxford Street.

Was the tramp pursuing them? Had he been angered by the way Mary had ignored him earlier? He might be dangerous ... in which case, she must move on, dragging Jason quickly along the street towards their next destination: Trafalgar Square, where they could enter the National Gallery and view all the virtuous masterpieces inside.

Improvising rather than using her map, Mary took a right turn, expecting to move back along the tourist paths her husband had instructed them to avoid. But then she found herself – and more dismayingly, found her son – in a grotty street peopled by feeble middle-aged men and gaudily painted women, each parading alongside shops selling red-light goods.

"Don't be alarmed, Jason," Mary said, her body tensing at the sight of a male mannequin in one window dressed in what she'd once heard was called a gimp mask, and little else.

"I'm not bothered, Mummy," the boy replied, his face looking confused. But Mary could hardly take seriously the testimony of a seven year old, and then led him away, beyond a woman whose dress was the exact opposite of her own in terms of length.

By the time they'd returned to a main artery of the city – Charing Cross Road, which, a quick consultation of her map informed her, led directly to Trafalgar Square – Joe had caught them up. The tramp in his wake appeared to have gone the way of the scarlet lady, leaving them free to explore the busy plaza and take photographs in front of fountains beneath the great English phallic symbol.

"Not *more* art," Joe protested as Mary directed them across to the gallery, and although his tone had been confrontationally playful, Jason had paid too much attention to his father's unacceptable attitude. How was Mary supposed to cope in the face of such irresponsible opposition? All the same, she steered her son and husband inside the grand building, relying on the likes of Da Vinci and Renoir to teach both about how beautiful the world could be.

Mary was never easily persuaded to separate from her son, but after becoming overwhelmed by Renaissance paintings, she momentarily overlooked the whereabouts of Jason. She eventually found him in the foyer with Joe, sniggering at Chinese tourists carrying more cameras than a posse of photographic journalists.

"What's the joke?" she wanted to know after reaching them and stepping back outside. She hoped they weren't laughing at her ... but her therapist had taught her to resist such paranoiac thoughts, and she tried hard to do so whenever possible. In truth, she remained moved by what she'd seen in the gallery, and was unable to hold her voice steady while cross-examining her family. "I mean, if you've got something amusing to share, feel free."

"Oh, stop sounding like a schoolmistress, Mary," replied Joe, his tone flippant and resigned. "We were just having some fun. I hoped you might join in."

Jason was still struggling not to laugh; the Chinese tourists had now emerged from the National Gallery, squabbling over something in incomprehensibly rapid Mandarin. As a younger woman, Mary had attempted to learn this language, but had soon given up after meeting Joe, who'd mocked her impractical aspiration and suggested that she concentrate on getting their first house into marketable shape. She'd acquiesced, of course, and when their son had come along, she'd switched her attention to the boy's development, making sure he turned out nothing like ...

"Joe, please, I'm only trying to make sure that – "

"Mummy, will you *please* stop arguing?" Jason intervened, and he'd surely been referring to both his parents, because then he added, "You're upsetting me."

Mary's husband smiled and was probably about to say something cutting when his mobile rang again and he snatched it out. More business talk followed, during which Mary had chance to stoop towards her son and ask if he was okay.

Jason replied with a quick nod, maybe to prevent her from detecting his suppressed frustration. Boys were like that, of course – uncritically devoted to their fathers. There was little Mary could do about that, and her therapist had suggested she shouldn't even try. Nevertheless, she was about to say something to turn the situation to her advantage when another person approached, his eyes about as untrustworthy as any Mary had ever seen. Indeed, after reaching Joe, this young man opened his grey jacket to reveal a row of small bags attached to one inner pocket, each bearing an illicit-looking substance.

Mary immediately moved away, blocking her son's view of the proceedings. She saw her husband shake his head, untroubled by the offer, and then pace towards her and Jason while still speaking on his phone about some sordid matter or another. It was probably just a nervous hallucination that made Mary spot the two figures she'd observed earlier – the tramp and the hooker – standing behind the drug dealer, but this nonetheless prompted her to move more quickly, steering her boy over a pedestrian crossing and then along a new road leading to other parts of this seedy city.

She didn't stop walking until they'd reach the Royal Courts of Justice, and then only because she felt safe within its authoritative proximity. A pair of scallywags was being accompanied out of its elaborate entrance, but now Mary felt less troubled, just one of a crowd of harried tourists consulting maps and seeking lunch. It was approaching noon, and after they chose a diner that sold healthy food as well as burgers, she felt herself settling into the daytrip. The close confines of the venue helped. Exploring London wasn't so bad, after all, she decided; she'd already survived – or rather, Jason had survived – a number of tricky situations. When Joe made a joke about the salad with which his junk food arrived, she even laughed with him and their son. Maybe she'd been worrying over nothing. Now she found herself even enjoying family life.

But when her husband insisted on them taking another tube ride to the capital's business district, her newfound confidence was compromised. There were no thugs here – no tramps or hookers or drug dealers – but she nonetheless sensed that many suited gents and made-up ladies in the area were trouble incarnated. There was something in their eyes Mary simply didn't trust; she'd always possessed a *nous* about this, refusing to ignore intuition, a survival technique during the difficult years of her youth. All the business people stepping in and out of big buildings with smoky frontages toyed with her nerves, making her feel protective of her precious son.

She hadn't wanted a child; this had been forced upon her by circumstance. She'd been seduced by Joe at an early age, little more than eighteen, when she'd known no better. He'd been tall, attractive and experienced, and in all her rustic simplicity, she'd felt genuinely flattered. It had taken her a while to get used to the sex he'd expected, but she'd eventually come to enjoy it, allowing its pleasures to overrule many nebulous risks. After falling pregnant, she'd grown frightened, but only by unknown dimensions of impending motherhood. She'd known that her husband was a good provider, seemingly drawing money at random from a world of which Mary had little awareness. Maybe it was ignorance of the source of their plentiful income that scared her – at least, this was what her therapist had suggested – but even so, she welcomed her monthly stipend and could cope comfortably with financial commitments.

But the more time that had passed – Jason's fractious early years – the less Mary had come to trust the world to which her husband was affiliated. There'd been constant phone calls, few from people whose voices sounded friendly, and when their pleasant semi in the Yorkshire Dales had been exchanged for a remote detached, her life had begun to feel less homely, the sense of threat more pervasive. Cars had replaced cars – Vauxhall followed by Mercedes followed by Bentley – and when clients were no longer restricted to the office and often invited back for dinner parties, Mary had started to feel her private life unravel.

72

Arguments had been common, after many of which Joe had fled the house, screaming arrogant accusations. Sometimes he wouldn't return for days, leading Mary to suspect other women. One night he'd come back in a odd frame of mind, and despite not detecting booze on his breath, she'd wondered whether he'd been taking drugs. Most folk in the finance game had recourse to such substances; this was a well-known fact. But it was that night – after Joe had, in typically grandiose mode, complained about her lack of ambition – that she'd decided to seek professional help for her psychological difficulties. In many ways, Joe was a negligent husband, but she suspected, on the basis of past experience, that the real problem lay with her.

The therapist she saw weekly agreed with Joe on some issues – that Mary overprotected their son, for instance – and with Mary on others: mainly, that Joe had let power arising from rapid success in business go to his head. These professional insights and advice had proved useful, and in fairness, her husband had tried to alter his bullish ways when she'd discussed them with him – certainly enough to encourage her to do the same with her fastidious ones. And now here they were, in London, a city of much experience, where Joe thrived and Mary cowered ... But the key question was which way would it all go for young Jason?

She observed her son, standing to one side of the mighty Thames. Her husband had entered one of the nearby buildings, hatching some scheme while excluding his family, like a patriarchal beast in a Victorian novel. Mary suspected that Joe wanted to keep them both from grubby truths involved in earning a living, but didn't such secrecy often result in unease? Would Jason soon wonder what went on in his father's private world, the way boys had done since time immemorial?

Mary joined her son near a wall, looking across what little of the city she could see from here. London had witnessed so much during its development, and its mismatching architecture reflected that. Her eye was drawn inland, to a horizon occupied by all the city's famous buildings: the gaudy Gherkin nearby, stately St Paul's Cathedral close to it, and the skeletal BT Tower at a distance.

At that moment, half an hour after leaving them, Joe returned and paced quickly their way. He had a spring in his stride, which implied that business had gone well. He was smiling broadly, an expression redolent of the buzz he was feeling and that at least pledged decent behaviour for a while – at least until he was in need of another fix of success.

"Ready to go?" he asked, holding out his arms to hug them, in full view of two suited figures who'd just emerged from the same

73

building he had. Joe had even put away his mobile phone. Mary wondered whether to trust him.

"I want to go in the London Eye," the boy said, responding enthusiastically to his father's uncommonly warm approach. "I want to go right up and see *everything*."

For some reason, this comment made Mary feel even more apprehensive and her hand tightened around his. It was surely just an imposition of fretful thoughts that made her see three other figures standing with the business people beyond her husband – the tramp, the hooker and the drug dealer … Indeed, after blinking and looking again, she saw nobody from the city's less palatable areas, nor even those smart office types.

"I thought we could first go to Shakespeare's Globe Theatre," Mary announced, her nerves far from steady after her latest half-hallucination. "It's not far from here. Then maybe we could take in the Tower of Lon–"

"He wants to go up the London Eye," her husband snapped, a little of his mean-spirited behaviour sneaking out, like a glimpse of the capital's underclass in some tourist-shunned backstreet. For one crazy moment, Mary felt as if Joe *was* the city.

As Jason had taken his father's hand, Mary had little option but to follow her family back into the tube system and then on a single ride to Waterloo, where they re-ascended into daylight to seek unrefined adventure.

And that was when they spotted the London Eye.

The slowly turning wheel did indeed resemble an eyeball peering back at Mary, watching her the way it observed all the city's inhabitants. It was like an eye of experience, a jaded peeper that had seen many wonderful and terrible things down the years. It was the capital's gaze burning a hole in her … and she looked away, took her son by the shoulders, and then hugged him tightly, as if she could protect him from a world he'd be unable to avoid in the long term.

Mary's first thought upon closer sight of the wheel was an echo of Jason's words earlier: *I want to go right up and see everything* … Sometimes her son sounded like her avaricious husband, thirsty for life and unwilling to compromise in terms of getting what he wanted. She wondered whether her therapist was right to suggest that denying people pleasures only made these more appealing. In short, was Mary doing more harm than good in keeping Jason from certain experiences? But then she overruled this concern, telling herself that her therapist was male and tended to side more with Joe than her. If this could be dismissed as yet more paranoiac behaviour, that was fine; it didn't necessarily make it untrue.

After joining a modest queue, Mary held her silence, hoping to avoid more rancour with her husband. But as the boy grew impatient to access the ride, she was unable to prevent herself from issuing further reprimands, the kind she believed youngsters should receive as often as possible.

But her husband responded with a scoff. "Stop being such a killjoy, Mary," he said, ruffling his son's hair and earning himself a cheeky grin in return. Then he added in a voice loud enough for others in the queue to hear: "You're more concerned about what people will think than simply letting Jason enjoy life."

There was possibly some truth in this – her therapist had certainly made the same observation – but Mary was reluctant to concede the point. By now, they'd reached the boarding area and others had thronged around them, a chaotic sea of faces. As Joe paced forwards to pay, she couldn't help assigning troubling identities to one group: a scruffy man wearing an incongruously smart sweater; a half-undressed woman smirking knowingly; a guy in a trench coat, possibly concealing illicit contents; two suited figures almost certainly discussing dirty deals; and finally, as Parliament was opposite this section of the Thames, a couple of furtive-looking politicians. But she decided that this was only another hallucination, and that her boy, who, as she and her husband were nudged aggressively aside, was now climbing aboard the London Eye, would be safe alone in the wheel, leaving her and Joe to sort out their issues.

And that was how their son ended up taking the ride with other people and not his protective mother, who'd do anything to save him from a world in which so many dreadful events occurred. She quickly said as much to her husband, who stood alongside the boarding area, puzzled by how they'd lost track of their boy.

"That was *your* fault," Mary exclaimed, watching the carriage that Jason had mounted trundle slowly upwards. "If you hadn't been arguing with me as usual, those other people wouldn't have barged past us."

"It'll do him good to be alone for a while," Joe replied, looking far from concerned about their son being with strangers.

Suppressing a mental image of the group of dubious characters, Mary added, "How do *you* know what's good for Jason? You're always too busy with clients to be a proper father."

"I work hard to earn a living. How else do you expect us to survive in this tough world?"

"I sometimes think that you and the people you deal with *contribute* to such toughness."

"What on *earth* are you talking about, Mary?"

She glanced up and realised that she'd lost track of the carriage her son occupied; it might any one of the rotating capsules overhead. The view would be incredible from up there, she thought with mounting unease. The boy was inside an experienced eye, surveying a city that thrived on the likes of her husband's duplicity. Nevertheless, she said nothing in response to Joe's question, and then turned back to look at him.

"One day," she said, almost tearful, "when our boy is a responsible man, you'll thank me. And I hope you'll be proud of him."

"I've got news for you, darling: I'm proud of him *now*."

She hesitated, caught out by his flippant response. Then her voice grew combative. "Yes ... so am I. Don't try to be clever, Joe. You're not in a business meeting now. This isn't a deal you're negotiating."

"Believe me," her husband replied, his smirk quickly fading, "you're more crafty and manipulative than any client I've ever known."

The comment was unexpected; he'd never make a similar accusation. Mary found herself speechless for several seconds, but eventually marshaled her thoughts. "Is that why you persuaded me to consult a therapist? To get a *man* on your side and prevent me from telling you more home truths?"

"Oh, this is the kind of paranoia I've come to expect from you down the years."

"Perfect paranoia is perfect awareness," she replied, and tried to prevent her mind dwelling on that disparate bunch of people who may or may not have boarded the London Eye with her son. She glanced up again at the turning wheel; all the capsules looked identical – how would she know which to approach to greet her returning boy?

Joe had just said something, but she'd missed it while privately ruminating.

"I beg your pardon?" she asked, suspecting that his comment had been disparaging.

But he didn't repeat it. Instead he adopted a different strategy, one possibly straight out of a business textbook. "Mary," he began, seeking to establish an intimate bond to get his nefarious way, "we both agree that Jason is our priority. What we don't agree on is the best way of bringing him up. So here's what I propose ..."

"I don't believe it. He's pitching a *deal* to me."

Responding to her laughter, which had drawn glances from many people waiting to take the ride, Joe scowled. Then he went quickly on. "What I propose is ..."

But at that moment, his mobile phone rang from one pocket of the jacket Mary had washed and ironed for him over the weekend.

Now Joe had a dilemma: should he prioritise family matters or acquiesce to a client? She watched him, realising that the power in their discussion had shifted her way. He squirmed for many seconds, during which the phone's ringing ratcheted up the tension.

"The *world's* calling, Joe," Mary said, her laughter undiminished. She felt unhinged, as if months or even years of anxiety were flowing out in a hurry. "Answer the call from the *world*, Joe! The *world* wants you! It wants to muddy you up, and once it's finished, it wants its wicked way with our *son*, too!"

"You're ... *mad*," he told her, snatching out the mobile phone, possibly as much to silence its nerve-shredding noise as to communicate with whoever was calling. "I'm thinking that medication might be the only answer ..."

As he turned to take the call, Mary stared out across the Thames at a city writhing with activity. It was as if she could see way above all the buildings up ahead, across a landscape stretching as far as the eye could focus. Now she felt *fused* with her beloved child, who was surely at the top of the wheel's cycle. She turned away from this spectacle, again realising that she needed nothing more in life than the love of her boy. Her marriage had always been full of tensions, even before their son was born. But Jason's arrival had resolved so much, offering her a focus in life. She knew that she was attractive and that this was all Joe needed her for: uncomplicated physical communion and an eye-pleasing magnet for potential clients – every one of them male, of course, just as her therapist was. They were *all* male, and had everything carefully plotted, because that was their nature, wasn't it? Even her own father had been manipulative, snuggling up to Mary in bed a little too closely after she'd grown too old for that kind of thing ... Well, she was determined not to let her son develop this way. She'd protect him at all costs, making him an honest man. He might even help her re-establish faith in this seedy, threatening world, a virtue she'd possessed as a child, before her drinking father and unsupportive mother had robbed her of innocence ...

"Mary! *Mary!*"

A man's voice broke into her reverie: it was Joe, her husband, who knew little about her past and the wellsprings of her anxieties. What would he do if she ever told him the truth. Leave her? Support her? Seek vengeance on her behalf? Mary refused to believe he'd resort to the first option, and doubted he'd pursue the last. But it was encouraging to feel that he'd try to protect her; after all, everyone needed support; it was what bound together people in the first place.

The surrounding city bloomed back into focus. She must have suffered a fugue, like those she'd often experienced as a younger woman, while pregnant with her boy. Mary looked up and saw Joe standing in front of her, holding her upright; he'd put away his mobile phone. How much time had passed since her last recollection? But that didn't matter, because she'd just noticed something else: the London Eye turning like a dilating pupil, like a telephoto lens zeroing in on some profound revelation.

Mary wrestled herself free of her husband's grip and immediately crossed to the boarding area. Many other people, none of whom had the same untrustworthy eyes as those she'd noticed earlier, awaited their ride, but first she must ensure that her son disembarked safely. A uniformed attendant paced forwards, but Mary shrugged her off; Joe, who'd followed quickly, offered the young woman – surely too young to understand the travails of motherhood – a quiet apology.

Then Jason's carriage came into view.

At the bottom, the doors slid open.

Mary had spotted her boy in one window, his head faced away, but as she moved forwards to take hold of him, he refused to turn. She had to climb onto the capsule, even as it started ascending again. Then, as her husband paid for her and Jason to take another trip above the capital, Mary noticed other people occupying this private chamber, this makeshift den of iniquity.

The doors had closed behind her, and Joe had failed to join her. Now there was just herself, the other riders, and her hideously transformed son.

The tramp lay in one corner, with a penknife rammed into his heart; his incongruously smart sweater was a wash of dark red. Opposite, her skirt ripped as if it had been torn violently down, sat the prostitute from Soho, her eyes rolling with intoxication; there were telltale holes in her exposed arms and her face was a compassionless ruin. The drug dealer occupied another corner, bagging up powders for the pleasure of two city traders in slick suits, both of whom looked pleased. Several politicians observed the scene, shaking their heads with moral rectitude while simultaneously exchanging cash and bundles of private-looking documents.

All the city's tawdry excesses were in evidence, personified by these living dummies, these automaton archetypes. That was Mary's first impression, and it horrified her. Then she did what she always did when confronted by such truths: turned to her child and hoped

78

that his touch would settle her reeling mind. She needed him as much as he needed her – perhaps more so, if she was being honest.

That was when the boy turned her way.

The casual clothing he'd worn earlier was gone, replaced by the kind of dark suit favoured by ambitious city-dwellers. Blood was splattered up both arms, and this was by no means the most disturbing sight. His fly was down and his belt unbuckled, and on the back of one jacket sleeve he chopped a small pile of white powder with a credit card. Moments later, snapping aside his stiff tie, he snorted this substance, drawing it deep into his skull to offer confidence for what he was about to say.

"Hey, everyone." His voice was high-pitched but much darker in tone than Mary had ever heard it. "I'd like you all to meet my mother. She made me what I am today."

All the people around Mary began grinning, their furtive eyes glinting in declining daylight. The dead tramp and the wasted prostitute seemed to twitch furtively..

Looking down at her corrupted boy, Mary said, "No … no … it wasn't *me*." She turned and glanced through the window, at the planet rolling from view. Her husband stood down there, using his mobile phone again, possibly bringing even more corruption to their tenuously secure lives. "It was *him*," she added with vitriol. "Him … him … *him*."

"Don't be so modest, mater," said a voice from behind, and even though its vocabulary had been transformed, Mary recognised the speaker as her previously innocent child. "I owe it *all* to you."

She heard the boy-man pace away and kick the dead tramp in the guts. Then he whispered something lewd to the prostitute, promising the same loveless brutality he'd recently administered. Finally he turned to the drug dealer, the city traders and the politicians, and added, "That's some fine Charlie, my friend. It'll help us guys conclude our furtive deal. The government will turn a blind eye, natch. Then we can all party like there's no tomorrow."

And it was only maternal duty, a willful blindness, that made Mary eventually join in.

THE BLACK DOG OF NEWGATE

Every corner of England, it seems, has legends concerning demonic black hounds, though as a rule these tend to be centred in rural areas. For this reason, readers might be surprised to learn that London has its own 'black dog' terror tale, though they'd probably be less surprised to hear that this monster's origins lie in Newgate Prison.

The history of this infamous house of correction, which stood at the corner of Newgate Street and Old Bailey from 1188 until 1902, is a horror story in itself.

Newgate was repeatedly damaged over the centuries – by the Great Fire of London in 1666, for example, and by the Gordon Riots in 1780 – but was always repaired, so its appearance changed many times. However, one thing that stayed the same was the prison's location and its reputation for being the worst hellhole any felon could be sent to. Everywhere in Newgate's interior there were chains, bars and bare, solemn brickwork. Its cramped, dark cells were designed to break the hearts of those confined there. Nothing had been made for comfort, and nothing was clean; vermin overran every room and passage, causing regular outbreaks of disease. The only light in the prison filtered through the main exercise yard, which was deep and narrow. Newgate's regime was never less than extremely severe, but in addition to this it was nearly always controlled by corrupt warders, who would use any method – from trickery and deception to sheer brutality – to fleece the prisoners of whatever paltry belongings they owned. Throughout its existence, Newgate was a byword for filth, despair and hopelessness.

So probably the last thing you needed to hear about, if you were about to be incarcerated there for the next 20 years, was the terrifying 'Black Dog of Newgate'.

This was no ordinary dog. It walked on two legs like a man, and was savage and carnivorous. For 400 years this ghastly apparition, to which locked doors apparently posed no obstacle, was rumoured to prowl the prison's gloomiest vaults, killing and eating any lone person it chanced upon. Various letters and pamphlets refer to its activities, though one, dating from 1638, tells how the monster – which in appearance was actually more like a werewolf than a traditional black dog – was created when, during the reign of Henry III (1216-1272) a young man being held in the prison on charges of sorcery was murdered by his fellow inmates, who then ate him because they were so hungry. One by one over the next few days, the malefactors were torn apart by the vengeful spectre, which the young warlock had summoned from Hell whilst in his death throes. In their panic, the prisoners responsible rioted and a number of them escaped, but the black dog followed them wherever they went, and in due course killed them all.

Of course, real-life cannibalism may lie at the heart of the Black Dog of Newgate legend. In the prison's early days, starvation was a regular problem, and it is highly possible that the most desperate prisoners would revert to eating each other. Violence within Newgate was almost never investigated by its authorities, and it doesn't seem beyond the bounds of reason that if the grisly remnants of cannibal feasts were occasionally found, these could easily be written off as the work of some ravening supernatural monster.

Not that this explains the creature's many later appearances, usually on the eve of executions, which were held outside the prison, just beyond the Debtor's Door. By all accounts, prisoners would quake in terror as they heard the awful beast padding along the cold, black corridors, grunting and snuffling at their doors, whining with a desire to devour their flesh. In 1596, one prisoner claimed to have seen it in its full gory glory, describing its feral canine appearance, and adding that it had a nest of thrashing snakes on top of its head and that it was accompanied by a sickening stench.

Even today, with Newgate a fading memory, the mythical monster is still with us. To the rear of Amen Court, close to St. Paul's Cathedral, a solitary chunk of architecture remains from the cursed penitentiary – a narrow stone alley called Deadman's Walk, once a passage leading to the gallows. The Black Dog is reputed to roam up and down this on certain nights of the year. Its low snarls and the clicking of its clawed feet are heard, and, when sighted, it is described as a shapeless blob which stinks disgustingly. Occupants of Amen Court have reported a similar terrible shape crouching on the wall overlooking the narrow passage, as if waiting to pounce on passers-by. It may no longer resemble the hybrid dog/man of legend, but these witnesses are in no doubt that it is the same evil spirit that was invoked in Newgate Prison all those centuries ago.

THE THAMES
Rosalie Parker

Old Father Thames – so the song has it – but she's more of a mother, that's what I've come to think. She started off young and beautiful, useful, the life-blood of the city. Then she was taken for granted, knocked around a bit. Now she's all used up, worn out, past it. But she keeps on flowing to the sea. Old Mother Thames.

I've watched the grey metal birds drone along the sluggish, moonlit curves of her, open their fat bellies and drop their loads – first the fire-sticks, then the whistling, booming two-tonners – on the wharves and factories, streets and houses. On the people, like me, who live and work here.

The Tate & Lyle sugar refinery's on fire. I can feel the heat. The bombing's been going on so long there can't be much left of the guts of the city – where the business is done, money conjured out of other people's graft. It's hard to remember what it was like before. Before the Blitz. It looks, and smells, like it might be the end of the world.

There are no fish in the river, she's too filthy for that. Just trash, the odd floating stiff – the ones who couldn't put up with it any longer, or who've been dumped there by someone who couldn't put up with them.

Few of us working girls will make old bones. I watch the tide shift the water up and down, backwards and forwards, the ebb and flow of living, of business – the business I used to be in – the oldest, dirtiest business of all.

I live a different life now. Just as tiring and difficult and dirty. But not the same. I don't miss the old life much – except her. Except her. Except her.

It feels like I've been watching such a long time. Watching and waiting. Watching the East End burn and waiting to see if Cally will step out of the ashes and come back to me and make everything right.

*

She showed up one evening at the start of the bombing, dressed for business in furs and a red dress, her mouth purple and ripe like cherries on the market. She was tall and slim, a lady, but her skin

82

was brown, her black hair coiled under her neat little hat. She looked like a picture in a magazine. It was cool, evening turning to night, and quiet – just me and her. Her eyes roved over me. She took out a long black cigarette from a silver case and let me light it for her.

"How old are you?" she asked, her voice all warm and silky, with something in it I didn't recognise.

"Sixteen."

"Her kohl-rimmed, almond eyes gazed at me and through me.

"Okay. Fourteen. I can look after myself."

"I'm sure you can, girl. I'm sure you can." She met my sulky glare full on.

She asked some more questions – where did we take the punters? Were we hassled by the coppers? Who did I have to look after me at home? She was cool as a cucumber about everything. She wasn't any kind of do-gooder. She said I looked nice in my little dress. She stroked my hair.

A gang of sailors came by, just off the ship. All mouth, but nice boys.

"Hello darlin', does your Dad know you're out?" "I don't fancy yours much!" "Who's the squaw?"

They laughed and joked around a bit. They were okay. They could see that Cally was a piece of class.

"Not much business tonight," I said, when they'd moved on. Cally stared up at the darkening sky. She took a long drag from her cigarette.

"It'll be a bomber's moon. We'll have action – of one kind or another."

A couple of soldiers rolled up, full of drink. Bursting for it. The big brown-haired one homed in on me.

"Well, little girl! Ain't you cute! How'd you like to do somethin' for me?"

I led him down the alley and finished him off in half a minute. He tried arguing about the money, but Cally showed up and put him right.

"She did her job, so pay her," she said, fixing him with her cool brown eye.

"And who the fuck are you?" he said. But he paid up all the same.

I didn't see her with her punter. He must have legged it pretty quickly after they'd done the business.

I thought – things are looking up. She'll watch my back.

I turned three more tricks before the raid started and took home good money for Pa. He had a drink and I found us something to eat.

We didn't go to the shelter. Me and Chrissie sat under the kitchen table and ate our cake and listened to the bombs dropping all around us.

*

I was hoping I'd see Cally again, but she didn't show. The next few evenings weren't easy. There was plenty of competition – a dozen girls worked my patch on a good night – although we were all friendly enough. We looked out for each other. There wasn't much to take home and Pa was sad, and then he was angry.

A few nights later she was back. She was wearing a black dress under the furs, with a sparkly brooch and sheer silk stockings. God knows where she got them. She was smoking one of her cigarettes.

"What would you like to do with your life?" she asked.

I shrugged. "I don't know. I was supposed to go to Petersfield – the school was evacuated, teachers and everything – but Pa needs me. He can't manage on his own."

She raised one of her long black eyebrows. "Can't he?"

"No. The bombing's done for him. He needs a drink to steady his nerves."

A big green motor drew up, headlights off in the blackout. A smooth-looking punter in a Homburg stuck his head out of the window. He took a good look at me. "Mmm. A nice little girl! Get in."

Cally put her hand on my arm. "I'll sit in the back."

"I don't need a bloody chaperone," he snorted. "It's not as if you're her mother, is it?"

Cally smiled at him with all her white teeth on show. He wound up his window and drove off. She watched the car turn the corner.

"You must learn when to be careful."

"I can look after myself," I said.

She stared out towards the river for a long time.

"What got you into this game?" she asked, at last.

"I dunno. I've always ... done it with men. Since I was ... it's no big deal."

She was staring at the water like something was going to jump out of it.

"What about you, Cally?"

"Oh, I've been at it since the dawn of time. You should make them use a johnny, girl."

"Hey! I'm clean! ... Some of them do. Some of them are nice. They cry afterwards."

"They still fuck you, child. You need to make sure you're safe."

84

"Do you like babies, Cally?"

"I was a mother. Not a good one."

"I'd like to have a baby sometime. A nice little baby to cuddle."

"Make it a bit later, that's all."

A tidy-looking chap in a brown suit took her off for a bit. When she came back she lit up another cigarette.

"Why do you do it, Cally?"

She plucked a shred of tobacco from between her teeth.

"I like to sleep with different kinds of people. Lots of people"

"You could have anyone you wanted. A super-looking girl like you."

"Not everyone likes Indian girls."

"You'd hardly know you're a darkie, you're so beautiful."

She laughed that tinkly laugh of hers.

"I can travel wherever I like, see who I want to see. No one tells me what to do."

"I'd like to get married to a nice boy one day."

She looked at me for a long while.

"Would you?"

"If I could find the right one. One that didn't mind too much."

*

Cally usually turned up when the other girls had moved on. I couldn't go with them because I had to keep an eye on Chrissie and Pa. In between punters she told me stories, about an Indian god called Shiva, and some battles and trials and things. There was a goddess, too. In her stories the women were in charge. She could be good, or bad, you never knew which. Sometimes she did awful things.

I told her about our street and how Mrs O'Driscoll was still singing her dirty songs when they pulled her out of the rubble.

She told me about the punters she'd had. She said she once did a chief inspector in a lift at Scotland Yard. He liked her so much that the next day he paid her a tenner to do his wife as well.

"Have you been with lots of women, Cally?"

"Quite a few. I like women's bodies."

"Why d'you stand out here, when you could be in a nice hotel, or a little flat up West?"

"Oh, it takes all sorts."

"You'll go away again, won't you? You'll go away and leave me?"

"I don't know. I might stay until the end of the War. It brings with it a certain ... heightening of sensation, don't you think?"

"It makes everyone randier, you mean?"

"That's it."

I reached up and touched her face.

"You're beautiful Cally. You really are."

She stroked my hair.

"Cally, my punters don't come back any more."

"Why do you think that is?"

"Perhaps I'm so good the first time they never need to do it again!"

"Maybe that's it."

*

I hadn't seen Cally for a couple of weeks. Pa's call-up papers had come and he'd been crying and carrying on and he went next door to see if Irene would take Chrissie and me in so we wouldn't be separated. She said a few choice things about the way I earned my living and Pa got angry and Alf and Tom had to drag him away.

Then one evening Cally was back, as lovely as ever in a blue dress that clung to her in all the right places, a sequined purse and matching silk shoes with little covered buttons. I gave her a cuddle and she cupped my face in her hands and tilted it up to the moonlight.

"Who did that to you, child?"

She could never be ugly, but her face was all set and hard.

"It's only a shiner."

"Who did it?"

"Just a punter."

"Which punter?"

"The smooth-looking one in the Homburg with the motor. He wanted to do some rough stuff. I got out of the car afterwards and ran away. It's all right Cally. I wasn't really hurt."

"What did he do to you?"

"Nothing I haven't had before. He kept talking about how much I was like his little girl."

She turned her face away.

"Have I done something wrong, Cally?"

"No. You've done nothing wrong."

She stroked my hair for a bit and I told her about Pa going into the army.

"Will your neighbour look after you and your sister?"

"I don't need looking after. Irene's all right. She'll take care of Chrissie when I'm working."

She opened her little bag and took out a silver flask with dancing figures all over it. I swigged a few sips of brandy. It went through me like fire.

"That's good stuff, Cally! Where d'you get it?"

"There's a chap I know in the War Office."

"Does he do something important?"

"Oh yes. He talks in his sleep."

She took a good, long swig herself.

*

A few nights later me and Cally were alone on the street.

It was chilly and quiet and the other girls had gone to the pub. The big green motor pulled up. The chap in the Homburg stuck his head out of the window and shouted over to me.

"Hello, dearie! Fancy earning a few more bob?"

Cally was beside the car before I could get there.

"How'd you like both of us? I can watch. Or you could watch us. Only another four bob."

His eyes flicked between me and Cally.

"All right, then. Four bob. Get in."

I sat in the front and she got into the back. He drove off, his hand wheedling up my skirt. Cally lit a cigarette.

"Where are we going?"

"You're a lot friendlier now there's a few bob in it for you. I'll drive to the wharf. It'll be quiet there."

The air-raid siren started up. He laughed in a funny sort of way.

"Not so quiet, maybe! But we won't let Jerry stop us, will we girls? We'll ride it out, won't we? Ha, ha! Ride it out!"

He laughed again while he parked the car, and wiped the sweat off his face. The water was a dark mirror in front of us. He leaned over and grabbed me by the hair.

"You know what I like, you dirty little bitch."

The first incendiaries rained down. I heard a small pop as the clasp of Cally's purse opened. She reached over the driver's seat and there was a flash of silver. A jet of blood spurted out of his neck and hit the windscreen. He sighed and slumped over.

She wiped the razor on her hankie and put them both back in her bag.

She said, "Do his flies up. We're going to put him in the river. She'll look after him."

I pulled myself out and helped drag him to the mooring. He slid in with hardly a ripple.

"Cally ..."

"None of them were fit to lick your shoes."

"But ... what are you going to do?"

Her eyes were still on the river.

"I think it's time to move on."

The tears came. I couldn't help it.

"What will I do without you, Cally?"

I rested my head against her. She stroked my hair.

"You'll be fine. Get yourself some War work. Ask your neighbour to help you."

"Will you come back?"

"I might."

"Please come back, Cally. I love you. What will I do without you?"

*

Chrissie's been evacuated to the school at Petersfield. She writes me letters sometimes, about the country people she's staying with. I think the city's just a bad dream to her now.

I've been working at the munitions factory for nearly five months. Irene's sister put in a word for me. I've made some friends – they're a good crowd. One or two have been more than friends – nothing serious – there isn't time for anything serious, the shifts are so long.

I've come to realise that you can get used to anything. Even the bombing. And the spaces where the girls don't turn up to a shift, or the next, and the empty chairs in the canteen.

I go for walks sometimes, if I can get away. I've seen a plant growing on the bomb sites. Fireweed it's called. It likes to get in first. It's tall and foreign-looking, with a big pink flower spike, all elegant and proud and alive. Sometimes there's so much of it you can hardly see the rubble.

Maybe she's sleeping with some general in a Yank hotel. Or sitting with her Indian gods, plotting some mischief to keep things on the boil. I don't expect she'll have time to come back to me, in this most damaged part of the big city. But Old Mother Thames, she's still running through it, washing everything out to sea.

THE OTHER MURDERERS

L ondon's name could be written in blood, it has hosted so many serial killers over the centuries. There are far more than we could detail here, but without doubt the most famous is Jack the Ripper, whose ritual slaughter and disembowelment of at least five (but maybe as many as nine) Whitechapel prostitutes during the autumn of 1888 has become iconic in the annals of crime.

Never named of course, let alone captured, and appearing in roughly the same time-zone as those two great works of Gothic fiction, Dr. Jekyll and Mr. Hyde (1886) and Dracula (1897), the Ripper came to assume the dimensions of a faceless and immortal monster who would terrorise generations of Londoners for long after his natural life should have expired, and has appeared repeatedly in books, movies and horror stories. Yet despite claims to the contrary, Jack the Ripper was not Britain's first serial killer. He wasn't even London's first serial killer. That dubious honour may actually belong to **John Williams** of Wapping, the so-called 'Ratcliffe Highway Murderer'.

In 1811, two incredibly violent attacks were made upon separate households off the Ratcliffe Highway, which ran through Wapping, one of the most impoverished districts in the East London docklands. In the first, a young couple, their infant son and a servant boy were horrifically slain – their throats cut repeatedly, their skulls crushed by the savage blows of a mallet – and all on a quiet evening in December.

There was consternation throughout the East End. Even in a neighbourhood as routinely violent and disorderly as Wapping, 'home invasion' type murders were quite rare, especially involving so many fatalities.

Only 12 days later, with Christmas fast approaching, the killer struck again, forcing entry to The King's Arms pub while its occupants slept. As before, the attack was driven by an apparent bestial rage, the publican, his wife and a female servant all dying under a hail of knife and cudgel blows, which left their corpses almost unrecognisable.

Even in an age untrained in criminal psychology, it became apparent that the motive here was not just burglary. There had to be a grudge involved, but who would hold such enmity against two unconnected families? The two local police forces – the Bow Street

Runners and the Marine Police Force, whose main task was protecting ships moored in the 'Pool of London' – were baffled. Neither was equipped with detective divisions or forensic units. However, they were smart enough to take note of a bloodstained hammer found near the scene of the first crime, with the initials JP inscribed on it. This led them to an Irish seaman, John Williams, who was known to be in dispute with the first family murdered, and who was suspected of having recently stolen a hammer from his friend, John Peterson. He was also accused of being seen with mud and blood on his clothes on the night in question.

Before he could be charged, Williams committed suicide in his remand cell at Coldbath Fields Prison. This was taken as an admission of guilt, and he was buried at the Ratcliffe Highway crossroads with a stake driven through his heart to prevent his undead husk continuing the horror. With no real explanation for the mass slayings, particularly those of the second family, not everyone was convinced that Williams was the culprit, but there were no more 'Ratcliffe Highway Murders' after his death.

*These days we are aware that many serial killers do their vile work simply for the pleasure the act itself gives them. Not that we understand it, and not that we don't feel utter fear and revulsion when it happens. When war broke out between Britain and Germany in 1939, and especially when the Luftwaffe shifted its attention from Britain's airfields to her cities in September 1940, the very last thing the authorities of London needed was another 'Ripper' scare. But that is almost what they got thanks to the activities of **Gordon Cummins**, a native of the city of York but now a Leading Aircraftman who was quartered in the capital.*

It was actually after the Blitz, in 1942 – but still during a period of sustained aerial attacks on London, with the air raid shelters in regular use, bomb damage in the streets and the blackout in full operation – when Cummins commenced a bizarre but deadly reign of terror, which in only six days was to claim the lives of four women. The first victim was found garrotted to death in a shelter in Marylebone on February 9th 1942. But the second, third and fourth – two housewives and one prostitute – were found in their flats in West London on the next consecutive nights, all their bodies displaying signs of steeply escalating violence; they too had been garrotted but in addition had been grossly mutilated with a range of implements, from razor blades to can-openers.

Despite police attempts to keep the public calm, the press dubbed the perpetrator 'the Blackout Ripper', and a full-scale panic appeared to be on the cards – after all, this maniac didn't just hunt streetwalkers; he had the temerity to enter private residences to commit his atrocities! However, two further attacks were then foiled, the women gamely fighting off their assailant, the first identifying an RAF uniform and the second hanging onto his gas mask container, the serial number of which led the police straight to Cummins's door.

Cummins's background did not suggest that he was a murderer-in-waiting. He had no known history of violence or sexual deviance, and did not even have a criminal record. But there was no question about his guilt. On arrest, his bedroom was searched and trophies which he had taken from his victims were found. New advanced fingerprint technology was also employed, and Cummins's prints were confirmed on several of the murder implements.

He was hanged at Wandsworth Prison in 1942, though some of the investigating detectives, the noted pathologist Bernard Spilsbury for one – who commented that the injuries on the bodies were the worst he had ever seen – found it hard to believe that Cummins had commenced his criminal career with such high levels of brutality. Many suspected that he had been active before but had simply got away with it. At least two unsolved murders of women in London during 1941 were later attributed to Cummins, though there was no official investigation in either case.

*While Gordon Cummins was still rotating beneath the trapdoor at Wandsworth, another London resident with Yorkshire origins, Halifax-born **John Christie**, was about to set new standards of odiousness with the series of sex murders that he would shortly commit inside his sordid home at 10, Rillington Place.*

Christie, a bespectacled little man with a reputation as a braggart and a martinet, was landlord of the soon-to-be-infamous tenement in Notting Hill, when, between 1943 and 1953, he lured various young women there under false pretences – usually having claimed that he was medically trained, or having impressed them in his capacity as a War Reserve Constable – and after rendering them unconscious with coal gas, raped and strangled them (though, as Christie was a necrophile, it didn't always happen in that order).

His total tally of victims is believed to be seven (though it may be many more), and this includes his wife, Ethel, whom he murdered in 1952. Two additional victims can be added to the list in the shape of his upstairs lodger, Timothy Evans, an uneducated Welsh lorry driver, who in 1950 was wrongly hanged for the murder of his wife Beryl (Christie's fourth victim) – mainly on the say-so of Christie as chief witness for the prosecution – and Geraldine, the Evanses' baby daughter, who Christie is also believed to have strangled, though he denied this latter crime to his dying day.

91

The weakness in Christie's plan always arose after the crime was committed.

Though a manipulative man who was undoubtedly skilled when it came to trawling for victims and arranging their destruction, he was very disorganised when it came to disposing of the evidence. Most of the bodies were either buried in his garden, under his floorboards or inside a recessed cupboard, which he simply locked and covered with wallpaper. In 1953, not having worked for years, and unable to endure the atmosphere in his squalid little flat, which was now inundated by the stench of death, Christie abandoned his home and attempted to vanish into London's legions of post-war homeless. But less than a week after a new upstairs tenant at 10, Rillington Place discovered some of the corpses, a sharp-eyed constable spotted Christie loitering on the Thames embankment at Putney, and took him into custody.

Christie was hanged at Pentonville Prison in 1953. Timothy Evans was posthumously pardoned, and his remains reburied in consecrated ground, in 1966.

*Of course it's often said that serial killers rarely resemble monsters, and while that wouldn't strictly be true with Christie – given his unlikeable manner and the dingy den he dwelled in – it is certainly true of the so-called 'Acid Bath Murderer', aka **John Haigh**, an insipid charmer and conman, who also used the chaos of the Second World War to mask his nefarious, London-based activities, and in the process murdered at least six people (but maybe several more).*

Whereas Christie's activities were driven by lust, Haigh was driven by greed. Despite later fallacious claims that he drank the blood of his victims, Haigh only ever seems to have had one interest during his adult life – benefitting financially as much as he possibly could from those around him.

Haigh worked at many jobs and attempted to start several businesses during the 1930s, but made a success of none. He was also pathologically dishonest, and served prison time repeatedly for fraud, theft and swindling. He finally seems to have settled on mass murder as an enterprise in 1944 when, operating first from Gloucester Road in southwest London and later from the glamorous Onslow Court Hotel in Kensington, he began befriending wealthy but gullible people, and after appropriating funds, investments, pensions and even property from them, killed them either by clubbing or shooting, dissolved their bodies in barrels of sulphuric acid and then poured the resulting sludge onto rubbish sites or down the drains.

92

Unlikely as it may seem, Haigh made this high-risk lifestyle pay to such an extent that he was able to live out the remainder of the war in considerable comfort. When peace arrived he had no intention of stopping; in fact, signalling an intent to step up the pace of his operations to an industrial level, he acquired a workshop in Crawley, West Sussex – little more in reality than a purpose-fitted murder unit (complete with acid-filled drums ready and waiting) – where he planned to bring many potential investors to 'see his inventions'. He killed and melted down three of them there before the game was up.

His final victim, a rich widow called Olive Durand-Deacon, had a friend, Constance Lane, who didn't believe that she would just leave the hotel where she lived without saying goodbye. The disappearance was reported to the police, who thought Haigh a suspicious presence among all these wealthy, elderly ladies. Background checks revealed his record for dishonesty, and soon they were searching his premises at Crawley, where they found evidence linking him to several missing persons, including Mrs. Durand-Deacon, and a gun that had been fired recently.

Once arrested, Haigh boasted that without a body no murder charge could be brought, but he had misunderstood the law of Corpus Delicti, which did not mean – as he assumed – a physical body (i.e. a corpse), but a 'body of evidence', and of that there was plenty. On learning his error, and hearing that forensic experts were recovering fragmentary body parts from outside his workshop in any case, he feigned insanity by claiming that he was a vampire. But the police didn't believe him, and neither did the jury.

Unlike John Williams, no stake through the heart was sought. Haigh's hanging at Wandsworth Prison in 1949 was deemed to be quite sufficient.

THE RED DOOR
Mark Morris

"**L**et us pray."

Although Chloe closed her eyes and clasped her hands together, she barely heard the words that her brother Luke was intoning. She had never had a panic attack, but as she stood among her family and her parents' friends she felt light-headed and jittery; felt her heart-rate increase and sweat break out on her body.

"Amen," Luke said finally, and although Chloe murmured the word along with everyone else it seemed like a husk in her throat, hollow and dry and hard to expel.

Her problem – if such a cataclysmic life-shift could be termed so mildly – had started even before her mother had been diagnosed with the liver cancer, which had taken most of the last year to kill her. Although her mother's unbearable suffering had made it even more difficult for Chloe to re-discover the path from which she had strayed, she firmly believed that her London life had been the true catalyst – or more precisely the fact that she had finally moved away from home two years ago, thus distancing herself, both geographically and ideologically, from her devout parents.

Not that her mother and father had been fire and brimstone types, intent on indoctrinating Chloe and her siblings with the notion of a vengeful and belligerent God. On the contrary, the God that Chloe had grown up with had been a merciful and loving one; a God that gave comfort and succour. As a small child she had thought of Him as a seventh member of the family – a kindly grandfather figure, whose influence was overwhelmingly benign. He was someone to whom she felt she could pour out her problems, someone who could always be relied upon to make things better.

It distressed her greatly, therefore, that she had recently begun to have doubts, not simply about the nature of God, but about His very existence. Back home in Buckinghamshire for her mother's funeral, she decided to confide in Joanna, her older sister.

On the night following the funeral the two girls found themselves sleeping in the bedroom which they had shared as children, the bedroom in which they had swapped secrets and gossip, and in which they had done so much of their growing up. Chloe found it nostalgic and yet at the same time, now that their mother was gone, desperately sad to be sleeping in her old bed, with Joanna in *her* old bed, just a few metres away. When the two girls had been small their mother had tucked them in every night after listening to their prayers. She had kissed them on the forehead and whispered, "Sleep well, sleep tight, may God protect you through the night."

The only thing whispering to Chloe now was the harsh wind in the branches of the denuded apple trees in the back garden. She listened to them scraping and rustling as she worked up the courage to speak, and then finally she whispered, "Jo? Are you awake?"

"Yes," Jo said immediately, as if she had been expecting the question.

"Can I ask you something?"

"If you like."

She was only two years older than Chloe, but Jo, who had always been considered the practical, pragmatic one, often acted as if the gap between them was much wider.

"Have your views changed at all since you left home?" Chloe asked.

"About what?"

"Well... about anything? God, for instance."

"No. Have yours?"

The response was blunt, and threw Chloe for a moment. Finally she admitted, "I think they have."

"In what way?"

"I don't know. I suppose I'm not as... certain as I used to be."

"You mean you don't believe any more?"

"It's not that, it's ... well, I'm not sure."

Jo paused for less than a second, and then she said almost crossly, "Well, either you do believe or you don't. Which is it?"

Chloe felt dismay seize her, felt herself shrivelling inside. I'm not going to cry, she told herself. But when she again said, "I don't know," her voice cracked on the last word, and all at once she was sobbing.

Lying in the dark, she half-expected Jo to move across to her bed, to offer comfort, but the older girl remained so still that Chloe might have believed she was suddenly alone in the room. Eventually Jo asked, "Have you spoken to Dad about this?"

With an effort Chloe swallowed her tears. "No. I don't want to worry him. Especially not now, when he's got so much to contend with."

"Probably wise," said Jo. Silence settled between them again, albeit one filled with the frenzied scraping of the tree branches outside. Then Jo asked, "What's made you have doubts?"

95

Chloe struggled to put it into words. "It's not one thing. It's an accumulation. I suppose when I was at home I saw evil as... I don't know... the Devil's work. Something separate from humanity. I knew it existed, I knew people did terrible things to one another, but it was as if it was this separate thing that bubbled up every now and again like ... like lava from a volcano."

"And now?" said Jo.

"Now I realise that it isn't like that. Living in the city I suppose it's made me realise that evil isn't always big and grand and uncontrollable. It's petty and vicious and banal. It's there in everybody. Every day, in one way or another, I come up against cruelty or cynicism or selfishness or envy or indifference. I was sitting on the tube the other day, and the day before there'd been delays on the District Line because a girl had thrown herself under a train, and this couple were griping about her, saying what a selfish bitch she was because she'd made them late for the pub."

"Welcome to the real world," Jo murmured.

"But why is the world like that?" protested Chloe. "Why, if God exists, has he let things get in such a state? A girl where I work was mugged the other week by two guys outside Ladbroke Grove tube station. People just walked past while one of the guys held a knife to her throat. And I read in the paper that a fifteen year old girl at the local school had been beaten up, and that even while she was lying on the pavement unconscious her attackers had carried on punching and kicking and stamping on her while other children laughed and filmed it on their phones."

She subsided into silence, aware that her voice had become stretched and almost whiny. Jo's response was as cool and considered as ever.

"God gave us free will," she said. "How we choose to live in this life will determine our role in the next one."

"But why?" Chloe asked. "Why give us free will if so many innocent people suffer for it?"

"We all need to be tested," said Jo.

"But why? That's what I don't understand. If God is all-good and all-powerful why does he need to make us suffer? Why put us through this at all?"

"To test our faith, of course. If we can suffer the hardships of life and still have faith in God, then we will prove ourselves worthy of sitting at His right hand. We have to earn our place in the Kingdom of Heaven, Chloe. If we didn't suffer the hardship and misery of our earthly lives we wouldn't appreciate the ultimate glory of life everlasting. We would be complacent, selfish beings, with no concept of good and evil, no perspective."

"But what about good people who don't have faith in God?" Chloe said. "What about people who don't believe in Him, but who are still kind and generous and loving to their fellow men? Don't they deserve their place in the Kingdom of Heaven?"

"Without God there is no Kingdom of Heaven," said Jo firmly.

*

Chloe spent the train journey back to London the next day gazing bleakly out of the window. How easy it would be to abandon her career and return home. She imagined herself withdrawing from the stress and responsibility of city life, of giving up her independence and becoming an unofficial housekeeper to her father. She could grow stout and spinsterish in the bucolic tranquillity of the village where she had grown up. And once there, surrounded by God's love, perhaps she would rediscover her faith, even if only by default.

These thoughts dismayed her even while they comforted her. Was her faith really so fragile that the merest test was enough to rattle it to its foundations? Jo had told Chloe that the real test of faith was to remain steadfast in the face of challenge and adversity, but it was easier said than done. Jo was tough, inflexible. Was it Chloe's fault that she was less robust than her sister? Was it a sin to be sensitive, to be lacking in confidence?

As the train drew closer to London, and the surrounding fields and villages were gradually superseded by urban sprawl, Chloe felt her spirits sinking still further. In recent weeks she had become obsessed with the notion that the very fabric of the city had become imbued with the decades of wickedness perpetrated within its confines, that the stones and bricks and timber of its buildings had soaked up every bad deed, every foul thought.

The walls and roofs of houses and factories and apartment blocks flashed by the grimy window, many of them old and crumbling and dirty, their facades stacked and angled haphazardly, as if the buildings they supported had been crammed in wherever there was space. Lost in her thoughts, Chloe barely registered them, and yet all at once something snagged her eye – something so fleeting that it was nothing but an impression, gone before she could focus upon it.

Nevertheless, whatever she had seen was unusual enough to lodge in her mind, as irritating as a sharp morsel of food stuck between her back teeth. As she disembarked at Euston her mind was probing at it, trying to bring it into the light, but it wasn't until she had sat on the rattling Northern Line tube to Tufnell Park, and had trudged the maze of streets back to the Victorian house containing her third-floor flat, and was fitting her key into the lock of the front door as the daylight faded into smoky dusk, that it suddenly popped into her mind.

It was a door. That was what she had seen. A door in a wall. The door had been painted a deep, shimmering red, though what had been odd about it – what had snagged her attention – was that it had been not at ground level but half-way up the wall. And furthermore, it had been upside-down.

That, at least, was how she remembered it. That was the image that had lodged in her mind. A bright red, upside-down door, half-way up a wall.

It was ridiculous, of course. That can't have been what she'd seen. And even if it was, there must have been some reason for it. It must have been a contrivance, an architectural gimmick, perhaps even part of some obscure advertising campaign. London was full of oddities, of things that didn't make sense. Some people loved that about the city – its quirkiness, its hidden corners, the fact that it was crammed with bizarre sights and bizarre stories.

By the time Nick called, Chloe had put the red door to the back of her mind. She ate some pasta and was washing up her plate, pan and cutlery in her tiny kitchen when her mobile rang. Thinking it might be her dad calling to make sure she'd got home okay, she went through to the main room, drying her hands on a tea towel, and retrieved her burring phone from her jacket pocket. Seeing Nick's name she almost didn't answer. But then she reluctantly pressed the 'Accept' button and said, "Hi."

"Chloe?"

"Yeah."

"Oh, it *is* you. I wasn't sure. You sounded weird."

"I'm just tired."

His voice grew soft, concerned. "Are you okay? How was it?"

"It was fine. As far as these things go."

There was a silence, as though he expected her to elaborate. When she didn't he said, "You're not all right, are you? Do you want me to come over?"

The thought wearied her. "Not tonight, Nick. I really am tired. I'm going to have an early night."

"Tomorrow then. Let's do something tomorrow. Take your mind off things."

She knew he was only trying to be kind, but she wanted to snap at him, 'Do you think I can just forget as easily as that? Do you think I'm that shallow?' But instead she said, "Yeah, okay, I'll see you tomorrow."

"This used to be a power station," Nick said, the wind whipping at his wispy blond hair and twitching the scarf at his throat. "It's pretty impressive, don't you think?"

Chloe gazed at the imposing edifice of the Tate Modern, the chimney stack high above her stabbing at the grim sky as if mockingly pointing the way to Heaven. Troubled, she turned her attention to the wide slope leading down to the entrance doors.

"I think it's ugly," she said.

"Really?" Nick looked half-surprised, half-offended, as if he was personally responsible for the building's design and construction. "Well, just wait till you see inside. It's amazing. Like a cathedral."

It had been Nick's idea to come here. He had wanted Chloe to see an installation in what he called, with a sense of ominous grandeur, 'The Tanks'. Since they had met two months ago, after Chloe's friend and work colleague Christine had all but bullied her into trying online dating, he had made it his mission to take her to all the places in London where she hadn't been that he thought were worth visiting. In recent weeks he had introduced her to the South Bank, to Highgate Cemetery, to Camden Market, and to several of his favourite restaurants. Chloe had tried to match his enthusiasm as he unveiled each new treasure, but she had thought the South Bank hideous, Highgate Cemetery depressing, Camden Market gaudily pretentious and most of the restaurants too expensive.

Nick was a nice guy, and had been nothing but supportive throughout the last days of her mother's illness, but Chloe had begun to wonder whether their relationship was really going anywhere. They had little in common – he loved London, she didn't – and she had so much to contend with right now that she couldn't help thinking the timing was all wrong. A year hence things might have been different, but currently Nick was less a pleasant distraction than simply one more thing to worry about.

"Isn't this amazing?" he said as they passed through the entrance doors and entered the vast, echoing space inside. Shivering, she tugged her coat tighter around her. In truth she felt nothing but dwarfed and daunted, and further away from God than ever.

"It's certainly big," she admitted.

"Come on," Nick said, taking her hand. "What I want to show you is this way."

The Tanks, located on level 0, had originally been a trio of huge underground oil tanks, and were accessed via a series of side doors arranged either side of a wide, dank, low-ceilinged corridor. The sign outside the door that Nick led her to bore the name of a Japanese artist – all spiky, sharp syllables, like jags of broken glass – and a long explanation about dreams and shifting states of consciousness which Chloe's eyes skimmed over without taking in.

The interior was dark, though not pitch black. However the lighting, such as it was, had been angled in such a way that it played with Chloe's perceptions, disorientating her, making her unable to tell where the floor met the walls, and the walls the ceiling. As a result she felt unsteady and uncertain, even a little sick.

"I'm not sure I like this," she whispered.

"It does take a bit of getting used to," Nick murmured. "But it's worth it. There's nothing here that can hurt you."

Ahead of her, Chloe could see shadows blundering about – other visitors tentatively picking their way forward. The room was full of ambient noise – slow, soft booms and the continuous echo of wordless whispers – and undercutting that, as though coming from a nearby but as-yet-unseen room, she could hear the drone of a voice speaking in a foreign language, its tinny quality suggesting that it was a radio or TV broadcast of some kind.

Edging forward, she was distracted by movement to her left, and turning she saw a number of figures, blacker than the darkness around them, standing in silhouette, their arms upraised. They looked to be pleading for their lives, or begging for help, but drifting closer Chloe realised that they were simply visitors like herself, standing on the other side of a thick glass wall which she had assumed, until she was close enough to touch it, was a continuous dark space. These people had their faces pressed to the glass and were peering through; Chloe could see the glint of their eyes in the gloom. From their blank expressions she guessed that the glass was one-way, that she could see them, but that they couldn't see her. The thought unsettled her, and she shivered and moved away.

It was only now, with a jolt of surprise, that she realised Nick was no longer holding her hand. When had the two of them disengaged? It must have been when she had stepped to her left, but she couldn't for the life of her consciously remember tugging her hand free of his grip. She peered into the gloom, but could not distinguish him from any of the other shadows bobbing ahead of her.

"Nick?" she said softly, but her voice was instantly swallowed up, incorporated into the ambient soundscape. She tried again, raising her voice a little, though oddly reluctant to draw attention to herself. "Nick?"

None of the shadows responded.

For a moment Chloe considered retracing her steps, waiting for him outside, but then she moved forward. He couldn't be more than a few metres ahead. He was probably waiting for her to catch up. She held her hands out like a blind woman as she tentatively placed one foot in front of the other. Remembering how the glass wall had been invisible until she was standing right next to it, she felt vulnerable, certain she was about to walk into or trip over something.

The shadows ahead seemed to be bearing left, like fish following the course of a stream, and so she moved with them, going with the flow. She realised she must have rounded a corner, for all at once the space in front of her opened up, and she could see the source of the droning voice, which had abruptly become louder. It was a television, icy blue in the gloom. It seemed to be suspended in mid-air, hovering like a ghost. On the screen a bespectacled Japanese man – possibly the artist – was giving what appeared to be a lecture direct to camera. However, as he spoke, white circular scribbles jittered constantly around his eyes and mouth, giving him a monstrous, corpse-like appearance. Chloe knew that the effect had been achieved simply by scratching circles around the man's features on each individual frame of film, yet in this environment the sight was unsettlingly nightmarish. A huddle of dark shapes was clustered around the TV, motionless as mannequins; they seemed to be hanging on the man's every word. Did they really understand what he was saying? Or could they see something in the overall work that she couldn't – something fascinating, even profound?

Feeling isolated, she peered into the shadows beyond the droning man on the screen, and her eyes were instantly tantalised by a shimmer of red in the distance. Drifting away from the throng around the TV, she moved deeper into the darkness. She wondered if what she was seeing was an illusion, whether it was even possible to pick out colour when there was no discernible light source. Certainly at first the redness seemed to shift both in and out of her vision, and in and out of the darkness, causing her to constantly adjust her eyesight. Then as she moved closer it seemed to rise from the gloom around it, to become more solid, and she realised that it was a door.

She halted in astonishment. Not only was it a door, but it was the door she had glimpsed yesterday from the train – or at least, like that door, it was upside-down, and positioned not at ground level but a metre or so above it. All at once Chloe felt frightened, as if she had stumbled across something very wrong, possibly even dangerous. Instead of backing away, however, she instinctively stepped forward, overwhelmed by a compulsion to touch the door, to check whether it was real. But before she could raise a hand, something hard slammed into her forehead, rocking her backwards and filling her head with sudden, unexpected pain.

Almost abstractedly, as if the shock had jerked her consciousness from her body, she became aware of her legs giving way, of her surroundings dissolving into black static. The only thing that prevented her from passing out was the sensation of surprisingly strong arms curling around her body, holding her upright. A particularly strident burst of static close to her right ear gradually resolved itself into a voice.

"Chloe? Chloe, can you hear me?"

Ten minutes later she was sitting in the café with a handkerchief which Nick had soaked in cold water pressed to her forehead. She could feel a lump forming there, the blood pulsing in thick, soupy waves just above her right eye. There was a clatter of crockery and Nick was back with tea and cake. She looked up to see his concerned face, and then turned her attention to the cup and saucer which he was pushing across the table towards her.

"Here you go," he said. "How are you feeling now?"

"Like an idiot," she admitted.

"How's the head?"

"Throbs a bit, but I'll be fine."

"Oh God, I feel so responsible," he said. "They ought to warn people about those glass walls. They're dangerous."

Chloe sipped her tea and said nothing.

"Maybe we should complain," he continued.

Chloe squinted at him. The electric light hurt her eyes. "Did you see anything through the wall?"

"Like what?"

She took a deep breath. "A red door."

"No. But then I was more worried about you." He looked at her curiously. "Maybe we ought to get you checked out. You might have concussion or something."

"I'm fine," she said firmly. "I just need a couple of paracetamols and a lie-down." She finished her tea and replaced the cup in the saucer with a clatter. "Sorry to be a party pooper," she said, "but I think I'd like to go home now."

*

"Hi, Dad, it's me."

"Chloe, my darling. How are you?"

"Oh... fine. A bit sad."

102

"Well, that's understandable. How was your journey back yesterday? I'm sorry I didn't ring. I felt exhausted once everyone had gone. These last few weeks have taken it out of me rather."

Chloe felt tears prick her eyes. She pictured her stout, bespectacled father, the wispy white hair receding from the pink dome of his head. Trying to keep the waver from her voice, she said, "Will you be all right in that big house on your own?"

"Oh, I'll be fine," he said with a confidence she suspected was entirely for her benefit. "My parishioners are spoiling me rotten. You should see how many fruit pies and lasagnes and goodness knows what else I've got in the freezer. And of course none of us are ever truly alone, are we? Not with God to see us through."

At first Chloe was unsure whether she could respond, but finally whispered, "No."

Her father's voice was suddenly full of concern. "Chloe, my love? Are you all right?"

She sniffed and swallowed. The tears which had been threatening to come brimmed up and out of her eyes, forming dark coins on the leg of her jeans as she leaned forward. Forcing out the words, she said, "It's just ... Mum. I miss her, Dad."

"I know," he said softly. "We all miss her, my love. But isn't it a great comfort to know that her suffering is finally over, and that she's now at one with God?"

*

"That boyfriend of yours been knocking you about?" said Christine cheerfully.

Chloe blinked at her. "What?"

Christine gestured at her forehead. "That lovely bruise on your bonce. Get a bit carried away in the bedroom, did we?"

Chloe hoped she wasn't blushing, though she rather suspected she was. Chris was the best of only a handful of friends Chloe had made since moving to London, but that didn't prevent her fellow copy editor from taking a perverse delight in poking fun at what she regarded as Chloe's naiveté.

"Believe it or not, I bumped it on a glass wall," Chloe said.

Chris's false eyelashes gave her widening eyes the appearance of Venus fly traps sensing prey. "I'm intrigued. Tell me more."

Ironically, for a magazine with a ceaselessly relentless publishing schedule and a strict remit to keep its finger firmly on the rapidly beating pulse of city life, the atmosphere in the *London Listings* editorial office was mostly relaxed and easy-going. Chloe would have preferred to have worked slowly and steadily through the week, but so much of what she did was reliant on the output of her colleagues that she had little choice but to adapt herself to the long-established regime and culture of the workplace. What this effectively meant was that for eighty per cent of the time she was either making or drinking coffee, exchanging gossip and twiddling her thumbs, and for the other twenty per cent she was engaged in a grim, feverish, to-the-wire race to meet her weekly deadlines.

Chloe told Chris about her and Nick's less than successful visit to the Tate Modern, though felt oddly reluctant to mention the red door. Already it was adopting the texture of a dream-memory in her mind, of something that, paradoxically, was both vivid and unreal. It disturbed her to think that the door might be a figment of her imagination, though the alternative was more disturbing still. She tried to console herself with the assertion that she had been under stress, that grief could play funny tricks with the mind, and that this was subsequently only a temporary aberration. She had even been trying to convince herself that 'seeing' a door was a sign of hope and optimism, that it was a symbol of new beginnings.

"I take it you still haven't shagged him then?" said Christine.

Chloe grimaced. "No, and I'm not planning to."

"You want to watch it, girl," Christine warned. "Even the nicest bloke in the world won't stick around forever if you don't give him a bit of what he needs."

Chloe looked away, trying to appear casual, though in truth she felt uncomfortable, out of her depth. If Christine ever found out that she was still a virgin, Chloe thought she might shrivel up and die of humiliation.

"I'm not sure if I'm really that into him," she said. "I don't think he's the man for me."

Christine rolled her eyes. "I'm not saying you should marry him, for God's sake. Just have a bit of fun while you can."

"But I don't think I even fancy him that much," Chloe said, trying not to sound defensive.

Now Christine looked pained. She shook her head slowly. "You know what your problem is?"

"I'm sure you're going to tell me."

"You're too picky. Ten years from now you'll be desperate to get a man into bed. And you won't be so fussy then, believe me."

Chloe shrugged, a dismissive gesture to hide the tightening in her stomach, and wandered over to the window. From up here on the third floor she could look down on the bustle of Tottenham Court Road, the continuous flow of people and traffic, and kid herself that she was removed from it all, that for the moment, at least, her world was an oasis of calm amid the chaos.

Directly across from the *London Listings* office was a row of unprepossessing retail outlets – a printer's, an office equipment suppliers, shops selling mobile phones, white goods, music and electronics equipment. Gazing out at the familiar view, Chloe suddenly gasped, as if someone had placed a cold hand on the back of her neck. On an anonymous patch of wall, between a sandwich shop and a display window packed with second-hand TVs, was the red door.

As before, it was upside-down, and was situated not at ground level, but about half-way up the wall. People were walking to and fro past it, partially obscuring it at times, but despite its unusual aspect no one appeared to be giving it so much as a second glance. Chloe stared at it unblinkingly for several seconds, her heart beating hard. Then she closed her eyes, and kept them closed for a count of five, before opening them again.

The door was still there. Immediately a thrill went through her, though whether it was a thrill of fear or excitement she wasn't sure. She shuddered, her arms bristling with goose bumps, but in her head she was thinking, *It is there. It is real.*

"Chris," she said, hoping her voice didn't sound odd.

"Yeah?"

"Come over here a sec."

"What for?"

"I want to show you something."

"What?"

"Just come here. It's easier to show you than to explain."

Behind her she heard Christine sigh in exasperation, but she didn't turn round. Now that she had established that the door was there, Chloe didn't want to take her eyes off it even for a second. After a moment she was rewarded with the sound of Christine's chair scraping back and her footsteps crossing the wooden floor.

"Okay. So what's so amazing?"

"Look across the road at that wall between the sandwich place and the TV shop and tell me what you see."

Christine was almost shoulder to shoulder with Chloe now, which brought her into Chloe's peripheral vision. Just as she was tilting her head to look where Chloe had indicated, a high-sided delivery van drove past on the opposite side of the road, temporarily obscuring their view of the red door.

When the van had passed, Christine shrugged. "I see a wall. What am I supposed to see?"

Chloe felt sick. "No," she moaned.

"What's the matter?"

"It's gone."

"What has?"

"What I wanted you to see."

Christine looked at her in exasperation. "Well, what was it?"

Chloe shook her head. "It doesn't matter now."

Christine's expression became an angry scowl. "Are you taking the piss?"

Miserably Chloe shook her head. "No I'm not. I swear I'm not."

"So what was it then?"

Chloe took a deep breath. "A door."

"A door?"

"Yes. A door in the wall." She groped for an explanation. "It must have been an optical illusion."

Christine's eyes bored into her. She looked as though she wasn't sure whether to respond with pity, anger or contempt. Finally she shook her head and turned away. "You're fucking weird," she said.

*

"Thanks for taking this so well," said Chloe.

Nick gave her a wry look and rubbed absently at the chipped veneer of the circular table. The pub was so cavernous that it seemed relatively empty, though they still had to raise their voices above the buzz of chatter which echoed off the high ceiling.

"I've never been one for screaming and shouting," Nick said, "though that doesn't mean I don't care. To be honest with you, I'm crying inside."

Chloe wasn't sure how to respond. Was he joking? "Really?"

"Well, maybe not crying, but … I can't pretend I'm not disappointed. I thought we had something. I thought we were getting on pretty well."

"We do get on well," Chloe said. She was briefly tempted to reach out and take his hand, but in the end she kept them folded in her lap. "And you're a nice guy, Nick, a really nice guy. You're good-looking, funny, interesting, kind …"

"Please don't tell me you're about to say 'it's not you, it's me'?"

The remark could have been cutting, sarcastic, but he said it gently, with a faint, sad smile. Chloe matched his smile with her own. "I suppose I am in a way. I'm just … not ready for a relationship. I'm cut up about Mum, I'm confused … to be honest, I don't know what I want right now. I've lived in London for two years, but I don't actually like it that much. I might even go home … or does that sound too much like giving up, admitting defeat?"

He shrugged. "It's entirely up to you. Ultimately you have to do what you think is best."

"I know." She sighed. "But the trouble is I don't know what that is."

He smiled, a warmer smile this time, and leaned forward. "You're a sweet girl, Chloe, and I understand about you not wanting a relationship right now, what with your mum and everything – but that doesn't mean we can't still be friends, does it? We can meet for drinks, days out; perhaps we can go to the cinema or the theatre now and again. What say we jettison the romantic baggage and just be mates?"

She looked at him sceptically. "And you'd be happy with that?"

"Yeah, why not? I do have girls who are just friends, you know. I'm not so desperate that I see every woman as a potential partner."

He looked sincere. "I'd like that," she said. "But what about the whole online dating thing?"

"I'll try again. If nothing else, it's a way to make friends – and you can never have enough of those. What about you?"

She wrinkled her nose. "I think I'll give it a miss. Not that this hasn't been nice, but it's not really my thing. My friend Chris kind of bullied me into it in the first place."

He gestured at her empty wine glass. "Well, now that we've got that sorted, fancy another?"

She hesitated. "Why don't we go back to mine for a cup of tea instead? It's on the way to the tube station."

He raised his eyebrows slightly. "Well, I don't know. Are you sure you'll be able to contain yourself once we're alone together?"

She laughed. "It'll be tough, but I have a will of iron."

It was a cold night, windy enough to propel leaves and litter along the street in loops and spirals. They walked briskly up Tufnell Park Road, turning left by the theatre on the corner. The illumination from the street lamps was splintered by a row of wind-blasted trees lining the edge of the pavement, casting a jittering kaleidoscope of vivid orange light and deep black shadow upon the ground. As they walked up Carleton Road, Chloe leaned in to Nick and surprised him by taking his arm. Ironically, now that there was no longer the pressure to become romantically linked with him, she felt more affectionate towards him, more at ease in his company. They were about half-way between the pub and Chloe's flat when a series of elongated shadows detached themselves from the darkness ahead.

Chloe tensed, unconsciously tugging on Nick's arm, but he said, "It's all right, come on."

"Let's cross the road," she whispered.

"There's no need. We'll be fine."

107

His confidence was reassuring, but Chloe still felt nervous. As she and Nick approached the hovering shadows, they began to move, sliding forward out of the darkness with a series of soft, snake-like rustles.

There were four of them, boys in bulky jackets and baggy jeans, hoods pulled up around their faces. One of them spoke, his voice both conversational and threatening.

"What you doin', man?"

Nick's reply was friendly. "We're just walking home."

Another voice came out of the darkness: "Oh yeah? Where you live?"

"Not far from here."

"Where exactly?"

Nick barely missed a beat. "I'd rather not say if you don't mind."

"Why not? What you think we gonna do?"

"I don't think you're going to do anything."

"You got a phone?" said the first boy.

"Yes."

"Can I borrow it?"

"What for?"

"Wanna make a call."

"Haven't you got a phone?" Nick asked.

The boy made a clicking sound with his teeth. "All out o' charge, innit?"

"What about your friends?"

The boys moved forward en masse. The one who had first spoken, the tallest of them, suddenly had a knife in his hand. "Never mind about them. Give me your fucking phone, man," he said.

"No," said Nick.

"Fucking give it, or I stab your fucking eyes out."

Chloe's throat was dry with terror, but she managed to croak, "Just give it to him, Nick. It's only a phone, for goodness sake."

Nick glanced at her, as if about to say something. As he did so, like a weaving snake sensing a chance to attack, the tall boy sprang forward.

Chloe screamed as Nick and the boy came together. There was a clash of bodies, a grunt, and then Chloe became aware of a dragging weight on her arm and realised that Nick was sliding slowly and silently to the pavement, his legs folding beneath him.

She clutched him for a moment, trying to hold him upright, but eventually had to let him go to prevent herself being dragged down with him. As Nick fell, the tall boy stepped forward and shoved Chloe in the chest hard. She staggered back, certain for a moment that she'd been stabbed and that the shock and the pain would kick in later. As she put a hand to her chest, expecting to feel the wetness of blood, the tall boy crouched over Nick like a hawk over a rabbit, picking at his coat and the pockets of his trousers, pulling out a phone, a wallet, keys. Then the boys were slipping away into the night, not hurrying, crowing over their booty, their victims forgotten.

Chloe scrambled forward, legs like water, heart and head pounding, lips gummed together with saliva that had dried to glue in her mouth. She reached out, touched Nick's body.

"Nick," she whispered, "Nick."

She touched something wet. She lifted her hand. It was black under the street light.

*

Nick's parents were Jean and Brian. His sister, who was in the second year of her 'A' levels, was called Liz. They arrived around four a.m., having driven down from Durham.

When they walked into the intensive care unit, Chloe rose from the chair beside Nick's bed and said, "Hello, I'm Chloe. I'm a friend of Nick's. I was with him when it happened."

Nick's sister looked down at her brother, white-faced; his mum burst into tears. Only Brian acknowledged her.

"How is he?"

"They think he's going to be fine," Chloe told them. "The knife punctured his lung, but he's had an operation, and they've patched him up. As you can see he's breathing on a respirator at the moment, but they ... they think he's going to be fine."

Her voice petered out. She was exhausted, emotionally and physically. She swayed on her feet, had to sit down again. Then Jean was stepping forward, grasping her hands.

"Look at you, pet," she said. "You're just about done in. Thank God you were with him. You saved his life."

Her eyes were wet with tears, but she was smiling shakily now, beaming with gratitude. Like Brian she was portly, her hair chestnut brown and worn in a way that made Chloe think of Shirley Bassey.

"I don't know about that," Chloe said. "I just called for an ambulance. Anyone would've."

"He'd have bled to death without you," Jean insisted. "Little life-saver you are."

Chloe didn't have the courage to tell her the truth – couldn't bring herself to say that if she hadn't arranged to meet Nick in the pub to tell him their relationship wasn't working out, and if she hadn't refused that final drink, and if she hadn't suggested he walk her home, then her son would never have been stabbed in the first place. Sitting beside Nick's unconscious form, staring at the transparent plastic mask covering his nose and mouth, and listening to the machines that were monitoring his life signs, Chloe couldn't help but think that this was all her fault, that if she hadn't been so selfish this would never have happened.

Suddenly, surrounded by Nick's family, she felt stifled, and pushed herself to her feet.

"I'll leave you to it," she said. "I'm sure you'd like to spend some time with Nick on your own."

Ignoring their protests she stumbled from the room. By the time she had pushed through the swinging double doors and was out in the corridor she was all but hyperventilating. She staggered to a chair with a pale blue vinyl seat and dropped heavily into it. The corridor outside the ICU was quiet, the only sound a faint buzz from the fluorescent strip lights overhead. Chloe slumped forward, closed her eyes, clasped her hands together. She didn't realise she was readying herself to pray until she actually started to speak.

"Lord, if you're there, and if you're listening, please help me. Give me the strength to overcome my doubts and believe in you again. I can't tell you how much the thought of losing my faith terrifies and upsets me. Without it I feel … cast adrift. But I can't pretend that I believe if I don't, I can't say I have faith if I don't feel it on the inside. Help me, Lord, please. If this is a test, or even a punishment, then believe me when I tell you that I want to overcome it, that I want my faith in you to be restored more than anything else in the world. But I can't live a lie, Lord. I need your strength, I need you to help set me back on the right path. Perhaps that's selfish of me, or weak, but that's how it is. I'm only human, after all."

Her voice trailed off. She didn't know what she expected to happen, but she felt just the same inside. Empty, lost. It was like a kind of darkness gnawing at her, devouring the light. Groggily she raised her head, her eyelids peeling apart.

The red door was on the other side of the corridor, directly opposite her, no more than half a dozen metres away.

Something rushed through her then – not faith, but a kind of tingling heat that was part awe, part wonder, and part raw, primal terror. For a split-second she wondered if this was it, the sign she had been praying for, but the notion had barely formed in her head before she was dismissing it.

No. This door was something different. Something wrong. Something unholy. She could sense it. She could feel it in her blood, in her nerve endings, in her very essence.

And yet she felt ensnared by the door too. Tempted. Tantalised. Repelled though she was, she had to know what was on the other side. Had to.

Almost unwillingly she rose to her feet. Took a step forward. The door seemed to throb like a heart, to call to her. As before it was half-way up the wall, upside-down. And now, up close, she could see that its paint was peeling and scabrous, that its wooden panels were cracked, its brass knob scratched and tarnished.

She took another step. She felt stuffed with heat, her eyes and throat pulsing, her heart like a drum whose vibrations shuddered through her body. Slowly she raised a hand, readying herself to knock.

"Our Nick's awake, if you want to see him."

The voice was like a slap, snapping her head round. Chloe gasped, blinking and swaying. For a moment her vision swam, and she thought she was about to pass out. Then the blur of colours and shapes tightened into focus, and she was looking at Jean, whose cheeks were flushed, and whose eyes were alive with excitement and curiosity.

Before Chloe could respond, Jean said, "Sorry, pet, did I startle you? What were you doing?"

"Nothing, I …" Chloe stammered, and turned her head back towards the red door. It was gone.

She sighed. She felt partly relieved, partly bereft.

"Nothing," she repeated.

*

When she woke it was dark. For ten or fifteen seconds she lay in bed, her mind almost comfortingly blank, trying to remember where she was, what had happened. Was it night-time? The early hours? For some reason that didn't feel right. Massaging her hot forehead with a cool hand, she sat up, groping with her other hand for her phone on the bedside table. She brought it up to her face, peered at the time: 7:13. Time to get up, time to go to work – but that didn't feel right either. It was only when she looked again and realised that it was p.m. and not a.m. that the memories came flooding back.

She had got back from the hospital around twelve hours ago, with barely enough strength left to stagger into her bedroom and collapse into bed, peeling off clothes and leaving them in her wake as she went. The adrenaline crash after the trauma of the previous

111

evening had caused her to sleep solidly and dreamlessly for the past twelve hours. Checking her phone again Chloe saw that she had a couple of missed calls and several texts, mostly from work, wanting to know where the hell she was. There was also a message from Nick, who sounded tired but okay, asking her if she was all right, and a text from Jo which said: *How are you? Feeling better after our talk?*

Still sitting in the dark, Chloe scrolled through her address book until she came to 'Home'. She selected 'Dial' from the Options menu and snuggled down into bed as the cricket-like burr at the other end of the line broke the silence.

"Hello?" Her father's voice was like honey. Emotionally raw after waking up, Chloe was shocked to feel tears springing instantly to her eyes.

"Dad, it's me. Can I come home?"

A moment of surprised silence. Then her father said, "Chloe, my love? Are you all right?"

"Not really," she said. "I'm not doing so well at the moment. Can I come home?"

"Well … of course. At the weekend, do you mean?"

"No, I was thinking now. Well, tomorrow. I thought I'd catch an early train."

"I see."

"Is that all right?"

"Well, yes. But what about your work?"

"They'll be fine about it," she said, not caring whether it was true or not. "They know about Mum. They said if I needed any time off …"

There was another moment's silence, and then her father said. "Right, well I shall expect you tomorrow. I'll look forward to it."

"Me too, Dad. And … Dad?"

"Yes."

"I need to talk to you about something. Something important."

"Right. Well, I shall look forward to that too."

Chloe rang off, feeling as though she had taken a step in the right direction, as though she had achieved something. Perhaps it was naïve to think her dad would solve all her problems, but talking to him would help, she felt sure of it. His was the voice of reason and compassion. He would untangle her muddled thoughts and put everything into perspective.

"I'm trying, Lord," she whispered. She threw back the duvet, crossed the room and switched on the light.

*

The door was back.

Chloe almost dropped her mug when she saw it. As it was, she jerked back from the window, slopping hot coffee over the back of her hand. "Ow!" she yelled, gritting her teeth as she ran through to the kitchen to douse the reddening skin in cold water. Once she'd patted her stinging hand dry with a tea towel she returned to the main room, sidling round the edge of the kitchen doorframe and keeping low, like someone targeted by a sniper. It was ridiculous to think she was being stalked by a door, and yet she couldn't help but feel that she was under scrutiny. She crept along the wall on bended knees until she was underneath the light switch, then reached up and snapped it off. With the flat in darkness, illuminated only by the glow of the street lamp outside, she felt marginally less exposed, though her heart was still thumping hard as she scrambled across to the window and jerked the curtains across, shutting out the night.

She rose, parted the curtains a chink with her finger and peered through the gap. She half-expected the door to have vanished, but it was still there, the peeling red gloss that coated it shimmering in the lamplight. It was on a section of wall that was part of the frontage of a second-hand furniture warehouse directly across the road from her apartment block. It was several metres to the left of the rolling metal shutter that was both wide enough and high enough to admit a sizeable truck, and that served as the warehouse's main entrance. As ever, the door was half-way up the wall and upside-down, and to Chloe it seemed to be flaunting its wrongness.

"You're not there," she muttered, and then, when that was not enough to dispel the image, "Go away, go away."

She let the curtain drop back into place, telling herself that if she ignored it, it would disappear, that next time she looked it would be gone.

She turned on the TV, checked her emails, made herself another cup of coffee, flicked through yesterday's *Metro*, even though she'd already read it. Try as she might, however, she couldn't put the door out of her mind; it was like an itch she was desperate to scratch.

Her flat was full of clocks – there was one on her kitchen wall, one on her computer, one on her phone, one on her DVD player tucked neatly beneath the TV – and every few moments she found her eyes straying to one or another, whereupon she would catch herself mentally calculating how many minutes had passed since she had last looked out of the window. She moved restlessly from room to room, sitting down for no more than two or three minutes at a time before feeling compelled to jump up and prowl again. Finally she tried to lie on her bed and close her eyes, but her mind was buzzing with anxiety, her stomach churning, and in the end she jumped to her feet, marched into the main room and twitched the curtain aside again.

The door was still there. Chloe gasped, feeling something between despair and fear curl inside her. She wondered whether, ultimately, she would be able to outrun the door, whether it was confined to London, and whether if she left the city and returned home it would somehow be unable to follow her.

She tried to glean comfort from that thought, though couldn't help but be aware that she was only speculating, and that sometimes the only way to overcome a fear was to confront it. Allowing the curtain to drop she made herself a promise: if the door was still there in an hour she would attempt to discover what lay behind it.

For the next hour she forced herself to sit in front of the TV, to stare at the screen, even though her mind was elsewhere and she had no idea what she was watching. For the last ten minutes her eyes kept flicking to the digital clock on the DVD player, and with a minute to go, she shuffled to the edge of the settee, hands braced either side of her. As soon as the green numerals changed, completing the hour, she shoved herself to her feet and rushed across to the window. Jerking aside the curtain she cried out, as though at a sharp stabbing pain, and felt her legs begin to shake.

The door was still there.

"Oh God," she breathed, unsure whether her words were an oath or an appeal for strength, "oh God." As she pulled on a jacket and gloves, the shaking spread from her legs, into her hands and belly.

"Come on, Chloe," she told herself, "you can do this."

She walked out of her flat and down the stairs, gripping the banister as though it was her only connection with reality, as though without it she would drift away and become lost. At the bottom of the stairs she hesitated a moment, then plunged towards the front door. As she twisted the Yale lock and pulled the door open, her heart was pounding so much it hurt.

Please be gone, she thought, *please be gone*.

She stepped outside.

And there was the red door, across the road, waiting for her.

Chloe descended the steps at the front of the house and moved down the path towards the gate. There were several seconds when the red door was hidden from view by the high hedge bordering the front of the property. *When I step through the gate, it will be gone*, she thought.

But it wasn't. She crossed the road towards it as though in a dream. She wanted it to flicker and vanish, wanted something to distract her so that when she looked back she would see only a blank wall. She reached the opposite pavement and the door was metres away. It looked as real and as solid as everything around it.

"One more chance," she whispered, and closed her eyes. She kept them closed for a count of ten, breathing hard and fast. When she opened them again there was the door, its surface red and peeling like burnt skin.

"Okay," she said, crossing the pavement in four strides. The door was directly above her now, its lowest point level with her chin. She reached out, forming her hand into a tight fist. When she knocked what would she feel beneath her knuckles? Wood or solid brick? If brick, perhaps it would break the illusion, snap her out of whatever was causing this.

She knocked. Knuckles on wood. The sound echoed away from her, as though carried along some unseen, impossible corridor.

Three, four seconds slipped by. Then she heard something beyond the door. Slow, approaching footsteps. She wanted to turn and run, forced herself to stand still. The footsteps stopped. The door opened.

Light spilled out. Chloe took a step back, screwing up her eyes. Through the door she saw a corridor, almost as narrow as the door itself. A cylinder on a thin pole jutted from a white floor about half-way along; much closer to her, just beyond the door, something large hung from what appeared to be a carpeted ceiling. She couldn't make sense of it at first, and then she realised that what she was seeing was upside-down. The cylinder on the pole was a lamp hanging from a ceiling flex. And the large, dark shape drooping from what appeared to be a carpeted ceiling like an over-sized bat was a figure, its feet planted firmly on a carpeted floor, to which upside-down furniture clung as if glued or nailed into place.

With the light behind it the figure was mostly in silhouette, though Chloe got the impression that it was a woman – small and hunched and wizened.

"Mum?" she said before she was even consciously aware that she had made the connection. "Mum, is that you?"

The figure remained silent. Chloe could not even hear her – if it was a her – breathing.

"What's happening?" Chloe whispered. "What do you want from me? Why are you upside-down? How can you defy gravity like that?"

The figure leaned forward. It creaked and rustled, as though made of parchment, as though it was nothing but a dried-up husk.

Its voice, too, was papery. "Gravity is an act of faith," it whispered.

"What do you...?" Chloe began, and then her eyes widened in horror. "No!" she cried. "No!"

And all at once her feet were leaving the ground, she was kicking at the air, she was falling. As she plummeted helplessly towards the infinite blackness of space, the night sky rushed up to engulf her.

THE DEMON BARBER OF FLEET STREET

I n the early 19th century, many parts of London were dangerous to explore. Footpads and cutpurses lurked everywhere. Fleet Street, a broad thoroughfare connecting the commercial heart of the capital, better known as 'the City', to Westminster and Whitehall, the centre of government, was less dangerous – unless you wanted a shave or a haircut. Because those who did, if they happened to stray into Hen And Chickens Yard, might be tempted to visit the barbershop of Mr. Sweeney Todd esq.

Todd was a skilled barber and an ingratiating presence, in fact something of a toady where the wealthy were concerned. But he also made a fortune from murdering them and stealing their money.

Todd's method was quite ingenious. He had installed a tilting armchair in his barbershop, and behind that a hidden trapdoor through which the bodies of those whose throats he had just slit with his razor could be dropped head-first into a pit, where later, amid rivers of blood and swarms of rats, he would strip them of all their valuables, before transporting them through a corridor to the basement of Bell Yard, where his lover and partner-in-crime, the notorious Mrs. Lovett, would dismember them and use their flesh to make meat pies – described in later pamphlets as "the worst pies in London" (though that apparently hadn't stopped people eating them).

Todd reportedly worked quickly and cut the throats of dozens of unsuspecting customers. He perhaps could have gone on indefinitely, but his downfall was the orphan boy, Tobias Ragg, whom he hired as a servant and eventually confided in regarding the heinous enterprise. Ragg went insane with shock, and the truth quickly got out. Mrs. Lovett poisoned herself before she could be arrested, though Todd was taken alive, and after a sensational trial, during which the jury swooned time and again to hear the horror of his crimes, was hanged in the year 1802, either at Newgate Prison or at Tyburn – the details at this point become sketchy.

This, as it stands, is the popular story, though how much truth it contains has long been disputed. It first appeared in 1846 in a serialised penny-dreadful called The String of Pearls, allegedly the work of Thomas Peckett Prest, a prolific writer of early pulp fiction (Varney the Vampire is also attributed to him). In that respect, most readers of the time regarded it as a straightforward horror story perhaps based on a kernel of truth. However, before this magazine

117

was issued, several other writers, Charles Dickens included, displayed a knowledge of the story. Dickens alluded to it vaguely and humorously in his novels *The Pickwick Papers (1837)* and *Martin Chuzzlewit (1843)*, but did not place it in a historical context. Dickens himself was born in 1812, only ten years after these events are alleged to have occurred, so it seems possible that if they really had done, he would have known and written more about them as a factual and serious event.

Of course, the Sweeney Todd story has been so popularised in recent times, with umpteen stage, screen and even musical adaptations, that it becomes ever more difficult to establish the exact circumstances of its origin. Some modern scholars have linked it to an incident in 1824, when a series of similar murder/robberies and subsequent cannibalisation of the remains were said to have occurred in the Rue de la Harpe in Paris, though that too has been dismissed as a fiction. In fact, thus far, no one has presented sufficient evidence to overturn the findings of a journalist writing in *Notes & Queries* in 1878, who stated that thorough checks in the *Newgate Calendar*, the *Malefactors' Register* and the *Old Bailey Sessions* revealed no trace of a prosecution or crime bearing similarity to those of Sweeney Todd.

His story is evidently one of those urban legends of the metropolis, so spectacularly ghoulish that it is enthusiastically told and re-told over the decades, constantly being embellished, and always coming with that all-important assurance that it is 'absolutely true'. The fact that it remains untouched by the sort of real horror and sadness that wreathes true-life London atrocities, such as those perpetrated by Jack the Ripper or the Ratcliffe Highway Murderer, perhaps suggests that most folk are well aware of this.

UNDESIRABLE RESIDENCE
Barbara Roden

I see that Transport for London is once again trying, somewhat half-heartedly, to find a renter to take over the Clapham North deep level underground shelter. It's not the first time they've tried, and I daresay it won't be the last, because I suppose they need to be seen trying to do something with the space. I doubt this go-round will be any more successful than the others. If questioned, we'd doubtless hear all about the unsuitability of the prospective renters' plans, or the ongoing problems with damp which make Clapham North unsuitable for document storage (the fate of most of the other deep level shelters). But there are other reasons why this particular shelter will never again be tenanted, in any way, by anyone.

I think that's because it's already tenanted, but I have no first-hand evidence; I've never been down the shelter, wouldn't even have known of its existence if it weren't for Mr. Harvey, my grade twelve literature teacher. In the sea of thirty-something, west coast, Liberal Arts-educated teachers who populated my suburban high school just south of Vancouver, Mr. Harvey was an island of old school, old country ways. He was just a few years shy of mandatory retirement at age sixty-five when I knew him, in the 1980–81 school year, and with his clipped British accent, regimental tie, and three-piece suits he stood out from the crowd like no other teacher I knew. He and I hit it off immediately, as I was one of the few students taking Literature because she wanted to, rather than because it was the only other course left in that block.

It seemed only natural that he'd be one of the chaperones on a school trip to London planned for the spring of 1981. I'd been saving for the trip ever since it had been announced; a devoted Anglophile, I wasn't going to pass up a chance to see the city which had played so large a part in my imagination since I'd first learned to read. Mr. Harvey, understanding soul that he was, leaned over and said to me, as our plane landed at Gatwick, "Well, you're home," and he seemed determined to ensure I had as wonderful a time as possible. To that end, he took my friend Liz and me out to the theatre, and then dinner at Fortnum's Fountain, on our fourth night in London.

It's something that would undoubtedly be frowned on now – a male teacher taking two female students out for the evening, complete with drinks in the play's interval – but Mr. Harvey obviously had no ulterior motive, and it was a highlight of the trip for me. The only thing that put a damper on it – quite literally – was the downpour which greeted us when we emerged from Fortnum's sometime just this side of midnight. There wasn't a taxi to be had, despite Mr. Harvey's best efforts to hail one, and finally I suggested that we make a dash for Piccadilly Station and take the Underground back to our hotel, near Paddington.

Mr. Harvey seemed reluctant, but we were all getting wetter and wetter, and there seemed no prospect of getting a cab, so he bowed to the inevitable, and a couple of minutes later we were plunging into the bowels of Piccadilly. After four days of travelling the Underground I considered myself something of a master of its intricacies, and led us all towards the Bakerloo Line platform.

Liz and I were relieved to be out of the rain, but I couldn't help noticing that Mr. Harvey appeared nervous. His eyes darted this way and that, and he was constantly turning to look behind us, as if searching for something he half-expected and didn't welcome. When we reached the platform he was careful not to venture too far towards either end, and when the sound of footsteps echoing along the passage behind us was heard he started visibly, only relaxing when a man and woman came into view. He was even more relieved when the sound of an approaching train was heard, and we took our places inside. The doors *whooshed* shut, and we were on our way.

Mr. Harvey was sitting opposite Liz and me, and something about the scene struck me as odd. It shouldn't have, because our teacher, with his obvious Britishness and familiarity with London, was the least out of place person in our group. Still, there was something not quite right about the scene, and it wasn't until we were halfway between Oxford Circus and Regent's Park that I was able to put my finger on it. During the time we'd been in London, Mr. Harvey hadn't once accompanied us on the Underground, which we used extensively. We'd all been given Underground passes, and as a way of moving a group of excitable Canadian students around London the Tube was unsurpassed. Yet Mr. Harvey was never there with us. He'd be waiting at whatever station we emerged from, ready to lead us to our destination, but to my knowledge he hadn't once set foot below ground during our trip.

It was a puzzle, albeit a small one, and something warned me that quizzing Mr. Harvey about it while we were below ground might not be a good idea. Besides, there was probably a perfectly reasonable explanation. Claustrophobia leaped to mind; there was something about being so far beneath the surface that was undoubtedly unnerving, if you thought about it for too long. I was curious, however, and when we emerged at Paddington I asked Mr. Harvey, as delicately as I could, why he didn't seem to like the Underground very much.

The rain had abated somewhat, so we weren't racing back to the hotel, and I had a chance to observe my teacher after I'd asked the question. He paused for a moment and looked at me thoughtfully, then resumed his stride.

"Fancy you noticing that," he said quietly. "I shouldn't be surprised, really, what with all the detective stories you read. In all the years I've been teaching literature no one else has ever written an essay about the Golden Age of the mystery story. It did make a change from endless ham-handed analyses of 'My Last Duchess' and *The Canterbury Tales*." He saw that I was about to say something else, and held up a hand to stop me. "Yes, I am prevaricating, because you're quite right, but now is neither the time nor the place to discuss it. I will, one day; but not now. With that you must be content."

There matters stayed for the next three months. I didn't forget it, precisely, but it was hardly at the forefront of my mind as the school year wound down and graduation approached. Indeed, I might have left school without getting an answer at all, if it hadn't been for Mr. Harvey bringing it up, one bright June day. It was after school, and I'd stopped by his classroom to drop off a textbook I'd found in my locker while doing some cleaning. I didn't intend to stay – there were term papers all over his desk, and he looked busy – but he waved a hand towards a nearby chair.

"Do you have a few minutes to spare?" he asked. "'Not many days will finish up the year' – to slightly misquote the Bard of Stratford – and you will be off to pastures new soon. And there is something I would like to talk about; a bit of unfinished business, if you will, pertaining to our trip to London in the spring."

I was all ears, as you can imagine. Outside the window I could see a groundskeeper on a lawnmower, describing lazy circles on the school playing fields, while the sun beat down and the smell of fresh cut grass drifted into the classroom. In my mind's eye, however, it was a damp London evening and I was shifting in my seat on the Bakerloo Line, wondering why Mr. Harvey looked distinctly uncomfortable. He had a bit of that look about him now, and for a moment there was silence. Then he cleared his throat, and began.

*

This all happened many years ago now (*he said*), long before I became a teacher. I was in the Army during World War II, with the 1st Battalion of the East Surrey Regiment. We'd been evacuated from Dunkirk in June 1940, and spent the next two years in England and Scotland, training, before our assault on North Africa in November 1942 as part of "Operation Torch".

As you can imagine, there were rather a lot of soldiers on the move all around the British Isles in those years, and it was sometimes difficult to find appropriate accommodation for them all. We knew we were headed north to Yorkshire in the autumn of 1942, but didn't know any details. At least I didn't, until I was summoned to the CO's office one morning.

"Ah, Sergeant. I would like you to meet Mr. Preston." The CO indicated a small, nervous-looking man whose luxuriant moustache seemed an attempt to compensate for his balding head. "Mr. Preston is from the War Office, and we have been discussing the arrangements for our journey to Yorkshire next week." Seeing my obvious confusion, he continued, "The Battalion will be forced to spend a night in London on the way north, and Mr. Preston would very much appreciate it – or so I gather – if the 1st Battalion were to be guinea pigs, as it were, for a new type of accommodation which has been built in the capital."

We both turned to look at Preston, who seemed uncomfortable with the sudden attention. When no one spoke he cleared his throat and swallowed, then let loose with a rush of words, as if he had been saving them up and wanted to get rid of them as quickly as possible.

"That's right," he said, his head bobbing up and down in time with his words. "Deep level shelters, built near existing Underground stations and designed to be used as accommodation. They were started almost two years ago, and the last ones have only recently been completed. Two parallel tunnels at every location, each one fourteen hundred feet long and divided in two horizontally, able to house up to eight thousand people at a time."

I tried to picture such a thing. "These were built to house troops?" I asked, somewhat incredulous.

"Not originally," said Mr. Preston. "They were conceived as shelters for Londoners, but there seems less public appetite for such things now, two years removed from the ravages of the Blitz, so it was thought they could be given over for use by soldiers on their way through London. They are all fully equipped with beds and medical facilities and" – he coloured slightly – "latrines and such, and of course they are very safe, so far underground. They can each be accessed from two above-ground structures, and from the platform of the closest Underground station."

Here Mr. Preston seemed to realize that he sounded less like a government official, and more like an estate agent trying to complete a sale. He subsided into silence, and after a few moments the CO took pity on him.

"Sergeant, I would like you to go to London and inspect this facility, which I understand is at – Clapham North, is it, Mr. Preston?" Preston nodded. "This particular facility has not yet been put to the test, and I do not want the 1st Battalion of the East Surrey Regiment to suffer as a result."

"Oh, I assure you that the facility is completely ready," said Mr. Preston with alacrity. "We would not be offering it to you if that were not the case."

"So you say, Mr. Preston. However, I was speaking with someone who had occasion to use one of your other shelters, at Belsize Park, within the past few weeks, and he was not happy with what he found; not happy at all. No mattresses, no bedding, and complete confusion as to how to gain access to the place. I will not have my men subjected to such treatment. They have been through enough as it is, with much more to come."

"I assure you that you and your men will have nothing to complain of, at Clapham North. All is in readiness."

"Hmmm." A simple utterance, on the CO's part, but it carried a wealth of meaning, as I knew only too well. "We shall see."

*

Thus it was that the same afternoon I found myself on a train bound for London, accompanied by Mr. Preston. Away from the CO's somewhat intimidating presence he was inclined to be a little more forthcoming, but not much. I did learn that the shelters were intended to be part of a high speed express route through London, after the war, and that only eight of the ten planned facilities had been built: those at St. Paul's and the Oval had had to be abandoned.

"Something to do with damage to the foundation of the Cathedral at St. Paul's, and water table levels at the Oval," said Mr. Preston, waving a hand dismissively. "I don't really know the details; it happened before my time with the War Office."

That seemed to be about all I was going to get from Preston by way of conversation, which suited me, I must admit. When you are a soldier in wartime there isn't a good deal of what would now be called "down time". Almost every minute of every day is accounted for, and in the company of hundreds of others, so chances to be on one's own are scarce. In truth, I looked on this as a little adventure, something out of the routine, and as such a thing to be savoured. How little I knew ...

When we arrived in London we took a cab to Clapham North Underground station. When we alighted Mr. Preston pointed to a structure, shaped like a block-house, not far off from the station.

"That is one of the above-ground access points for the shelter; the other is entered through those buildings over there." He pointed towards three squat brick buildings a hundred or so yards away. "They house the lifts and staircases, and ventilation shafts for the shelters. However, we shall be entering through the station itself."

This was a relief to hear, as it had begun to rain rather heavily, and the prospect of standing in the out-of-doors while Mr. Preston fumbled for a key was not a pleasant one. We therefore turned away from the street, and entered Clapham North station.

Mr. Preston spoke a few words to the man at the ticket counter, who barked something to a subordinate, who in turn scurried away. He returned a minute or so later with a middle-aged man who walked with a pronounced limp in his left leg, and who was introduced as Mr. Bradley, the stationmaster. When I was introduced in my turn, he snapped off a smart salute.

"Pleasure to meet a fellow soldier, Sergeant Harvey," he said, and patted his bad leg. "Got this at the Battle of Cambrai. Blighty wound. You could say I was one of the lucky ones."

"Yes, yes, Mr. Bradley," said Preston impatiently. "The sergeant is here to inspect the deep level shelter, prior to his battalion's arrival. Quite why this is necessary I do not pretend to understand, as I have assured his colonel that all is in order and the shelter is fully ready to be occupied, but – " He shrugged.

Mr. Bradley eyed him keenly. "It's funny you should say that, Mr. Preston, because I've been wanting to have a word with someone about that shelter. You say it's in order, but if that's the case, I'd like to know who's been a-making such a ruckus down there?"

"Ruckus? What on earth do you mean?"

"I mean the noises down there, like as if a gang of navvies was laying track or summat. I'm not the only one who's heard it, neither. I thought it were just some last minute work going on, but if all's in order then who's down there, and what are they doing?"

Mr. Preston looked from the stationmaster to me and back again, as if the answer would appear on our faces, but when none was forthcoming he contented himself with a shake of the head.

"Perhaps there *have* been a few things – minor, of course – that needed doing," he offered, somewhat feebly. "When was the last time you, or anyone else, heard anything?"

"Three nights ago, just afore the end of my shift. There's been nothing since then, leastways not that I've been told. And that's another thing. We only ever hear anything late in the evening, just as the station's about to close. Why would anyone be working down there so late?"

"I really have no idea, Mr. Bradley. But if the last time you noticed anything was three nights ago, and nothing has been heard since, then I would suggest that whatever was happening has finished, and that the sergeant here will see – as I have maintained all along – that the shelter is completely habitable. Now, it has been a long day, and I would like to get this over with as quickly as possible. I have no wish to keep you from your duties any longer, so if you will excuse us – " Mr. Preston gave the merest nod of his head to the stationmaster, and began walking towards the escalator. "This way, Sergeant Harvey."

"Just a minute, sirs," said the stationmaster, and Preston stopped with a *tsk* of annoyance. Bradley made his way to the ticket counter and had word with the man behind it, then returned to where we were standing. "I'm as good as off duty now, and Reynolds there knows where to find me if there's trouble. I'll come with you, if you don't mind. Like to have a look down there myself."

"Very well, if you must," said Preston with a sigh. "I had no idea I would be leading a tour group."

*

The platform entrance was an unmarked, locked door, for which Mr. Preston produced a key. When the door swung open an unpleasant gust of warm, dampish air wafted over us, and we peered down to see a wide flight of concrete steps disappearing into the darkness below, illuminated at intervals by weak pools of light.

"At the moment we only have a minimal number of lights on, but of course that will change when the shelter is inhabited," said Mr. Preston, who seemed somewhat hesitant about plunging into the depths. He took a deep breath. "Follow me, then," he instructed, jumping a little as Bradley closed the platform door with a *clang* behind us, and we began making our way down.

There were four flights of stairs in all, and as we got closer to the bottom we could see that they opened into a wide space extending left and right before continuing down on the far side, a

125

distance of some fifteen or so feet across. Mr. Preston stopped us before we could cross this space, and gestured around him.

"Here it is, the deep level shelter," he said. He probably meant the words to sound grander than they did, but was defeated by the immensity of what we saw, an immensity into which his words fell and vanished as they were uttered. I had been trying to imagine what an underground shelter designed for some eight thousand people would look like, but the reality eclipsed anything I had been able to picture.

We had emerged into a tunnel which stretched away on both sides of us for as far as the eye could see, before gently curving away in the distance. Both sides were lined with rows of metal bunkbeds, three high, running perpendicular to the wall on one side, horizontal on the other, with a narrow walkway snaking between the two rows. Each bunk was equipped with a thin mattress and some had blankets neatly folded on the end. Mr. Preston gestured to them with a satisfied smile.

"I told you that all was in order, Sergeant," he said, unable to keep a hint of smugness out of his voice. "I think that your battalion will find everything here to your satisfaction."

I had to admit that it did look very tidy and business-like. "What other facilities are down here?" I asked, and Mr. Preston waved a hand.

"If you continue down the stairs" – he pointed across the shelter – "you find yourself on the lower level of the tunnel." He saw the look on my face. "Oh yes, there is a second level. The design is unique, I am told; two circular tunnels placed one on top of the other, the lower level of the top tunnel bisecting the top level of the lower one." He turned into the passageway and began walking to the right. "Further access between the levels can be had through these staircases, situated all along the shelter." He pointed to where a low stone wall interrupted the line of bunkbeds to the right of us. "They are meant to be used in cases of emergency only, however. Now, if you will follow me ..."

We followed silently behind Mr. Preston, the only sound our footfalls along the cement flooring. Even the stationmaster, whom I suspected of being a garrulous soul under normal circumstances, was quiet. Suddenly the silence was broken by a rumbling noise, which grew louder and louder with every second. Both Preston and I started, but the stationmaster only grinned.

"That's a train above us, coming into the station," he said. "And before you ask, Mr. Preston, no, that isn't the noise I heard. I've worked here long enough to know where sounds are coming from, and what I heard was definitely coming from underneath me."

126

We continued on our way, and eventually saw light spilling into the tunnel ahead of us. We found ourselves in an intersection with a smaller tunnel, which ran at right angles to the one we were in.

"This is one of the two main cross tunnels," said Mr. Preston. "As you can see, the main shelter tunnel continues on for a distance. If you were to turn left here, you would eventually find yourself in the upper level of the other shelter tunnel, with a medical post on the far end. But we shall turn right."

We did so, and Mr. Preston gestured to his right. "Men's and women's latrines," he said. "There is also space designated for a small canteen. Nothing fancy, you understand, but food can be brought from the surface and warmed."

"You saying they'll be bringing food all this way?" asked Mr. Bradley. "It'll need warming and all by the time it gets here."

"No, Mr. Bradley, there is a much less circuitous route for getting supplies down here. This." We had come almost to the end of the cross tunnel, and in front of us could see a circular metal chamber enclosed by a metal grille. "This lift goes all the way to the surface, to one of the two entrances I pointed out to you, Sergeant. On either side there are, as you can see, staircases. They give access to alternating levels of the shelter, and also proceed to the surface. Although the lift can hold up to four people, its main use is for the transportation of supplies and equipment. If you were to go down the stairs to the left, you would gain access to the lower level of this shelter, and also to the plant and control room, where the ventilation, electricity, water, and sewage systems are monitored and maintained. You see, gentlemen, we have tried to think of everything." Preston led us back to the deep level shelter tunnel. "In the event of an emergency, the facility is completely self-contained, and could support eight thousand people in relative comfort for up to five days. What do you say, Sergeant Harvey? Do you think your colonel can have any objections now?"

It was difficult to find any, and I shook my head. "No, my report will be completely favourable, Mr. Preston. I cannot find any fault in the facility or the accommodation."

From above us came the sound of another train passing over our heads. It was odd to think that we were below the trains, and it made me think of the only possible objection, which was that anyone suffering from claustrophobia might not fare well in such an environment. However, the noise obviously reminded Mr. Bradley of something else.

"But what about those sounds, Mr. Preston?" asked the stationmaster. We were by now making our way along the deep level shelter tunnel towards the staircase to the platform above us,

127

and he was perhaps trying to reassert some of the authority which he felt was rightfully his as we approached his domain. "We didn't imagine them."

"Oh, I daresay there is a perfectly rational explanation," replied Preston. "Some last-minute minor work, as I suggested earlier. If such work was being carried out, then the men would have used the lifts, and you would not have seen them."

"Well, I'd appreciate it if you could find that out for me, sir. I know as some people have been making unauthorised use of the Underground stations and tunnels, and there's all manner of disreputable people about, looking for somewhere safe of nights. Some of them might've made their way down here."

Mr. Preston stopped. "The idea is preposterous. But if it will satisfy you, I shall make enquiries." We had reached the base of the staircase by now, and Preston pulled a watch from his pocket. "My goodness, is that the time? I'm afraid you have missed your last train, Sergeant Harvey. I had no idea we had been so long below ground. Do you have somewhere you can stay for the night?"

"No, I don't," I replied. "However, I'm an old hand at making do." As I said the words, I glanced round me. "Indeed, I could do far worse than stay here." I patted the nearest bunk-bed.

"Here?" both men said simultaneously. "You can't be serious, Sergeant," continued Preston.

"I'm deadly serious," I replied. "The colonel wants a full report, and I can't think of a better way to make sure he gets one. Besides, if there is someone down here who shouldn't be, I'll be in a perfect position to winkle them out, and solve Mr. Bradley's little mystery. Two birds with one stone."

"Why, that's very sporting of you, Sergeant," said Mr. Bradley with enthusiasm. "And if Mr. Preston here gives the word I shall spend the night down here as well, and that way we can spell each other, and be sure not to miss anyone. As a soldier, I'm sure you'll agree that two heads are better than one in a case like this."

Preston looked from one of us to the other, then shrugged helplessly. "I really do not think this is a good idea, but I can do little to stop you if that is what you want."

"That's settled, then," I replied. "If you'd like to join me for a bite of supper and something fortifying, Mr. Bradley, we can prepare ourselves for our evening's adventure."

*

As I had suspected, the stationmaster knew of an excellent establishment not far from the station. It was still pouring with rain when we emerged from the station, and I congratulated myself on not having to venture any further than was necessary in order to find lodging for the night. Somewhat to my surprise, Mr. Preston asked if he could join us. He had no wedding band, and I suspected that he lived alone, and was rather welcoming of a chance for some company of an evening. Even more surprising was when, as we drained our glasses at the end of the meal, he stated his intention of joining us for the night.

"As I seem to find myself in the position of having to 'sell' these shelters to prospective users, it would be as well for me to have first-hand knowledge of what they are like from the perspective of someone using them," he said by way of explanation.

I will admit that I had not been completely happy at the prospect of spending a night alone in that vast space, and knowing there would be three of us made me feel better. I am not – or was not then – a nervous man, but there had been something about the shelter which had unnerved me. In addition to the sound of trains from overhead, I had been conscious of the occasional skittering noise close to hand; not loud enough to remark upon, and almost certainly caused by rats, but jarring nonetheless. Plus I had been aware of a feeling that there was always someone just out of my sight, in the curve of the main tunnel in front of or behind us, or pulling back into the shelter of one of the emergency staircases or cross tunnels. More than once I had caught myself turning to look behind me, and noted Mr. Bradley doing the same thing, although neither of us had said anything. If this was what had prompted the stationmaster's offer of company that night, I was grateful for it.

By the time we arrived back at the station it was full night, and the streets were almost deserted. There was not a soul on the platform, and the one train that pulled in as we stood waiting for Mr. Bradley let off no passengers. Eventually the stationmaster returned, and we saw that he was carrying three powerful torches.

"Don't know as there are any down there," he said, jerking his head towards the stairs, "but they might come in handy. Also fetched a bottle of something – medicinal, you might say." He patted the pocket of his overcoat. "Never know when that might come in handy and all. Just checked with Reynolds, and he says it's been quiet. Last train'll be along soon, and then they'll be closing up for the night. So lead the way, Mr. Preston."

Was it my fancy, or did Preston hesitate for a moment between turning the key and opening the door? If the man was having second thoughts, though, he said nothing, and a few seconds later the stationmaster was once again closing the door behind us, and we were making our way down to the deep level shelter.

The atmosphere seemed changed somehow, but I attributed this to the fact that it would be several hours before we once again saw the daylight. However, almost as soon as we were standing in the main shelter I heard the same skittering noise I had noticed earlier, only louder now. The other men obviously heard it too, and we looked at each other for some seconds.

"Rats," I said finally, and Bradley nodded his head.

"Crafty beggars," he replied. "I should know."

"But where on earth could they be?" asked Preston, clearly puzzled. "There are no signs of them."

"Oh, they get themselves everywhere, Mr. Preston," said the stationmaster, his tone conveying a wealth of knowledge on the subject. "You wouldn't be surprised, if you'd worked below ground as long as I have."

"Indeed! Well, I shall get someone to look into the matter as soon as possible," said Preston, who seemed to take the rats as a personal affront. "If we can build something such as this, we should certainly be able to keep it free from ver ... what on earth is it?"

He and I had been facing Bradley, whose gaze had shifted from Preston to somewhere past both of us. We turned and peered down the tunnel, which was empty.

"I thought I saw something down there," muttered Bradley. "Must have been a shadow."

"I'll go take a look," I said, and was glad when Bradley added "I'll come with you, Sergeant."

"Ridiculous waste of time," I heard Preston mutter, but he fell into step behind us, and we made our way along the tunnel.

Only every fourth light was on, which certainly did create ample opportunity for shadows. Just to be sure, we shone our torches between the banks of bunkbeds and down the emergency stairwells as we passed them, but there was no one there. We went as far as the cross tunnel which led to the lift, but there was nothing to be seen in either direction, and it struck me that if there *was* someone down there who should not be, the odds of finding them were not good. There were simply too many tunnels and levels and staircases for someone to duck into or hide in, and in that vast and shadowy warren three men had little chance of flushing out an intruder who did not want to be found.

I suspect we were all thinking much the same thing, but no one wanted to be the person who suggested we call it a night and abandon our plan. We made our way in silence back to a spot near the staircase to the station, in unspoken accord that this would be where we spent the night. Bradley and I chose lower bunks on one side of the tunnel, with Preston in a lower bunk on the other. We made desultory conversation for a few minutes, and listened to another train rumble over our heads.

"That'll be the last of the evening, gents, nothing more to disturb us tonight," said the stationmaster.

We then decided to take it in turns to keep awake.

"I'll go first," I said, "then you, Mr. Bradley, and then you, Mr. Preston. Thank you, Mr. Bradley" – as the stationmaster passed me his bottle of something "medicinal" – "I think I shall. If anything happens I'll be sure to wake you."

"Nothing *will* happen, Sergeant," said Preston, settling himself on his bunk. "I shall see you in the morning."

*

For a time the only noise to be heard was that of my two companions as they tossed and turned in their beds. Now that the trains had stopped running there was no hint of a sound from above, and it struck me what a self-contained world it was, down there in the shelter. It would be different, I told myself, with hundreds or thousands of others down there, and for a few minutes I amused myself trying to picture the scene with not two, but two thousand, restless people trying to get themselves off to sleep.

My companions had finally settled themselves when I heard the skittering noises again. They seemed louder, and I told myself it was only because the silence was so much more absolute than it had been. When the noise showed little sign of abating I got up and made my way down the tunnel, trying to identify where it was coming from. There were obviously ventilation pipes throughout the shelter, and spaces for wiring; the rats must have made their way into those. I knew what Mr. Bradley meant when he said they were crafty beggars who could get anywhere, and I mentally wished Mr. Preston luck in any attempt to get rid of them.

I had, by this time, gone some distance down the tunnel, and turned to make my way back to my companions. I could see the spot where they were, marked by light coming down the staircase, and was surprised to note that one of them seemed to be awake, for a figure was standing by the bunk where I knew Bradley was sleeping. Thinking he had got up and noticed my absence, I was on the point of calling out to him, when I became aware of a louder than usual skittering sound beside me, seeming to come from the wall itself. I looked there, expecting to see a rat, but saw nothing, and when I once more turned down the tunnel the figure was gone.

Doubtless Bradley had seen me, and gone back to bed. He must have been one of those fortunate men who can, once awakened, fall back into a deep sleep, for he was breathing deeply and regularly by the time I got there. I sat down on my bunk for a few minutes, then got up again and walked a ways in the other direction.

I had not intended to go far, but I was restless, and the alternative was sitting and waiting until it was time to wake the stationmaster for his shift. So I continued down to where the cross tunnel led to the lift at one end, and connected with the other shelter tunnel in the other direction. We had not been that way, and I fancied seeing how far it was, so with a last backward glance towards where the other two lay sleeping, I set off down the passage.

Either it was more poorly lit than at the other end, or the lights were dimmer, but it seemed to get darker and darker with every step I took. I had still not reached the connection with the other shelter when, with no warning, what illumination there was disappeared altogether as the lights flickered once, and then went out.

Thank goodness I had remembered to bring my torch with me, and I silently blessed Mr. Bradley for having provided us with them. I snapped it on, and my silent blessing turned to an audible curse as I saw, highlighted in the ring of light cast by my torch, a face close beside me.

I saw it only for a moment, for the torch dropped from my hand, and when I picked it up (noting with profound thanks that it had not broken in the fall) the face was gone. Just then the lights came back on, and I saw that I was completely alone in the corridor.

I say that I only saw it for a moment, but I can still picture it vividly in my mind's eye. Whether it was a man or a woman I cannot say, for the face was so thin and pinched, as if through hunger or illness, that it was impossible to determine a sex. There was no colour to it anywhere; even the lips were a sickly greyish-white. The only part of it that registered anything like colour were the eyes, which were a featureless dull black, and two white teeth – not together – which could be seen through the pallourless lips.

I was grateful that the possessor of the face was nowhere to be seen, and after a few moments' thought I realized that it must have been little more than a hallucination. There had been no more than three or four seconds between my first sight of the face – which had been so close I might have reached out a hand and touched it – and picking up my torch and seeing that the face was gone, and there was no way anyone could have made it to either end of the cross tunnel and turned a corner, out of my line of vision. Besides, in the profound silence of the shelter I would have heard the sound of running feet, and there had been nothing.

I no longer had any desire to proceed towards the other shelter tunnel. My one thought was to get back to my companions and wait quietly until it was time to wake Bradley. I therefore turned and headed back the way I had come, pausing only once, when I thought I heard a slight noise in the cross tunnel behind me. A quick look showed me there was nothing there, and I continued back to my post.

The next hour passed relatively uneventfully, except for the occasional sound of the rats (as I thought of them). Once I heard what sounded like a faint cough from further down the tunnel to my left, but a quick investigation showed no one there. All in all, I was glad when my watch showed it was time to wake Bradley and let him stand guard.

I debated what, if anything, to tell him, and eventually merely said that I had heard rats, and suggested that as the power had gone out for a brief time he should probably not stray too far from us. This he agreed to, and I stretched out on my bunk and closed my eyes.

I did not expect to fall asleep quickly, but I must have, for the next thing I knew someone was shaking me by the shoulder.

"Sergeant Harvey! Wake up, Sergeant!"

I was awake in an instant, and sat up to see the stationmaster crouched beside the bed. His face was pale, and his breath was coming quickly.

"What is it?" I asked, swinging my legs over the edge of the bed.

"I don't know, Sergeant, but it sounds as if someone's playing silly buggers further down the tunnel. It stopped just afore I woke you, but … ah! There it is again!"

It was a horrendous *clanging* noise, and I could think of no more apt term than that used by Bradley earlier in the evening: "As if a gang of navvies was laying track." That was clearly impossible, and my mind groped for a logical answer. "It sounds as if someone is knocking over rows of bunks," I said to the stationmaster, and he nodded.

"That's what I thought when I heard it, Sergeant. It were further away then, but it sounds as if it's getting closer."

A figure appeared beside us, and we both jumped. It was Preston, who was clutching his torch and blinking his eyes, staring at us.

"What is happening?" he asked, his voice higher and thinner than usual. "What on earth is that horrible din?"

"We think there's someone knocking over bunks," I replied, realising as I said it how ridiculously improbable that sounded.

"*Is* there? Well, we will soon put a stop to that." He turned and peered down the tunnel. "Where is it coming from? Ah, I see, down this way," and he turned and headed towards the right, in the direction of the cross tunnel we had already visited. Which was odd, because to me – and to Bradley, too, according to the look on his face – the noise was clearly coming from our *left*.

The only answer was that there were several other people with us in the shelter, and that thought made me go cold. There were only three of us, and I did not fancy our odds against a group that could potentially be much larger and clearly knew the intricacies of the shelter better than we did. I had my Webley with me, but the other two men were not armed; indeed, I doubted whether Preston would know what to do with a revolver even if he had one.

I turned to Bradley, keen to get the old soldier's take on the situation, but to my surprise he was walking as fast as he could down the tunnel to my left. I heard him call over his shoulder: "This way, Sergeant, I think we have the blighters just down here!" at the same moment that, away to my right, I heard Preston cry: "Sergeant Harvey, come with me, I think I have them pinpointed!"

Then I, too, heard something from below; more crashing, the sound of which was clearly coming up from the emergency staircase just ahead of me and to my right. Bradley had already passed it and was clearly not turning back, so without thinking I headed towards the low wall and the stairs concealed behind it.

It was not until I was at the top of the steps, ready to plunge into the darkness below, that I realized the stupidity of my actions. Moving back to the centre of the tunnel, I could see Bradley far ahead of me to my left. Preston was out of sight on my right, and here was I, about to go willy-nilly into – what? "Divide and conquer" is a well-established military principle, and it was clearly in play here; only *we* were to be the conquered.

"Bradley!" I called out, trying to be heard over the din, which was increasing in intensity every moment. "Mr. Bradley! Stop a moment! Wait!"

He obviously heard me, for I saw him stop and turn. Then he seemed to freeze, staring at something that was hidden from me, and I heard him scream: "That face! That *face!*"

I knew beyond doubt what he had seen, and I ran towards him as fast as I could. When I got to where he was standing I found him staring at an otherwise blank patch of wall between two rows of bunks. It was not until I grasped him by the shoulder that he turned to look at me, and I could see that his face was pale, and dabbled in sweat.

"It was right there, Sergeant," he said, his voice low and trembling. "I swear it was – the most ghastly face I ever did see. I didn't imagine it!"

"I know you didn't," I replied. "I saw it too, earlier." I glanced around, not really wanting to, but needing to be sure. "Look, do you see any signs of a disturbance?"

Bradley looked round him, even more reluctantly than I had. "No, Sergeant. Nothing's been disturbed; but where is that noise coming from? And what's making it?"

The latter question was one that I was in no mind to deal with at that point. "I don't know, Mr. Bradley. But I do know that we need to leave, now. Wherever it's coming from, and whatever's making it, we aren't going to be able to deal with it. Sometimes retreat is the only sensible option, so I suggest we do just that."

"Where's Mr. Preston?"

"He went the other way. I'll go and get him; you get to the stairs as fast as you can, and wait there for us."

I turned away from the stationmaster and began to run down the tunnel, looking back just once to ensure that Bradley was indeed following me. Curiously, the noises near us – both further down the tunnel, behind Bradley, and on the lower level – were diminishing rapidly, while the noises further along towards where Preston was seemed to be getting louder and louder. At the time I put it down to the fact I was moving away from the one, and closer to the other, but now – now I'm not sure. I think it was because Bradley and I were beginning to sense the truth, while Preston – mercifully for him – wasn't.

I passed the staircase to the platform, resisting a fleeting urge to turn to my right and head up it, and continued along the passageway down the centre of the tunnel. Far in the distance I could see Preston, close to where the cross tunnel entered the main shelter. He had stopped, as if unsure in which direction to head, and I called to him, trying to make myself heard over the din and my own gasping, for I was running as hard as I could now, fearful of I knew not what. He obviously heard me, for he stopped and turned, and I heard him call in return: "Hurry up, man, they're just down here. We'll catch those miscreants yet!"

As he said this a figure emerged from the passageway to his left and stood beside him. I stopped and stared, trying to make sense of it. It was clearly a person, but instead of clothes it was garbed in what I could only think of as a sheet, which covered it from head to toe. I could make out little of its features at that distance, but I could see that where the face should be there was a gleam of white, stark and cold. I knew it was a face, though, of sorts, for where the mouth should have been there was a gash, cold and black, which drew upwards, and wider, for all the world like a ghastly expression of glee.

I screamed. There is no other word to describe the sound that came from me. Preston was still turned towards me, seemingly oblivious to the figure which stood almost shoulder to shoulder with him. There was no way he could *not* see it, I told myself, no way he could be unaware of its presence. And then I wondered what the effect on him would be if the figure should suddenly decide to make itself known to him ...

I did the only thing I could think of. With one quick movement I unholstered my Webley and took up a shooting stance. Preston's face registered shock and fear at the same time, but I barely heard the words "For God's sake, are you mad?" before I took careful aim and fired to the right of him.

The report of the revolver in that confined space was awful indeed. I have no idea where the bullet ended up, but when I lowered my arm I could see that the figure had vanished, and Preston alone was standing in the tunnel. There was no sign that anything was, or had been, near him.

I resumed my run, and did not stop until I was beside the War Office man, who seemed nearly apoplectic with rage. I cut him short with a ragged: "We have to leave here. Now."

"But what on earth was that outrageous display about? You could have killed me!"

"Didn't you see it? Beside you?" I asked, knowing the answer.

"There was nothing beside me! But I do know, Sergeant, that I am going to report you, as soon as this affair is over."

"You do that, sir," I replied, tugging on his arm. "But right now we have to leave."

"Leave? Why?"

"Because there's something down here, Mr. Preston." I was still tugging at his arm, but he was holding his ground.

"Yes, of course there is! And as a representative of the War Office, I intend to find those responsible. They went down there, I think." He pointed in the direction of the lift. "There were several of them. If you will not accompany me, Sergeant, then at least allow me to go back up to the station, so that I can call for reinforcements. We will either catch them down here, or ensure that they are apprehended when they try to leave at the surface."

"That's fine, Mr. Preston. We'll go back up to the station and get help there." Anything, so long as I got him moving towards the staircase. "Let's go and get Mr. Bradley."

"I fail to understand you, Sergeant Harvey. You were the one who was so keen to spend the night down here, and now you seem to want nothing more than to ... *ahhhh!*"

I can't do justice to that scream. I simply can't. I had been standing beside him, in more or less the place that the ... figure ... had been; that is to say, with the cross tunnel to the lift shaft stretching out behind me. Preston had been looking straight at me, but he had shifted his gaze so that it was over my shoulder, looking behind me. That was when that scream was wrenched out of him, and I turned to look at what he had seen.

A row of figures, standing silently across the tunnel, with more jostling behind them, as if seeking the best vantage point. They were all dressed – if you can call it that – in sheets, and they all had that same look of gleaming white about the face and hands. There was also that same look of insane glee about their mouths, inasmuch as fleshless, toothless openings can be called mouths.

At least he's seen them too, I thought to myself, as I grabbed one last time at his arm. "Mr. Preston. *Now*. Let's go."

He needed no further urging. The two of us turned as one person and began running along the tunnel. In the distance I could see a figure – Bradley – waiting, and I remember that I was trying to judge the distance, thinking to myself *Eighty more yards; seventy; sixty ...*

A cry sounded behind me, and I stopped in my tracks. Preston had stumbled and fallen, and I turned to him. As I did so I saw that the lights in the tunnel, far in the distance behind him, were going out one by one – blink, blink, blink – coming steadily closer to us. I reached Preston just as the light above him went out, and dropped to the ground beside him as what I can only describe as a wild, screeching mass passed overhead and further along the tunnel towards Bradley.

All was confusion after that, as I reached for the torch that I had stuffed into my pocket. I felt Preston moving beside me and saw his torch click on, then a dim pool of light further down the tunnel where I knew Bradley was. "What the bloody hell was that?" I heard him cry.

"I don't know," I called back, "but you should ... for God's sake, get down!"

For it was coming back. You know how, when a train is about to enter an Underground station, the air pressure changes? It was like that. Whatever it was, it was coming back. I yelled at Preston to stay down, and we felt it pass above us like an express train. I could picture this happening indefinitely, with us pinned down to the floor, so I made a decision.

"Mr. Preston, we have to run for it, now!" I urged, tugging at him. He leaped up like a startled rabbit, and the two of us were haring down the passage, our torches making bobbing patches of light on the floor ahead of us, and Bradley's ragged voice calling encouragement.

But we would not be fast enough. I knew it as soon as I felt that drop in air pressure again, and gauged that we were still some way from where a pool of light indicated Bradley's location. I yelled again: "Get down!" and dropped to the floor.

And then it was that I witnessed one of the most incredible sights I have ever seen. Rather than fall to the ground with me, Preston stayed upright, and as I turned and shone my torch upward I saw that he had planted his feet in the corridor and was facing the oncoming mass. "No! *No!*" I heard him cry as that force swept over us again.

His figure was silhouetted against the blackness of the tunnel, and together our torches were turned into that terrible mass. Faces leapt out at us – one, then another, then another – all of them with that same terrible grey-white countenance, all of them grinning. Preston stood his ground for as long as he could, and then I saw him tossed to one side like a carelessly discarded toy.

Then all was silence.

It took me a moment to register the complete lack of noise, as deafening in its way as the tumult of moments ago. Then, as I struggled to my feet, I saw that the lights were blinking back on, one after another, until the entire tunnel was again illuminated.

I heard footsteps behind me – Bradley, approaching as quickly as he could – as I moved towards where Preston lay, crumpled against a row of bunks. For several moments I feared the worst, but as I bent over him I saw his eyes flutter, and realized that he was still breathing, although raggedly. One leg was bent at a horrible angle, and Preston lifted his head long enough to take it in.

"Well, a limp isn't such a bad price to pay, is it, Mr. Bradley?" he managed to say, before unconsciousness took him in its merciful arms.

*

There isn't much more to say, really. I went for help, as it was clear that it wouldn't be possible for the two of us to move Mr. Preston without risk of further injury, and it was felt that a man in uniform might have a better chance of procuring immediate assistance. He was taken to hospital, where it was decided that although the injury to his leg was grave, he would – with time, and some effort – be able to walk again. I visited him in his office, some weeks after the event, and found him unwontedly thoughtful.

"I have had a chance to … ask a few questions, Sergeant Harvey, and have found something that may be of interest. Are you at all familiar with Defoe's *Journal of the Plague Year*?"

"As it happens, Mr. Preston, I have read that work."

He cocked his head to one side. "You surprise me, Sergeant. Well then, you will know that Defoe speaks of Plague pits, as they were called, being filled with four hundred, six hundred, as many as eleven hundred bodies each. As the Plague raged, more and more of these pits were needed, and in many cases they were constructed hastily, and their locations were not recorded. Can you imagine how it is that many of these locations have since been found?"

"I would say through the building of the London Underground, Mr. Preston." Which only stood to reason, when one thought about it long enough. All those burial grounds, unrecorded and undisturbed for more then two centuries, until someone else decided to burrow into the ground underneath London …

"You are quite correct, Sergeant Harvey. In some cases lines have been diverted around these pits, once they have been discovered; in others a straight path has been taken through them, as there was no other option. What would you think the chances were that the deep level shelter at Clapham North goes through such a thing?"

I thought for a moment, back to that terrible night of a few weeks earlier.

"I would say that there was a very good chance of that indeed."

Mr. Preston looked at me for a moment, then nodded and turned to the window. A weak sun was pouring its rays through the panes, but it was a blessed sight for all that. "I told you, I think, that similar shelters were started, and then abandoned, at St. Paul's and the Oval. I wonder, now, if the official reasons given for their abandonment are not … well, not quite truthful."

*

I don't know much about what happened at Clapham North after that; the war rather got in the way of further investigations on my part, and not long after it ended I left England for good. I don't think the shelter was much used, either by troops or by the general public, even after the onslaught of V1 and V2 bombs in 1944 made such underground shelters popular once more.

I do know that when I reported back to my CO, not long after my own experience, I gave a strong indication that the deep level

139

shelter at Clapham North would *not* be suitable for the 1st Battalion of the East Surrey Regiment. As you might understand, I gave him a somewhat … selective account of what had happened, but the Colonel – who was Scottish on his mother's side – perhaps read more into my statement than was actually there. He declined to ask many questions, but could not stop himself from saying, "I take it that Mr. Preston is not happy with this particular outcome."

I paused a moment. "I think, sir, that you will find Mr. Preston more than understanding of the situation."

And apart from that journey with you and Liz, in March of this year, I have not travelled on the London Underground since.

NOSFERATU IN HIGHGATE

It is hardly surprising that Highgate Cemetery in North London has provided the set for many a horror movie. The Victorian necropolis, now famous for its rows of decaying sepulchres and overgrown mausoleums, is a faded Gothic masterpiece. It also has a history of supposed occult activity, not least the mysterious case of the 'Highgate Vampire', which made the national press in 1970.

Highgate Cemetery has long been rumoured to be haunted, and not in a pleasant or amusing way. The alleged sightings there are extremely spooky. For instance, a female figure occasionally spotted flitting about among the tombstones is said to be the shade of a madwoman searching constantly for the graves of the many children she murdered in life. A skeleton in rags has several times been reported standing on the other side of the cemetery's barred gate. A tall figure with glaring red eyes allegedly comes and goes among the catacombs, and is extremely menacing if met at close-hand. But perhaps most interesting of all are those legends connected with Highgate Cemetery that seem to imply vampirism.

English mythology in general rarely mentions the mainly East European phenomenon of nosferatu, but Highgate appears to be an exception to that rule. Whether this owes simply to its Grand Guignol appearance, or something more substantial, is uncertain. In the mid-1960s, a Highgate woman went on record to describe nightly attacks made upon her in her bedroom by an unknown male, who left puncture wounds on her neck. Other witnesses reported encounters around the exterior of the cemetery with a pale, waxy-faced man found drinking the blood of dogs he had killed; when approached once, he leapt athletically over the cemetery wall and vanished. There have also been several instances of corpses being disinterred in the cemetery and left lying around on the paths, two of them holding hands and another with its head severed – the police put these desecrations down to the acts of vandals or occultists.

However, Highgate's reputation for housing a vampire went stratospheric in early 1970. The previous December, amateur investigators had commenced a series of late-night vigils there, and in the February admitted to having witnessed something strange – a tall, spectral figure in the darkness, which badly alarmed them. This led to massive renewed interest and a rash of similar sightings. That same month, the Hampstead And Highgate Express took things a *little further when it reported another investigator as saying that they were dealing with an actual vampire, the blood-drinking revenant of a Wallachian nobleman who had been brought to England in his coffin in the 18th century and buried in London. The investigator allegedly voiced a fear that this nobleman had been aroused by modern Satanists, and that he would need to be disposed of in the traditional way – by being staked through the heart or beheaded.*

The investigator later insisted that, though he had made statements to this effect, there was much journalistic embellishment in the story. Nevertheless, the media's interest was kindled. The following March, news broke that dead foxes had been found in the cemetery, drained of blood. Some investigators were still reluctant to use the word 'vampire', though perhaps inevitably, with Hammer Horror movies in the ascendant, and new celluloid additions to the Dracula mythos arriving in the cinemas each year, the idea that a traditional vampire was active in one of London's largest and most atmospheric cemeteries caught the public imagination.

A mass vampire hunt resulted on Friday March 13th that year, during which hordes of enthusiasts scaled the walls of the cemetery, causing much disturbance to local residents. One investigator would later write that he and several companions purified a vault that night with garlic and holy water, but made discoveries which eventually led them to a derelict house in Hornsey, where they disposed of a vampire by cremation.

No real evidence has been offered in support of these claims – and some of them sound suspiciously like the sort of melodrama familiar to us from vampire movies – but they certainly add colour to what seems to be an old Highgate tradition that is quite unique in the annals of English supernatural mystery.

THE HORROR WRITER
Jonathan Oliver

S imon emerged onto the pavement from Leicester Square tube, and swore softly as he once again found himself on the wrong side of the road. He took slow, steady, calming breaths, and waited for a break in the traffic before crossing over.

If he were to be honest with himself, Simon would have to admit that Charing Cross Road was the only part of London he knew relatively well. The rest of the city was something of a mystery, accessible only to those adept at deciphering the arcane tangle of multi-coloured lines that make up the tube map. He knew that it was considered a classic of design; a complex system rendered in supposedly simple terms. It was just that every time he looked at it, a strange, buzzing itch would start to build in the centre of his skull, and the lines would blur. Getting around in London was not something Simon was very good at, and he very much hated being lost; hated the panic that arose as he felt control slipping away. Charing Cross Road, then, was a sanctuary, with its easy access to theatres, cinemas and, most importantly, bookshops. Sadly there weren't as many of the latter as there had once been. Of late they had been closing down with depressing regularity. The last time Simon had ventured into the city, he'd found that one of his favourite literary haunts had been turned into a Subway.

He was somewhat surprised, therefore, to find a second-hand bookshop where he was almost certain there hadn't been one before. After all that had happened recently, Simon found such a discovery more than heartening. Perhaps this weekend would prove to be a considerable improvement on the week that had preceded it.

At first glance, the store seemed rather minimal, so narrow it was almost as though the buildings that flanked it had been pushed aside to accommodate it; rather like a paperback being squeezed in between two hardbacks on a tightly packed shelf, Simon thought. Behind a window fogged with condensation, a display held a few tatty Dan Browns, a mildewed stack of Catherine Cooksons, and a couple of Stephen Kings that looked as though they had been chewed upon. What Simon could see of the shelves to either side of the cluttered counter seemed no more promising. However, he had a rule about bookshops, and that was to never walk past one with which he was unfamiliar.

He opened the door onto an almost tropical heat and a fug of tobacco smoke. Behind a desk piled high not just with stacks of books, but also half-empty takeaway cartons and endless cigarette butts – and flanked on both sides by two furiously buzzing two-bar heaters – sat an unkempt man, rolling a cigarette and glaring down at a paperback with a broken spine.

"What is it, squire?" said the man, without looking up.

"Yes, I rather wonder if you have a particular volume of short stories. It's very rare and the title ..."

"If we do, it will be through the back."

The man gestured to a darkened doorway at the rear of the shop.

"The back?" Simon said.

"Here," the man rose to his feet, and placed his cigarette behind his ear. "Let me get the lights for you."

He waddled over to the doorway, reached within and flicked a switch.

A series of lights in metal shades blinked and stuttered into life, illuminating the corridor beyond. Lining the passage from floor to ceiling, as far as Simon could see, were row after row of bookshelves.

"This do you, squire?"

"Oh yes," Simon said. "This will do nicely."

"Just don't go getting lost."

Simon chuckled at that, but when he looked up, he saw that the man wasn't smiling.

*

Simon's delight at finding such a wealth of literature was dampened when he realised that there had been no attempt to place the titles in any kind of order. Several hardback collections of Elizabeth Barret Browning's poetry sat next to a manual for a Ford Focus. A long line of Gabriel García Márquez novels was broken by four well-thumbed copies of *The Joy of Sex*. However, Simon found that a great deal of pleasure could be derived from the thrill of the hunt – the search for hidden treasures – and so he continued on, undaunted, between the stacks.

As he got to his knees to pry out a promising looking paperback from a low shelf, he noticed that a book had been inserted into the stack the wrong way round, and pulled it out with a view to correcting the oversight.

The copy of *Dracula* began to crumble in his hand almost immediately, spilling gritty dust into his palm. Before it fell to bits, a single page drifted out intact and fell at Simon's feet. He was about to leave it where it was, shaking his head that a book could be so poorly looked after, when he noticed that something was written onto the margin of the text.

Find me. Help me.

Simon had found all sorts of things within the pages of second-hand books – train tickets, faded family photographs, a single condom still sealed within its packet – but this was the first time he'd ever seen a cry for help.

He looked up at what sounded like the distant howling of wolves coming from somewhere near the front of the shop, only to find the internal doorway through which he'd entered shrouded in darkness. Had the owner shut up for the day and forgotten all about him?

"I say, excuse me!" Simon said, as he starting heading back between the shelves. His footsteps were halted by an icy blast of wind and the renewed howling of wolves. He was certain, then, that something was moving within the darkness beyond the doorway.

Simon turned and ran, his hurried flight given impetus by the scrabble of claws on floorboards behind him, fear snatching his breath.

A sharp left-hand turn brought him into an almost identical corridor and Simon was half-way down it before he realised that he could no longer hear the sounds of pursuit.

Surely someone was playing a trick on him? This was clearly some elaborate practical joke; perhaps a camera had been cleverly secreted within the binding of one of the books.

"Very good," Simon said loudly. "Very convincing and certainly a little frightening. You got me."

When he was answered only by silence, Simon made his way back down the corridor and turned the corner, to find an avalanche of books completely blocking the passage beyond. He was certain that he hadn't heard the books fall. Maybe whatever had been chasing him had upset them. The mound of books reached almost to the ceiling. It was clear that dismantling the barrier would take some time, and so Simon decided to head deeper into the shop, hoping to locate an alternative exit.

A short while later he breathed a sigh of relief when he came to a door, stencilled across which were the words *Fire Exit*. He pushed the metal bar, but instead of being greeted by a gust of damp air and the sounds of traffic, he was faced with yet another book-lined passage.

For much of Simon's life, books had been a source of comfort and inspiration. A house wasn't properly furnished unless it contained at least a few bookshelves, and Simon's house had perhaps more than most, along with precariously stacked piles of paperbacks yet to be read or filed away. He loved to be surrounded by books, yet now he found the smell of old paper almost cloying, the aroma faintly reminiscent of an ossuary he had once visited while holidaying in Florence.

The corridor in front of him was a little lower than the one that preceded it and as Simon stepped down the floorboards creaked ominously, as though there was an enormous, hollow space beneath his feet. The shelves that marched away into the distance were uneven; some bowed out into the passage, while others shrank back, hiding their titles in shadow. How could such a vast and unlikely library be contained behind the squalid shopfront that had first drawn him in?

Simon reasoned that if he were trapped here for the time being – he tried not to think of it as being lost, anything but that – he may as well take an interest in the books. Perhaps he'd come out of this with a rare treasure to show to his fellow enthusiasts.

There were no words on the spine of the hardback he took down from a shelf and the cover was blank, giving no indication as to its contents. Inside, there was no title or copyright page. Instead, the text started right away and Simon began to read:

What a strange book. What was this anyway? He considered that it may be fiction, though of some experimental sort. Ordinarily, he would have little patience with such a thing, but Simon found himself curiously drawn into the text. As he read, he was distantly aware of the darkness rising around him, of the absolute silence that had closed upon him, like two soft, warm hands clamped firmly over his ears. No matter, *he thought, because the words had him now and it*

was only by focussing on the smell of books and the vaguest thread of panic worming its way up his chest, that Simon tore himself free and threw the tome to the floor. It landed on its spine, its blank pages brazenly open.

"What ... what is this?" Simon said, backing away.

The pages started to turn, slowly at first, but they soon sped up, moving faster and faster with a hiss that sounded like dry, malicious laughter.

Simon turned to find the fire door firmly shut. With no way of opening it from this side, he had no option but to flee. He didn't care where his footsteps took him, as long as it was away from that damnable book.

He jerked to a sudden halt as he came to the top of a precipitous flight of steps. Looking down, he saw that the stairs were made not of wood, but tottering stacks of books. Each step was uneven, some deeper than others, making Simon's stomach churn at the prospect of descent. But he could still feel those terrible blank pages at his back; still feel the influence of that wicked book as it sought to draw him in, and so he started down the steps.

The stacks shifted alarmingly beneath him and Simon grabbed the shelves to either side for support, only for his flailing left hand to punch deep into the guts of a rotten book. Steadying himself, he grimaced as he wiped his hand on his sleeve, shuddering as something with more legs than he was comfortable with skittered across his arm. He looked at the book he had destroyed and could just make out the words on the broken cover – *Metamorphosis, Kafka.*

From somewhere far above him came a chittering sound and a noise like a vast insect slowly picking its way across a wall.

Simon hurriedly resumed his descent, praying that whatever had emerged from the book wouldn't find him.

The depth of the book steps became such that he had to get to his knees before lowering himself down each one. As Simon was negotiating a particularly deep stack, he felt the tower of over-sized hardbacks tilt alarmingly beneath him.

The step settled with an exhalation of dust and a mouldering stench of rot before thousands upon thousands of pages suddenly crumbled and he found himself falling. Simon's cry was quickly absorbed by the tide of paper that carried him down into the depths.

*

Simon's watch had become detached in the fall, so he had no idea of the time. There were no windows down here; the only light was provided by the ubiquitous bulbs in their metal shades.

He had fought to the surface of the book pile, to find himself in the middle of a corridor, broken floorboards forming the edge of the pool he floundered in. On a breath of foetid wind he could hear the sounds of claws on wood and the skittering of huge insects.

He fought his way out of the pool and ran – his breath burning in his lungs, his limbs heavy. Simon considered that whoever had trapped him here was using books against him, or rather the things to be found within their pages. Perhaps, then, if he found some books with more pleasing content, his progression through this maze of literature would be less fraught.

No sooner had Simon thought this then he came to a brightly decorated area, equipped with small plastic chairs surrounding low plastic tables, scattered with crayons and paper. Low bookshelves held a selection of brightly coloured titles. He picked an annual from a shelf and smiled.

"Good old, Rupert. Perhaps you'll see me through the maze," he gasped.

Only when he opened the book did he realise his mistake, and his blood ran cold as something snuffled and wheezed its way towards him.

*

Simon was five, perhaps six, and it had rained all summer. His misery at not being able to go outside was compacted by being stuck indoors with his Aunt Erin. Erin clearly didn't understand little boys and her palpable discomfort around him only added to his misery. One afternoon, as the rain thundered against the windows and Simon listlessly flicked through a comic he had already read five times, Erin leapt to her feet with an exclamation of "Of course! Toys!" His elderly aunt hurried up the stairs to return several minutes later with a water stained cardboard box.

"I must have been given him when I was about your age," she said, lifting the flaps of the box. "I loved Rupert the Bear when I was a child."

The manky stuffed toy that Erin handed Simon reeked of damp. Its checked trousers had long since fallen prey to moths and when he took the toy from his aunt one of its button eyes fell out, a torrent of sawdust spilling from the hole it revealed.

*

As the wheezing, threadbare creature stumbled towards him, Simon's screams were much the same as they had been on that rainy day all those years ago. Sawdust trickled from Rupert's empty eyes as it pawed weakly at his legs, the red stitches of its makeshift smile snapping open as it attempted to talk. And other things followed the bear, childhood terrors that Simon had forgotten or suppressed; things that had been created to bring simple joy but which had, for whatever reason, filled him with fear.

Simon overturned bookcases as he backed away, throwing crayons and toys as though that would deter the horrors that pursued him, exhorting him to play, asking him for cuddles as they held out their moth-eaten arms.

Simon overturned a rotting bookcase in his panic to get away, flinching at the shower of tiny worms that spilled from the dusty, honey-combed planks. As he scrambled over broken hardbacks and torn dust jackets, he could hear something wheezing just behind his ear, and a smell like things left for too long in the darkness enveloped him.

In the end, however, it wasn't difficult to outpace the childhood nightmares; most of them were falling to bits or struggling to run on legs that were little more than stumps. Simon only stopped running when a painful nausea gripped his stomach, reminding him that he wasn't as fit as he used to be. He leaned against a shelf as he caught his breath, making sure not to catch sight any of the words on the spines of the books that towered over him.

How had he got himself into this terrible mess? He'd had an awful week at work and he'd thought that a Saturday spent shopping for books would have cheered him up. Even so, when he'd woken this morning he'd found it difficult to get out of bed. It had taken most of his energy to shove a meagre breakfast into his mouth and shamble down to the station. On the train journey into the city, Simon had found it hard to concentrate on the book he'd taken with him, nodding off over the same paragraph time and again. In fact later, on the tube, he'd only awoken just in time for his stop. And there had been someone …

Simon frowned, as a memory suddenly surfaced.

There had been that strange man beside him on the tube, wearing the shabby raincoat and stinking of tobacco.

Simon had heard him whispering to himself as he sat down, and the man had leaned against him, slumping in his seat as though he were drunk. He had attempted to ignore the man, burying himself in his book, only to begin drowsing over the same paragraph. There had been a brief moment of darkness as the carriage's lights flickered; a sudden lurch as the train took a sharp corner. At first Simon thought he had just dreamed it, but now he felt increasingly certain that the man next to him had taken the book out of his hands and covertly replaced it with another.

Was it possible, then, that he had somehow become trapped within the pages of this new book? Had the man on the train ensnared him with words?

If this were the case – and after everything he had faced within the maze, it was no stranger an idea than any other – Simon had to break out of the book.

Could he write a book of his own, perhaps? Simon quickly dismissed this idea when he realised that he didn't have anything to write with. Also, the sounds coming from further down the corridor suggested that he didn't have time for such a response. What, though, could pull him out of the book? Simon looked frantically about himself, and he was just beginning to succumb to panic when a misspelled word on the spine of a nearby novel gave him an answer.

Of course: typos.

Nothing ruined a story more than badly edited text. Simon was a stickler for correct grammar – his brother had once drunkenly referred to him as 'a Grammar Nazi', at a particularly unpleasant family gathering – and he detested seeing the English language misused. However, more often than not, a novel would contain at least one typo. But which should he pick from the many texts that surrounded him?

As he was pulling books from the shelves, Simon saw the shadow of an elongated, many-jointed leg creep up the wall further down the corridor. He could smell a stench that reminded him of visits to the zoo, and hear someone weeping. He didn't have long, but every book he opened appeared to be perfectly in order. Simon refined his search, and chose the cheapest and most lurid looking paperback he could see. And there, fifteen pages in, he found a particularly egregious passage. Simon focused on the broken words and

when, would this train get tere? He was already to late for his meeting. There had been reports of rats' in the tunnels on the news. But this didn't panic him. Simon closed his eyes for a moment

and then snapped them open as the tube screeched around a tight corner. Beyond the windows a cascade of sparks lit up the tunnel wall. Simon looked down at the open book in his lap, and the blank pages almost drew him back in. He fought their pull and closed the book with a snap. The noise seemed unnaturally loud, but it wasn't loud enough to wake any of his fellow passengers.

Hunched over open books, swaying with the movement of the train, sat six men and seven women, their closed eyes oblivious to the text moving across the pages before them.

None of them awoke to his pleas or rough handling, and when he tried to wrench the books from their grasps, he found them to be as immovable as statues.

With a squeal of brakes, the train came to a sudden stop as it emerged into a station. The doors hissed open and Simon flinched as a squall of pages blew into the carriage. Making sure not to catch a glimpse of anything written upon the leaves swirling around his ankles, he stepped onto the platform.

He tried to ascertain where he was but the words on the battered blue and red sign would not stay still long enough for him to read them. There was only one exit from the platform and Simon took it as the train hissed out of the station, taking its cargo of insensate readers with it.

Rather than finding an escalator leading to the surface, as he had desperately hoped, Simon came to a stairway leading down. He supposed that he should have been thankful that the flight wasn't composed of mouldering books, but even so, he felt the ice-cold breath of fear as he descended.

The bottom of the steps led into a short passage, which itself lead to a vast circular chamber lined with books to an impossible height. As dismayed as Simon was to be surrounded once more by books, it was not the millions of pages that dried his mouth in an instant and set his heart racing – and he could hear the whispering of the text within each tome, calling to him – it was instead the column of formless darkness that sat at the heart of the library.

Before this seething mass of nothingness stood a desk upon which lay a book, its blank pages open. Simon stepped forward and a chair slid from the side of the room, its legs scraping noisily over the rough stone floor, before coming to a halt in front of the desk. The invitation was clear enough and though he really didn't want to, he didn't see that he had any choice other than to sit.

There was nothing written on the pages of the book, but the anticipation the volume projected was palpable.

"Who are you?" Simon said.

Words began to form on the paper, wet ink slowly drying as the text unfurled across the page.

One who needs to be read.

"I don't understand."

In being read, I become.

"All those things in the bookshop, was that you?"

No, Simon. All those things were you. I merely make real what is within you.

"But why me? What have I ever done?"

Simon was all too aware that the note of hysteria in his voice made him sound like a whining child, but he was also all too aware that he was talking to a book.

Perhaps he would wake to find himself in a secure unit, babbling to the padded walls.

The words before him were still and Simon was about to get up from the desk when the text began to write itself once more.

Because you used your imagination. You used words against me. Nobody has done that before. You are more than just a mere reader.

"What do you want from me?"

I want you to write a book, Simon.

"And if I refuse?"

Then you will be as those you saw on the train, captured by the story, possessed by the text.

"But why would you want a book? You're surrounded by books!"

The story that we'll tell together will be unlike any other. And each one who reads the tale will bring me closer to being. And then, Simon, we can control every story. Together, Simon, once I have been brought out of the story and into the world, we can tell the world what it truly should be.

Simon thought about the dreadful freefall his life was in; slipping from one mediocre job to the next, each month barely having enough to pay the rent. He thought about the despair he felt as he watched the news each night, the anger that things never turned out the way they should. His parents had told him that he could be anything he wanted to be, but the world seemed to have a very different idea. Simon had always wished that he could tell the world to just stop. Stop and do things properly.

He didn't want to be trapped by his petty and meaningless fears. He didn't want to be like those cattle on the train that had brought him here, swaying uncomprehendingly over the words that had caught them.

"Okay," Simon said. "Okay. I will be your writer."

*

And in the end it was all so very easy. There was no staring blankly at the page and waiting for inspiration to strike. Simon sat at his laptop in his tiny bedsit, and the words just poured out of him. And though this was essentially a collaboration, though he was constantly aware of the whisper of the words as he dreamed onto the page, Simon felt that he owned at least some of this tale.

When he sent the manuscript out, he had to admit that there was a part of him that wished that was that; that he was done with the story now and it would perhaps leave him alone. A month later when the first offer came, he was so shocked by the proposed advance that he almost accepted it then and there. But no, his collaborator said, more will come.

And they did. And soon Simon was a very wealthy man.

In what seemed to be no time at all, he was sat behind a desk at Foyles on Charing Cross Road before a pile of paperbacks, pen in hand. The queue snaked out of the bookshop and stretched as far down as the Palace Theatre.

A pretty young girl smiled shyly at him as she handed over her book to be signed. As a crimson pall rose from her neck and across her cheeks, she mumbled something.

"I'm sorry," Simon said. "I didn't quite catch that."

"I said ... where do you get your ideas?"

Simon grinned, and glanced towards the shadow that stood just behind his right shoulder.

He couldn't wait for the reviews.

BUTCHERY IN BLEEDING-HEART YARD

In old London, incidents of barbarous cruelty were commonplace.

Throughout the history of the metropolis there have been murders and massacres of every description; mayhem so gory that it is scarcely possible to picture it. A good number of these terrible events were judicial in origin – there were burnings, boilings, beheadings, whippings, gibbetings, hangings, drawings and quarterings, and even drownings when villainous buccaneers were shackled along the mossy bricks of Pirate Dock to await the high tide. Then there was the more common-garden type of atrocity – the rippings, stranglings, poisonings, shootings and bludgeonings, as perpetrated by madmen and maniacs; these too proliferate through London's past.

However, in the late 16th century one truly appalling attack was launched upon an eminent citizen of London, which did not so much astound the city because of its gruesome nature – though it was gruesome, it was almost indescribably gruesome – but because it was also, supposedly, a supernatural occurrence.

Elizabethan England was the heyday of the social climber. Throughout the Tudor period, the old traditions of the medieval age were swept away piece by piece; one no longer needed aristocratic lineage to do well – ambition and intellect would sometimes suffice, and under Elizabeth I, a far more benign figure than her father, Henry VIII, or her older sister, Bloody Mary, the risks for those forcing their way into the upper echelons of society were much less than they once had been. The queen herself appointed administrators on the basis of talent as much as pedigree, and would consciously protect them against the guiles of more established courtiers.

Once such pair was Sir William Hatton and his wife, Lady Elizabeth, a handsome young couple whose determination to join the elite was legendary and whose success in this matter was quite astounding. William Hatton was chiefly renowned for his dancing skills, and yet he achieved very high office, reportedly serving Elizabeth I as Chancellor of England. In fact, so pleased was the queen with Sir William that she granted him a huge boon – an extensive tract of land in Holborn, called Ely Place. This had once been the private residence of the Bishop of Ely, but now the Hattons could do with it as they wished. They renamed the district Hatton

Garden and constructed an impressive manse, which they called Hatton House, from where, as true socialites of their age, they would entertain regularly and lavishly. Of course, it wasn't long before rumours were circulating that the Hattons owed their unbridled success to more than mere ability. Lady Hatton, it was whispered, was a Satanist, who in the early days of her marriage had performed a black magic ritual, summoning the Devil and making a pact with him, promising her soul in return for success on Earth. As England was now entering the era of the witch hunt, these kinds of stories – whether true or unfounded – could have been very damaging, but the Hattons were shielded by powerful friends and simply laughed the whole thing off.

However, it seems they had one enemy against whom there was no protection, and here lies the secret behind the Hatton legend's longevity – because the incident that followed would become a staple of Gothic stories for centuries to come.

On an unspecified date in 1596, the Hattons held a masked ball at their grand new home, and the great and good of the capital attended. All types of costumes, some of a truly extravagant nature, were on show. By all accounts, the only thing that prevented Queen Elizabeth herself from appearing was her age and ailing health (though it is also known that the queen was regularly advised by the occultist and magician, Doctor John Dee, and rumours still hold that, for reasons he kept to himself, he strongly recommended she avoid Hatton House on this particular night).

At around midnight, Lady Hatton was apparently distressed by the presence of one particular guest – a tall figure in a black hood and robe, wearing a menacing pair of iron gauntlets. Not long afterwards, Lady Hatton was seen conversing with the hooded figure and then leaving the premises in his company, heading out into a paved enclosure called Bleeding-Heart Yard. A few minutes later, a cry of 'Murder!' drew the other guests outside, and they were aghast at what they saw.

Lady Hatton had been horrifically murdered, her head dashed on a water-pump and her body disgustingly mutilated: the limbs severed, the throat cut repeatedly, her heart torn out and left by her side.

For so brutal an assassination of such a celebrated person there is surprisingly little evidence of a criminal investigation. Suspicion was apparently cast on the Count of Gondamar, Spanish ambassador to England at the time and 'a noted schemer in the cause of Popery', while the Bishop of Ely, who had apparently taken the loss of Ely Place hard, also came under scrutiny. In addition, there was a theory that Lady Hatton might have had secret *lovers – witnesses insisted that the mystery fellow in the hood had been known to her, and had caused her great anguish when she'd first set eyes upon him. However, no arrests or interrogations were reported in the case, so it is perhaps no surprise that gossip came to implicate the Prince of Darkness himself – Satan, looking for revenge because Lady Hatton, having attained all she'd sought on Earth, had now been seeking to wriggle out of her demonic bargain.*

This supernatural tale gathered momentum when additional rumours held that, in the days following the murder, the pump in Bleeding-Heart Yard would give out blood if operated at midnight, and that other curious-looking folk – presumably witches and warlocks – were beginning to assemble there as if visiting a shrine. There was a very belated sequel in the 1820s, when a strange woman – apparently insane, dressed in rags and covered with filth – approached Hatton House, where ever since the murder a large horseshoe had been kept nailed over the main door. This weird beldame spat upon the good luck charm, and cursed the occupants of the house, which by this time had been subdivided into hovels for paupers, saying that she could "do no harm while it remained to protect them".

This is the myth. But how much of it is actual truth?

It is difficult to investigate the case over such a distance of time, but a brief review of the few known facts will expose many inconsistencies in the story, including a possible confusion of historical characters. First of all, many of the achievements credited to Sir William Hatton (including the dancing) may actually have been the work of his uncle, Sir Christopher, while Lady Elizabeth Hatton is in some accounts of her life reported to have died from natural causes and been buried in 1646 – so she could not have been murdered in Bleeding-Heart Yard in 1596. In fact, the date of the murder itself varies depending on who is telling the story. One version holds that a woman – not necessarily Lady Hatton – was torn to pieces on that ill-fated spot, but much later on in 1626. The very name, 'Bleeding-Heart Yard', has no sinister background, but was adapted from the Bleeding-Heart Inn, which occupied the site in medieval times and bore an inn-sign depicting the Virgin Mary weeping beside the Cross.

There is ambiguity about even the basic tenets of this story, and much of that may be down to one Richard Barham, who, writing as 'Thomas Ingoldsby', was a popular urban folklorist in the Victorian era. Barham usually based his tales on crumbs of truth, but tended to embroider them with fantastical elements for the entertainment of his readers. His account of the Bleeding-Heart Yard tragedy first appeared in the New Monthly Magazine in 1843, and became the *accepted version of events. How much of it owes purely to his imagination is uncertain; but though no written accounts of the killing of Lady Hatton predate the 19th century, the story was widely known in London long before then.*

PERRY IN SERAGLIO
Christopher Fowler

Perry knows how to handle women, alcohol, fast cars, drugs, deals and dialogue. Perry knows where to eat this week, where to shop next week, and where to avoid from last week. Perry has a sixth sense that tells him where to be seen, and how often. On the city streets, Perry's more than smart. He knows the ropes and bends the rules and plays the games a lot faster than anyone else he knows. Perry has style and wit and charm and cannot be seen through because he believes in himself.

Perry learnt the hard way.

Perry was a product of the seventies, a hot commodity in the eighties, and in the nineties he's his own best salesman. Perry sold out early to avoid disappointment. He knows that the success of a man is measured by the price of his toys, so Perry has a lot of toys. Perry's latest toys include a Porsche, a personal CD/DAT player with built-in graphic equaliser, the latest Hewlett-Packard personal computer, a studio flat in Kensington Church Street, and for the last two weeks a girl named Josie. Perry would like a Hewlett-Packard pocket computer with a lightpen that you can plug into a video display unit, a purer drug source, a larger apartment and another girlfriend, preferably not called Josie.

Perry is twenty-nine years old, genteel, London-based, heterosexual, slim, dark haired, dark eyed and upwardly mobile. He does not appear to have a job, and yet he makes a living. Perry buys a little, sells a little, helps a friend in need a little, and still never gets up before noon to do so.

Perry is never lonely. He has a lot of friends in an area where his movements are known. Perry exudes charm without grease and friendships without attachment. Perry appears in the photographs of others. Laughing in night clubs, his eyes shining red in the Polaroid's flash. Leaving restaurants with his white scarf curving gracefully across the shoulder of his jet dinner suit. Across wine-stained acres of tablecloth, between green jeroboams, flashing wide white teeth, hair brushed smartly above glittering black eyes.

Perry has been around the world. He's lived in New York. He's done the drug scene. He's been through EST. He went on a health kick. He crashed his jeep and 'reassessed his lifestyle'. He looks after his friends but never gets involved. He is not an admirable person yet he earns something close to respect from those who meet him. He has no morals save a peculiar set of standards bred for him by the experiences of the last ten years. That was when the city still held excitement for Perry. Women were thrilling. Conquest was worth it. Clubbing was hip. Being recognised gave a buzz. The social whirl was exactly that. Now Perry sometimes wonders whether he could stop it if he tried. What is about to happen to Perry has never happened to anyone before, but will now start happening to quite a few people. Perry always likes to be the first. Unfortunately, this time he really is.

CLICK.

"Perry, it's Marsha. We'll be at The Zoo later. The table's booked for nine thirty. Come along if you want or we'll see you later at Abe's. Love you."

CLICK.

"Hello? I hate these damn things. Perry, it's Michael. Give me a ring when you get home. It doesn't matter now late. Just call me. I *hate* these things."

CLICK.

"Perry! Perry! You there? Shut up, you guys, I'm trying to … Perry, we're over at Don's and there's this party to celebrate … what are we (indistinct) … Yeah, it's Human Rights Day in Equatorial Guinea and Constitution Day in Thailand so that seems like a good enough … (indistinct) What? Oh yeah, Diane says to call her."

CLICK.

"This is Josie. You're never in, do you know that? Did you get my message last night? Where were you? I waited over an hour. Look, I'm not going to sit by the phone waiting for you to call, OK? I'm going over to Abe's tonight if you want to catch me. Bye."

CLICK.

"Perry, this is Michael again. Listen, I'm really …"

CLICK.

Consuela had ironed his socks again. Maybe it was a Mexican tradition. The place had looked as if Hurricane Betsy had passed through on a drink binge four hours ago, and was now spotless. Consuela was a gem. Maybe he should pay her more. He cut a line of coke on the mahogany dresser, snorted it, wiped his forefinger over his gums, wiped the mirror and stood it back in place. His image turned to face him. His eyes were dark and tired. He looked waxy and unhealthy. Time for a trip to the tanning parlour. His skin had a faint sheen of sweat on it, but the room was cool. Some days he felt he was losing the edge on his looks. Today was one of those days. It would dark in a couple of hours. Artificial light was kinder. It had been a long week. A lot of partying over the bank holiday, and not a lot of sleep. After forty-eight hours straight through, he'd still had to drop a quaalude to take a nap. He was too tired too much of the time. He'd have to learn to relax more.

Perry reset the answering machine. It was unusual for Michael to call twice the same day. Perry and Michael had been to school together, had sat next to each other in class for seven whole years, and yet now seemed to have nothing in common. Michael was studious and quiet, hated crowds and noise. Hardly an ideal companion for someone like Perry. He made a mental note to call Michael in the morning.

Now, what had he been doing before stopping to check his messages? Hadn't he been picking out a jacket for tonight? Perry wondered if he was having another memory lapse. It was the oddest thing, but twice this week he'd stopped dead in the street, unable to remember where he was heading, or why. Perry thought hard. He looked across the bedroom, blinds still locked shut from yesterday or the day before. No wonder the ficus died. He'd ask Consuela to look out for a silk one. Unopened letters lay fanned across the duvet cover. That was it, he had been about to check his mail. The envelopes yielded restaurant bills, computerised credit card expenditure forms, thank-you notes for a party given last Saturday, details of the winter fashion previews, a gallery opening and an invitation which read:

SERAGLIO
The Ultimate Opening Night Party
For The Ultimate Party Club.
Saturday November 17th 1986
11 St. James's Street London W1
Doors open 10 p.m.
Please bring this invitation with you

Today's date was Friday, November 16th.

*

"Nobody *I* know, darling. As much as one *abhors* the mention of anything so sordid as money, does it say how much it is to get in?"

"No mention on the card. Perhaps the invitation gets you in for free."

"I hardly think so, Perry. When was the last time you got something for nothing? I mean, apart from something you had to remove with antibiotics."

"Well, what are you doing tomorrow night?"

"I *was* planning on changing the colour of my hair. It said magenta on the box, but this is much nearer mauve, I swear. Do you think I should have my nose bobbed?"

"How you manage to turn the conversation back to your looks every time is beyond me, Diane. I thought you'd already had your nose bobbed?"

"Don't be a bitch, Perry. That was Paula. She was having her eyes lifted and thought What The Hell? That girl doesn't have a single feature left in its original place. She daren't stop smiling for a second. My other line's flashing, I must go. Why don't you come around and pick me up at nine, there's a dear."

*

Perry had a coffee for pep and a joint to mellow out. And two aspirins, as an afterthought. He turned the invitation card over. SERAGLIO. Sounded as if it might be full of Arabs. He wondered who the owners were, and why he hadn't read or heard of this place opening up. Not that it really mattered, because he knew he would be there tomorrow night when it opened. He always was.

The evening passed in the smoke-hazed basement of a Fulham Road restaurant, where the interesting legs descending the iron-runged ladder had turned out to be Josie's, and therefore less sexually stimulating than if they had belonged to a stranger. Josie joined the table, and came along with them to Abe's, and then to a new club in Bayswater called The Palace. Perry took some speed, and snorted a couple of lines in the bathroom. Someone mentioned that Michael had been in looking for him.

The next morning, Josie had left by the time he awoke. He looked terrible and felt worse. On Saturday afternoon he went for a sauna and a sunray treatment. By early evening he was ready to face another long Saturday night. He had forgotten to turn on his answering machine, and he'd forgotten to call Michael. He tried now. No answer. From six until eight he lay on the bed eating pizza and watching old video tapes on fast-forward.

Perry shaved and showered, smoked a joint, drank a couple of glasses of wine.

The telephone rang, but he switched it into the answering machine and turned off the volume. Diane walked in just as he was knotting his tie.

"I thought I was coming to pick you up."

"You were, but Sarah picked up this funny little croupier last night and has turned the lounge into a den of fornication. Poor dear, she has absolutely no sense of discrimination. It never pays to dabble with tradespeople." Diane brushed the hair out of her eyes. Thick blue-black sideburns curled around almost to her nose.

"What do you think? Give me one of those, there's a dear."

She hitched up her skirt and gave a twirl. Beads clattered and swung. She took a joint from Perry's hand and pulled heavily on it, blowing the smoke to the ceiling.

"Are you feeling okay? I must say you look a little tired and ..." a pause while she held back a cough, "a little wasted, if you don't mind my saying so."

"I'm fine," Perry answered irritably as he slipped on his shoes. "Come on, let's get out of here."

Seated in the car, Perry loosened the collar of his shirt. His neck felt sore and chafed, probably as a result of his sunray treatment. They drove to a bar in Covent Garden and collected some friends before making their way to St James's Street. Leo, a model, Sammy, an actor, Lynda, who did nothing, and a strange, silent girl who was introduced as Lotte, or at least something which sounded like it.

The entrance to the club was small and bathed in crimson. Its exterior was deserted, but once they had passed beyond the entrance desk they heard the muffled thump of music filtered from the tall mirrored doors enclosed in the far walls. Perry's shoes sank into plush redness as he peered ahead into shafts of light and dark. Before him, black-clad waitresses stood before lounging guests, mutely awaiting their instructions.

"Pretty place," said Diane as she checked her hair once more in her pocket mirror. Perry was walking ahead, checking things out, obviously impressed. He gestured about himself.

"Pretty's right. Like the carnival in *Pinocchio*, with more subtle lighting."

"I never saw *Pinocchio*." Diane slid her mirror away, and looked up.

"Read, darling, not 'saw'. Come on then, I'll buy you a gin."
Perry grabbed her hand.

The bar counter lay before them, spotless and white, almost surgical in appearance. The barmen were of vaguely Eastern extract, and slipped silently between the frosted columns behind the counter shaking cocktails and dispensing change trays. Perry pulled himself free of the crush at the bar and handed Diane her drink.

"It's damned hot in here." He wrenched open his collar and slid the back of his hand across his forehead. "Why on earth have they got the heating on?"

"Perry, darling, you must be feverish ... it's positively freezing. Look!" Goosebumps extended from Diane's shoulder to the mouth of her glove.

High above them, the word SERAGLIO shone in pulsing red neon, brushing heads and shoulders with seductive light. Cigarette smoke turned slowly in swathes towards the dark of the ceiling.

"Don! Don! Over here!" Diane was waving her arm above her head and pointing downward.

"Perry! Hey, you missed a great party last night. Diane." Don bussed Diane on one cheek, then the other. Don was tall, black skinned and black leather clad. His hair was slicked back into shiny loose curls and woven with beads. He appeared to have several people with him, although the insouciance of their introductions belied their acquaintance with anyone in the room. Champagne appeared, along with fresh glasses. The group insinuated itself through the crowds and up to the tall mirrored doors set into the walls beyond the bar. In front of one of them stood a bouncer of such sinister aspect that Perry involuntarily took a pace back.

"Come on, let's go through to the dance floor." Diane was tugging at his sleeve. As they moved forward, the bouncer lightly pushed back the enormous glass doors with his palm and waited for them to pass through. Perry found it hard to take his eyes from the glistening dark features of the man's face.

The dance floor was vast and filled. An unrecognisable dance mix pounded from banks of speakers imprisoned in a chromium trellis. The temperature had jumped at least twenty degrees. Many of the dancers had removed their shirts, their frenzied gyrations spinning them through kaleidoscopes of light. Don and his friends moved onto the dance floor as lasers criss-crossed beams and planes of red and blue, erupting into flowers of brilliance whenever cigarette smoke drifted into them. The girl called Lotte crossed to Perry's side.

"I love this song – let's dance." She pulled at his arm.

"No, I want to wait a while." He shook his sleeve free and stepped back from the floor. Over by the side table Diane stood tapping long artificial nails on the side of a glass. She waved in the direction of the bar.

"Let's get another drink." She led the way. At the bar she ferretted into her bag, withdrew a vial and slipped it to Perry.

"You can do it at the bar, no one will notice. The spoon's attached." He nodded and ducked his head, snorting once, twice. His nostrils stung immediately.

"What are you cutting that with?" Perry rubbed the sides of his nose. "Christ!"

The music changed. Videoscreens were lowered. Something was being projected, he could not decipher the images from this angle of the room. Other people came and joined them, hurling fragments of conversation over the pounding music. Perry removed his tie, rolling it up and slipping it into his jacket pocket. His shirt was soaked in sweat. Pulling some napkins from the bar, he undid his top three buttons and mopped up. Diane took his jacket. He was wiping the top of his neck, watching Diane fold the jacket over her arm very slowly, first one sleeve and then the other. His eyes moved from the jacket, upward along her sleeve, to the spikes of her hair and to the glint of chrome from the bar counter, to the black-suited barman polishing a glass. Perry watched him sliding his cloth around and around the glass. As it passed the rim, there was a glitter of light which splintered through to his eyes, penetrating, he felt, to the very depth of his optic nerves. The barman was staring at him and smiling, his lips conveying silent mirth, his eyes revealing none. Perry wrenched away his gaze.

"Heard a word I've been saying. Are you all right?" Diane asked, her brow furrowed.

"Yeah, fine. Come on, let's go and dance."

*

"Half a hit, that can't do you any harm."

"Acid always leaves me wasted the next morning."

"So what are you rushing to get up for tomorrow, hey?"

Don pressed the tiny white slip onto Perry's tongue. Across the room, a singer appeared up on the stage, and launched into a fast song which sent everyone onto the dance floor. Perry found himself in a sea of bodies swelling towards the front of the stage. He felt suffocated, unable to move. Shoving his way out of the crowd, he emerged at the edge of the dance floor in a burning sweat and dropped down onto a chair against the back wall. Lotte, Don and

Lynda emerged to join him after the last song. When a waiter appeared with a tray of drinks, Perry paid. He looked up into the face beyond the lip of the tray, into the blank eyes, and felt the room shift. Now Diane was in the corner, whispering and laughing with Don. She caught his eye, came over and touched his shoulder.

"Can I have the keys to the car, Perry? I won't be a minute."

"Sure, here." Perry shook his keys loose from the lining of his jacket pocket.

The music pounded on around him. An androgynous electronic voice sang the word 'sex' over and over again. Perry turned around on his seat to face the dance floor – and found himself facing Josie. Her hair was plastered flat on her forehead. She looked sad and pale Perry was confused.

"Josie, where have you …"

"Perry, it's Michael …"

"Been meaning to call …"

"Perry, he's killed himself."

"What? What are you talking about?" he said stupidly.

"This morning. He jumped out of a window. He's dead."

Perry stared. The room shifted once more.

Josie talked on, but he could not hear her. He could see her lips moving, but the damned electronic sex-sound just hammered over her words. He felt sick.

"Got to go to the bathroom …" Perry staggered to his feet.

Under cold white globes set into the ceramic tiles of the toilet he splashed his face with water, and the rocking of the room slowly subsided to stillness. He carefully rebuttoned his shirt and combed his hair, then walked back into the heat of the night club.

*

"She was here a minute ago. I was talking to her!"

"Don't shout at, me, Perry. I'm not deaf!" Diane swilled down the last of her glass and passed him back his car keys.

"She was here. She said something about Michael."

"Drugs, Perry, drugs. You must have been hallucinating." Don wagged his fingers in front of Perry's face. "None of us have seen Josie since yesterday."

"You are so tense, Perry. Really," said Diane. "Let me give you a massage."

"I know I'm tense. Do you have a 'lude on you?" Perry held out his hand.

"Oh no you don't," warned Diane. "Not if you're driving back."

"I'll leave the car here, I promise."

165

"Well ..." Diane looked unsure. "All right. But only take a half, OK?"

"The man's a walking pharmacy!" Sammy laughed and moved off to the bar with Lotte.

*

"All right, don't make a big deal out of it. I just slipped."

"You hit the deck with a bang, darling, never mind 'slipped'. Let's see your back. Turn around."

Diane pulled at the back of his jacket. Perry had been on the dance floor. One moment he had felt fine, then the room shifted again and he had lost his footing.

"I'm great, honestly. Just get me a beer, would you?" His mouth was dry and sore, his throat stinging from having to shout all the time. "I'll come with you, give you a hand." He felt the back of his jacket. Stitches had torn along a seam. His spine was tender, a bruise swelling. He stood behind Diane as she joked with a waiter. Beyond her shoulder the bar mirrors threw back distorted flashes from the dance floor. He looked up slowly. Sheets of polished metal probably, not glass at all, not the way they twisted and stretched his reflected form. The mirrors made him look almost inhuman, blurring out his hairline, darkening and cracking his skin, sinking his eyes back to flat red dots until it seemed ...

"Diane, do I look all right to you?" He touched his hands to his face.

"A tad less than your usual stunning self, I must say." Diane's smile faded. "How do you feel?"

"I don't know." He accepted the drink from her and walked away from the bar. "Do I look ... different?"

"Perry, I really haven't a clue as to what you're on about. You look a little, well, tired." She gestured at the ceiling. "Not that one can see a thing under these lights."

*

The music changed tempo. Dazzling beams of red trapped his eyes and seared his brain. As the beat of the music grew faster, revolving lights flicked up onto a huge mirrored ball and hurled shards of colour to the corners of the room. He covered his eyes with his hands. With his skin prickling and the bile rising in his throat he turned and stumbled to the bathroom once more, the beer glass dropping from his hand with a huge bang. Back in the coolness of the tiled room he bowed his head over the sink and tried to be ill,

166

but nothing would come. The edges of the basin were hard and icy against his palms. He could feel perspiration trickling into his ears. His throat felt as if it were on fire. He tore at the collar of his shirt, sending the buttons skittering over the floor. The bathroom appeared to be filled with mist. He could barely make out the outline of his body through the condensation on the mirror. Scrubbing the glass with his sleeve, he stared in disbelief at what he saw.

His eyes appeared to be filled with cataracts, his skin waxy and grey. Overhead, the globe light buzzed and flickered. The room tipped. The image in the mirror changed as rivulets of water ran down. The buzzing of the light moved inside his head.

He fell back from the sink to the floor, cracking his head against the wastepipe behind. Clutching the basin before him, Perry hauled himself onto his feet and ran an exploratory hand above the nape of his neck. His skin was numb and burning. He squinted hard at the mirror again. The back of his neck was wet and warm.

Outside, somebody was trying to get into the bathroom. He must have locked the door. He took his hand from his neck and looked at it. The fingers were red. He brought them up to his face and raked the flesh of his cheeks, looking into the mirror which seemed to show the skin of his face peeling and flaking in glistening grey flakes under his nails.

"Hallucinating again … I just have to maintain," he thought feverishly. "Get fresh air. Get …" A streak of pain cut along the side of his head, through his throat, spearing his chest and shoulders. Now he grabbed his head and screamed, the sound reverberating from the metal fittings around him. He withdrew hands which held hair and skin and blood, forcing himself to look up into the mirror.

Through watery smears of condensation he barely recognised his form, a shapeless red and grey mass topped with a bloody knot of hair. He clutched at his face once more, the skin seeming to move beneath his hands. The sink below was filling with skin and bloody liquid. He coughed hard, then harder. Something sinewy entered his throat, then his mouth. His cough fell to a guttural barking deep within.

Now his arms burned. Frenzied, he scratched at the backs of his hands until they were raw but for the band of skin beneath his Rolex. As he clawed at his arms, the pain burned away to a deep fierce fire, glowing inside his chest. He tore off the remains of his shirt and dug his clogged nails into the skin beneath.

*

167

"Why don't you go and look for him?" Diane shouted into Don's ear. He might've passed out in the john, or something."

Don obediently loped off across the thinning dance floor. Diane looked at her watch. It was nearly three thirty. She picked up her marguerita. The ice in it had melted, the salt smearing down the side of the glass. She looked at it distastefully and pushed it to the far side of the table.

Don reappeared at her side.

"He's not in there. Must have gone home." Don's eyes moved with the dancers as he talked.

"The bastard's probably on the make again. He'd hate not scoring on his first trip to somewhere new," said Diane sourly. She noticed that Don's gaze had twisted away in the direction of the washrooms. "What is it?"

"Well, it looks as if there was quite a fight in there earlier." He looked at Diane. "You know, blood and stuff. You think Perry was in a fight?"

"He's a lover, not a fighter. He could talk his way out of any situation." Diane stood up. "Come on, give me a ride to your place."

Don stood and linked his arm in hers and together they pushed their way out of the room.

"I like this place," said Diane. "It's got a friendly atmosphere." She turned to Don. "We'll have to come here again."

*

CLICK.

"Perry, where *are* you? I've been trying to get hold of you for days. If you don't want to see me just say so, but pick up a telephone to do it, OK? This is Josie again, and *you* can call *me*, because I'm giving up."

CLICK.

"Perry, this is Abe. I've got some primo stuff here waiting to be enjoyed, so come on over. You like, you buy. Take care of yourself."

CLICK.

"Perry, it's Marsha. I suppose you heard about Michael. Wasn't it terrible? I guess you're feeling low, so call me in a few days. Bye."

CLICK.

"Perry, Diane again. Where the hell are you? I came around, didn't you see my note? I'm sorry about Michael. How did you know about him? I'll call you tomorrow."

CLICK.

The message machine records and records. Soon it will reach the end of the tape. Soon it will be dark. Behind the machine is the bedroom wall. Beyond that, another apartment, wherein more city dwellers ready themselves for the night ahead. And further beyond is the well of the building, a square dark hole filled with staves of wood, rubble and trash. In a corner of the well is a triangle of hardboard, warped by fungus and soaked in the evening rain.

Beneath the hardboard lies a ramp of corrugated iron, crusted with rust and filthy growths of mould and dirt. Below this are a number of dented sticky paint pots, strung together on a length of rope. Inside one of the pots is a piece of rancid hamburger. A rat approaches, raising itself on its back legs to pause and sniff the air. It moves on, scurrying from pot to pot, peering over the rim of each until it discovers the pungent meat. Gingerly, it enters the pot. As soon as it does so, it senses danger. Now its feet are stuck fast in the paint. Frantically it bangs from side to side trying to free itself, squealing with fear as the rope is released and the pots fall together with a clatter.

There is a heavy movement in the darkness of the corner. Dimly, a shape appears. A scaly shambling thing approaches, half covered in rags, blank red eyes flickering about itself. Suddenly it leaps upon the pots with animal ferocity, tearing at one and then another until it discovers the fat, paint-smeared rat cowering from its grasp. Bony claws pull at the sticky wriggling meal with a grunt of satisfaction. Deep within the scaly wetness, intelligence sparks. A half-thought flickers, trying to make a joke about the advantages of tinned food, but it is fleeting. The concentration of its efforts turns to the fulfilment of a far more basic need.

Later it will try to find a new place in which to forage. Perhaps tomorrow it will try once more to face the daylight. In time it will adapt. One thing it knows for sure. Perry's in Seraglio forever.

*

169

Marsha raised the wine glass by a delicate stem and swilled it gently, listening to the ice cubes as they clinked.

"You never told me," she said as she watched the ice. "What is it exactly that Perry does for a living?"

Diane thought for a moment before reaching for her glass.

"Oh," she said nonchalantly, "he's Something in the City."

THE MONSTER OF HAMMERSMITH

Today, Hammersmith is a thriving ward of inner West London, sandwiched between the equally bustling districts of Shepherd's Bush and Fulham. In the early 19th century it was less built-up, but still a crowded and lively neighbourhood. It was also a scene of utter chaos – for at night a monster was believed to roam its foggy streets.

It was in the winter of 1803 when stories began circulating that a horned something, apparently half-man and half-cow, was leaping out at unsuspecting women and trying to haul them off into the shadows. The bizarre events continued well into 1804, but the descriptions given weren't always the same. Some witnesses reported the cow/man hybrid, but others described a white-sheeted figure, while some said it was like a man but that it glowed in the dark. In all cases, the perpetrator was regarded as extremely hostile, howling at its female victims and physically assaulting them. Vigilantes soon took to the streets, though this in itself had a fatal outcome when one of them shot and killed a workman returning home at night covered in white dust. The vigilante responsible was sentenced to death by a judge who was not sympathetic to citizens taking the law into their own hands, though this penalty was later commuted to imprisonment with hard labour.

The real culprit was finally apprehended wearing a calf-skin, and named as a local boot-maker called James Graham; a neighbour had given him up, concerned that his foolish 'pranks' were getting out of hand.

And yet this wasn't the end of the story. Bewilderingly, the 'Hammersmith Monster' reappeared in 1824, and a further series of assaults took place – a white-sheeted figure again leaping onto women late at night, though his time he was more aggressive. He had sharpened claws, and would use them to tear off clothing and lacerate the victims' faces and bodies.

Because of the time period that had elapsed since the last outrage, links were now made with a well-known Hammersmith haunting of several centuries: a glowing spectral form said to glide across the graveyard of St. Paul's Church every few decades or so. Officers were posted at night, many in the vicinity of the church, though, not surprisingly, a human agency was again detected when a young farmer was caught in the act of attacking a woman while wearing a sheet, and was subsequently jailed.

171

But still the case of the Hammersmith Monster would not rest.

In 1832 it returned yet again, wearing a long white robe and with talons for fingers, which it employed to rip off female clothing. After several such offences, a suspect was apprehended and prosecuted by the newly-formed Metropolitan Police, rumours later emerging that he was a gambling man who had been assaulting women as part of a ridiculous wager to purloin their clothing.

Looking back on these events they seem almost comical to us, yet in a more superstitious age people were very alarmed. One of the women assaulted in 1804 reportedly died of fright. A fear held by many was that the real Monster of Hammersmith was never actually captured because he was of supernatural origin, and that innocent men were sent to prison in his place. Memories were even stirred of the so-called 'London Monster', an unknown assailant who, between 1788 and 1790, terrorised the whole London area by grabbing women from behind, and slashing through their clothing with knives in order to wound their buttocks. A man called Williams had been imprisoned for that, but the attacks had continued for some time afterwards.

The idea that copycat criminals could be at large was less prevalent then than it would be today. The sense of power that serial attackers derive from causing terror among their target populace – a terror that would be reinforced by a neighbourhood's reputation for already having a resident ghost or monster – would be seen by modern criminologists as a strong motive for the maniac's mantel to be taken up again and again by different perpetrators.

Whatever the circumstances in the 19th century, the strange tradition of a prankster hanging around the benighted streets of Hammersmith, jumping out on lone women to frighten and assault them, turned very sour indeed in June 1959, when the naked body of a prostitute was found beaten and strangled, and dumped on the banks of the River Thames at nearby Chiswick. A further seven such homicides were to follow in the Hammersmith district before the series ceased of its own accord in 1965, coincidentally with the suicide of a leading suspect (though officially the murders still remain unsolved).

Of course there is no link between the 19th century Monster of Hammersmith and the case of 'the Hammersmith Nudes', or 'Jack the Stripper' as the press dubbed him, but it is one of those strange and unpleasant accidents of fate that both these characters were active in the same urban district. It is certainly difficult to take the 19th century attacks lightly when one remembers the far more terrible attacks that followed in the 20th.

172

SOMEONE TO WATCH OVER YOU
Marie O'Regan

Emily glanced over her shoulder again, hoping to find nothing – but her shadow was still there, keeping pace. She sped up, annoyed to find that the increased tempo of the tap-tap of her heels was making her feel worse, not better – the fact that they'd picked up a gruffer echo was something she tried to ignore. She was only a few feet from the stairs leading down to the exit now; and she cursed her penchant for sitting at the front of the train – all it had done was leave her with further to go to get to safety.

The lights in the waiting room went out, and she moaned – thank God she was at the stairs now. What on earth had possessed her to wait till the last train home when she knew damn well how dark it got on the platform at this time of night? East Finchley was a beautiful station, but it was also the first station going northwards that wasn't underground – and when the staff switched the waiting room lights off, it got dark quickly.

She heard her pursuer's breathing quicken and grow ragged as he started to run, and she launched herself at the stairs with little thought of how hard it would be to keep her balance at that speed. She clattered downwards, praying someone would hear her and come to investigate – but no one did. Towards the bottom she tripped, and felt herself grasped by strong arms – her rescuer stood her up and moved on before she had a chance to register who it was; her only impression was of strength and the cloying smell of tobacco smoke.

Then he was gone. She stood in the corridor and stared upward, scared her pursuer would still follow – there was a scuffle up there, then a cry, and finally the sound of squealing brakes as the last southbound train was brought to a sudden halt. An alarm sounded and she blanched, knowing what had happened. She just didn't know to whom. A shadow moved at the top of the stairs, and she saw a man's silhouette against the lights of the incoming train – a tall figure in a long, dark coat; a hat obscuring his features. He seemed to look down at her, just for a moment, and then he was gone.

Now staff arrived. She found herself shouldered to one side as guards ran up the stairs, and a very nervous young man tapped her arm, tried to shepherd her back towards the ticket offices, and the way out. "If you'd come this way, Miss ..."

173

She nodded, and allowed herself to be led. From behind her came the unmistakeable sound of someone throwing up.

*

As she walked into the office next morning, chatter stilled – she saw heads turn as she passed by, eyes drop as she sought to engage them and find out what was so interesting. Then she saw her boss, George Burrows, appear at his door and beckon her into his office, and her heart sank.

"If I could have a word, Miss Lane," he said, and stood back to allow her entrance.

She nodded and swept past him, trying to ignore the nervous muttering that swelled behind her.

He followed her in and indicated the chair opposite his, and waited 'til they were both seated before he continued. "I'm surprised to see you in this morning," he said, his tone kind.

"You are?"

"You've been up most of the night, after all," he went on. He registered the incomprehension on her face and smiled. "This is a newspaper, Emily, surely you realised we'd hear of a death on the line?"

Realisation dawned, and Emily was embarrassed. "I didn't think. I mean, I knew you'd hear about the body on the line, I just didn't connect the fact you'd find out I was on scene, as it were."

"You're tired, of course," George said. "There's no reason for you to be up to speed with the office at this hour." He pressed a button on his intercom and spoke to his secretary. "Can you bring those files in, please, Carole?"

The door opened almost immediately, and Carole swept in with a manila folder clutched to her frail chest, tattered pieces of paper creeping from its edges. She smiled at Emily, before a "humph" from George dissolved her grin and sent her scuttling back to her desk.

George opened the file, and took out various clippings – placing them side by side on the desk before her. 'You're not the first one, you see."

"I'm not the first one...? I'm not following you."

He tapped the clippings, impatient now. "Look! It's right there, see?" He sighed at her confused expression, and sat back. "I wouldn't be a million miles from the truth if I said you were about to be attacked before this happened, am I right?"

Emily stared. "How...?"

174

"Look at the clippings," he said. "There have been a number of instances of 'phantom rescues' over the years; yours is just the latest."

"Phantom what?" Emily laughed. "I'm sorry, but just because I got the willies late at night on a train platform doesn't mean I was attacked."

"What were you scared of? Last night, on the platform?"

Emily laughed. "It sounds stupid now, but I thought someone was following me."

"And you felt threatened, yes?" George was bending forward now, his hands clasped in front of him, a finger on his lips.

Emily nodded. "Of course. A woman on her own, late at night, no one around … and someone's walking behind you, at the same pace as you, speeding up when you do…" She stopped, spooked all over again, her mind back with the events of the previous night, the man's heavy footsteps catching up with her own, each heel tap accompanied by a deeper echo …

"Of course." George sat back, satisfied he was right. "And then someone appeared, out of the night, and saved you."

"He saved me from falling, I suppose," she conceded, "but I hadn't actually been attacked, had I. I just got scared."

George shook his head. "I believe you were about to be attacked, and if you're honest," here he stared at her over his half-rim glasses, his expression serious, "so do you."

Emily attempted a smile, but failed miserably. "Because it's happened before, right?"

"That's right," he nodded. "Read the clippings."

The clippings were of varying age, she saw, from issues of the paper as far back as the 1970s. All told similar tales – a young girl leaving the station late at night, complaining of a sense of being followed – a man attempting to catch up with them. All the girls had been grabbed at the head of the stairs (she'd been lucky, she realised, to get down them without being caught) and pulled towards the darkened waiting room. So far, so unsurprising. The odd fact was that, in each case, the girl concerned spoke of the smell of pipe smoke, and strong arms wrestling them away from their attackers … and a brief glimpse of a manly shape in a long dark overcoat with square shoulders and a hat, brim down over the eyes, as it descended upon their assailant; a style that had been old-fashioned enough to stand out, even then.

Stapled behind each of these clippings was a shorter article from the following day – a tale of a body on the tracks, no sign of a struggle. One girl had seen her rescuer fall onto the line alongside her attacker, and screamed until help came – but the railway workers thus summoned only found the body of her attacker; there was no trace of anyone else having been at the scene.

She placed the clippings back in the folder, congratulating herself on the fact that the shaking in her fingers was almost imperceptible, and let out a breath. "They can't all be the same."

"And yet the similarities just keep stacking up."

"Someone's exaggerating, making things up."

George sat forward, frowning. "That doesn't track though, Emily, does it. Different people, different times ... yet all tell of a man in a coat and hat."

"Doesn't have to be the same man," Emily pointed out.

"I'll grant you that in the forties a lot of men wore dark coats and hats," he said. 'But what about since then? And all of them smelled of pipe tobacco?"

"Lots of people smoke," she tried ... but she could see George already shaking his head.

"Not pipes," he said, sighing. "It's a very different smell, as you know. And besides, not that many people smoke anymore, compared to then. I mean, look at films – in the seventies everyone was doing it. Not these days, though; these days if a character in a movie smokes, he's usually a baddie."

Emily had no answers. "I didn't really see anyone," she said. "Just felt his arms, and smelled the tobacco."

"So you do admit it was tobacco and not a fag you smelled?"

"I have to, don't I," she said. "It was Dad's brand, Old Holborn."

"And the man was wearing a long coat, and a hat, just like the other times?"

Emily nodded. "I don't know what kind of hat, though ... the name, I mean. It was like those old films – with that actor Dad loved. James Mason."

George laughed. "God, that's right – he did, didn't he?"

Emily stared out at her colleagues; all staring in, amazed he was laughing. "George, they're looking."

He frowned again, but the corners of his mouth were twitching, and Emily knew he'd be laughing again before long. He and Dad had been two of a kind that way, and she felt his loss all the more keenly when she was with her uncle.

"All right, lass," he said. "Best get out there and investigate this, eh? We wouldn't want everyone knowing the cub reporter's my favourite niece."

She smiled, then scraped her chair back and stood up. Leaning forward to pick up the files she whispered, "Can I come and see you and Auntie Ann on Sunday?"

"Course you can," he said. "Can't see you doing a roast, somehow."

She grinned and held the files tight as she turned, forcing herself to look serious. "See you then, then."

*

Two hours later, poring over the files she'd found in the paper's archives, Emily was forced to admit George had been right. East Finchley station had, over the years, been prey to a number of these incidents – the earliest one she'd found had happened in October of 1972 when a seventeen year old girl had been coming home from a day visiting family in Camden Town. She'd been followed as she got off the train, and grabbed before she reached the stairs leading down to the exit. The only witness had been a middle-aged man in a black overcoat and a grey hat, who'd shouted for help and run to her aid. The two men had scuffled, and in the melée the girl had been thrown to the floor. She'd struggled to her knees just in time to see the older man grab her attacker as he made for her once more, knife in hand. In the struggle, both men had apparently overbalanced and fallen on to the tracks, into the path of an oncoming train. Both had died almost instantly.

No one had listened to the victim's protestations that her saviour hadn't fallen; he'd *pulled* her attacker down onto the tracks, and held him there as the train bore down on both of them. Emily didn't believe it either; who would willingly go to their own death, when all they'd had to do, really, was knock the attacker down and pin him there until help arrived – which in a staffed underground station shouldn't have taken more than a minute or two?

She spent another hour going through various other reports from over the years, but none seemed to quite fit the facts of what she'd been told by her uncle. There was a long and dispiriting list of the usual muggings, fights and accidents – some resulting in death, others in injury – none of these mentioned the man in the hat and overcoat.

Looking at the clock, Emily was surprised to see it was almost four o'clock; she hadn't even taken a lunch break, or had a coffee. No wonder she felt sick.

A shadow appeared at her left side and, looking up, she saw her uncle there, frowning again. "Any progress?"

She shook her head. "Not much; the usual list of violence – brawls, attacks, not much else." She reached into the hanging drawer on her right and drew out her handbag. "Do you mind if I go home a bit early? I've got a thumping headache."

177

"I'm not surprised," he answered. "You haven't left your desk all day, and you can't have got much sleep last night." He started to walk back to his office. "Go home, get some rest, but clear your desk first."

She nodded. "I will. Thank you."

"Bright and early tomorrow, mind," he called. "And I'll expect some progress tomorrow, alright?"

She groaned. She knew she'd better have something he could run by the end of the next day, but had no idea what to write. She trudged towards the exit, shoulders bowed. She'd worry about that later.

*

Twenty minutes later she was sitting on a train, heading back towards East Finchley. She glanced at her watch, and was comforted to find it was only four thirty. There should be plenty of people about when she reached her destination.

Sure enough, she hit the beginning of the rush hour, and East Finchley was teeming with people as she got off the tube and headed for the stairs. She couldn't help being over-cautious, jumping when anyone got too close – which earned her more than a few dodgy looks from people who couldn't decide if she was on drugs, drunk or just plain crazy. She was starting to think they might have a point – perhaps she was mad, after all. As she turned left at the bottom of the stairs, heading towards the ticket barrier and the High Road, she caught a glimpse of a hat. A very old-fashioned hat that looked uncomfortably familiar. The crowds parted and she saw that the hat belonged to an elderly gentleman, being buffeted towards her by the evening tide of commuters.

She stood back to let him pass, earning herself a few choice comments in the process, but she didn't care – he looked worried enough without being accosted by a loon of a woman demanding to know where he'd got his hat.

Keeping her head down so she didn't find herself getting into even more trouble, she made her way out to the High Road and hopped on a bus heading towards North Finchley. Twenty minutes later, she was letting herself into her flat above a shop just off Tally Ho Corner, trying not to fall over the cat winding its way between her feet and purring. "Come on, puss," she said, nudging the animal gently with her toe. The cat jumped and started off towards the kitchen. Emily laughed as she followed, shedding her jacket onto the bannisters as she followed. "You've got me right where you want me, don't you?"

Later, dinner cooked and eaten, cat fed and watered, Emily found herself channel-hopping as she thought over the events of the previous twenty-four hours. She felt such a fraud – it wasn't as if the man at the station the previous night had actually attacked her, after all. She'd been scared, yes, and he might well have tried to drag her off if the man in the hat hadn't …

Hadn't what, exactly?

She'd felt someone. She had. The feel of his body as he pulled her upright and the smell of pipe smoke that rose from his damp wool coat; she couldn't have imagined that. She examined her arms, and was a little surprised to find no trace of his clasp. He'd *hauled* her to her feet; surely there should be a mark? Something to show the strength of his grip? Whoever had been following her had definitely felt his strength – her rescuer had swept him off the platform to his death. Hadn't he?

She tried to focus on the TV screen before her, aware she'd just missed something important. Offering up a silent prayer of thanks to the great god Sky Plus, she picked up the remote and rewound. The local news was on, and a reporter was standing outside East Finchley station, microphone in hand, with a suitably solemn expression on his face. He was reporting the apparent suicide of a young man the previous night – a Warren Lytton, nineteen years old, a history of minor problems with the police; a couple of mugging convictions that seemed to consist more of aggravated shoving than outright violence, no one had been hurt, shoplifting … nothing too sinister.

Someone just off camera was shouting, and Emily strained to hear what was being said. No use; whoever it was had been pushed out of range of the microphone, and all she could make out was raised voices. A female voice, shouting, and more voices speaking in a conciliatory tone. The reporter stopped speaking, and in the silence that followed Emily heard quite clearly: "My boy wouldn't kill himself! He wouldn't do that!" The report cut back to the studio, and the newscaster shaking his head in disapproval.

Emily turned the TV off, her stomach churning. She ran for the bathroom and just made it in time before she doubled over and lost her supper. She sank to the floor, shaking, and wiped the sweat from her face. So it was being labelled a suicide. Perhaps it even had been, who was she to say? She couldn't help feeling a sense of relief that it was over – she'd been dreading more questions by the police. They'd been lovely to her, calming her down and taking her home – but no one had taken her story of the man in the hat seriously, that was obvious. She supposed in the absence of any sign of someone else at the scene they'd had no choice – no one else had even seen him.

She found herself crying, and rubbed her face clean of tears. She would not let this get to her. It was done, and she could move on now. She'd file a piece in the morning about the suicide, and that would be the end of it.

She smelled pipe smoke, and flashed back to the tunnel – she *had* seen him, she knew. So why had no one else?

*

The next morning found her at her desk bright and early, typing up the report of Warren Lytton's apparent suicide – she felt someone standing beside her and looked up to see George, reading the copy as she typed it.

"What about the attack?" he asked.

Emily shrugged. "What can I say? There's no record of anyone else being seen at the station at that time, just this guy. Who knows? Maybe he slipped off the platform running away."

"You don't believe that."

"No," she answered. "I don't. But I don't want to look like an idiot, or crazy."

He said nothing.

"Would you?" she pushed.

George stared at her for a long moment before nodding. "Fair enough." Then he was gone.

Emily sat, nonplussed, not entirely sure from their exchange whether she should go ahead and file the piece or not. Gradually the office started to fill up, chatter replacing the peace of a few moments before; not making things any easier to focus on. Someone laughed and she whirled round, the voice familiar, but no one seemed to be responsible – most of her colleagues were by now seated at their desks, concentrating on the monitors in front of them.

She tried to work out why the laugh was familiar, but to no avail – it had been a man's voice, of that she was sure; probably an older man, but no one in her immediate area fitted that description.

Her nostrils filled with the scent of Old Holborn and tears welled up as she thought of her father; she'd loved to sit on his lap as a child, and this smell brought her back to those days in an instant. Yet no one around her was smoking.

She gave up, and sent her article to her editor, then closed the screen down. She needed some air.

As she left the building, someone jostled her, and as she automatically apologised she realised this was no accident. Her attacker's mother stood before her, her expression furious. Emily glanced back over her shoulder to see if anyone was on hand to help should it be necessary, but she was on her own.

"Excuse me," she said, and moved to side-step the woman.

Mrs Lytton, however, was having none of this. She stepped in front of Emily once more, her eyes narrowed.

Emily wondered if she thought this made her appear more intimidating, and bit down on the smile that threatened to bloom. Perhaps she'd have found it more frightening if she hadn't found herself looking down at the older woman.

Mrs Lytton took a step forward, not content 'til she was close enough to share Emily's breath, something Emily found vaguely distasteful, but not particularly scary.

"My boy didn't kill himself," she spat.

"Emily nodded. 'You might be right,' she said before adding with uncharacteristic cruelty: "But he's dead, so we can't ask him, can we?"

The woman gasped, and now she didn't look threatening – she looked heartbroken, and Emily felt heat blossom in her chest before spreading to her face. How could she have said that?

"I'm sorry," she said. "I didn't mean it to sound so …"

"Fucking cruel?" Mrs Lytton interrupted, and Emily had the grace to look sorry.

She nodded. "I'm sorry he's dead, I really am. But it's not my fault."

"Then whose is it?" the woman wailed. 'Who killed my boy?'

Emma sighed, and steeled herself for the inevitable response to what came next. "I didn't see anyone," she said. "I just heard a cry, and then the alarm. I was running away."

"From what?"

"From Warren." The woman hissed as if scalded, and Emma hurried to apologise. "I'm really sorry, but he was chasing me … and then he was gone, and I heard him yell … and then there were brakes, and …"

"Stop it!" Mrs Lytton screamed, raising her arms as if to fend Emily off. "Bloody stop it, you lying bitch!" Her hand was up and planted firmly against Emily's cheek before either of them knew it was going to happen, and then she was gone, leaving Emily alone and sobbing, hand raised to the livid imprint on her shocked face.

Emily caught a whiff of that tobacco again, and shook her head. "No," she said. "Please don't." The smell faded, and she breathed out a juddering sigh of relief. "I'm going home," she said, to no one. "Alone."

No one followed.

Emily's piece came out the following day, and her phone started to ring as people realised she'd been involved.

The article made no mention of the attack she'd been sure was about to follow, but did mention her presence at the station; she found herself to be a celebrity, and decided – with her uncle's permission – to stay indoors for a few days, until something else of interest happened and she was no longer 'interesting' to the gawkers and on-lookers that had crawled out of the woodwork.

*

A few days later Emily found herself making her way home alone once more, having spent the evening at a local theatre for a review of a play being put on by the local amateur dramatics society. *Blithe Spirit*. The joke wasn't lost, but Emily didn't think she'd ever find that funny again.

As she left East Finchley station, she saw a man leaning against the wall, hat pulled down low over his face, shoulders hunched against the cold. She slowed, then drew herself up and hurried forward – she'd be safe inside.

The man stood up as she approached, and as he lifted his head she saw she'd been scared of nothing.

"Uncle George," she said. "I wasn't expecting to see you here."

He smiled. "I thought you might want some company. Seeing as it's late."

"I'm glad you came. It's a bit quiet tonight, isn't it?"

George nodded, and took her arm. "Come on, we'll take the bus."

Emily found herself propelled down the hill, towards the bridge. "I normally get the bus at the next stop up," she said, trying to pull away. "It's a bit dark this way."

The bus stop they were heading to was closer, she knew, but she didn't like going under the bridge where it was dark. And there was a stretch of road just beyond the adjacent pub that was bordered by gardens with overhanging bushes – she preferred to be more visible, especially after …

George sighed, impatient. "It's all right, I'm with you." And kept pulling her on, past the bus stop they should have waited at.

As they reached the corner of Bishops Avenue, George pushed her to the side, and she found herself by a house with a low fence – and a lot of foliage.

"What are you doing?"

George laughed. "I thought we could take a bit of a walk."

"Why down here?"

George's grip on her arm grew painful, and she got ready to scream.

"Uncle George, what's going on? You're scaring me!"

"I'm sorry, love," he said. "I didn't want to do that. I just wanted you to see. I want you to make everyone see."

"You're not making any sense," she said. "See what?"

George nodded at the house, but had the grace to loosen his grip. "He lived here."

"Who did?"

"Your saviour. You were right; he's done this before – and it's time people knew."

Emily turned to stare at the house – unprepossessing in the gloom, she could see, nevertheless, that it was neglected. An air of loneliness pervaded its surrounds, making it stand out from the expensive, well-tended houses that adjoined it. "Who lived here?" she asked.

"A man called Arthur Fuller. I went to school with him, or rather your dad did. They were a couple of years below me."

"He knew Dad?"

"Very well. They were mates."

"What happened to him?"

George's eyes glittered as he started to talk. "He was killed. Walking home one night, late, he saw a girl being attacked by some thug at East Finchley station. Decided he had to have a go, save the girl." He laughed, the sound bitter in his throat. "Bloody idiot."

Emily didn't quite understand. "Why was he an idiot, if all he did was try to help someone?"

"The girl was your mother, and Arthur knew her, of course."

Emily stared.

"You look like her, you know," he said; and tried to touch her hair.

She flinched.

George grinned, his teeth bared white in the dark. "You see? You're just like her."

She took a step back, and he gripped her arm tighter.

"It's not like she was going out with your dad at the time," he said. "She was fair game."

"Oh, George," Emily moaned. "You were the thug?"

"So the papers called me. I just wanted a kiss, that's all. But she wouldn't be quiet."

"And Arthur heard her? Came to help?"

George nodded. "I always felt bad that he got hurt. "I just pushed him off. I didn't see the car coming."

The smell of Old Holborn surrounded her now, and she felt herself relax. They weren't on their own any more.

George took a step towards her, and Emily stiffened. "I want you to tell his story," he said. "I want people to know he's still saving people."

"Why?" she asked. "Because you feel guilty?"

George nodded. "That, yes, and because people should know it wasn't just an accident. He was a good bloke, and he tried to help your mum. Just like he's still trying to help people."

Emily took George's hand, and peeled his fingers away from her arm, one by one. "I can't do that," she said. "It wouldn't be right."

"Why not?" he demanded. "Why shouldn't he get some recognition for what he did?"

"Because then they'd know what you did," she said, and saw the realisation dawn in his eyes. "And, even worse, what you nearly did to Mum."

George launched himself forward and pushed her towards the busy road.

She felt herself falling, but was overwhelmed by the scent of pipe tobacco, even as she felt herself being set back on her feet. She stood, gasping, as she saw the cloud darken around her uncle, a smoky figure reaching out for him and drawing him towards the main road. A bus was hurtling up the hill towards them, but she couldn't make a sound – and it was too dark for them to be seen, just yet.

George was trying hard to break free, but to no avail. As the bus drew close, the cloud solidified, and Emily saw her saviour, hat pulled low over his face, dark coat pulled tight around him. He pushed George down, and both men fell under the oncoming vehicle – brakes squealed, someone screamed, and Emily found herself witnessing everything this time, at close range, as Arthur held him there.

She saw George's hand, protruding from underneath the front of the bus – blood trickling towards the kerb. There was no sign of the rest of him. The hand twitched, just once, then was still. A woman who'd been walking up the main road was screaming: scream after scream pealing out, with barely time to breathe between. The bus driver was sitting in his cab, head buried in his hands – the few passengers were staring forward, shock etched on their faces. She could already hear the sirens.

Emily staggered to the kerb and threw up, and when she looked up, he was there. He smiled at her, and touched his fingers to his hat

– an old-world gesture. The smell of Old Holborn caused her stomach to clench, and she vomited again. When she looked up again, he was gone.

She couldn't tell the story, she realised. And not because it would ruin her aunt's life, and her parents' memory. She couldn't tell the story because then everyone would know about Arthur – and much as she hated the idea of him continuing his vendetta, she hated even more the idea that he wouldn't be able to help any more girls daft enough to wander home on their own in dangerous places.

THE BLACK DEATH RETURNS

The original Black Death, which first struck England in 1348 and killed two thirds of the entire population, was so dreadful and inexplicable an event that it was deemed at the time to be the work of the Devil or maybe even the work of God – a scourge unleashed across the land to punish a nation of sinners. When it returned to London several centuries later, in 1665, it was understood to be a pestilence – a naturally occurring biological disaster, which had no supernatural origins. However, that did not mean the population of the metropolis was any better equipped to resist it.

In truth, the Black Death – or Bubonic Plague, to give it its true title – had never really left. Caused by the 'Yersinia pestis' bacterium, it could be transmitted through the bites of fleas dwelling in the fur of the black rat, a vermin that flourished in the open sewers, filthy, narrow backstreets and rotted thatch-work roofs of England's medieval and post-medieval cities. There had been severe outbreaks in London in 1599, 1603, 1625 and 1636, but it was the 'Great Plague of London', 1665-66 (the last one to date in Europe), which was most reminiscent of the original visitation.

It first reared its grisly head in April 1665, in the London docklands and then in the Drury Lane area of St. Giles-in-the-Field, two districts both noted for their cramped living conditions and extreme poverty. It is no surprise that those dwelling in the worst grime were the first affected. But the Black Death never discriminated between rich or poor. All through that first summer it spread like wildfire, eventually engulfing the entire city in a manner not seen for centuries. This time the citizens attempted to fight the illness, hiring qualified doctors and nurses, and organising outdoor hospital wards, where, quite reasonably, it was hoped that sunlight and fresh air would aid patient recovery. But inevitably mistakes were made. For example, acting on inaccurate information that the infection was spread by cats and dogs, the Lord Mayor of London declared a cull on the city's pets – the great irony being that it was cats and dogs who were keeping the city's rat population down.

Other attempts to manage the catastrophe created even more nightmarish scenarios.

Afflicted families were locked in their own homes, their doors and windows nailed shut, for at least 40 days, which almost invariably meant that those among them who were not infected

186

would also die. Death itself could only be verified to the parish clerks by volunteers or condemned criminals, who would visit the homes in question, load all corpses onto the death-carts and roll them through the streets, calling out a warning that they were passing through to the burial grounds. Often these strange, damned folk, nearly always blind-drunk in order to perform their task, would first have looted the houses in question, and in some cases were suspected of having murdered plague survivors in the process. London's winding, corpse-strewn streets were constantly fogged by the smoke of 'purification fires', the flames of which were fed with bizarre mixtures of pepper, tobacco and frankincense in order to create foul-smelling fumes to ward off the sickness.

And in the midst of this infernal scene, doctors and physicians moved back and forth in long, dark capes, wearing face-masks fitted with heron-like beaks packed with herbs of healing, but terrifying people rather than reassuring them because they resembled angels of death. However, there were acts of heroism too. Though many of the well-to-do fled the city, others did not. Most London aldermen remained at their posts, including the Lord Mayor, Sir John Lawrence. Diarists Samuel Pepys and Henry Foe stayed behind also, determined to keep a truthful record of events, which would later prove helpful to medical science.

By the September of 1665, an average of 7,000 Londoners were dying from the plague each week. It must have seemed as if Armageddon was upon them. By good fortune a very hard winter was to follow, the relentless ice and snow taking a huge toll on the rats and their fleas. But it would be almost another year, in September 1666, before the Great Fire of London burned down a large portion of the old medieval city, finally ending the epidemic. Many writings afterwards spoke of a capital left empty: bones and carrion in side-streets, grass growing from cobbled courts, the River Thames, normally so busy, now bereft of traffic. Almost certainly, many of these references were exaggerated, though the grim facts speak for themselves: in total, 120,000 Londoners had succumbed to the disease, which was almost a quarter of the great city's population.

Just imagine what it would mean if such a percentage perished today.

THE OUTCAST DEAD
David J. Howe

*I have heard of ancient men, of good credit, report that these single
women were forbidden the rites of the church, so long as they
continued that sinful life, and were excluded from Christian burial if
they were not reconciled before their death. And therefore there was
a plot of ground called the Single Woman's churchyard, appointed
for them far from the parish church.*
'A Survey of London' by John Stew and edited by
Henry Morley. 1598

*Southwark lies low; the greater part being some six inches beneath
the level of the Thames. To these retreats out-laws, debtors, thieves
and rascals of every breed resorted; laying for Southwark the
foundation of that questionable character it has never wholly lost.
Originally a refuge for insolvents, it soon became a settlement for
the vilest refuse of humanity. Deeds of darkness were committed
with terrible frequency.*
'Historical Souvenir of the old Borough Road Baptist Chapel',
founded 1673. c1900

Milly paused outside the tube entrance and shuddered.
There was no traffic on the sodium-washed streets,
and the only sound was the mournful whisper of the wind
in the trees on the other side of the road.

She looked around: no taxis, no idea where she could go, except
for taking the tube back to her own familiar part of London. There
was only one problem. She was claustrophobic, and the thought of
descending into that dark maw filled her with dread.

She cursed herself. Why did she think that coming across
London to see Jake, her ex-boyfriend, would be a good idea? Her
friends had warned her against it, but, stubborn as ever, Milly had
felt that something could be gained from it. Even if it put them on
proper speaking terms again. She had been wrong. From the start
Jake had been unresponsive and distant, and when he finally talked,
after a couple of Jack D and cokes, it was only to ask if she could
lend him some money.

So that was what it was all about, Milly had thought. He just
wanted her to cough up again for him – which was the whole reason
they had split up in the first place. She didn't want to be the 'Bank

of Milly' any longer. Quite apart from the fact that she couldn't afford it. With rent and food and utility bills rising at what seemed like an astronomical rate, not to mention the petrol costs for her car – essential as she really didn't like using public transport – she was rapidly in danger of ending up homeless.

And so the bastard had shouted at her, she had shouted back, and before she knew it, she was sitting on her own in an unfamiliar pub, in an area of London she had never visited before.

A few stiff drinks later, and she realised she had stayed a little too long, and with the clang of a bell, was encouraged onto the streets.

Now she had to get home.

And to do that, she had to take a tube.

Her heart was pounding at the thought, so she swallowed and stepped towards the entrance. It was dark and uninviting; space seemed to compress around her, and the air thinned, making it catch in her throat. She thought she saw something pale flit through the darkness, but when she turned her head it was gone. She looked up and down the street.

Under one of the streetlights she caught a glimpse of a person, but they were shadowy and moved away in a strange loping motion. Milly squinted but there was no further movement.

She composed herself and stepped forward. She could do this. Once on the train it would be easy, and she could navigate the various lines and changes to get back onto familiar ground.

Milly smiled to herself. 'Silly Milly' they used to call her, but she was stronger than anyone knew.

With a determined step, she walked down the flight of steps leading underground. Her heels clacked as she crossed the marble entrance hall, and located a ticket machine which would allow her entry to the tiled halls and passageways that would lead to the platforms.

She could do this.

*

The platform was deserted.

Milly sat on her own and looked at the display board, which suggested that the next train would be there in around ten minutes.

This was shown as the first train, and there were no second or third trains noted. *Maybe this was the last one out tonight?* Milly wondered what time the tubes stopped working. She had a feeling that they ran all night, but what would be the point of that? Trains crossing London twenty four hours a day, ferrying nothing but ghosts and abandoned newspapers from place to place. They had to stop them at some point.

Another memory surfaced. Workers called 'fluffers'. She remembered seeing a newspaper article or television documentary about people who cleaned the tracks of debris. So many tons of human hair gathered in the tunnels every day, blown there by the air sweeping down the platforms ahead of incoming trains. If it wasn't removed ... then what? Maybe there would be giant hairballs tumbling along, knocking passengers from their feet as they waited for trains.

Milly smiled at the visual image. She was feeling okay.

One minute.

Milly noticed a slight change in the air. A trembling as though something was stirring. She stood and moved to the glass walls that protected her from the edge of the platform, glancing around her as she heard a metallic thrumming in the rails below. She was trying not to think about the tunnel roof curving above her. How that supported however-many metres of earth, rock and concrete above her head. How that could come pressing down on her, stopping her from moving.

She realised that she was holding her breath, and released it with a sigh.

Through the glass partition and down the ink-black eye of the tunnel, she saw a light. Distant but getting closer.

The train was coming.

The air started to stir and move down the tunnel. She liked the feel of the coolness against her skin.

The sounds intensified and with a rush, the train swept into the station.

Milly tried to catch a glimpse of the driver, but there was only the impression of a figure sitting up front. The image imprinted on her mind as the train passed by was of a face that was smeared, one too few – or too many – features to be wholly comfortable. Milly thought that maybe he had been holding his hand over his face or something.

The train drew to a halt, and after a moment the doors hissed open, the corresponding glass doors on the platform also opened. Milly paused for a second, but no-one got on or off. The whole place was silent, as though in anticipation.

She stepped through the nearest door into the carriage, and gripped a handrail tightly. This was the moment she had dreaded. The train smelled of oil and grease and an underlying miasma of human dread. Milly looked up and down the carriage. There seemed to be no-one else on it. She moved further into the train, and sat on one of the seats facing the other side of the carriage. That way she could see the expanse of the compartment and feel that she was perhaps slightly less enclosed.

Milly looked at her hand, which was gripping the rail beside her. Her knuckles were white. She drew in a deep breath, and released it and her hand slowly.

The train was still sitting in the station. Perhaps even at this time of night, they had to keep to a schedule. A lot of the track and signals would be automated, and even with no passengers, the network needed to keep running, like a child's train set which keeps on going even when unattended.

The doors hissed shut, the rubber seal between them pressing together like lips as they trapped her inside.

Milly breathed slowly, concentrating on not getting into a panic. The last thing she needed on a totally deserted train was a panic attack. She felt calmer, and looked around again. There was still no-one but her on the train.

With another exhalation of air, the train started to edge forward. Milly saw the platform sliding past outside the window. Her eyes followed the wall as it moved away.

There was someone standing there.

Milly twisted her head as the train gathered speed and entered the tunnel. The edge of darkness cutting off the external light as the carriage moved forward.

Milly could not believe what she had seen. She moved to the other side of the carriage to try and crane her head back down the train to see if she could see anything. But the train was in the tunnel now, and there was nothing but the faint image of the tunnel walls passing by, illuminated from inside the carriages.

It was a woman. Milly was sure it had been a women. But she had been topless, her breasts out and showing. What's more, she seemed to be cradling a baby in her arms.

Milly was positive that no-one had been on the platform with her, and there was no way that anyone could have entered it without her seeing.

What's more, as with the driver of the train, Milly felt that the woman was ill, or that something was physically wrong with her. Her head, in the brief time she had seen it, had been crossed with red marks, lesions of some sort.

She shook her head. She was imagining things. There couldn't have been anyone on the platform, let alone a naked woman with a baby. Perhaps she had seen the image on a poster on the wall, and in her stressed state had imagined that it was a real person? That had to be it.

191

Milly returned to her seat and sat down. The train seemed to be moving slower and slower now. She could clearly see the wall of the tunnel outside. The stanchions of iron, which were holding the arched passage in place; the endless cables, which were held to the wall with grips every few metres. She could make out the colour of the cables every so often, in places where they were newer, or where the grime from the trains had been wiped off. There was one red cable, and two smaller ones which seemed to be a green or a blue, depending on where they were. Milly watched them pass by, hypnotised by the movement.

The train slowed still further, and then came to a stop.

There was silence.

The train jerked a little and moved forward again at a crawl.

Out of the window, Milly saw the tunnel wall fall away as the train entered a larger underground space. In the light from the windows, she could just see the wall on the far side, and a number of boxes and crates piled up in a jumble across the floor. There didn't seem to be a platform here though, just this open space.

The train groaned as though in pain, and came to a halt again. Milly looked out the window at the area beyond. It was like something on one of those fairground rides, where a small carriage takes you into the past: *See the miners digging for gold! Witness the discovery of oil!*

Only here there were no waxwork tableaux, and no anodyne commentary about the weight of the sacks, or how many children it had taken to sew them.

There was a poster pinned to one of the walls. It looked like a skull and crossbones, but Milly couldn't be sure. She looked closer, and could make out some words printed beneath the image: something about Crossbones Graveyard.

Then the lights on the train went out.

*

In the total darkness, Milly panicked.

She let out a squeal of terror and staggered backwards. Her leg twisted and she fell back onto the seats. She could feel her skin starting to itch as the walls of the carriage pressed in on her. She squeezed her eyes tightly closed and sat still, focussing on her breathing. As her pounding heartbeat slowly returned to normal, she wondered what was happening.

She opened her eyes to see that some dim lights had come on, obviously some sort of emergency lighting, allowing her to see the interior of the train.

192

She looked around, but there was nothing to see. The carriage was quiet and the train was silent. She wondered what was going on. Had the train been parked up for the night now, on the assumption that no-one was on it? Was there a power failure?

She shuddered as the roof of the carriage seemed to dip down towards her. She knew the signs. She needed to keep control of her breathing or a panic attack would send her to the floor … and with no-one to help her, this was something she had to avoid.

She wondered how long she should sit there. She rummaged in her bag and pulled out her mobile phone. The light from the screen illuminated her face. No signal.

She noted that it was just before one in the morning. Not that this fact cheered her at all. It might as well have been the middle of the day for all the difference it made.

As she stuffed the phone back in her bag, something ran past the window outside.

Milly started, and looked at the dark space. All she could see was her reflection in the curved glass, distorted and lit by the dim lights inside the carriage. There seemed to be nothing else outside.

A pale shape flitted again across the glass. Milly wondered if it was just her own reflection bouncing and moving with her. Surely it couldn't have been the pale shape of a child, which was what it had most resembled?

There was a muffled thump from somewhere, and Milly jumped as it reverberated through the train. Were they about to set off again? She waited but nothing happened.

The air was starting to grow a little stale, and Milly could smell something sweet on it. It was Parma Violets, she realised. Her grandmother had given her them as a child, and she still associated that sweet taste and smell with her family. Why could she smell Parma Violets?

There was another bump, and the carriage seemed to rock slightly. Milly stood up. She could sit here all night she realised. Maybe she should make her way to the front of the train and see if the driver could offer any help. She suddenly remembered that all the carriages had a pull cord to alert the driver or guard to any problems.

She moved over to the closest sliding doors and located the lever pull on the wall to the side. She grasped it with her hand and pulled. Nothing happened.

She pulled it again, perhaps expecting to hear a jingling bell, or an alarm, but it seemed to be completely dead.

There was nothing for it but to make her way along the train.

She collected her bag and moved down the carriage towards the front. The whole experience was slightly surreal, she thought. She had not travelled by tube for many years due to her fears, and the first time she set foot on one, this happens. Typical really.

The silence was eerie, and in the half light, Milly's distorted reflection loped and followed her along the train. Milly kept catching sight of it as the head bulged and pulsed, as though something were trapped inside trying to stretch its way out.

She stopped moving and looked around. There was nothing there. No sound. But the reflection continued to make its distorted way along the train! She muffled a cry with her hand. There was something anaemic and deformed tracking her progress along the outside of the train. She tried to make out what it might be through the window, but it flickered and vanished. She had seen a distended head, and arms which seemed far longer than they should be. The creature's gait was loping, as though its hidden legs were not working quite as they should.

She looked back down the carriage she had traversed and saw nothing. She let out a long breath, and thought that perhaps her claustrophobia was making her see things, making her own reflection seem to have a life of its own.

She recalled an occasion when she had tried to get something from the small closet under the stairs in her boyfriend's house, how she had felt suffocated, and how she had been convinced that there had been something else in the house behind her, ready to push her into the tight space and lock the door on her.

Milly pushed her hair from her eyes and tried to calm herself. She shut her eyes and waited until her breathing had returned to normal. Then she opened her eyes.

Standing at the far end of the carriage was a figure. It had not been there before. It was clothed in black and carried a long staff in one hand. In the dim light it was hard to make out any detail, but Milly could see that it was not human. Its face was distended and black, eyeless slits perched above a long, hooked, tapering nose which extended far from the head. It looked as though the whole of the lower face had been pulled out into a point. It was terrifying.

As she stood there, staring at the thing, it took a step towards her.

She needed no more encouragement. She turned and hurried to the door at the end of the carriage. Through the glass panel, she could see the dim lights in the next carriage, and she hooked her hand around the handle and pulled. The door would not open.

She made a small squeal of panic and pulled again. Why wouldn't it open?

194

She looked behind her and saw that the hideous figure was stepping towards her. One step at a time. As though it was engaged in some horrific game of statues – except that when she looked back, it continued to move rather than being frozen in place.

She suddenly realised that the door handle had to turn to open the door, and she twisted it one way and then the other.

A sweet smell reached her nose, something putrid and rotting. Something well past its prime. She heard the gentle rustle of material as the thing stepped closer and closer to her, its staff tapping on the metallic floor of the cabin in time with its steps.

She pulled the door again and it opened. She threw herself through and grabbed the handle of the door to the next carriage. That opened as well, and she slammed both behind her, leaning her back against the door and breathing heavily.

She turned and looked back through the glass.

The distended face was gazing straight through at her.

She realised that the figure was wearing a mask, a full face affair which gave it an insectile look, with the slitted eye holes and the nose and mouth area pulled out into a beak-like proboscis.

After a moment's thought, she pulled a comb from her bag. She jammed the plastic implement into the handle, stopping it from turning. That would keep the door shut for the moment.

Milly turned and headed up the carriage. Like the previous one, this was empty and quiet. She could see that the door ahead seemed to be the one to the driver's area – it had no glass panel, and a sign proclaimed that passengers should not enter.

Milly ignored the sign, and tried the handle. This one was locked. She tried to operate it in the same way as she had the previous one, but it was stuck fast.

She then noticed that another sign mentioned an emergency unlock panel, which was situated alongside. There was a small glass sheet blocking access to a control lever.

Without thinking further, she smashed the sheet with her elbow, and pulled the lever. There was a satisfying *click* from the door.

She grasped the handle, and this time it opened.

Milly nervously looked back along the carriage. There was nothing there, but there were shapes once more moving alongside the train outside the windows. Fast and ethereal, they brushed up against the glass before vanishing into the gloom. Milly caught sight of faces and hands, none of them normal, fingers missing, misshapen mouths and eyes, bone white skull fragments surrounded by weeping flesh.

She pulled the door fully open and stepped into the driver's cabin.

At first she couldn't understand what she was seeing. Unlike the rest of the train, it seemed to have been decorated in red ... but then she saw the streaks on the front window, and felt her feet stick to the floor as she stepped in whatever was pooled there.

In a moment's clarity, she saw the gore streaked body of the driver. It was lying over the front of the carriage, one flayed, skeletal hand ineffectually clutching the dead man's handle. The body was still clothed, but the flesh seemed to have been ripped and scored from his body as though by some grotesque clawed implement.

She stepped back involuntarily, and her feet trailed in the pool of blood which was underfoot.

How could this have happened? It was like some bad horror film.

She looked up and out through the red stained glass at the front of the train and saw shadowy figures moving outside. As before there was something hideously wrong about them, but in the gloom and through the blood she couldn't see properly. She whimpered and backed from the tiny room, the walls suddenly crashing in on her, the ceiling plummeting close.

She felt her breath catch, and her hand trembled as it clutched at one of the support posts in the carriage. She steadied herself, and fumbled for her phone. If only she could call for help. The screen lit her face up, and again she saw that there was no service.

She selected someone at random from her contacts list and tried anyway, but the phone was silent in her hand. No connection could be made.

She dropped it back in her bag.

Milly moved shakily to the nearest door and glanced out.

Strangely, and despite what she had thought she had seen before, all seemed still and quiet.

There was a sudden hissing sound as the air in the hydraulics was expelled.

Milly abruptly stepped back, expecting the door to open, but it didn't.

She banged it with her hand. Why did nothing ever work!

Then she realised the problem, and gripped the two sides of the rubber seal between the doors, heaving them apart. They reluctantly slid aside, letting a rush of stinking air into the carriage.

Milly coughed and wrinkled her nose. She pushed the doors fully open and looked down.

There was around a four foot drop to the ground. There was nothing moving out there, and no sounds at all. Milly started to wonder if she had imagined it all. Perhaps a lack of oxygen in the carriage or something? She looked back at the front of the train, and could see the red splatters on the floor inside the driver's cabin. She hadn't imagined *everything*.

Milly crouched down and sat on the edge of the doorway, dropping herself to the ground below. She paused and listened. Nothing.

The area she was in was dark and wreathed in shadows. The only light was coming from the windows of the train, and the emergency lighting was weak.

She stepped away and made her way across the ground towards a pillar arrangement in the centre. Maybe there was a flight of stairs up or something.

The light dimmed the farther from the train she got, but her eyes were adjusting to the gloom, and she could make out shapes. Stacked boxes and piles of what looked like rubbish were littered around.

At the pillars, she could see the poster that she had spotted from the train. It was a black and white photocopied image. The main picture was of a skull and crossbones, and under that, in large black lettering were the words:

THIS IS STILL THE CROSSBONES GRAVEYARD

Milly looked closer at the smaller words which ran across the bottom of the poster. They explained that the Redcross Way area had been a pauper's graveyard in the sixteenth century, and that London Underground were digging it up to make way for an extension to the Jubilee Line. Milly frowned. She'd not heard of this before.

She realised that the poster must have been brought down here by one of the London Underground workers. Perhaps they had been put up around the outside of the area by protestors.

There was an echoing, sliding sound from somewhere distant, and a *clattering,* as though an object had been dislodged and had fallen. Maybe there were rats down here? Milly looked around her. She didn't much fancy meeting a horde of furry creatures in the dark.

There was another sound: a slow dragging, like a sack being pulled across the ground.

"Who's there?" Milly called, her voice catching and weak. She chided herself for sounding so pathetic. "Is there anyone there?" she called again.

The silence that followed was deafening, and Milly realised that she was holding her breath. She let it out slowly, and then jumped as the dragging sound came again.

She stepped away from the wall and looked around her. It was dark and there was nothing to be seen. She pulled her phone from her bag once more and switched it on. The light from the screen cast a pale glow in front of her, and she stepped towards the darkness. There had to be a way out of here. There must be some steps somewhere – after all, workmen had to have got down here to build the railway.

The light hit a rocky wall, and Milly turned to follow it along. She passed sacks full of unknown objects tied with string, and rough wooden crates with their lids securely nailed shut. Her feet crunched gently on the gritty floor as she went, and every so often she heard quiet scuffling sounds which caused her to pause. *It has to be rats*, she thought. Did she read somewhere that there were more rats in London than people? Or was that an urban myth?

She had nearly reached the other side of the space, when she saw something move.

A pale shape flitted quickly from behind one of the crates, and she caught it out of the corner of her eye.

She looked closely at the area, holding her phone out in front of her like a talisman. There was no more movement, and all seemed quiet. So she swung the phone back in front of her again.

And it illuminated a deformed and grinning skull.

Milly screamed and jumped back, the light from the phone bouncing all over the place.

Standing right before her was a figure draped in filthy, rotting rags. Its hands were raised for balance, and it was swaying from side to side. Its head was a skull, bare bone and grinning teeth, with dark sockets which seemed alive in the flickering shadows. There was black flesh hanging off the skull and strands of fine hair covering the gleaming white pate.

Milly stepped back, eyes fixed on the figure. It had to be a trick. Something from Hallowe'en which the workers had used to scare each other as they did whatever they did down here.

But then it stepped towards her. Milly saw that one foot was deformed and broken, and it dragged across the ground under the creature.

Milly noticed that its bony taloned hands were stained with gore. Black blood and strands of hair were hanging down. She swallowed and stepped back again.

Her foot caught on something, and as in the carriage, she felt herself toppling over, arms waving wildly. She crashed down backwards with a thump.

She scrabbled with her feet, momentarily winded, and saw that she had tripped over one of the sacks, which had burst open, spilling a selection of items on the floor. There were skulls and bones of all shapes and sizes. Some recognisable like ribs and pelvis, the long humerus, the tibia, fibular and femur of the legs, and others smaller and less identifiable, like vertebrae and perhaps carpal and tarsal bones from the hands and feet.

Milly kicked them aside as she tried to get away from the shadowy horror which was still lurching slowly towards her.

Her phone was on the ground beside her, thankfully still working, so she snatched it up, and cast the light around her, trying to see which way to go.

To her horror she saw the legs and feet of other deformed and skeletal figures, all moving towards her. Shuffling slowly. Some hopped, using lengths of wood as makeshift crutches. Some crawled, and in the weak light Milly realised that these were children, their legs withered and useless.

She let out a squeal and scrambled to her feet. Her legs felt bruised and grazed as she staggered away.

The darkness encroached on her, and the light from her phone cast a dim pool. She saw another wall, and hurriedly made her way along it. And then there was a door.

Milly twisted the handle, pulling it open. She dashed through and pulled it shut behind her.

It was even darker in this area. In the light from her phone, Milly could see a passageway in front of her. Walls of plaster leading away into pitch darkness.

Milly hurried forward. Her heart was thumping, the sound echoing in her skull. She could feel another panic attack building up. Behind her she heard a scraping sound as the door was opened, and shuffling, scrabbling noises as hands trailed along the plaster walls.

She whimpered, following the passage as fast as she could. She felt, or thought she felt, insects crawling on her arms. She brushed them reflexively, her hands trembling.

Suddenly, the passageway ended, and Milly was standing before another open area.

There was a shaft of sickly yellow light from the ceiling high overhead, and it illuminated a pit which was filled with bones and skeletons and other rubbish: rags and filthy clothes; drinks cans and bottles; paper and indefinable lumps of litter. The outpouring of an overpopulated city.

Milly looked back but could see nothing in the darkness of the corridor behind her. There was no way forward. She was standing on a platform above the pit. She looked down and could see that the pit was about six feet below her, and that there was an iron ladder dropping into it.

She turned and pushed her way off the platform and onto the ladder, which she descended as quickly as she could.

As her head ducked below the edge of the platform, she could see feet shuffling into sight. At the bottom, her feet crunched on the bones and rubbish at the edge of the pit.

She looked around. Where was the way out?

She staggered and felt her foot give way under her. She fell with a scream, tumbling backwards. She emerged a moment later, dripping with stinking effluent. The bones and rubbish she realised had been floating on a deep pool of sludge. She didn't even want to consider what was in it.

She waded to the edges, and tried to get out, but every time she tried, her feet slipped, and there was nothing to get a purchase on. She scrabbled harder, but her feet skidded on the sloping sides.

There was a thud and splash behind her, and she looked back to see the pit heaving in the middle. Then another pale shape fell from above.

She looked up and saw with horror that the creatures from the corridor above, were, one by one, falling into the pit. They weren't jumping, but being pushed by the weight of those behind them. Milly cried out in panic. She had to get out of there. She felt something brush her ankle, and she pulled it away, but then something else touched her.

She realised that the deformed corpses were still moving, and making their way for her under the floating layer of skeletal remains.

She screamed and tried again to get out of the pit. But the sides were too sloped and too slippery, and she couldn't gain any purchase.

She screamed again as a hard bony hand grasped her ankle, and a grinning, dripping face raised up out of the ichor to stare into her eyes.

She saw madness and poverty, a life of drudge and hopelessness reflected back at her. Then the face twisted, and she recognised revenge and hatred. London had failed these people, and their bodies had been piled into a paupers' graveyard to rot and be forgotten as the outcast dead. But they had not forgotten, and when

200

the opportunity came, they would have their revenge, one person at a time.

A shape moved on the far side of the pit, and Milly saw that the figure from the train was standing there. It watched her impassively through its distended mask.

With a start she remembered where she had seen it before. Old books of London, where those who worked with the diseased and hopeless dead wore primitive masks to try and protect them from sickness. The pointed snout and distended head were all part of the outfit developed for these plague doctors.

Milly shouted for help, but the figure just stood there.

Suddenly Milly was dragged below the surface. She struggled and thrashed, bones and rubbish flying around her.

The dark fluid filled her mouth, and she spluttered at the rank taste. Bile rose from her stomach and she was sick, coughing and flailing as she tried to regain her footing.

More figures landed on top of her, and more hands clutched and picked at her wrists, arms and legs.

Milly felt herself being dragged down. She flailed and kicked, but as fast as she freed herself from one set of fingers, another latched onto her.

She felt her head go under again, oily, filthy water flooding her nose and mouth. She screamed underwater, the sound muffled and echoing through her ears.

The pool thrashed and bubbled.

A buzzing sound filled her brain, as though a thousand tiny ants were burrowing into her head. Her eyes burned as she frantically looked around under the surface, desperately trying to escape.

She tried to draw a breath to cry out again, but the water filled her mouth and she tried to cough again, drawing in more and more of the poisonous liquid.

She moved helplessly, a black mist coming in across her eyes. Claustrophobia crashed in on her, panic flared momentarily.

Then it stilled. A final trail of bubbles rose to the surface, releasing Milly's final breath into the air, and the floating detritus settled.

At the side of the room, the masked, cloaked figure turned and walked off into the darkness. The Outcast Dead quietened and returned to their slumber. Until the next time.

'There is in this part a great concentration of evil living and low conditions of life that strikes the imagination and leads almost irresistibly to sensational statement ... the palm for degradation was, at the time of our inquiry, still to be given to the group of old

201

courts lying between Red Cross Street and the Borough High Street
... Of this spot I have the following note written by one of my
secretaries: "Women with draggled skirts slouch by, their shawls
over their heads. Undergrown men hang about. As I passed along
three women stood gossiping on a doorstep; one of them was
suckling a child openly with bare breasts. She showed no shyness.
All were of the lowest type. Many evil faces, and a deformed boy
with naked twisted leg completed the picture." ... The character of
these places varies somewhat in detail, but in general it is lowness
and wickedness that impress here rather than poverty: and the
lowest depths of degradation are found in the registered common
lodging-houses, which are still numerous.'

'Life and Labour of the People in London' by Charles Booth
assisted by Jesse Argyle, Ernest Aves, Geo. E Arkell, Arthur L
Baxter and George H Duckworth. c1900.

WHAT STIRS BELOW?

The London Underground is one of the largest subterranean transport systems in the world, and is certainly the oldest. Work first started on it in 1855 and it opened in 1863, a single railway line running between Paddington Station and Farringdon Street. Since then of course it has gone through many transformations, constantly expanding in every direction, including downward, until it is now a vast, multi-levelled transit labyrinth covering the entire Greater London area and encroaching into several counties beyond.

Not surprisingly, it has seen disasters of every sort, from cataclysmic train crashes to murders, abductions, accidents, suicides and unexplained disappearances. Though in the 21st century it is rightly regarded as one of the best-operated, safest and most secure underground railway systems on the planet, during the 150 years of its existence the overall loss of life on the London Underground has been massive. In addition, over the years its excavation has caused the demolition of numerous graveyards, crypts, burial vaults and plague pits, so perhaps it is no surprise that the Underground's ghost stories are too numerous to recount in a simple one-off entry like this.

Suffice to say there is scarcely a station on the Underground network, or a stretch of tunnel, which does not have its resident phantom, and – from the wraith of the murdered actor William Terriss, who supposedly walks the platforms at Covent Garden, to the shrieks of women and children killed during an air-raid at Bethnal Green, to the ice-cold threat that manifests itself in the lower passages at Embankment – these unearthly presences appear to cross the entire supernatural spectrum from the benign to the tragic to the malevolent.

Of course, despite a plethora of audio and photographic evidence, none of these phenomena to date have been proved to really exist, though the witnesses tend, in general, to be reliable: London Underground managers, patrolmen and cleaning and maintenance crews, rather than passengers who might not be fully aware what they have experienced. Given the busy state of the network – during daytime hours it is teeming, and even late at night there is often much staff activity – we rarely hear tales of individuals who have been terrified on the Underground, but there is no denying the eeriness of some of its myths.

Perhaps the most shudder-inducing of all is that of the so-called 'Dead Body Train'.

Rumours persist that a tunnel closed to normal public traffic once ran from the Royal London Hospital to a destination unknown, passing only one regular station en route, Whitechapel, at which it never stopped. This is because its only passengers were corpses: hundreds of them, stacked either in coffins or burlap sacks depending on which garrulous old ex-Underground employee you talk to. This Dead Body Train has allegedly been out of service since around 1900, so it could not have been used, as someone once suggested, to transport excessive numbers of World War Two bombing fatalities to hastily built crematoria. Nor could it have been constructed in response to some dreadful epidemic. Victorian London was rife with, among other illnesses, cholera and small pox. But these were quantifiable calamities, which did not cause an undue panic for the health services at the time. There was no plague in London in the 19th century. Likewise, the horrific Spanish Flu pandemic, which killed millions, did not become a menace until two decades after the Dead Body Train allegedly ceased to run.

There is no official document confirming the purpose or even the existence of this macabre vehicle, and no physical evidence ... except a curious bricked-up tunnel at Whitechapel Underground Station, which though it can no longer be entered, apparently leads in the direction of the Royal London Hospital. There is some confusion among former Underground employees as to what this inaccessible passage once was. Some argue that it did indeed lead to the hospital, but that it was a walk-through for ordinary patients. Others say that it was nothing more than a maintenance tunnel, but a few state baldly that it was the route of the Dead Body Train.

If the tale has no spark of truth in it, it is not easy to see where such an elaborate fiction might have originated. One possible explanation lies in the story that, during Victorian times, spare rooms at Whitechapel Station were used as a temporary mortuary when the facility at the Royal London Hospital once became overcrowded. There is also the not insignificant case of the London Necropolis Railway, which opened at Waterloo Station in 1859 in response to lack of graveyard space in the city centre, and existed solely to transport the recently deceased overland to Brookwood Cemetery in Surrey. These funeral trains continued to operate until the Second World War, when heavy bombing destroyed the railway lines and sidings. There was nothing sinister about them; facilities existed at Waterloo for mourners, and religious services were often held there, but this might have influenced the Dead Body Train legend, and Whitechapel – the decayed neighbourhood at the heart

204

of the old East End, with its gruesome history of Ripper murders –
would have been the obvious place to locate such a grim tale.

And yet if it is untrue, little more than a carefully fabricated
urban myth, why is it that late at night at Whitechapel Underground
Station, staff still report the sound of a train when no train is in
motion, trundling along tracks that no longer exist, through a dark,
arched passage which has long been blocked off and is filled only
with dust and cobwebs?

THE BLOODY TOWER
Anna Taborska

S hakil had more in common with Jim Morrison than Osama bin Laden, so it came as something of a surprise to his family when the front door splintered with an ear-rending crash at four o'clock one Sunday morning, and a naked Shakil was dragged out of bed, handcuffed and pulled out into the darkness.

It was a year since the Prime Minister had given his speech in Parliament to accompany his new anti-terrorism legislation, and a year since the ravens had flown the Tower.

*

The birds had been restless all morning. The Raven Master tried in vain to persuade Thor the talking raven to say "good morning". At around midday, about the time that the Prime Minister sat down amidst a deathly silence a little over two miles away, Thor croaked something that might have been construed as sounding rather like "Nevermore!" and took off – half-flying, half-hopping, taking the other ravens with him.

"Thor! Thor, come back!" The Raven Master ran as far as he could after the departing birds. Another Yeoman Warder joined him, disturbed by the desperation in the older man's voice. "Don't worry mate, you know they won't get far with their feathers clipped". But the Raven Master wasn't convinced.

*

A year later and the ravens weren't back, the Crown Jewels had been removed, the tourist attractions ousted, the Yeoman Warders sacked, and the Prime Minister had his own little Guantanamo right here on British soil – in the heart of the capital.

The Tower – in reality a collection of twenty-four towers and various other structures – was nothing if not perfect for the job at hand. It was as if the ancient buildings had been waiting for seventy-five years for blood to flow down their walls once more. The Tower's last victim had been shot on 15th August 1941: a hapless German spy who broke his right ankle while parachuting into Ramsey Hollow, Huntingdonshire, and was duly court-

206

martialled and executed before he had managed to do any spying. Josef Jacobs's executioners had been considerate enough to allow him to sit before the eight-man firing squad – made up of members of the Holding Battalion, Scots Guards – as his injured leg made standing difficult. The coroner noted during the autopsy that Josef had been shot once in the head and seven times around the white lint target that had been pinned over his heart. The poor man was buried in an unmarked grave at St. Mary's Roman Catholic Cemetery in Kensal Green, Northwest London, and, to add insult to injury, earth was later thrown over his grave, allowing for the cadavers of total strangers to be buried on top of him.

*

Shakil had enjoyed history at school, and under different circumstances would perhaps have been interested to know that he was being driven into the Tower of London complex, but by the time the tear-stained blindfold was removed from the eighteen year old's eyes, he was already in a damp, dark cell, and his only thought was one of fear for his life.

He spent his first half hour shouting for help and looking for a way out, then footsteps resounded and three guards appeared.

"Shut up, you piece of shit! And stand up for The Warden."

The Warden was dressed in an Armani suit and very shiny shoes. His accent was an uneasy fusion of public school and East End wide boy, explainable by the fact that his daddy had paid for him to go to public school, but the boy had not been bright enough to get into university, and had instead used his financial leverage to hang out with bankers, gangsters and aspiring politicians. His money and dubious connections had finally landed him his current position, and he intended to abuse every inch of his power.

"Congratulations," the Warden intoned sarcastically to the frightened teenager on the other side of the bars. "It is my duty as Warden to welcome you here. You are officially the first detainee of the Tower of London Detention and Concentration Facility."

"I didn't do nothing!"

"Shut up when the Warden's speaking!"

The Warden continued by assuring Shakil that during his stay he would not only give up his terror cell, but would also help them to fine-tune the system they were creating.

"But I didn't do nothing!"

"I am referring, of course, to the Government's new anti-terror system."

"But I didn't do nothing."

207

The Warden laughed. "Get him scrubbed up," he told the guards.

*

Even as Shakil was told where he was, his family had no idea whatsoever. It was seven in the morning and they had already been waiting two hours at the local police station to speak to someone who might know something. The duty officer told them to come back at nine, when the chief superintendent would be in, but they refused to leave. It took all of Mr Malik's diplomatic skills to stop his wife and daughter ending up in the holding cells, as panic for Shakil made it impossible for the women to sit still and wait in silence.

When the chief superintendent finally turned up at half past nine, he tried to go straight into a meeting, and this time it was Mr Malik whose nerves gave way.

"What have you done with my son?" he shouted repeatedly at the top of his voice. The police station was filling up with other distressed members of the public by now, and the chief superintendent decided that in the interests of public relations it would be best to assist the Malik family rather than incarcerate them. He made a couple of phone calls, and finally informed the Maliks that their son was being held on terrorist charges at an undisclosed location.

"Terrorist charges! Shakil? Do you even know what you're talking about?" Shakil's sixteen year old sister Adara yelled at the chief superintendent, while Mrs Malik suddenly felt faint and her husband had to hold her up.

"Calm down, Miss Malik." The chief was starting to seriously consider locking up the lot of them – public relations or not. If the son was a terrorist, then there was a good chance that the rest of the family were as well.

"Shakil – a terrorist? Look, my brother's greatest ambition is to strip at hen parties. How on earth could he be a terrorist?" Adara was hysterical, and Mr Malik tried to calm her down, while holding onto her sobbing mother.

"Mr Malik," the chief superintendent said, putting on his most professional smile. "Why don't you all go home and once we know something more about your son, we'll contact you."

*

Eventually Mr Malik decided to take the remains of his family home, to regroup and think where to appeal for help. On the way home, Adara replayed the events of the previous night in her mind, and tried to think of anything that could have contributed to her brother's abduction by the Met's Anti-Terror Squad.

Shakil and Adara had been invited to a party. There had been a long discussion with their dad, who hadn't wanted Adara to go. Shakil argued that if his father trusted him with the keys to his car and to his explosives warehouse, then surely he could trust him to bring his sister home safely.

"Your sister's not a car." But Mr Malik lost the argument, as his wife joined in on the side of the children, and the siblings went to their friend's party.

After about half an hour of chatting to each other and the hostess, a blonde girl had come up to Shakil and asked him where he was from.

"East End," Shakil gave the girl his sexy smile.

"No, I mean, where's your family from? You're not English."

"I'm Pakistani."

"Oh ... Are you a terrorist?"

"Maddy!" Their hostess's embarrassment was painful to see.

"My dad says that all Pakis are terrorists," explained Maddy. Adara and the hostess exchanged glances, wondering which one of them was going to deck her first, but Shakil merely thought hard for a moment, then said, "I don't know about anyone else, but I *am* a terrorist – a terrorist of the heart."

The girl processed the information for a while, then laughed. Adara rolled her eyes, while Shakil explained to Maddy that his name meant 'sexy' in Arabic. Adara caught Shakil's eye and put her finger in her mouth, making like she was about to vomit. Shakil got that mischievous glint in his eye, and added, "Lots of Pakistani names have Arabic origins, and most of them mean something. For example, 'Adara' means 'virgin'." Everyone looked at Adara and laughed. "Does not!" Adara stuck her middle finger up at Shakil, eliciting more hilarity. The blonde whispered something in Shakil's ear, "Let's see what you got then, Mr Terrorist," and went to kiss him, her hand straying downwards towards the boy's crotch. But just then Shakil's favourite *Doors* song came on the stereo, "I love that song!", and he was off – leaving Maddy to wonder whether her low-cut top was showing enough cleavage.

*

As Adara recalled her brother dancing to *Light My Fire* in front of a room of admiring girls and jealous boys, his shoulder length black hair glistening under the dim lighting, Shakil was hosed down with freezing water and his fine locks were shaved off by a brute of a guard who doubled as the prison's 'hairdresser'. Shakil had been very proud of his hair, and the sight of it falling on the stone floor, and the bald, bleeding reflection staring out at him from a mirror that was shoved in front of his face with the words "Who's a pretty boy, then?", broke him. What with the fluorescent yellow jumpsuit he'd been forced to don after his 'shower', in place of his customary jeans, Nirvana T-shirt and leather jacket, the old Shakil was no more.

*

Then Adara remembered that a couple of the boys at the party had started a conversation about making bombs. One of the boys said that it would be easy to make a home-made bomb, while the other disagreed. Shakil had piped up, saying that you could make a detonator really easily out of just about anything – even a mobile phone. Shakil knew a lot about explosives, as his father was an engineer, specialising in demolitions, who was often asked by the council to demolish traditional areas of the East End so that developers could turn them into car parks or high-rise hell holes for the underprivileged.

"You see, son," Adara had heard her father say to Shakil more than once, "You could be blowing things up too, just like your old man, if you just went to college and studied engineering, instead of playing guitar and thinking about girls all day."

Maybe someone had reported Shakil's stupid teenage conversation to the authorities. How sick would that be? What kind of a world were they living in if you couldn't even chat at a party without being abducted by the police several hours later?

"Mum, we gotta go back ... Dad ..."

"What is it, sweetheart?"

"There was some stupid conversation at the party last night about making bombs."

"Oh God." Mrs Malik was starting to feel light-headed again.

"We have to go back and explain that no way would Shakil make a bomb; he just knows about explosives because of Dad's job."

"Okay, sweetheart, we'll go back and tell them," said her father.

"But what if they take your father away as well?" Mrs Malik had aged ten years in the last few hours. "What if they don't give us Shakil back, but take away your father too?"

"We have to try," Mr Malik was adamant.

So Adara and her parents went back to the police station – that day, as they would every day in the weeks that followed.

*

The interrogation had not lasted long, as after several belts around the back, chest, face and head, Shakil was already unconscious.

"We'll have to do something about your technique," the Warden told the interrogating officer. "This isn't going to work. I'm seriously thinking we need to look at the equipment we have at our disposal, starting with that weird looking thing in the basement."

The weird looking thing in the basement was a Scavenger's Daughter – the one claim to fame of one Leonard Skeffington, Lieutenant of the Tower of London during the reign of King Henry VIII. Mr. Skeffington must have been either a very bored or a very unpleasant man – perhaps both – for it would have taken him no small amount of time to come up with a device that matched the infamous rack both in terms of the pain and the damage it caused its victims. And having a day job at the Tower of London, Mr. Skeffington would have had ample opportunity to observe both instruments in practice. While the rack stretched people until their limbs were dislocated and then torn from their sockets, the Scavenger's Daughter compressed them – in a foetal position – until they bled from their orifices and their bones broke.

Had the Warden displayed any interest in the Tower's rich history, or had he taken the time to speak to the former Chief Yeoman Warder of the Tower or any of his staff before having them thrown out of the complex, he would have known all about the Scavenger's Daughter, but – perhaps luckily for Shakil – he hadn't and he didn't.

*

Now a breeze with no discernible source stirred in the torture chamber. The ropes on the rack creaked and shadows flitted uneasily around Mr. Skeffington's invention. Eddies of dust formed and whirled out into the corridor, swirling around the feet of a guard who'd been trailing slightly behind the Warden's guided tour of the Tower complex. Bob shivered as the temperature suddenly dropped, and hurried to join the others.

It had been a long tour, but the Warden was still going strong and was just now explaining to the Home Secretary and the heads of MI5 and MI6 his plans for the redevelopment of the Tower.

"As you know, the Prime Minister has informed me that the war on terror will require the detention and interrogation of many more suspects than previously thought." The Warden was positively beaming at the attention he was getting from some of the country's most important men. "So I am having plans drawn up for a large number of holding cells with bunks. We are now about to enter phase one of the project, but once all the work is complete, the Tower will hold more inmates per square metre than any other prison in Europe."

"And how much time do you think you'll need to finish the project, Warden?" asked the Home Secretary.

*

Several hours later, and the cold wind that had started in the torture chamber now stirred the ropes on the row of gallows outside the White Tower, causing them to creak and swing. Had an observer chanced upon the scene, he or she might have had the impression that something heavy, yet unseen, was dangling from them.

Bob was on guard duty, patrolling the southern part of the Tower complex. He was in the basement of the Wakefield Tower, consciously avoiding the torture chamber and trying not to spend too long gazing into any of the dark corners, when he heard a child crying – a boy.

Bob froze, listening intently. "Hello?" The sobbing came again and Bob moved cautiously towards the sound. "Hello?" A second boy called out something – Bob couldn't make out what. "Who's there?" Bob walked towards the voices, but as he did so they seemed to move away. "Wait!" A flurry of footsteps and Bob followed, determined to find the boys. He couldn't understand for the life of him what they were doing in the Tower, and in the middle of the night as well.

Bob followed the crying up the stairs to the ground floor and out of the building. As he stepped outside, he saw two small figures ahead of him. He hurried after them, calling to them. They disappeared into the Bloody Tower, and Bob went in after them. He didn't see them again, but followed their voices up to a room on the first floor, where all trace of them disappeared. Confused and disconcerted, Bob was searching the room when he heard a blood-curdling scream in one of the adjoining chambers. He rushed next door and stopped short as he saw something coming rapidly towards

212

him from the far end of the room. It was like a mist emerging out of the darkness – a mist that transformed into solid matter, as a screaming woman, dressed in what to Bob looked like a ball gown, came running in his direction.

Bob shouted at the woman to stop, but she kept running at him and kept screaming. The guard drew his weapon. "Stop or I'll shoot!" The woman kept coming and Bob panicked, shooting at her a couple of times. As she reached him, the woman finally dropped – facedown – right in front of the shaking guard. Bob closed his eyes for a moment and sucked in air through his mouth; in his fear he had forgotten to breathe. He bent down and checked the woman's pulse – nothing. That was when he noticed the gashes on her back; fragments of whitish backbone protruding from all the blood. He'd only had time to discharge two rounds at the woman, so why was her back slashed a dozen times? Bob looked at his gun, puzzled. Perhaps the new ammo they'd been issued splintered inside a person? He felt bad about killing the woman. He put his weapon away and went to report the incident.

Back in the White Tower, Bob was hurrying to see the Warden, when he bumped into the Head Guard.

"What's wrong, mate?" Pete looked concerned. "You look like you've seen a ghost."

"I just killed a woman."

"What?"

"I just shot a woman. She was coming at me. I told her to stop, but she wouldn't listen. I think she was crazy."

"Bob, what the hell are you on about?"

"I killed someone. I have to go report it."

"Whoa, whoa. Hang on a sec there, mate. Look, don't take this the wrong way, but ... have you been drinking?"

"No. No, I haven't." Bob tried to get past the older man, but Pete was having none of it.

"Look, if you killed someone, then there's a body, right?"

"Right ... Now let me past. I need to see the Warden."

"Let's go and check that there's definitely a body. You don't want to bother the Warden and get yourself sacked if this is all just in your head."

Pete wouldn't let it go and eventually Bob found himself on his way back to the Bloody Tower.

"This is a strange place," Pete was saying. "Sometimes people see things. My brother knew someone who was a Yeoman Warder here when it was still a tourist attraction. And he said that one of the other Warders left after something tried to strangle him in the Salt Tower – something nobody could see."

213

"Well, I definitely saw someone," Bob was getting upset again, "and I shot her." But when they got back to the Bloody Tower, there was no dead woman anywhere to be found.

*

A couple of hours later, around two in the morning, Crewes and Hampel were on guard duty in the White Tower. Crewes decided to check out the armoury. It was like Christmas come early. The gun in his holster forgotten, Crewes was soon happily swinging a poleaxe around the chamber.

"What the fuck are you doing, man?" But five minutes later Hampel too had a large grin on his face and a poleaxe in his hands, and the two of them were giggling like schoolboys and re-enacting some light-sabre battle or other from an early episode of *Star Wars*.

Neither of them noticed the shadow that fell across the threshold, nor the huge masked figure that entered the room, nor the massive axe it was holding. Crewes didn't even have time to discharge his gun or swing his poleaxe, but neither did he see what was coming. Hampel was less fortune for, although he got to fight briefly for his life, he also got to stare death right in the eyes and see the scant light glint for one blinding moment on the axe's head before it came down and sideways.

*

As the masked figure strode back to the Hell from which it had come, axe in one hand and the fruits of the night's labours in the other, Shakil was lying shackled on the floor of his cell. He was running a fever, slipping in and out of consciousness. In one of his lucid moments, he became aware of a delicate scent, quite out of sorts with the damp, musty chamber that was his new home. He shouldn't have smelled anything, as he could hardly breathe through his pulverised, blood-encrusted nostrils, and yet he did. The scent was sweet and floral – like a woman's perfume, but weak and distant.

Shakil's swollen, cracked lips moved incoherently as he found himself trying to hum a tune: "Sweet Jane. Sweet, sweet Jane." Shakil knew the song so well, but in his present delirious state he couldn't remember who it was by. His failure to remember distressed him and he wanted to cry, but then that scent wafted by again, closer this time. *The Velvet Underground*, Shakil remembered and smiled.

214

Just then the air in his cell stirred slightly and eddies of dust started to rise and twist. Shakil tried to change position, but only succeeded in causing a fresh stab of pain in his head and chest. He lost consciousness for a moment, then regained it as a soft, cool hand tenderly stroked his face.

"Mum?" he whispered before drifting off into a gentle sleep. But the woman who knelt beside him was not his mother.

*

The boy could not have been much older than her. His skin, dark compared to the pale young men of the court that she had been used to, made a stark and fascinating contrast with the whiteness of her own hand. There were even darker patches on his skin, where they had hit him, and bloody marks on his face and body.

The girl with the heavy embroidered dress and the long, reddish-golden hair continued to stroke Shakil's face, gazing at him with sadness and compassion. A tear fell from her eye onto the boy's cheek, and he stirred for a moment, then fell asleep once more.

As the grey light of dawn filtered in through the tiny barred window at the top of the cell, a gaping wound opened up in the girl's neck and started to bleed profusely. She grimaced in pain and put her hand up to her neck. Her already pale complexion turned white as a sheet and she faded away to nothing. A tear rolled down Shakil's cheek, but he slept on.

*

The following morning Shakil woke up to his cell door slamming open, and freezing cold water under pressure forced him against the wall of his cell. He was thrown a bowl of slop to eat, and he crawled over to it, stiff and feverish.

While Shakil tried to eat, his family were down at the police station again, being told that if they persisted in asking questions about him, they would be arrested as well. They followed their visit to the police with a trip to the offices of *The Guardian*. After a long wait, a sympathetic journalist informed them that if Shakil was being held on terror charges, then it was probably at the new detention centre in the Tower of London. This being the case, there was nothing *The Guardian* or any other newspaper could do, as there was a Government injunction against reporting on the Tower. Any journalist caught investigating issues relating to the complex would be imprisoned, and there would be repercussions against the editor and other staff at his or her newspaper.

215

"I am very, very sorry for your son and for your family. But the only help I can give you is to tell you to forget about your son, or you will end up in prison yourselves, along with your daughter."

"I will not forget about my son!" raged Mrs Malik as her husband and daughter escorted her out of the building – just as they would escort her out of various newspaper, police, human rights organisation and government buildings every day in the weeks that followed.

*

Shakil's second interrogation was even shorter than the first. The boy only just managed to reiterate that all he'd done was to take part in a general drunken discussion about explosives at the party, that he wasn't part of a terror cell, and that during his summer trip to Pakistan his uncle had taken him sightseeing with his aunt and cousins and not to a terror training camp, when Pete came in to report that the bodies of two guards who had been on duty late last night had been found in the Armoury.

"What?" For the first time since anyone in the room could remember, the Warden looked shaken.

"Crewes and Hampel, sir. We found their bodies." Pete looked white as a sheet and seemed unsteady on his feet. "At least, we think it's them."

"What do you mean, you think it's them?"

"The heads sir ..."

"What about their heads?"

"They're missing, sir."

"What?"

"I said ..."

"I know what you said, man!" The Warden pushed his seat away from the table so violently that it toppled over, and the interrogating officer dived to pick it up. "Take me to the bodies, and organise a search for the heads at once. Use the dogs." As the Warden swept out of the room with Pete in tow, the interrogating officer piped up in a feeble little voice, "Excuse me, sir ..." Despite his fear, pain and confusion, Shakil couldn't believe how the interrogator's whole demeanour changed when he spoke to the Warden.

"What is it?"

"What shall I do with *him*?" The interrogator nodded in Shakil's direction.

"Take him back to his cell. We'll continue this later."

*

Shakil was thrown back in his cell, amidst his usual protestations that he hadn't done anything, that they'd made a mistake and that he wanted to call his parents; and guards with dogs were dispatched to look for the missing heads.

The search came to an abortive end when the dogs were taken to the Salt Tower. As soon as the shadow of the tower fell on the two Alsatians, they started to whimper like puppies. And as their handler dragged them towards the threshold, they bayed and jumped about, trying to pull away from the building.

"Come on, you little bastards, we're going in!" But Jeffries didn't stand a chance. Max dropped into a crouch and started backing away, eyes fixed on the dark entrance to the Salt Tower, while Theo let out a plaintive howl, bit Jeffries on the hand and, when the shocked handler let go of his leash, ran in the opposite direction like the hounds of Hell had been loosed on his fine black pedigree tail – now tucked between his legs, right under his belly, and fleeing for its dear fluffy life.

While Jeffries led the disgraced Max back to the kennels, then rounded up Theo and gave him a good hiding, the other guards entered the Salt Tower and searched it top to bottom, but found nothing. By dusk the heads still hadn't turned up. A discussion flared up as to whether police and crime scene investigation teams should be brought in from the outside, but the Warden categorically refused, on the general rule of thumb that "What goes down in the Tower, stays in the Tower." The search for the heads would resume in the morning. For now, all guards were to be extra cautious and patrol only in pairs. The guards grumbled amongst themselves that Crewes and Hampel were in a pair when they were murdered, but nobody dared contradict the Warden. And so night fell.

*

Bob was patrolling the Wakefield Tower with Pete. There were only ten minutes left until the end of the shift, but Pete couldn't wait that long.

"I need to take a leak, mate. Wait for me, won't you?"

"Sure." But as soon as Pete disappeared around the corner, Bob heard the heartbreaking sobbing of a child – the little boy from the night before. "Pete? Pete!" But Pete couldn't hear him and Bob couldn't wait, as the child's crying receded down the corridor, joined by the voice of the older boy. Bob threw one last, undecided glance in the direction of the toilets, then took off after the boys.

Bob followed the voices and footsteps, calling out to the children as he spotted them heading out of the building. He couldn't see them clearly in the darkness, but the little one looked about ten, and the older one couldn't be more than twelve or thirteen. What the hell were they doing here, and where were they hiding during the day? It wasn't that much of a surprise that the dogs hadn't found them – Max and Theo seemed to be about as much use as his late aunt's toy poodle – but the massive hunt for Crewes's and Hampel's heads should have unearthed the boys' hiding place. Then again, the heads hadn't turned up, so perhaps where the heads were so too were the boys ... what a horrible thought. And speaking of Crewes's and Hampel's heads ... as Bob followed the boys into the Bloody Tower, he suddenly realised the folly of what he was doing. He stopped for a moment and thought about turning back and rejoining Pete, but then the little boy cried out somewhere in the darkness ahead of him, so he drew his gun and hurried inside.

*

Pete came out of the toilet and returned to the place where he'd left the younger guard. He called out to his colleague, then glanced at his watch and figured that Bob must have gone back to the guards' quarters. "Thanks for waiting," he muttered under his breath, and followed suit.

*

The boys were gone. By the time Bob realised that he was in the same chamber as he'd shot the woman in, it was too late – the woman was running at him from the far end of the room, shrieking. Bob's brain stalled, but his automatic pilot engaged and he pointed his weapon at the woman, shouting for her to stop. This time he did not fire and, as the woman drew closer to him, Bob noticed that she was not looking at him – she was running in his direction, but not actually at him. Now she was close enough for Bob to see the terror and madness in her eyes. As the screaming woman reached Bob, he jumped back, weapon raised, ready to let her pass, but she fell bleeding to the floor, exactly as she had the other night when he'd thought he'd shot her.

When Bob recovered enough to lower his weapon and think rationally, he bent down and studied the gashes in the woman's back. It was obvious now that he wasn't responsible for them. It was as if someone had hacked into her from behind, over and over while she was running away. Bob looked in the direction from which the woman had come, and that was when he heard the footsteps – heavy and getting closer. Then a sight more monstrous than anything he

218

could have imagined appeared at the far end of the chamber. Striding rapidly towards the guard, giant axe in hand, was a mountain of a man, with a black hood-like mask over his head, holes cut out for the eyes – and the eyes unblinking, deathlike, yet burning with a malevolence that could only have come from Hell itself.

Bob fought to keep a hold of himself. "Stop or I'll shoot!" The monster paused for the briefest moment, looking directly at the guard. Bob could have sworn that the fiend smiled beneath his mask, before moving forward again with added determination. As he approached Bob, he raised his axe. "Stay back!" Bob took aim and squeezed the trigger, but his gun jammed. He tried not to panic; he managed to unblock the gun, and discharged several shots at the approaching giant. He kept shooting, but the monster kept coming. Bob was still shooting as the axe came down. The last thing he saw was the room spinning over and over, and then his own headless body slumping to the ground, then receding in the distance, as his head was picked up and carried off into the darkness.

*

Shakil had fallen into a restless sleep. He dreamed that he was in a different cell. There was a window at eye level and he looked out of it onto the patch of land known as Tower Green. A scaffold had been erected there and Shakil could see a small crowd gathering. Then he saw a procession of people walking from the White Tower in the direction of the scaffold. Among them was an elderly man, leading the most gorgeous girl Shakil had ever seen. She was slim and petite, with a beautiful face, rendered very pale against her jet black dress. Her hair was hidden by a silk scarf, but a lock of it had escaped, and shone once reddish, once golden in the cold February sun. She held a small book in her hand, and walked like a goddess or a queen might walk.

As Shakil watched, the girl was led towards the scaffold. Shakil expected her to take a place among the crowd, but the elderly man led her up the steps, onto the wooden structure itself. That's when Shakil noticed the large block of wood, and the huge, monstrous-looking, hooded man who stood in the shadows at the side of the scaffold, holding a massive axe. Shakil looked at the girl, who addressed the crowd and read something out of her book, and then the reality of what was going to happen dawned on the boy and he felt sick. As he watched, the girl removed her scarf and coat, and handed them to one of the women attending her. Then she took a handkerchief and tied it around her eyes. Shakil tried to open the window, but it was stuck. He rattled it in a desperate attempt to get it open, but to no avail. He shouted, but nobody could hear him. He was forced to watch helplessly as the beautiful girl kneeled, then panicked as she couldn't locate the block by touch alone. Shakil watched in horror as someone from the crowd scaled the scaffold, and guided the girl's hands to the chopping block. She calmed down, and lay her head upon it. The masked man stepped out of the shadows and raised his axe.

*

As the axe came down, Shakil cried out and woke up. His relief that it had only been a dream dissipated as soon as he realised where he was. As his eyes adjusted to the dark, he saw a figure watching him from a corner of his cell. He pulled back, frightened, but then he recognised the girl from his dream. The gentleness emanating from her dispelled Shakil's fear in an instant. Confused but unafraid, he watched the girl draw closer. He could smell her perfume, and wondered why it was familiar. The girl touched his face and Shakil closed his sore eyes for a moment, then opened them again and gazed into the girl's sad face. He reached out and touched her reddish-gold hair, smiling back when she smiled at him.

The first light of dawn crept into the cell. Pain clouded the girl's delicate features and a thin red line appeared on her pale neck. Shakil watched in horror as the girl put a hand up to her neck, and blood oozed out between her fingers. Shakil started to panic, and the girl held out her free hand to him, trying to reassure him even as she fought to stem the flow of her own blood with her other hand. As she bled, the girl's features became soft and blurred, and she faded away, leaving only a pool of blood on the floor; a second later that too was gone.

Shakil pushed himself back against the cold damp wall of his cell and sat there, shaking. He was still sitting there when the guards came to hose him down.

*

"We're going back upstairs now," said the Warden, "but bear in mind that this is where we'll be having our little chats from now on if you don't tell us what we want to know."

Shakil's hands were handcuffed behind his back and his ankles loosely chained together. He was speechless following the interrogating officer's demonstration of the rack, unable even to protest his innocence, which he'd done at every given opportunity

220

up until now. The Warden took Shakil's silence to be an admission of guilt, and congratulated himself silently on his first small victory over the youth. The interrogating officer, on the other hand, was still miffed that the plaques about the torture instruments had been removed – along with all the other tourist information – as his urge to try out the Scavenger's Daughter was growing daily, but he couldn't for the life of him figure out how the damned thing worked. If only someone had told him about *Google*.

Back in the interrogating room, the officer ordered Shakil to name the other people in his terror cell. Shakil was still unable to speak, and the Warden thought that perhaps he'd been wrong: the stubborn little shit was not on the verge of spilling the beans after all; his silence was merely a new and irritating resistance tactic. The Warden nodded to the interrogating officer to get physical. The interrogator grinned and was about to take a swipe at Shakil when Pete appeared, and informed them in a trembling voice that the body of Bob Dawson had been found in the Bloody Tower – the body, but not the head. The Warden had no choice but to order Shakil to be taken back to his cell.

"You are one lucky son of a bitch," the interrogating officer hissed in Shakil's ear as Pete led the boy out of the room.

*

Shakil was left alone for the rest of the day, as everyone in the Tower complex was preoccupied with the search for a psycho killer and three missing heads. The boy spent much of the day lying on the hard stone floor. At night he couldn't get to sleep, and when he finally did, he dreamed about the execution again. This time he was right there, standing among the small group of people at the foot of the scaffold. As the executioner moved towards the girl and raised his axe, Shakil started screaming, "Stop! Let her go!"

The hooded monster turned away from the girl and headed towards Shakil.

"Run! Go! Now!" The girl's voice rang out over the agitated whispers of the crowd. She had raised her head from the block and, the blindfold still over her eyes, moved her head around, as if trying to locate Shakil through sound alone. "You can't stop what will happen to me. It will go on happening over and over – as long as the Tower stands."

The executioner went to descend the scaffold, axe raised, eyes on Shakil.

"Run! Please go! Now!" So urgent was the plea in the girl's voice that Shakil ran.

He woke up to the familiar sound of his cell door slamming open. As Shakil was hosed down, his family were preparing to see a woman from Amnesty International. By the time they had arrived at the Amnesty office, and the woman had said that she would try to help them, but it would be a slow and difficult process, Shakil was already strapped to the rack in the basement of the Wakefield Tower.

"I don't know!" he half screamed, half pleaded.

"You don't know their names?" asked the Warden, as the interrogating officer got ready to tighten the ropes one more time. Shakil was stretched out on the iron frame, his feet secured at one end, his hands at the other. The replica of the sixteenth century original worked just fine. The lever on the central wooden roller allowed the interrogating officer to turn the rollers at the head and foot of the rack simultaneously, pulling the ropes that secured Shakil's hands and feet in opposite directions.

"I don't know what you're talking about!" The interrogating officer was about to turn the roller again, when Pete came running in and informed the Warden that Jeffries was missing. If looks could kill, the filthy look that the interrogator gave Shakil would have dispatched the boy to the next life for sure.

"What shall I do with him?" the interrogator asked the Warden.

"Leave him where he is."

Luckily for Shakil, the ropes on the rack were not stretched tight enough to do any serious damage, but as the day wore on, the agony of having his arms pulled taught over his head grew. At lunchtime a fly found its way into the basement, and tortured the sweating, suffering boy by buzzing round his head and sitting on him, again and again; every time he managed to move enough to dislodge it, it would be back. This carried on for about an hour until the fly grew bored and flew off to find some dog shit to feed on. Half an hour later Shakil's nose started to itch for no apparent reason, and the boy squirmed, tried to blow on his nose and did whatever he could to alleviate the itch, but it persisted for a good forty minutes, driving him crazy, and then suddenly it eased. By teatime his muscles began to cramp painfully and Shakil cried out in pain and fear.

As darkness fell, the chamber changed. Shadows moved around Shakil, and he could hear whispers and moans in the dark corners. Despite his great discomfort, exhaustion overcame him and he almost dozed off, but the approach of heavy footsteps brought him wide awake. The night was at its darkest now, and Shakil peered into the darkness near the chamber door with growing trepidation. The footsteps grew louder, the shadows and whispers around Shakil stilled, and a terrible silence fell on the chamber.

Shakil struggled against his bonds as the footsteps came closer. Then the chamber door swung open, and in the scant light from the corridor Shakil saw the silhouette of a massive man. As the giant entered the chamber, Shakil recognised him: it was the hooded monster that had cut off the girl's head in his nightmare – it was the executioner, and he had seen Shakil, and was advancing towards him, raising his axe.

Shakil thrashed about on the rack, crying out and twisting madly from side to side. An image of his parents and his sister flashed into Shakil's head, and he was sure he was going to die. When a white mist formed before his eyes, he thought he was passing out, but the mist quickly solidified and took on human form. It was the girl from Shakil's dreams – the girl who had visited him in his cell – and she now stood between the boy and the executioner, small and slender, but more corporeal and stronger than the other night.

The executioner went for the girl immediately, but she ducked his blow and fled from the chamber, leading him away from Shakil. The boy shouted out in protest, but the executioner and the girl were gone. Shakil struggled on the rack again, terrified for the girl. Eventually he exhausted himself and gave up. Tears for the girl welled up in his eyes, and he closed them. Then all of a sudden there was that perfume again, and a gentle, soothing presence was in the room. The girl was back. She touched Shakil's face and chest; she touched his hands and studied his bonds closely.

Ever since the presence of people in the Tower at night had disrupted the fine balance between the living and the dead, the girl had found herself increasingly able to interact with the physical world. For many years those who walked in the Tower during the day and those who walked there at night had been separate. Now the order was destroyed and the girl, and the realm of nightmare in which she resided, had entered the waking world. And she had fallen in love again – and again her love was doomed.

Jane Grey had been fifteen when she was bullied into marrying a young man she hardly knew, but she had grown to love him. Nine months after their wedding, she had watched from her confines in the Tower as he was taken for execution and brought back a while later – his rag-covered head rattling around beside his headless body in the horse-drawn cart. An hour later, Jane suffered the same fate. Her crime: being too young to withstand the machinations of her ambitious parents and powerful in-laws, who had made her queen of England for nine days, incurring the wrath of the rightful heir to the throne.

Jane loosened Shakil's bonds and let him down. The boy's body slumped, his arms temporarily useless, and he fell into the girl's arms. Drawing on his life-force to give her strength, Jane led Shakil out of the dark building.

*

Jones was checking the area west of the White Tower when he spotted the prisoner whose head he'd shaved leaving the Wakefield Tower with a girl in an old-fashioned dress. He raised his weapon, shouting for them to stop, then gave chase.

Jane and Shakil fled towards Traitor's Gate and the River Thames beyond. The only obstacle in their way was the portcullis on the south side of the Bloody Tower. The pins-and-needles had eased, and Shakil had enough feeling back in his arms to work the ancient mechanism that pulled up the seven hundred and fifty year old spiked gate. He and Jane ran under the portcullis just as Jones was catching up with them. The guard paused for a moment, taking aim at Shakil's back. There was a loud creaking noise as the mechanism holding up the portcullis gave way, and the two and a half tonne structure came crashing down, its spikes impaling the guard through his head and his shoulders. He held onto his weapon a moment longer, and then it fell from his hand. His body remained upright, fixed by the iron spikes, surprised eyes staring ahead.

Jane and Shakil ran down the steps leading down to the water-logged Traitor's Gate. Water levels had risen in the last few years, the river's tides had increased in strength, and the land beneath the water-gate had been worn away. The bottom of the gate no longer sat on the mud beneath the water, but hung free in the water itself, the gate now held up by the solid walls on either side of it. As Shakil inspected the bottom of the gate, he understood why the girl had brought him to this spot.

"We just have to swim under it," he said to the girl. "I'll go first, then I'll help pull you under the gate."

Shakil lowered himself into the freezing water and went under, using the bars to pull himself down one side, then up the other side of the gate. He came up, gasping for breath, and stood chest-high in water, shaking from the cold. He reached out to Jane through the bars.

"You just have to get down and under the bars, and I'll help pull you up," he told her.

224

Jane gazed at Shakil, sadness and longing in her eyes. As Shakil watched, her features began to soften and fade. She turned from the boy and fled back towards the Bloody Tower, disappearing before she reached the top of the steps.

"I'll come back for you," Shakil called out to the night.

*

The Warden and the interrogating officer were returning from the site where Jeffries's headless body had been found. The multiple lacerations on the dead guard's back and the lengthy blood trail leading up to the body suggested that Jeffries had managed to run a fair distance before succumbing to the killer's axe.

"I'm going to have to get the police involved." The Warden looked defeated.

"We'd better get the prisoner off the rack," the interrogator reminded him.

"Christ, I forgot all about him. Let's go and get him ourselves. There are hardly any guards left, for God's sake." The two of them went down to the torture chamber, but Shakil was nowhere to be found.

"Goddammit! Goddammit!" The Warden's vocabulary – never huge – shrank to one word.

After a final search of the Tower complex by what was left of his staff, the Warden finally called the police and admitted to having a terror suspect on the loose and a bunch of dead guards with missing heads.

*

The executioner was not happy. The pathetic slip of a girl had outfoxed him, robbing him of the head of the traitor on the rack. It was his duty to collect as many heads for the Queen as possible – and he would have to hurry if he was to get a decent quota before daybreak.

*

Shakil made it back home before dawn. His luminous yellow jumpsuit was almost dry, but he had to ditch it as soon as possible. He used the last of his strength to scale a tree at the back of the house, and quietly opened his sister's bedroom window. He gazed at Adara, longing to hug her, but what was the point of waking her up? Things would never be the same again, and it was best not to get her hopes up. He looked in on his parents, also sound asleep. Then he went to his room and changed his clothes. He noticed an old history book from school and quickly flipped through the pages, looking for something. And there it was: a reproduction of Paul Delaroche's painting of the execution of Lady Jane Grey. Recognition and sadness crept into Shakil's eyes. "Jane."

Shakil moved swiftly and silently to his father's study, opened a drawer and took out the keys to his father's office and warehouse. He put on a long, loose-fitting coat, and tucked the jumpsuit under it – he would dispose of it later, away from the house, preventing any repercussions against his family. He took a final look at his sleeping parents, then went into Adara's bedroom and left quietly through her window.

Adara woke up, looked around her room and shivered. For a moment she had the vague feeling that something wasn't right, but sleep quickly reclaimed her and she sank back onto her pillow.

Shakil disappeared around the corner just as the first police cars pulled up.

*

The Warden and the interrogating officer were on their way to the Warden's office in the White Tower, when their path was cut off by a brick shithouse of a man, carrying an axe in one hand and Jeffries's head in the other.

"Shit!" The Warden froze for a moment, and the interrogating officer was first to draw his gun.

"Drop the axe!" But the giant didn't drop the axe; he raised it and ran at the interrogator. The interrogating officer emptied his gun into the giant's chest, then turned and ran towards the Wakefield Tower. The Warden paused long enough to ascertain that the killer was following the interrogator, then ran as fast as he could in the opposite direction.

*

The interrogating officer ran down the stairs to the basement. Before he knew it, he found himself in the torture chamber, cowering behind the Scavenger's Daughter and listening to the heavy footsteps coming closer. He'd barely had time to reload his gun when the heavy door of the chamber swung open, its hinges breaking, and the executioner strode in, Jeffries's head still swinging by one side and the axe held firmly on the other.

226

The guard emptied his gun into the advancing giant's head and chest, then fell to his knees and started to pray. The executioner raised his axe over the guard's head, and then thought better of it. He placed the axe and Jeffries's head carefully on the ground. Then he grabbed the sobbing interrogator by the back of his neck and the seat of his pants, squeezed his head down towards his knees, and thrust him into the Scavenger's Daughter, fastening the iron bonds with ease.

"So that's how it works." The ridiculously inappropriate thought slipped into the interrogator's head before the monster tightened his bonds, forcing blood from his nose and mouth, and cracking his spine.

The executioner contemplated his handiwork for a moment, then picked up his axe and cut the man's head off.

*

The Warden had locked himself in his office and was calling the police again when he heard heavy footsteps approaching. He put the phone down and stood very still, hoping the footsteps wouldn't stop outside his office door, but they did. There was a moment's silence, and then an ear-splitting thud as the axe came splintering through the thick wood of the door. The Warden thought he was going to have a heart attack. For some reason all he could think of was Jack Nicholson breaking down the bathroom door in *The Shining*. Then he remembered that the door on the far side of his office led to an adjoining chamber, which in turn led back round to the stairs.

As the executioner burst in, the Warden was already leaving through the back and heading downstairs. As he ran for the main entrance leading out of the Tower, the Warden ran straight into the escaped prisoner.

"You're back!"

"Yes, I'm back." And Shakil opened his jacket, revealing the vast amount of explosives strapped around his waist, and the detonator in his other hand. The Warden turned around, planning to go back the way he'd just come, but the executioner was striding towards him, axe in one hand, Jeffries's and the interrogator's heads in the other.

The Warden turned back to Shakil.

"We can make a deal. I can get you released from here." Shakil looked the Warden in the eye and raised the detonator in front of the man's face. "No!" The Warden raised a hand in protest and backed away as Shakil placed his thumb over the detonating button. "Please, don't. I have a wife and kids." The Warden didn't have a wife or kids. In fact he hated both kids and women, only using the latter sporadically when his urges got the better of him. But Shakil wasn't to know. The Warden sensed the boy's hesitation. "I have two kids, and a third on the way." Shakil's thumb wavered over the detonator.

The Warden held the boy's gaze. He didn't see the axe rise behind his head; nor did he see it swing down and round. But he felt the sharp pain in his neck, and then the world span and became red and orange, as the Warden's head went one way and his body went another, flailing arms lashing out in reflex action and grabbing Shakil's hand, pushing the boy's thumb down on the detonator.

*

Debris flew everywhere: stone, timber, metal, body parts and shards of glass. Among the body parts were severed heads, which fell – some of them burning, all of them thudding – to the ground.

Had there been any witnesses at that early time of the morning, and had those witnesses looked closely, they might have noticed orbs of light and strange wisps of mist rising from the burning ruins and merging with the dawn sky.

Police, fire trucks and ambulances were on the scene within minutes; news vans not much later.

*

Adara woke up to the sound of the news on her television.

"Police are puzzled by the disproportionate number of heads among the remains…"

She sat up, startled, convinced that she'd switched her TV off the night before, and saw her brother standing before her. He wore his favourite leather jacket and smiled at her, pushing a thick lock of shiny black hair away from his eyes. Adara's grogginess was instantly replaced by astonishment, then pure joy. She smiled back at Shakil and reached towards him, but he faded away, revealing the television with the newsman still reporting on the explosion.

Adara cried out and burst into tears.

"The authorities believe that the explosion was an act of terror. Many will no doubt be saying that the Prime Minister's new anti-terror legislation has already been justified; some that it is still not enough."

As Adara stared at the television uncomprehendingly, several ravens hopped past the reporter's back and perched on a nearby wall, overlooking the burning wreckage.

228

SOURCES

All of these stories are original to *Terror Tales of London* with the exception of 'The Soldier' by Roger Johnson, which first appeared in *Mystery For Christmas*, 1990, 'Train, Night' by Nicholas Royle, which first appeared in *3:AM London, New York, Paris*, 2008, and 'Perry In Seraglio' by Christopher Fowler, which first appeared in *City Jitters*, 1986.

FUTURE TITLES

Ｉf you enjoyed *Terror Tales of London*, why not seek out the first three volumes in this series: *Terror Tales of the Lake District, Terror Tales of the Cotswolds* and *Terror Tales of East Anglia* – available from most good online retailers, including Amazon, or order directly from http://www.grayfriarpress.com/index.html.

In addition, watch out for the next title in this series, *Terror Tales of the Seaside*. Check regularly for updates with Gray Friar Press and on the editor's webpage: http://paulfinch-writer.blogspot.co.uk/.

CPSIA information can be obtained at www.ICGtesting.com
Printed in the USA
BVOW04s2215180714

359370BV00001B/81/P